the
Tangled
Bridge

ALSO BY RHODI HAWK

A Twisted Ladder

RHODI HAWK

the Tangled Bridge

TOR®

A TOM DOHERTY ASSOCIATES BOOK

NEW YORK

This is a work of fiction. All of the characters, organizations, and events portrayed in this novel are either products of the author's imagination or are used fictitiously.

THE TANGLED BRIDGE

Map by Jackie Aher

A Tor Book
Published by Tom Doherty Associates, LLC
175 Fifth Avenue
New York, NY 10010

www.tor-forge.com

Tor® is a registered trademark of Tom Doherty Associates, LLC.

Library of Congress Cataloging-in-Publication Data

Hawk, Rhodi.
    The tangled bridge / Rhodi Hawk.–1st ed.
        p. cm.
    "A Tom Doherty Associates book."
    ISBN 978-0-7653-2497-9 (trade paperback)
    ISBN 978-1-4299-8592-5 (e-book)
    1. Women psychologists–Fiction.   2. Family secrets–Fiction.   3. New Orleans
(La.)–Fiction.   I. Title.
    PS3608.A884T36 2012
    813'.6—dc23

2012019877

First Edition: October 2012

Printed in the United States of America

0 9 8 7 6 5 4 3 2 1

For Hank

Acknowledgments

I'd like to thank Sheriff Greg Champagne and his officers at the St. Charles Parish Sheriff's Office for taking time to answer questions and share information about investigative procedures.

Also, my heartfelt gratitude goes out to Joanna McAdam for assistance in getting to the final draft, and to my fellow Candlelighters: Robert Jackson Bennett, David Liss, Joe McKinney, and, of course, Hank Schwaeble.

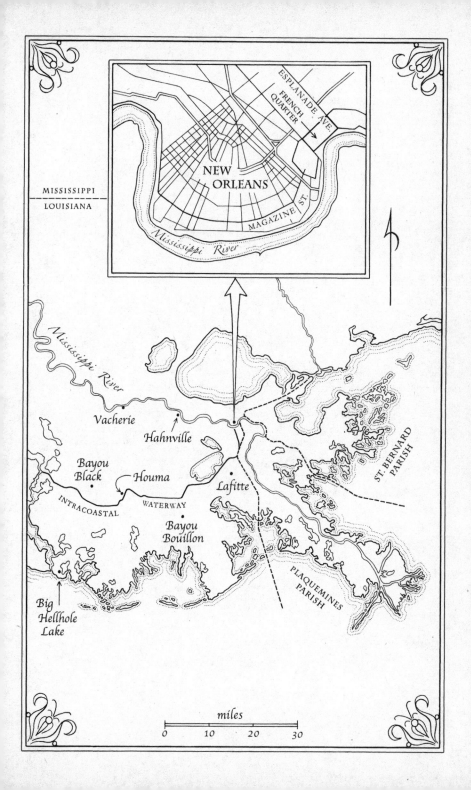

ESPLANADE AVE.

FRENCH QUARTER

NEW ORLEANS

MAGAZINE ST.

Mississippi River

MISSISSIPPI
LOUISIANA

Mississippi River

Vacherie

Hahnville

Bayou
Black

Houma

INTRACOASTAL   WATERWAY

Bayou
Bouillon

Lafitte

ST. BERNARD PARISH

PLAQUEMINES
PARISH

Big
Hellhole
Lake

miles

0   10   20   30

the
Tangled
Bridge

NEW ORLEANS, NOW

ONCE, WHEN SHE WAS ten, Madeleine brought home pockets full of potatoes she'd found behind the school cafeteria. Mother was already long gone by that time, and Daddy had been away for weeks, so potatoes were a nice break from the usual scrounging. Madeleine and her brother Marc were getting sick of redfish from Bayou Black.

Zenon had come that day, too, escaping his own empty kitchen. He was also their brother, but none of them knew that yet.

That was a good long while ago. Long before they'd learned how to separate their ghosts from their bodies and walk the briar world with its winding, shadowed river. Before Zenon had become a murderer.

Madeleine remembered how she'd stood on the step stool and laid out one potato for Marc, one for Zenon, and the last for herself. All three potatoes were sprouting tails. The boys had watched while Madeleine took the first one and lopped off the end where a long, snaking root had been growing.

"Three blind mice!" Marc had said. "She cut off the tail with a carving knife!"

They'd laughed, all three kids, laughed themselves dizzy over a bunch of sprouted potatoes.

There were no parents around that fall, not anywhere.

Now, two decades later, Madeleine wondered about Marc's baby, out there somewhere, semi-orphaned. The child was most certainly safe, she told herself. Marc was dead, Daddy was dead, and Zenon was as good as dead. The baby's mother had gone and hidden with it somewhere in Nova Scotia. That was good. She should hide. Madeleine didn't want to know where they were.

"Three blind mice!" Marc had said way back when.

She thought of it every time she saw a potato.

t w o

NEW ORLEANS, NOW

ADELEINE HAD LAIN DOWN in her own bed and slept hard, very hard, but when she awoke she was not in her bed. She was in the passenger seat of her truck.

Ethan was asleep behind the steering wheel. They were parked somewhere dark—it didn't look like it was anywhere near Madeleine's place or Ethan's. She rubbed the corners of her eyes, blinking, waiting for sleep to fade so she would recognize where she was. But no, this didn't make sense. She was supposed to be at home in bed.

Is this a dream?

She put her hand on the gearshift, solid and real under her fingers. No dream. Her hair was slick with sweat. Last thing she remembered she was lying in bed, Ethan breathing evenly next to her, and now she was . . .

No idea. She looked through the windshield. Just shy of daylight out there. The truck was parked on a gravel shoulder off some road, beyond which a chain-link fence wrapped around a boat dealer's lot. On the other side, a sharp grassy rise ran along the road like the berm to a sandstone quarry.

She was still wearing her bedclothes: a tank top and drawstring cotton shorts. But there were sandals on her feet. Keys still in the ignition.

In the driver's seat, Ethan groaned and then blinked awake.

"Is the doctor in?" he said.

"Which doctor?"

"Witch doctor! Just my luck." His eyes were puffy but he was smiling at her.

"What . . . are we doing here?"

He rubbed his face. "I don't know. We were at your place and sometime in the middle of the night I wake up and you was gone. Found you gettin into the truck."

She listened, bewildered, trying to dig out a memory from last night:

Tick tick tick tick.

Ethan reached for her and she held his hand to her face, grateful for the comfort of it. Even though she'd grown used to the lapses in time—a few hours here or there—this was the first time she'd truly wandered off.

He said, "Couldn't let you go driving around in your sleep so I took away your keys. But then you just got into the passenger side instead. You told me where to drive you. Don't you remember?"

She hesitated, shaking her head. "I don't . . . Maybe. What happened after that?"

"Then we drove here."

"Where's here?"

"The levee, I think. You wanted to go outside, but I wouldn't let you, so you sat there arguing with someone I couldn't see."

"Who?"

He shrugged. "Couldn't tell, honey. Just assumed it was a river devil. Severin, I guess."

Madeleine reached over and turned the key so she could roll down the window. The mosquitoes were waiting. They'd been lapping at the dew on the glass. In the fresh predawn breeze, she smelled silt and also something acrid: smoke. Campfire smoke gone cold.

She said, "Hobo fires."

"Probably, yeah. This part of the levee. What all do you remember?"

"Just . . . I remember I was looking for something. A bird."

She frowned, because that wasn't entirely true. She wasn't just looking.

She said, "But that was . . . you know, briar. River devils. I didn't realize my actual flesh-and-blood body was in on it."

"Well, maybe it's just a plain old case of sleepwalking."

She looked away. Sleepwalking! Wouldn't it be nice if it was as simple as that?

Her gaze swept the grassy rise. At the top, an asphalt bike trail formed a spine along the levee's ridge. It looked like a beast curled around the Mississippi River. Streetlights illuminated only the trail and left everything beyond it in darkness.

She couldn't see over the rise, down to the underbelly. Down there, she knew, was the reason she'd come here. The tick-tock bird. Something had gone terribly wrong down on that river, somewhere among those hobo camps.

Ethan said, "Well, baby blue, I guess we oughtta head back now."

He raised his hand to the ignition, but she stopped him. His eyes flickered. He was feigning puzzlement, but he knew good and well they weren't done here.

She said, "I'm sorry, honey. You know we gotta check it out."

～✦～

NO REASON TO BE cold, but she was. There had been a sweatshirt behind the seat, which she now hugged close around her even though
there was no chill to the air. Damp, yes, without being hot nor
cold. It'd be hot as soon as the sun came up. Real hot.

As they ascended toward the hike-and-bike trail, Ethan reached
for her hand, and in doing so brought more warmth than the
sweatshirt had. Their sandals left dew prints—dotted parallels from
Madeleine and a dot-dash that matched Ethan's limp. A high school
football injury had once put him in a wheelchair with little hope of
ever walking again. But as he'd worked through college, his muscles slowly responded to relentless physical therapy until he got to
the point where he could walk on his own. Now a limp and the
occasional ache were all that remained.

He said, "I don't like it. It's dangerous."

"I can use pigeonry if I have to."

He gave her a sidelong glance.

Behind them, a neighborhood lay hushed in the day's first glow:
shotgun cottages and potholed streets bathed in amethyst. The
Mississippi was just a stretch of blackness ahead.

They reached the asphalt spine and she scanned the river's edge.
The camps were likely somewhere in the black woods along the
banks below and to the left. Overhead, an electrical tower supported
a network of wires, and beyond that the pumping station routed
pipes from the river. They continued moving down the slope toward what her nose judged to be a bog.

Three blind mice . . .

The rhyme was stuck in her head now, but that was the point,
wasn't it? Music calms the savage breast. Usually worked to distract
Severin. Too bad it had to be a blood rhyme. Always a blood rhyme.

"Why're you so quiet?" he asked.

"Shh."

"Why shh?"

She answered in a whisper. "Because if there are people out here,
it's best we find them before they find us."

"Woman, you gonna put me to an early grave."

She squeezed his hand. The neighborhood's glow vanished behind the rise. Full darkness, here, and this was good. It forced her to draw from her other senses. Because she wasn't kidding herself—this really was dangerous. Even with pigeonry.

Pigeonry was the word they used for the way Madeleine could place thoughts into other people's minds. It stemmed from what Mémée, Madeleine's grandmother, had called "pigeon games." Mémée and her siblings used to practice briar skills like pigeonry by working on simple subjects, such as birds. The children of the briar could make pigeons fly, walk, or stack one atop the next by implanting thoughts into the birds' minds.

The sound came. She paused. The sharp clicking. Over to the right. It eclipsed the other bird calls.

Ethan paused, too, and looked at her. She nodded in the direction of the sound. He turned to look. So dark, though. They could see nothing.

Click click click.

Not like any bird or insect she'd heard before and she'd grown up on a bayou. More like something she'd hear in the river devil's bramble. It made her feel stealthy, catlike.

Ethan put his lips to her ear and whispered, "I'll check it out. You stay put."

She nodded, because she didn't want to go see for herself. She didn't fear the thing she heard. She feared what it brought out in her.

Ethan moved off into the darkness.

Her toes were now wet. She took a step and felt the earth softening beneath her. A bog. A haven for mosquitoes . . . and leeches, too. She rimmed the soggy part and made for the woods. Didn't like being out in the open like this.

The scent of cold smoke grew stronger. Ethan was probably still close by but she couldn't see nor hear him, and the tick-tocking had stopped, too. Perhaps she could take a quick check of the camp before Ethan got back. She was thinking that, yes, this place was dangerous, but they weren't the ones in danger. Not if they were careful.

She walked with hands outstretched, catching branches and easing between them. Dry wood snapped beneath one foot and she paused, listening.

The birds were very loud now. The predawn cacophony. She could hear nothing else out there. She ventured again, but with the next step came another snap. This was no good—she needed to move in silence. She bit her lip and took another step, sliding carefully without picking up her foot so that she moved without a sound. Much better.

But then she heard a third snap. This one hadn't come from her own footfalls.

THE GROWING DAWN WAS now illuminating the river. Though dim, she could see a silhouette, a human form much larger than herself. Not Ethan.

Madeleine froze. Her eyes strained, fingers splayed and ready. She zeroed in on that silhouette and seized control.

Put both hands on the nearest tree.

She waited.

The sound of snapping branches near that silhouette: far too close. She moved so that he was backlit by the Mississippi, and she saw that he was obeying the pigeonry—both of his hands were pressed against a tree.

She asked aloud, "What are you doing out here?"

"Just sleepin, lady, I ain't hurtin nobody."

She stepped closer. She could tell he was a black man, much darker than herself, with short hair that was almost completely gray.

She tightened her mind's grip on him. "Is that really all you're doing out here? Tell me the truth."

"I ain't lyin. Got up to take a pee. Was just headin back to get my things and clear out."

She stared, believing him, because the way he was holding that tree indicated that he was fully susceptible to the pigeon exercise. He probably didn't even know why he felt compelled to hang on like that.

She released him. And then, taking a step closer, she realized that she recognized him. He was a busker who played the harmonica. Used to sing on the streets with her father. She'd even fed him herself when her father had brought him home for supper on occasion.

"You're Shalmut Halsey."

He peered at her, his posture relaxing. "My God. Maddy?"

"Hey!" Ethan's voice, sharp.

Madeleine turned toward him and found his hand. "It's alright, Ethan. Shalmut here's an old friend."

"I thought you were going to stay put," Ethan said.

"I meant to. What did you find?"

"Nothing. There was a camp, but no one in it. Looked like whoever was there had just left."

Madeleine turned back to Shalmut. "You know anything about that?"

Shalmut said, "Sure: the little blind boy, Bo Racer, and his mama."

Madeleine cast a glance back toward the levee; dawn was growing stronger with every moment that ticked by. She was beginning to feel foolish.

Shalmut asked, "Whatch'all doin out here, Maddy? This ain't no place for you."

"Tell you the truth, Shalmut, I have no idea."

He exhaled, and it smelled like booze. He was staring at her with an intensity that made her feel grateful the sun hadn't made its full way to the horizon yet.

Shalmut said, "Yes you do. Some'm wrong. You got the insight, just like your Daddy before you, God rest his soul."

She said nothing.

He slapped the back of his neck. "Y'all come on, these woods is fulla muskeetas."

They followed him, and Madeleine spotted the place where the blind boy and mother must have been: a thick quilt and a carved wooden stick—just the right height for a boy to use as a cane. He and his mother must have left in a hurry.

Madeleine, Ethan, and Shalmut continued past it to where the trees opened up before the Mississippi, then walked along the shoreline. The birds were at the peak of their morning frenzy.

"Still enough smoke to keep the bugs away," Shalmut said, indicating the charred skeleton of a campfire.

He looked from Ethan to Madeleine. "Y'all wanna tell me why you really here? Never know. I may be able to help."

But before Madeleine could answer, she heard a woman's slow, fractured voice: "Well, look who's here."

Madeleine spun around.

The woman was heavyset and tall, about six feet, with long frizzy hair. Madeleine stumbled backward in reflex.

"Jesus!" Shalmut turned and retreated a few feet into the woods.

The woman was grinning. Madeleine stepped backward, clamping her thoughts onto the woman's mind.

The tree. Put both hands on that tree.

But the woman didn't respond to the implanted thought. Instead she took a step forward.

"Hunting that little boy same as me, Maddy?" Her voice was deep and cigarette cracked.

Madeleine didn't know her. It felt disorienting the way she spoke her name, but having worked with countless homeless folks around the city, people she didn't know often recognized her.

More disturbing was the fact that she couldn't get a hold on this woman's mind. And that she kept moving closer.

Madeleine said aloud, "Stop right there."

Ethan stepped between them, his posture tense.

The woman laughed. "Whadjoo bring him along for? Gotta travel light."

"God, look at her hands," Shalmut whispered.

They were filthy. Worse than that. In her right hand she clutched a beer bottle with a broken off neck, and from fingertips to elbow: thick black streaks. Even in the growing dawn Madeleine could see that it was blood.

Stop moving, stop, STOP!

That strange grin widened. "Oh no you don't. This here's *my* pigeon."

Madeleine jerked her head toward the woods, scanning the trees.

"Who you lookin for?" The woman took another step forward.

"Stop right there," Ethan said, hand blocking her.

Madeleine asked, "Who are you?"

"You ain't recognize me? Gotta look past this old lady crack whore."

"Y'all, we got to get!" Shalmut whispered.

The homeless woman spoke again. "They's good hunting round here, yeah. You been lookin for the blind boy, like me? He's slippery."

Madeleine tore her gaze from the sticky bottle and cast an involuntary glance in the direction of the camp where the quilt and the little cane had been.

The woman was looking toward that direction, too. "Yeah, well, I'm done for now." Her gaze swiveled to Shalmut. "Maybe I'll use him next."

She blinked once, and then tossed the bottle onto the cooling embers. Her expression slackened. And then she looked up with a furtive glance from Madeleine to Ethan and then beyond to the north, pausing, her face pinched in thought. Maybe even fear.

Madeleine realized that the hold had lifted. She tried again to snag the woman's mind.

Sit down on the banks, hands on your knees.

This time, the pigeon exercise took. The woman knelt down.

Madeleine breathed a sigh of relief. "It's OK. She's alright now."

She scanned the woods again, her eyes wide and her ears tuned. Nothing. No one else there.

Shalmut was right by her side. "We got to get!"

Madeleine shook her head.

Ethan agreed with Madeleine. "No, we can't leave. Not yet."

The woman was still kneeling near the blackened camp.

"Who are you?" Ethan asked her.

She answered with a hint of confusion in her voice. "Alice."

Madeleine said, "How do you know me?"

"Know you?"

"You asked me, did I recognize you?"

Alice said nothing.

Madeleine tried, "Just a moment ago. You called me by name."

No reply.

And then Madeleine asked, "Did you kill someone last night, Alice?"

Silence, and then, "Yes, ma'am."

"Jesus, God almighty," Shalmut whispered.

Alice cast a glance at Madeleine's eyes and then her gaze fell to the shore beneath her knees. "Ain't sure if he's dead, but I tried."

"How many people did you kill?" Madeleine asked. "One?"

Alice looked back over her shoulder and a lock of frizz fell over her eye. "Yeah, just the one."

"Why? Why did you?"

"I don't know that, ma'am. Can't say that I recall. I remember I's lookin for a boy, though. He'uz in a car at first, and then he's out in the woods somewhere. Couldn't get'm."

"Who exactly did you kill?"

"I don't know. Someone got in my way."

Shalmut was watching with round eyes, his hand curled at his lips as though he was trying to blow warmth into it.

"Tell us where the body is," Madeleine said.

Alice pointed north. "Just over yonder on the banks."

Shalmut said, "I'm gonna move along, y'all. This don't in-volve me."

"Don't leave, not yet," Ethan said.

Alice was still kneeling. She closed her eyes and started to pray in that gravelly voice.

Madeleine said to Ethan, "We need to find out if that person's still alive. I need to go check. And then Alice is gonna want to go talk to the police, won't you Alice?"

Alice continued to pray without answering, but Madeleine knew she would obey the directive when the time came.

Ethan said, "You're not going over there alone."

"Well we can't leave Alice by herself."

Ethan breathed through his teeth. "Mr. Halsey. Would you please wait here with Miss Alice while we go look for the body?"

Shalmut's eyes were wide and fierce. "With *her*?"

Madeleine said, "Yeah. Just watch her. If she gets up from that spot, you can leave."

"Good God, good God. I just wanna move along, that's all." Shalmut turned and stepped into the woods, but then he paused, ad-dressing Madeleine. "Come on, baby. I can't just leave y'all here like this, not with your father lookin down on us from heaven. Let's all move along together and let the police sort it out, yanh?"

"Please wait, Shally," Madeleine said. An unenforced request.

She knew Alice wasn't going anywhere. She was completely under Madeleine's will. Shalmut, however, she'd leave to decide for himself. He was free to disappear into the woods if he wanted.

She and Ethan followed in the direction Alice had indicated. The rhyme kept cycling through her mind.

See how they run.

Ethan said, "Next time you go sleepwalking, remind me to bring my cell phone."

The shoreline wound around a bend, and they found him: a

reclining male figure about fifty feet away, heavy dress shoes worn down so that the sole had flopped forward on his right foot. She could see his legs and nothing more. From the torso up, he was tangled in a broken green umbrella that looked like it had once been attached to a patio table. Probably served as shelter out here. The foot with the flopping shoe was resting in a burned-out campfire similar to Shalmut's, still emitting a small amount of smoke.

They drew nearer, saw the arm twisted up around the head. His hand was splayed atop his scalp, his mouth open. Blood on his face. A tear at the throat. It looked like he was missing his right eye.

Madeleine wheeled away.

Steady now, she told herself. *Not a time for cowardice.*

"Alice must have gotten him in the eye first, then the neck," Ethan said.

Madeleine made herself turn back around. "Well. He certainly looks dead."

"Probably. But just to be sure . . ."

Ethan was leaning over the body. Madeleine kept her gaze fixed on that flopping shoe while Ethan took the man's pulse.

"Nothing. And the body temperature's already dropped." He withdrew his hand and it came away wet.

"OK, enough. Police now."

She turned, fighting a rise of bile and hoping Ethan wouldn't see how unnerved she felt. She walked in the direction of where Shalmut and Alice were waiting somewhere further down the shoreline.

Ethan caught up with her and took her arm. "You alright?"

She nodded.

He asked her, his voice soft, "Is this what you saw when you were in the briar last night?"

"No. I didn't have anything to do with it!"

"Of course not. I didn't say that."

He was looking at her carefully, as though he wasn't sure what kind of question he really wanted to ask. And she didn't know how to explain.

She said, "Not much happened, there was just that bird call. I was following the clicks. I don't know why."

"Alice used the word 'hunting.'"

She said nothing. What could she say?

Ethan asked her, "Do you have any idea what's really going on here?"

Madeleine glimpsed the flop-soled shoe again, shaking her head. The streetlights went out up above on the hike-and-bike trail. Light enough now.

"All I know is, that poor guy lying there wasn't the intended victim. And that woman Alice, she's not really the one who killed him."

three

HALMUT HAD STAYED WITH Alice. Ethan had waited with both of them while Madeleine went to the Circle K and asked the manager to call the police. They arrived shortly thereafter and like moths chasing the blue-and-white lights, neighbors gathered to watch. Now the police were interviewing witnesses, with various sections of the woods cordoned off and Alice in handcuffs sitting in the back of a cruiser. Madeleine took it all in. She knew that Alice had been used like a puppet to commit that murder, but she didn't know what to do about it.

Madeleine toyed with the idea of consulting the river devil. She didn't want to think of her as Severin anymore. In fact she didn't want to think of her as a "her" anymore. This was a river devil. An "it." Thinking in terms of name and gender made it feel human. River devils weren't human.

"Ya daddy woulda been proud a you."

It was Shalmut, shuffling up to pat her shoulder.

Madeleine gave his hand a squeeze. "Proud of what, Shal? I haven't done anything."

"You coulda just let it all be. Most wouldn't a bothered with folks like us."

"I'm not so sure about that."

He said, "It's true. People give up on us, I know. We give up on ourselves so who else gonna care? Bible says the Lord helps those who help themselves."

Madeleine looked at him and then over at Alice. Both had trouble with booze. Maybe other substances, too. On the street, most folks were addicts or had mental disorders.

Shalmut leaned his back against the truck and put his hands on his thighs. "You ain't tryin to save us or sweep us away. For you it ain't like givin up cuz you one of us. Used to be. Ain't tryin to be disrespectful in sayin so."

"I know, Shally."

"You talk to him ever? Your ole man?"

Madeleine gave him a careful glance. Some people believed she could commune with the dead. Or predict the Super Bowl score or any manner of things. All her secrets had come out last year during Zenon's murder trial. Seemed like admitting to talking to river devils would be scandalous enough, but the public liked to attach other ideas to that, thinking her a psychic of many stripes. Or a crackpot. She'd set up a Web site and accepted the help of a few volunteers (angels, as she liked to think of them) to sort through the hundreds of letters and e-mails. The messages were pretty much categorized according to what the inquirer wanted; most just wanted to tell their own stories.

"I talk to Daddy, Shal. But maybe not in the way you mean."

He looked offended. "Whatchoo talkin bout, 'the way I mean.' I'm talkin about a quiet moment and you say a little prayer. That's what I mean. Put a flower or a nip of something strong on his stone pillow."

But he added, "Course if they's any sonofabitch gonna come back from the dead and raise the roof out here, it's Daddy Blank."

Madeleine laughed, and Shalmut guffawed so loud it drew glances from the officers. He tipped an invisible hat to them.

She grinned. "Why don't you stick with us for a while, Shal? You could stay with Ethan, or I could ask around, see if I can find you a room for a few days."

"That's awful kind a you, Darlin, but I'm OK."

"Then how about a ride somewhere?"

"Naw, I don't think I need to see this through. You alright now."

"Did the police finish up with you already?"

He shrugged. "They don't need to talk to an ole man drinks too much. Ain't seen nothin ain't heard nothin. I think they want to talk to your doctor-man next."

He pointed, and Madeleine looked. Ethan was standing with a detective who'd already questioned her and whose name she'd already forgotten. The poor guy was wearing a suit jacket in this heat.

For the police, this was a cut-and-dry case. Madeleine wished her friend Vincent was here. She'd chance telling him a bit more about what she knew. Vincent wasn't a detective but he was on the force, and he might be able to help.

"Too hot to be wearin . . ." she started to say to Shalmut, but he was gone.

She looked around, but no sign of him. Just the neighborhood and the boat sales lot and cars passing on Leake Avenue, an unfortunate name for a street that ran along a levee. Neighbors had satisfied their curiosities and were turning back to their homes. There were some cyclists along the hike-and-bike trail.

Down below, pitcher plants adorned the bog with late season blooms. Madeleine thought about all the mosquitoes that had been buzzing near that soft, damp earth, and wondered how many of the insects had followed the pitchers' scent and into the drowning traps. Ants, flies, and even small frogs seemed to fall for the attractive illusion the pitcher plant created, inviting its victims deeper into its belly.

Occasionally a stoic beetle might bore its way out of an already weakened plant. But usually, once the pitcher had its prey, it kept it.

Madeleine felt eyes upon her. She didn't even have to look up to know that the river devil, Severin, was there.

❧❧❧

TO MADELEINE'S EYES, SEVERIN looked like a little girl. The voice was light and cherubic, and so at odds with what it was. Severin tapped fingernails along the pickup as she walked around the bed, grinning in that manner that looked more grimace than grin. Bare feet, bare body, silver-gray and filthy.

"You called for me," Severin said.

"Did I?"

But of course Madeleine hadn't. In fact she'd never summoned the river devil, ever, and likely never would.

She said in her mind, "I didn't summon you. I was just thinking about you."

But Severin said, "To think is to summon. It seems you wish to see about last night. As to why it was such."

Madeleine looked over toward the policemen and the remaining onlookers. No good consorting with Severin in public. Madeleine would look like a lunatic. Even if she spoke only in her mind she'd lose track of the physical world around her—not respond if someone spoke to her, exhibit wild expressions and posture.

"No. Later," Madeleine said.

"A thing such as this. You think it could wait, so?"

Madeleine swallowed. Severin was right. If she waited she might lose track of whoever or whatever was behind Alice's behavior last night.

Severin slipped a small, grimy hand into Madeleine's, and guided her to the pickup's door handle. Madeleine pulled the handle and climbed inside the truck.

Or rather, her *physical* body did.

She settled back onto the seat and closed her eyes. Tugged. Feeling the light wobble, prying her ghost from her body.

Madeleine left her shell behind and followed the river devil back in the direction of the Mississippi, where otherworldly thorns were already starting to stretch, and blacken, and curl into tunnels.

four

*P*ATRICE LAY IN HER bed waiting for the four o'clock rooster. The night was still night, and it was a quiet one. Even Marie-Rose was silent. No noise but the clock ticks. Patrice counted them, waiting for Sunday to emerge.

The lovely thing about Sundays was that they were perfect—perfect in the ways of God, not man. On Sundays, the heart went to grace. Of course, that didn't prevent the river devils from coming around. Patrice had once hoped it might. Was a time, Patrice and her sister and brothers were not permitted to go to church—their mother had forbidden it though Tatie Bernadette had secretly told them about Lord Jesus. Mother had never allowed church because she had a black heart and wished to lead her children away from God, away and down into the depths of the bramble world, that the children might learn shadow magic to serve her.

But now, their mother was gone. After Papa had died, Patrice had used her skills to banish her mother to New Orleans. The children had been going to church for many months now.

And yet Patrice recognized the ugly irony of it: The river magic that was an abomination in the eyes of God was the only thing that kept their mother at bay. Patrice knew this had to stop. The river magic had to stop. The children had to find a means to escape their mother without using river devil ways. And to do that, Patrice knew, they would have to leave Terrefleurs. They would have to hide.

Today in church, Patrice would have to pray for courage to do this. She didn't know how to leave Terrefleurs, the only home she'd ever known. She was the oldest at fourteen; Guy and Gilbert were both eleven; and Marie-Rose, the youngest, was only seven years old. Where would they go? How would they feed themselves?

They could try living off the land. At least the boys were good hunters. Guy was, anyway. Frog gig, fishing pole, slingshot, it didn't matter; he never came home empty-handed. And since Papa died, Guy had also begun using the rifle. He was good with it. They'd all started calling him Trigger. If you were just talking about him, it was Trigger. But if you were talking about the twins together, it was Guy and Gilbert.

Patrice rolled over and looked at the rumpled heap of bedding where her little sister, Marie-Rose, was sleeping. Marie-Rose always tossed and turned through the night, sighing and muttering and laughing, sleeping about as peacefully as a toad in a dragonfly swarm. She even sassed in her sleep. Usually, when Patrice lit the lamp by the four o'clock rooster's crow she'd find Marie-Rose with her feet on her pillow and her head buried deep under the quilt. Were it not for Patrice's insistence that Marie-Rose sleep with a kerchief wrapping her hair, the child would awake each morning with so many snarls on her head she'd look like she was starting to cocoon.

Patrice smiled, listening. Still dead peace. Still too early to wake her. Where was that rooster?

On Sundays, the children rose and washed and donned their best clothes—Trigger always needed a little nagging but the others got themselves ready and were taking breakfast by dawn—and they all went to church with Tatie Bernadette and Francois and the other Christians on the plantation. They sang and clapped and praised and praised. A far cry from pigeon exercises.

The rooster crowed.

Patrice drew up on her elbows. It wasn't right.

The crowing hadn't come from the four o'clock rooster. This one was different. One of the later ones.

It was crowing a second time as Patrice reached over to the bedside table and lit the kerosene lamp. The room glowed to wakefulness. A tiny speck of brown on Patrice's pillow, brown like blood, and her hand went to the back of her neck. A broken welt there. Probably a bug bite that she'd scratched in her sleep.

She looked to the mantel clock and caught her breath: 5:30! An hour and a half later than it ought to be.

Patrice threw aside the quilt and scrambled to her feet.

Tatie Bernadette was staying with a sister and was to meet them at the church, which meant that Patrice was to help make breakfast this morning. She now only had an hour to bathe, dress, and make breakfast for all the workers.

"Marie-Rose," Patrice started to say . . .

But her sister's bed was empty. The quilt lay balled in the middle of the bed. Straps dangled to the floor. Rosie hadn't been strapped in last night. There hadn't seemed any need.

Patrice pulled a wrap over her shoulders and opened the door, heading for the pantry, and saw Gilbert.

He said, "I know, Treese, it's late. The second I heard that other rooster I knew you'd be in a fit."

"Where's Marie-Rose? You see her?"

"Naw. What happened?"

Patrice just shook her head and adjusted her wrap.

He said, "You go ahead and start getting ready. I'll look for her."

"What about Trigger?"

"I woke him up."

"*Got* him up?"

Gil shrugged but did not reply. Which meant Trig was probably still sleeping. Gil opened the pantry door, stepping out to look for Rosie. Drizzle out there. Not rain. Not full rain. Patrice hadn't even heard a pitter-patter the whole time she'd been lying awake.

She hurried to the men's parlor and flung open the door. "Trigger!"

He was sprawled facedown on his bed, looking like he'd lost a brawl with the linens. He groaned but did not move.

Patrice grabbed a tail of sheet and yanked. Trig thumped to the floor with no protest and no resistance. He did manage a whimper.

She said, "Starch up. It's late."

"Honey, why you got to be so hard?"

She left him to it and rushed off to get ready.

❧

WHERE HAD ROSIE GOTTEN off to?

The girl might have gotten a start with chores, or maybe she'd just gone to get something to eat. Gilbert would find out.

Patrice washed and dressed and tried not to think too much about it as she made it to the kitchen house and started breakfast. No biscuits this morning. They'd get eggs and coffee and porridge from last night's leftover cornbread. Milk, too. If someone had done the milking.

The door swung open and closed with plantation workers filing in, the lanterns casting a honeyed glow against the whitewashed walls. Terrefleurs did have electricity but its use had fallen off after Papa died, when the flood took away power and illness left the overseer, Francois, unable to keep up with the knobs and tubes. An outlet in the parlor of the main house still worked, and the children used it to listen to the radio.

Patrice worked as fast as she could but she was slow. This was not her usual chore.

The workers kept shuffling in. Their hair and clothes were studded with droplets of mist.

Finally, Patrice was nudged aside by a woman and her daughter, Eunice, who was Patrice's age. Patrice used to play hide-and-go-seek with Eunice and a small pack of farm brats before Patrice's mother forbade interaction with plantation children. After that, Eunice grew into something of a stranger even though she lived right here on Terrefleurs. Already she was working half days in the fields.

"Go on ahead now, Miss Patrice. We'll take it from here," Eunice said.

"But I wanted to make the breakfast today."

"You don't have to be cookin no breakfast. You the mistress these days."

"It's the ways of Jesus Christ, who taught that a master must humble himself in service, even to those who are his servants."

Eunice's mother laughed. "Well you tell Mr. Christ that all the servants gonna starve to death if they have to wait on the master to cook these eggs."

Always it seemed that serving God in one way meant denying Him in another.

Patrice returned to the main house without having taken anything to eat, and went straight to the men's parlour to see if Gil had found Rosie. But Gil wasn't there. Trigger, however, was. Still tangled in those wretched linens on the floor where she'd left him.

"Guy!"

His body snapped. She folded her hands and looked away as he struggled to his feet and donned his trousers. When she looked back he was squinting at the clock.

"I'm sorry, honey. Is it as late as that? I was just . . ."

She shook her head. "It doesn't matter. We won't be attending service this morning. Marie-Rose has gone missing."

His expression drew up. "That so?"

And from behind her, she heard Gil's voice: "Yeah, it's so."

He was soaked through, standing in the doorway, and he pulled off his shirt as Trigger was shrugging into his suspenders. Backward reflections of one another, those boys. Stick-framed, blue eyes, and catlike faces, but with light black skin and hair. Just like their sisters.

"On the wander," Gil said.

"You certain?"

"No sign of her anywhere. Nobody's seen her."

Trigger flung himself into the chair with a laugh and pulled on his boots. "Aw, come on you two! She's alright. Y'all worry like ninnies."

Patrice looked at him.

His preadolescent voice cracked somewhere between a boy's laugh and one that sounded like a girl's. "Oh, for God, Treese, you gotta know she ain't wandered far."

"Hasn't."

"She *hasn't* wandered far. Couldn't have. Come on, now. How much distance is one little girl gonna cover on a bramble stroll in the dark?"

Patrice said, "She'll be in her nightclothes. And it's drizzling out there."

"I know, I know. Which is why I'm gonna run get her and bring her back. While y'all load up and head on over to church."

Patrice shook her head. "Not today."

"Yes, today. How many times does Rosie go on the wander?"

Patrice lifted her gaze to the steamed window. The answer was: often. Often enough to keep straps on her bed.

Trigger said, "It ain't never . . ."

"Hasn't."

"*Hasn't* never . . ."

"Hasn't *ever*."

"Woman! *It hasn't ever* taken more than an hour to find her. And if I check through the briar I'll have her in just a few minutes. Y'all're talkin about missin church for nothin."

Patrice thought about it and found his words to be truthful. Trigger was a far better tracker than Gil, and if he'd been the one to have gone after Rosie first thing she'd probably be home by now. Trigger had river water flowing through his veins. He was more at home out in the woods than he ever was here in the house.

Gil was standing bare-chested with suspenders dangling loose at his legs and a fresh shirt in his hands, more bones than boy. "He's right, Treese. Let me take you on over to church this morning and let Trigger handle all this."

Trigger put a hand to Patrice's shoulder and was leading her to the door. "Go on get ready now."

She said nothing, letting him steer her. He had the good grace to hide a patronizing expression but she knew he thought her nervous. She took the doorknob in her own hand so that she might be the one to close it.

But then she paused, looking back at Gil. "Did you look in on the four o'clock?"

Gil shook his head. "That ole rooster's gone."

"Dead?"

"Probably. Fox must have carried him off."

Patrice looked at him, dark skin gleaming with water in lamplight. She felt a trickle at the back of her neck and touched blood where that scratch was. Must have opened the wound.

Trigger took gentle hold of the door and closed it on her.

five

NEW ORLEANS, NOW

SEVERIN LED MADELEINE DOWN to the banks of the Mississippi. Madeleine steeled herself, thinking the river devil was going to take her back to the murder site, but instead Severin walked straight into the water: step by step, eyes forward, like a parishioner about to be cleansed anew. Her hair trailed behind her on the water's surface. Madeleine looked back. The trees had already stretched so tall, and the thorns had spread so that there was no visible rise of levee, no hobo camps. The sun had gone, too—disappeared behind the mist of the river devil's world.

"You're going to show me *exactly* what happened?" Madeleine asked.

"So, to see!" Severin turned to her with bright eyes, a child excited to go for a swim in the river.

The water felt cool on Madeleine's skin even though it wasn't real. Her body was still sitting in the pickup while the rest of her was descending into the water with Severin. The silty river bottom squished beneath her as she first walked, then swam toward the center.

Severin was treading water, facing her. She reached out and took Madeleine's hand.

"Ready?"

Madeleine nodded. Severin dove down, and Madeleine took a breath and dove after her. The water was clear and gray like the briar mist above the surface. Easy to forget that what she saw was part illusion. Were this actually the Mississippi, it would be the colors of a toad. They went straight down, and then Severin paused, floating like a marionette on strings, and Madeleine paused with her. And then Severin plunged down even further.

It seemed pointless. Diving down to the bottom of the river. How did that answer any questions? Madeleine was tired and growing irritated, and she wouldn't even be here were it not for the urgency of the situation. She didn't like bending the rules of the bargain with Severin. A bad precedent.

But instead of reaching the river bottom, when she dove down she broke the surface again. Suddenly down was up. And everything had changed.

This world was still a briar world. But it was rooted in a place that was not the least bit familiar. The sounds out here were not those of the Mississippi River, not even Louisiana. The shoreline was not muddy banks—there were rocks, and grassy estuaries cut with broad red channels for a rise and fall of tide.

"What is this?" Madeleine asked.

"Wolfville."

Madeleine frowned. There were seabirds, and also briar creatures that hovered in her periphery before disappearing when Madeleine looked directly at them. Exhausting, trying to distinguish briar world from a more familiar kind of reality.

They were swimming toward shore. Sandpipers scattered as a merlin swooped into their midst. The birds did not avoid Madeleine, though. She might as well be a breeze passing among them. She saw them up close in a way she'd never before experienced. Every detail, from the color patterns on their feathers to the nostrils and small black eyes. She reached out and touched a beak. Could feel the rigidity of it but couldn't move it. The sandpiper did not react to her touch.

When they reached dry sand, things changed. It was in the way she and Severin moved. Each step was as though they crossed a mile, their surroundings blurring past though their bodies moved slowly and carefully. Madeleine kept her gaze on Severin so as not to go dizzy. They stopped in front of a white two-story house, an old salt box, with hummingbirds buzzing mounds of red dianthus in the front yard. A sign read SWEET WILLIAM INN.

"What's this got to do with last night's murder?" Madeleine asked.

Severin didn't reply but instead led her up to the house, walking through the front door as though they were ghosts, and up a flight of stairs. A bed and breakfast, it seemed. Severin turned at the landing and led her through a very small door which concealed a second set of stairs, this one dark and very steep. Dangerously steep. They were heading into the house's attic. At the top of the stairs, a baby gate. They passed through it.

Madeleine could hear a woman's voice as she spoke on a cell phone. "No Mama, we're fine. I don't pay rent. Nuh-uh. I clean the rooms and me and Coop stay for free."

Sun poured through the window in a trapezoid pattern where a playpen stood. Madeleine could see a little boy sitting amid foam blocks with letters and numbers stitched on them, playing with a stuffed green dinosaur.

Madeleine stared at the child, unable to move, because though she'd never seen him before she knew at once who he was. This was her nephew.

◦◦◦

MADELEINE GRABBED SEVERIN'S ARM. "What're you trying to pull?"

"Only what you asked to know!"

"I asked about the murder!"

"And so you see."

"You trying to tell me that baby has something to do with last night?"

Severin made a face and pulled free from Madeleine's grasp. She alit on the beveled board siding and climbed like an anole. Up, up along the wall, which angled to a ceiling that matched the peak of the roof. A person could stand upright only beneath the peak; everywhere else the ceiling slanted too low.

Severin darted up and over to where the baby's mother was curled up on a battered couch with a cell phone pressed to her ear. Emily Hammond. The one who had fallen pregnant by Madeleine's brother Marc, just before he killed himself. Emily had fled all the way to Nova Scotia to escape the darkness surrounding Madeleine's family.

"Yeah, Mama, Cooper's playin with the dinosaur you got him," Emily was saying.

Madeleine looked at the little boy, who was knocking the dinosaur against the blocks.

"Cooper," Madeleine murmured, and she knelt down to hook her fingers in the fabric of the playpen.

The little boy looked up and cooed, smiling, and Madeleine could swear he was looking directly at her. He tossed his head with an inhaled laugh. He was clearly a LeBlanc: blue eyes and African skin. Points at the brows. So much like his father. Like Madeleine, even.

Madeleine felt her eyes go hot. She would have liked to know this little guy. But it was too dangerous. *This,* here and now, just being here was unthinkably dangerous.

She had to turn away. "Severin, I mean it, we have to leave these people alone."

"It is a glimpse, yes, a whisper at most." The river devil crept back along the seam of roof joists to peer into the playpen.

The beveled wood that lined the walls looked original, and the house had to be around a hundred years old. The attic itself was crudely finished out for a living space. No insulation. Probably hot in the summer and cold in the winter.

Emily had her head tilted and was laughing into the receiver. Madeleine had gone to school with her. The sun pouring through the window reflected off the playpen and filled Emily's face with gold, her blond hair falling in loose, short waves.

Emily looked across at her son and sat up, saying into the receiver, "Yeah, the landlady's real nice. Watches Coop while I'm in class. We got everything we need."

And then Emily's expression changed. She rose to her feet.

"Hey, Mama, let me call you back."

Emily was staring at her son as she closed the flip phone. Madeleine followed Emily's gaze. Severin was curled behind the little boy, whispering into his ear.

Madeleine pushed her back. "You get away from him!"

Severin sprang out of the playpen and retreated up along the ceiling, her face both angry and satisfied. "They do not listen so easy. These you must whisper when they are young."

"What did you say to him?"

"Nothing of a matter. It is a practice only, that over time he might listen."

Emily Hammond put a hand to her mouth. Madeleine looked back at Cooper. He'd arranged his foam blocks into the letters A–U–N–T–I–E.

Emily snatched her son out of his playpen. "Who's here? Who is it?"

Her eyes were wet. Cooper looked dazed but did not cry.

"Get us out of here!" Madeleine said.

Severin crept forward. "He is the last child of the briar. It is a thing that leads to another, and what you asked to know."

"But what's that got to do with that murder on the levee?"

"The training. Only the training for a far tomorrow."

Severin scrabbled across the ceiling and over to the stairs, down to the third step. Madeleine looked over the railing. Blood was seeping from beneath Severin's toes. Her lips pulled back in a smile, and then she scaled the wall again, pausing in the corner at the ceiling.

Emily was turning in a circle, her eyes searching. "Madeleine! Madeleine LeBlanc!"

Madeleine looked at her.

"I know it's you, Madeleine. You're his only aunt. I remember when we were in school. You were just like any other kid. You wouldn't have hurt anyone in those days."

Madeleine wished she could tell her, *I'm not here to hurt you.* But that would be a lie. *This* was hurting her. *This* was hurting little Cooper. Just by knowing where he was, it opened him up to the briar where knowledge flowed in the collective.

"Leave us alone, Madeleine!" Emily cried. "All you people, you leave us alone!"

And then she rushed for the stairs, knocking the baby gate aside.

Madeleine stepped toward the railing. "Don't!"

But Emily was descending much too fast for the steep, narrow stairway, and with little Cooper clutched in her arms.

Emily's feet slid out from under her and her head knocked back against the third step, the one where Severin had left droplets of blood.

Emily made a guttural sound, her arms protecting Cooper's head. But she rose and pulled open the door at the base of the stairs. Blood on her hair and shirt. Madeleine listened as her footfalls descended the second set of stairs and out the front door.

Severin was still smiling.

six

ENON LAY WITH HIS hospital gown gaping enough at the neck to expose a few clusters of chest hair and a sharp collarbone. He'd lost weight, Madeleine thought. His face looked slack except for the eyes—they seemed to be smiling . . . almost. An oddity of the human brain that certain facial muscles created recognizable patterns, such as joy, even when the lips or cheeks couldn't form a smile. In Zenon's case, not only was a true smile impossible, he wasn't even able to blink for a yes or no response. That meant he was either oblivious to his surroundings or unable to communicate. Or both.

Zenon's current state was the result of Madeleine's first awkward attempts at pigeonry. It had happened after Madeleine found out that Zenon had committed murder. She had gone to the police, testified against him, and afterward he'd sworn he would kill her. His briar skills were already honed sharp—much more than hers—and she'd understood that the only way to escape him was to kill him first. And so, she'd used her newfound skill of pigeonry to send a fellow prisoner after Zenon in the facility where he was incarcerated. What Madeleine had intended was that Zenon should die. Instead, the other prisoner she'd used to attack Zenon had broken his spine without killing him. An implanted thought often changed once inside a "pigeon's" mind.

As a result of the attack, Zenon would live out the rest of his life like this, staring at the ceiling, unable to speak. Possibly not even able to think.

The stark hospital room bore no sign that Zenon existed as anything other than an extension of that institutional bed. No personal effects. Not even the quilt she'd once brought him. Even the thick curtains were drawn as though natural sunlight might bear some contaminant.

Madeleine opened the curtains and let the sun fill the room, washing over the sterile fluorescent lighting and causing her to squint. She pinched the bridge of her nose and closed her eyes for a moment. She'd at least managed to change her clothes since dealing with the matter at the levee and then going into the briar with Severin. By the time she'd returned to her body, Ethan had already finished talking to the police and had brought her home. She must have been in a rambling state before she came to. Hated to think of Ethan seeing her like that all the time.

A short blond nurse appeared in a shapeless pink uniform that looked like it was made from the same material as the bedsheets.

"Hi there!" the nurse called out as if addressing an auditorium full of people instead of one single woman and a catatonic man. "Looks like we have a visitor today! You family?"

Madeleine shrugged. "Half-sister."

"That's real good. I'm Vessie. We're taking real good care of your brother here."

Madeleine nodded as Vessie reached for the IV hook and took down an empty plastic bag.

"He looks like he's smiling," Madeleine said.

"Probably because he's happy to see you. He wishes you'd come to visit more often."

"I doubt that."

"He does! Everyone loves visitors."

Madeleine took a step closer to Zenon as Vessie replaced the empty IV bag with a full one. That ghost of a smile on him—and it wasn't an illusion—was probably just a response to what he saw in his own private dream world. Maybe he was even somewhere in the briar tunnels. Unlike Madeleine, Zenon might actually like it in there.

She narrowed her eyes and touched his hair just above his right ear, pulling off a curled, dried bit of something. "What's this?"

Vessie widened her grin. "Oh, ha ha! Looks like a leaf!"

"He's confined to his bed. Where would he have ever been near a leaf?"

Vessie shrugged. "I thought he needed a little fresh air."

"You took him out?"

"Just around the grounds."

"Isn't that against policy?"

Vessie's grin slipped a fraction. "That's just red tape. If it's in the patient's best interest, hon, they'll look the other way. I'm just trying to give him the best care possible."

Madeleine looked back toward the window. Cars in the parking lot, on the streets. People.

Vessie was folding back Zenon's sheet to reveal his legs had grown thinner and paler since he'd become bedridden.

"You can't take him out again, ever," Madeleine said.

Vessie looked up. "What?"

"If he weren't in this hospital he'd be incarcerated, awaiting trial for multiple murders. I'm serious about this. He can't go out."

Vessie's lips parted, her brown eyes wide and livid. "You can't be serious!"

"I'm very serious."

The nurse gawked for a moment, then flung her arm in the direction of Zenon's shrinking body. "Well just look at him! He can't even go to the bathroom on his own! What do you think he's gonna to do, rob a bank?"

"I understand that you meant well. But if you take him out again I'm going to have to report it."

Vessie huffed, drawing herself up a notch. "Fine." Her hand swept up and tucked a cropped blond curl behind her ear and then reached down to seize Zenon's leg. She started moving it in bicycle circles.

Madeleine's cell phone buzzed inside her bag, and she turned toward the window to take the call. It was Ethan.

"How you holdin up, sweetheart?"

"I'm alright. I'm here at the hospital in Zenon's room."

"Good God, baby, why'd you go there of all places?"

"Chloe insisted on meeting me here."

Silence, then, "You couldn't just get some sleep and wait until tomorrow to talk to her?"

"No, considering what happened at the levee last night, I think it's important to talk to her immediately."

"But they got the old woman, Alice."

"Yes, but . . ."

She glanced over her shoulder where Vessie was pressing Zenon's knee to his chest and then straightening it again, Zenon's ghost smile still in place. Vessie laid down the leg with exaggerated care and moved to the other side of the bed.

Madeleine lowered her voice and turned back toward the window. "You know good and well there was something else going on. Something about the way that woman Alice acted."

The windowsill was dotted with husks of flies. Two live ones were popping against the glass. In the reflection, Madeleine caught Vessie watching her. She was slowly rotating Zenon's arm.

It occurred to Madeleine that Ethan had been silent a beat too long.

"Something wrong, baby?" she asked.

He said, "Well, I'd checked in with your buddy Vinny on the task force like you asked me to. Said they had two other murders last night. Unrelated. Both suspects confessed on the spot and got taken into custody."

She considered this. "In New Orleans? That doesn't seem that unusual."

He paused. "Yeah, well, Vinny said the other two suspects were homeless folks, too. So were the victims. Homeless on homeless, three totally unrelated in the same night. No fights, nobody stole anything from anybody else, no motivation anywhere to be found. That's never happened before."

Madeleine tightened her grip on the cell phone. "Oh."

"Didn't want to tell you just yet, but I figured you'd be hot if I didn't."

"I appreciate it."

Ethan cleared his throat. "Well, St. Jo's is doing a roundup, trying to bring everyone in off the streets and keep'm safe."

"Good."

"You gonna get some rest once you finish up with ole Chloe?"

"No baby, I'll just wait til tonight."

He grunted. "What are you gonna do?"

"Better head over to St. Jo's, see if I can help with the outreach."

"Now listen up, Madeleine, you ain't gonna be no damn good to no damn body if you don't get a little sleep."

"Not going to require too many cognitive reasoning skills. Just bringing some hard luck folks in off the street."

"Any way I can talk you out of it?"

" 'Fraid not."

"Figures." He sighed, then, "I'll go with you."

"No need, baby, you got too much work to do there at the clinic."

"And let you run around blight buildings by yourself so you can gather up all the street folks?"

"I—I just figure you got labs."

"I knew you'd be hardheaded and I already cleared my schedule."

She chewed her lip. Bringing Ethan along could either be a good thing or a bad thing. But beneath it all, she'd be relieved to have him. "Alright then."

"Meet you at St. Jo's in an hour."

"Sounds good. And Ethan?"

"Yeah?"

"Thanks."

"You're welcome. I love you."

"I love you, too."

She hung up. She could still see Vessie working Zenon's arm in the window's reflection. Those two other killers—she wondered if they were people she knew. And she wondered if she knew the victims. Either could have been friends of her father, or former patients from when she'd still carried on her practice at Tulane. Now she was living off what was left of her dwindling estate while she volunteered for St. Jo's and tried to figure out how to regroup after her lost career. It had been almost two years but it seemed like a whole other life—before the river devil had made it impossible to be a psychologist.

Before she'd used the pigeon game to strike Zenon down.

Before Daddy had died from an overdose in an abandoned building in Iberville.

Before before before. So much had changed in such a short time.

Vessie laid down Zenon's arm and picked up his other leg.

Madeleine thought of those black woods at dawn. That clicking sound.

"MADELEINE."

She turned to see her great-grandmother, Chloe LeBlanc, entering through the doorway.

Chloe's iron hair was puffed into a knot at the nape of her neck, and she gazed at Madeleine with black eyes and ancient dark skin, a paper napkin rumpled in her fist. Despite the heat, a white cotton quilt lay folded over her knees. Pushing her wheelchair was her attendant, Oran, an albino black man.

Madeleine looked back at the bed where Zenon lay, and saw that each time Vessie raised his leg to complete the bicycle rotation she exposed his genitals.

"Vessie, could you please continue his exercises another time?"

Vessie's eyes snapped, her lips in a tight white line. She opened her hands with a melodramatic flourish, dropping Zenon's leg as if it were a rotten ham bone. The room was quiet. Vessie moved for the door but then halted.

"Likes'm closed," she said, and darted back to the window, snapping the curtains shut.

The room went dark. Where the two panels met, a white line of sunlight glowed.

Madeleine, Chloe, and Oran watched as Vessie strode out of the room. Oran shifted on his leg as though he wasn't sure what to do with himself.

Chloe thrust a finger at the blanket on her knees and Oran took it and unfolded it over Zenon.

Madeleine recognized it. "That's the quilt I'd brought him. The one from the cottage on Bayou Black."

"We cleaned it," Chloe said.

Madeleine took a corner of it and helped Oran spread it over Zenon, pattern side down. Oran moved quickly as though he wished to get it over with.

He spoke to Chloe in a whisper. "Shall I wait outside, then?"

"No. You stay here," Chloe replied, then said to Madeleine, "What is this you must discuss? You've thought again about learning your devil?"

Madeleine eyed her but didn't answer immediately. The two flies vibrated in the space between the window and the blackout curtains.

"Not really," Madeleine said. "We have a bargain now. Severin and I. Seems to be working."

Chloe's face drew to a sneer, and before she could say anything, Madeleine added, "I want to know if there are any others. Something happened last night. Led me to believe that someone was using the pigeon game."

Chloe was watching her with fascination. "Is this true? How do you know?"

"I can't be sure. It's why I wanted to talk to you. Do you know of anyone with these abilities, outside our family?"

Chloe spread her hands. "The only two living are right here in this room."

Chloe didn't know about little Cooper, Marc's son, of course. Madeleine let her gaze fall on Zenon. She didn't like that smile in his eyes. She wished he'd close them and go to sleep.

Chloe said, "Madeleine. You pretend so much. Why you come to me with stupid questions? You can learn answers to much better questions, in a way that no one else in the entire world can. You alone can exist in the briar with your river devil. This is a gift you squander."

"Right now I just want to know if there are others like our bloodline."

"Others! Stupid! No, girl, our family is all there is. You still don't see? This is why it is powerful. If others could do what you can it would undermine you. Outside your bloodline, the lumens are the only ones who can tap the briar. That is why they weaken you."

Chloe leaned forward. "You really want to know? You learn the ways of your devil, yanh? The river devil shows you answers even to stupid questions."

Madeleine listened, refusing to be fazed. The bargain with Severin was working well but Madeleine knew that if she let her frustration escalate, Severin would come looking for her.

"This is serious, Chloe. There was a murder last night."

"Listen, Madeleine, you know I can help you. We start with the stupid question, yanh? 'Are there others,' you ask. So. Tell me, what do you know now?"

"What do I know?"

Chloe said, "Tell me everything in your mind now."

Madeleine blinked at her, thinking. "I was speaking to Alice, a homeless woman who'd killed a man, but she didn't seem to be in charge of her own body and mind. And—"

"Ah, see! Look how you hold back. You talk about something that does not matter."

"It does matter! Chloe, I—"

"Listen! It does not matter because you have already given care to this thought. You hold a magnifying glass too long and it only serves to burn the object. You drop it, and look at the rest. Forget this homeless woman."

"I just don't understand what you're getting at."

Chloe said, "What is in your mind right now, right here, as we stand in this room?"

Madeleine sighed. Still unclear what Chloe was getting at, she gave it a shot. She stepped outside her thoughts and backward-examined them. So many things there, not the half of which she cared to expose to the likes of Chloe.

Madeleine said, "Alright. I don't like that nurse. I don't like the look on Zenon's face. I heard a clicking noise this morning and I can't get it out of my head. There are dead flies in the window."

"That's better," Chloe said, and waved at Oran.

He moved across to the window where the flies were, seeming to be relieved at having a task to fill. Madeleine stepped back.

Chloe said, "You are not telling everything in your mind, Madeleine. I can see there is more that is hidden."

Madeleine did not meet her gaze.

Chloe said, "But you do not have to. Not this time. You have taken a look yourself."

Oran was running his finger along the window track. The two living flies were buzzing and bouncing off the window, too sluggish to notice him. He retrieved the last of the dead flies from the sill and then closed a fist around the two that were still bobbing. Madeleine watched, repulsed.

Chloe said, "Now, back to the stupid question, 'Are there others like your bloodline?' Does it feel the same? Does this question matter to you so much?"

Madeleine threw an exasperated scowl at her. "Yes. It matters!"

But as soon as she'd said it she realized it wasn't so.

Chloe was right. Madeleine was posing a trumped-up question. She wasn't really looking for others like herself, not at this moment. The heart of the matter was something else. It formed a stone of dread in her stomach, and perhaps she'd been trying to deflect focus.

"Throw them away, Oran, and wash your hands," Chloe said.

He obeyed.

Madeleine said, "It's just that when I found the woman who'd done the killing, she recognized me even though I didn't know her."

Chloe sagged as if Madeleine had just greatly disappointed her. "You cannot let it go, eh?"

Madeleine said, "And the woman, Alice, said something about using Shalmut next time. Not sure what she meant by that."

"You are so stubborn."

"I was with her for a while. I didn't exactly conduct a thorough examination, but aside from slight dissociative tendencies, she didn't show any signs of dementia."

Chloe waved a hand. "You always talk like a doctor of the mind, Madeleine, but you know nothing. I can help you manage your devil and learn the briar."

"I've been managing on my own."

"Ah! So, how long before your river devil takes you so deep into the briar that you don't know where you are anymore? What will you do, hope your man can keep you on a leash?"

Madeleine balled her fists at her sides.

Oran turned away and hesitated, then shuffled toward the

doorway and leaned against the wall, his golden orange hair glowing beneath the direct light from the recessed fixture. He looked like he wanted to break from the room.

Madeleine said, "We've worked out a schedule. Severin only comes during certain windows of time, and I give her my full attention when she does. After that, she leaves me alone so I can function in the real world."

"Oh, you believe that, do you? Tell me, Madeleine, do you really think that river devil will continue to honor your bargain? How long do you have before you're at her mercy?"

Madeleine frowned. "I don't know that I have a choice."

"Of course you have a choice! You let me help you. I have watched so many generations fall away to madness. The only one who never went mad was him." Chloe waved at Zenon. "He kept sharp. He let me guide him."

"He was a murderer. And he tried to kill me, too, if you recall."

Madeleine looked down at Zenon and saw the lightness had finally disappeared from his eyes. "She took him outside. That nurse who was in here. Took him out for fresh air."

The old woman said nothing. She coughed, bringing something forward from her lungs, and spat into her paper napkin.

Madeleine said, "I told her not to do it anymore."

Chloe seemed nonplussed.

Madeleine looked at Zenon and said, "He used to listen to foreign radio stations. Where they spoke in languages he didn't understand. Said it helped him stay sharp."

"He studied. He learned much. Now it is up to you, Madeleine, you are the last."

Madeleine flinched, thinking again of little Cooper, but she would never tell Chloe about him.

"I say, you are the last, yanh?" Chloe said, and she was watching with a fixed stare.

Madeleine nodded.

Chloe lowered her voice to a growl. "Bah! A waste. You do not care what happens! Generations of children who squander gifts."

"I didn't ask for any of this."

"You didn't ask! You have a gift; it is your duty to use it. You too lazy. You should make babies with that worthless man and bring them to me. I will raise them to be gods."

"If I ever did have a child, Chloe, you can bet I would keep it far away from you."

Chloe leaned forward in her chair, eyes bright. Madeleine wondered if the old woman really could live long enough to raise a child. Already, she was supposedly 116 years old. She looked like she'd stopped ageing altogether once she'd reached eighty. Which child of the bramble had helped her do that?

"Listen to me, Madeleine. You listen, girl. You will go mad. I tell you this, you will go mad."

Madeleine stared, her mouth going dry.

Chloe lowered her voice. "Your river devil plays along with your silly bargain as a way to draw you deeper into the briar. Your body will be an empty shell while your mind flies away. Maybe forever."

Madeleine could feel tears pricking at the backs of her eyes. She tore her gaze to Zenon. His chest rose and fell, rose and fell. She dared not look at his face.

Chloe said, "You go on and on about something meaningless, one drunk vagrant kills another drunk vagrant. You pretend that is important. That is housecleaning. If you want to keep from going mad, you have one choice. You come and learn with me."

seven

*B*O RAMIREZ FIRST FIGURED out the clicking thing when he was really young. Couldn't say exactly how old. At that time, he could pretty much find his way by feel and by listening to regular sounds. The air-conditioning blower. Cars passing. Wind in the trees.

Kids at school were either nice to him or mean. Some of them were really mean. Bo couldn't play much with the regular kids because he was a special needs for being blind. That's how he met Ray. The only other one with a physical handicap. Bo would go running on the playground and crash into Ray's wheelchair, and they'd both go butt-over-bean onto the pavement and sometimes even get bloody.

Ray never gave him hell about it, though, as far as Bo could tell, because in the early days Ray couldn't speak, only sign. Bo couldn't sign, only speak. And because Bo was blind he couldn't see what Ray was signing even if he knew sign language, which he didn't. Not at that point anyway. Bo did Braille and he mouth-talked, and that was it. So if Bo crashed into Ray's wheelchair and Ray was hacked off about it, Bo never knew because Ray had no way to chew him out. They got along great.

One day Bo was running on the playground and heard Ray's wheels going, and he grabbed Ray's wheelchair and ran with him. They flew like that for a few seconds until Bo ran them off the pavement into the grass, at which point they crashed, both of them rolling butt-over-bean again. Ray lurped up his lunch and Bo got in trouble. They were best friends from that point on even though they couldn't talk to each other yet.

The clicking discovery seemed like a small thing at first, but really it changed everything.

Bo'd discovered it accidentally one day when he got in trouble. He'd been chasing a cat and crashed into his mom while she was bringing in the groceries; caused her to drop an entire jug of milk and a lettuce. The lettuce was washable but the milk was for spoil. Anyway, his mom stuck his butt in the corner. She'd always told him to slow down because it was dangerous for blind kids to be running around. Said he's liable to break his neck one of these days.

So he was standing in the corner, bored stupid, and he was running his hand along the bumpy wall and making all kinds of noises with his mouth. Farm animal sounds, motor sounds, tick-tock sounds—making clicks. That's when he realized that when he clicked at the wall it sounded different from when he clicked at the middle of the room.

That's all at first. Could just tell when he was standing in front of a wall.

He took to clicking at everything, remembering how the tone of the click sounded different depending on what he was clicking at. His mom said he sounded like a clucking chicken. He could eventually tell the difference between a wall and a curb or a car, and then he could tell the difference between a car and a truck.

The school put all the special needs kids together which meant that older kids, some of them way older, were stuck playing with the littler kids like Bo and Ray. There were about twelve kids altogether, of which most were learning disability. Those kids were all pretty nice. They liked to play hard like Bo did. But some of those kids weren't really learning disability, they were just plain fools who spent all their time huffing paint. And those ones, Oyster and Mako and them, they were older than Bo by about six years.

The paint huffers threw rocks at him on the playground. Told Bo they were playing baseball and he had to use his cane like it was a bat. Bo knew it was just their excuse to pelt him with rocks. Later, they quit pretending there was any game at all and just beat on him, threw rocks, stole his pack, even stole his shoes once, and always they stole his cane. They would steal his cane and break it, steal his cane and smear it with dog shit, or take it from him and beat on him with it. They stole his sunglasses, too. Bo had to wear sunglasses because it looked funny in the place where his eyes ought to be.

Bo missed the sunglasses but didn't care about the canes. Even without the huffers he'd lose a cane here or there or somewhere. He only carried them because his mom made him. Even now she made him carry one, even though the clicks were way better for seeing than the cane.

After Bo and Ray became friends, the bigger boys started beating on Ray, too. Mako seemed like the meanest one but Oyster gave him the mean ideas. Sucker punch the blind kid because he couldn't see you coming. Run up behind the deaf kid in the wheelchair because he couldn't hear you and he couldn't chase you down.

Bo would swing back, and he built up real fast reflexes. Managed to clock Mako or one of the other boys every now and then. But not often.

The clicking, though, was starting to really pay off. He crashed a whole lot less. And he crashed Ray less, too.

One day Mako snuck up behind Ray and smashed him in the face with his backpack so hard Ray's chair went sideways and he fell out.

But Bo figured out what was happening with his clicks and he chased Mako and knocked him good in the ear. Mako went down. Bo went down after him. But Mako was so much bigger and he turned it back and rang Bo's bell. And then the other huffers came after him, too. Teacher showed up and put everyone in detention except for Ray. So all in all you couldn't say Bo won the fight because he was pretty much getting his butt handed to him except for one or two good punches, but still, things changed after that. The huffers would still come over and sock Bo or Ray every now and then but it was less often.

After a while, the huffers stopped coming to school. Bo had no idea what they were doing if they weren't going to school, but good riddance. His mom always said every cloud had a silver lining and it was true. Even though the huffers pretty much made his life miserable, Bo had had to be so extra careful when they were around that he'd become an expert at seeing with his clicks. Could run like the wind without crashing into anything, could even chase a soccer ball.

Now and again he'd still come across the huffers. Found out they didn't only leave school, they'd all left home. On purpose! Bo and his mom sometimes had to leave their home and spend the night wherever because his mom's roommate needed some privacy. Bo didn't mind camping out with his mom like that, but guaranteed he'd never do it on purpose.

eight

VACHERIE, 1927

PATRICE AND GIL RODE their horses along the wet main road to Vacherie. In the same way they used kerosene lamps instead of electric lighting at Terrefleurs, the primary mode of transportation was still horses even though they had Papa's automobile. It required gasoline and upkeep. If Papa were still alive, though, they'd be using electric lights and the car. Despite his madness he'd managed to keep things running.

"You think we'll be late?" Gil asked.

"We might be," Patrice said.

She watched as his gelding trotted along with its smooth gait. Sugar Pie, the mare Patrice had chosen to ride, had a more jaunty way; it made Patrice's legs a bit stiff. At least the drizzle had stopped before they'd set out.

She said, "We'll need to get serious about leaving Terrefleurs."

"I know," Gil said.

"If we're very careful, I think we can be ready in three months' time."

"Three months? How do you figure?"

"We just need to come up with a plan."

He seemed to think this over but said nothing. The horse hooves beat against the gravel in a rhythmic accompaniment to first light.

Patrice said, "The primary thing is money. We'll need to save up as much as we can. A hundred dollars, I think."

He turned and looked at her, his blue eyes slanting. "We could take up horse wrangling."

"Be serious!"

"I'm trying, honey, I just don't know where we'll find a hundred dollars. Mother still handles all the money even though she's off in New Orleans."

"We could sell eggs. . . ."

She did a quick calculation. Even if they could sell a dozen eggs a day at 25 cents a dozen, that only added up to a dollar every four days. Which was about $7.50 a month. At that rate, it would take them over a year to save to a hundred dollars. And that was assuming the hens could actually produce a dozen eggs a day every single day, in excess of what went to the workers.

She shook her head. "Maybe six months. We'll just have to come up with a way. A hundred dollars in three months' time, that's $33.33 each month for two months, and $33.34 for the third month."

"Might as well be a thousand."

"Or . . . we can pull it off in six months if we only save $16.66 a month."

"You really think we can hold mother off for another six months?"

"I . . . don't know. Maybe. Yes, we can probably hold her off that long."

"Well, alright. But even so, even if we can save up all that money, what'll we do once we've got it?"

"We just have to make a plan."

"What kind of plan?"

"You know, what to take with us. Where to go. What to do for shelter. Horses or car."

"Car!"

"We'd have to get it running first and I'd be the only one who could drive."

"You can't drive, you're a girl."

"Hush up. At least I can see over the steering wheel."

And Patrice thought, six months seemed like an eternity now. But six months ago Papa was still alive, and Mother presided over Terrefleurs. Over the children. Terrefleurs was now coasting along like a raft with no one to guide it. A lot could happen. They had to make that money in six months or they would be mother's slaves forever.

She secretly believed they'd find a way to do it in three.

~~~

PATRICE AND GIL SAT in the back pew. They'd arrived late to church and had had to slip in after the service had already started. Reverend Turner looked smaller from this distance. Tatie Bernadette was sitting way up at the front. This was new. The children and Tatie usually sat together somewhere in the middle. Tatie was easy to pick out even from behind where not an inch of skin showed, because every Sunday she wore the same violet dress and the matching violet hat with the silk rose pinned at the base, and if there was a chill she used a shawl. No shawl today.

Patrice stared at that distant violet glow and thought of Rosie. From experience, Patrice knew that Marie-Rose would be fine. Trig would find her as promised. Just another wander. Rosie wasn't the only LeBlanc child to physically walk off when the briar closed around her, but she was the most frequent one to do it. Their mother had started in on Rosie when she was still so young.

Thank God their mother was gone for now. This thought did not take the Lord's name in vain. Truly: thank God.

At the other side of the church, on the pulpit, Reverend Turner was talking about King Solomon in the days before he came to glory. The wicked days.

Patrice stifled a yawn and stole a glance at Gil. He was looking toward the reverend, but in truth his gaze was leveled at the dust motes that glimmered like wood fairies in the morning light. Most buildings had the windows angled so they never took a direct ray of sun. A dead stare of sunlight could heat a room to the steam boil in under ten minutes. This was probably why most parishioners took the first Sunday service, when those rays still seemed more a miracle of God than a torment of Hell. Patrice hated to think what the ten o'clock service might feel like.

Something was out of place. She looked beyond the reverend, then realized the altar had been removed from the great basin. So there'd be a baptism. Reverend Turner wasn't one to take the flock down to the river the way some did. Patrice tried to scan the pews for the newborn who was to be baptized but found only her fellow parishioners' backs.

From the pulpit, the reverend spoke of how King Sol had taken to idolatry, turning against God, and in doing so had split his kingdom in two: Christians and idolaters.

And then he bade the flock rise and turn in their hymnals to page 662. The piano sounded off with the opening chords of "Holy, Holy, Holy!", and Gil had the hymnal open to share between himself and Patrice just in time for queue.

Holy, holy, ho-ly!
Lord God almighty!
Early in the morning our song shall rise to Thee

Patrice didn't need to read from the hymnal. She often sang this one to herself at home. Song was not a thing their mother had allowed them to engage in, either. Songs came from the radio and from the cadence the workers sang in the fields. Her mother had kept Terrefleurs openly practicing in river magic, while Christians like Tatie Bernadette had privately maintained their faith. Privately until now, when all was open, and river magic had become the faith that was frowned upon at Terrefleurs.

What would mother do if she heard Patrice singing a Christian song right now?

Patrice smiled.

Cherubim and Seraphim
Falling down before Thee

She tilted back her head and lifted her voice straight to God, somewhere up in heaven, where maybe poor lost Papa had finally found comfort.

Gil's voice rose alongside Patrice's. He set down the hymnal and took her white gloved hand as they sang together. She smiled at him, but then:

A dried spot of blood on the back of his collar. She angled her head to take a closer look. A scratch just below the base of his skull. She stopped singing.

He caught her examining him. Frowning, she turned to show him the same scratch at the back of her own neck. The one she'd woken up with. The one that was supposed to be a bug bite.

He stopped singing, too.

Patrice drew her gaze toward the front of the church where Tatie Bernadette stood short and round in that violet Sunday dress. But next to her, next to her . . .

Holy, holy, ho-ly! tho' the darkness hide Thee,
Tho' the eye of sinful man Thy glory may not see

A spindly woman standing with Tatie. Not Tatie's sister. The hair was pulled snug up under a cloche hat. A dress that dipped low beneath the nape. And along that dark skin, a light trace, visible even

from the back of the church. A scar. A snaking zipper of a scar—
Patrice knew even though it was not fully visible—that traveled
down below that collar line.

Mother.

⚜

PATRICE FELT A HAND on her arm. Gilbert was trying to pull her down
to the pew. She realized that she and Reverend Turner were now
the only ones left standing. The song had ended and the reverend
was segueing into the baptism.

Patrice balled her fist and funneled her gaze on the back of her
mother's head. *You stand and leave—*

But she clamped the thought in midstream.

Not here. Not here.

Not in God's house.

She couldn't bring herself to use devil's magic here.

She was still on her feet.

"It's blasphemy," she murmured, feeling helpless.

Gil rose and took hold of her elbow, whispering, "Let's sit now,
honey."

She turned to look at him full in the face. He must not have realized it yet, that their mother was sitting up there with Tatie Bernadette.

There were ways in which Patrice could talk to him so that no
one else could hear. Ways in which she could cast her mother out of
God's house. To invoke such things as that, though, no matter how
pious the intent, it was all still—

Gil had an arm around her waist but he was no longer trying to
pull her down to the pew. Because he finally saw his mother, too.
There, up at the pulpit, Reverend Turner was taking Maman by
the hand. The reverend was speaking of baptism. Sin washed away.

Patrice shouted, her voice breaking across the pews:

"NO, SIR, DO NOT WASH THAT WOMAN!"

The entire congregation turned to look at Patrice. Paddle fans paused. Even Reverend Turner paused.

Patrice called out, "Reverend Turner, that woman is not clean. She must not touch that water."

Mother lifted her gaze from the front row, then turned with her hand still in the reverend's and ascended the steps to the pulpit where the basin waited. The reverend looked bewildered but he followed her.

"Stop!" Patrice shouted.

"No, child. No, honey!" Tatie Bernadette called to Patrice from the front pew.

"She must not touch that water!"

"Quiet your mouth!" Tatie Bernadette was now pushing her way out of the pew.

The parishioners looked back and forth from Tatie Bernadette to Patrice as they argued across the church. No one but the reverend ever spoke during service.

"She is unclean!"

"She has repented!"

Reverend Turner was standing frozen on the pulpit. Mother was by the broad white basin, taking off her shoes. She'd grown smaller over these months.

Gil was pulling at Patrice again, but this time he was pulling her toward the aisle.

She moved with him, calling, "My mother, Chloe LeBlanc, is not repentant. This is blasphemy! THIS IS BLASPHEMY!"

"Quiet yourself!" Tatie Bernadette used fists and elbows to charge down the aisle.

The reverend had recovered himself and now was opening his arms in Patrice's direction. "The Lord welcomes all . . ."

Patrice shouted, "He welcomes those who accept Him as their Lord and savior! That woman has done no such thing. If she said she has, she is lying!"

"I accept Jesus Christ," Mother said.

"No!"

"You hush now!" Tatie Bernadette grabbed Patrice's arms and whispered through jowls. "Your mother has found Jesus at last! Now that is the truth!"

"I will not tolerate this blasphemy!"

And, pop! Tatie Bernadette slapped her.

Patrice stepped back, addled, and then her fury regrouped and condensed itself into ball lightning.

She thrust her finger toward the reverend, her voice shrill. "You let her touch that water you will sully the Lord's house!"

Gil had his stick-thin arms around Patrice's waist and was urging her backward.

She fought him, searing her gaze across the gaping, gawking faces of the congregation. "If any of you, if any one person here lays hands of prayer on that woman, you are inviting devils! Into your hearts! Into your homes!"

Gil dragged her backward through the doors. Outside to white light. Clouds rolling overhead and sunlight drenching them from beneath with silver.

Gil let Patrice go, then. He shut the doors and turned to look at her, hands on hips. Nearby on the cracked shell drive, the horses nickered.

And then the church doors swung open again and Tatie Bernadette stormed out, letting them bang shut behind her. "What do you mean making a scene like that, girl? And in church!"

"It should be a spectacle! You can't permit her to work over the church like that, it's blasphemy!"

"You quiet your mouth. How dare you talk about blasphemy? You yourself took a baptism just a few months ago!"

Patrice stepped toward her *tatie*. "What does she want from you?"

"Want? She only wants salvation, girl, just like you did."

"Why?"

Tatie softened just a touch. "Now that's a fine question, 'why?' "

"Why now? Why after all these years? You know why *we* couldn't be baptized. Because *she* wouldn't let us. So what's changed for her?"

"Maybe it's a miracle."

"Come now, Tatie, she must be asking something of you. Please tell me what that is."

Tatie did not reply for a very long moment, her eyes solemn, and then: "She wants Jesus, petite Patrice. That's all. She just wants to be saved."

Patrice shook her head, her cheek still burning from where Tatie had slapped her, and before she could stop herself, she pried. God forgive her. She pried right into Tatie Bernadette's heart. Because she knew her dear *tatie* was lying.

She saw it. The intention was there: Tatie Bernadette wished to bring Mother to God. But there was something else, too. She intended to act on Mother's behalf in some way.

"What are you doing, there, girl?" Tatie Bernadette whispered.

Patrice swallowed.

Tatie said, "You talk of blasphemy, but you workin those river devil ways. Ain't ya? Right here in front of God's house."

Patrice said nothing. Devil's magic, still a sin whether at God's house or her own.

Tatie Bernadette turned and hefted herself back up the stairs, through the doors, rejoining the congregation in its celebration of the baptismal sacrament. The doors banged shut once again.

Patrice turned her back on all of them and cast her eyes to the sun, a searing white tunnel through the clouds. She let it burn her vision to tears.

Gil touched her arm. "That outburst of yours. Seemed more like something Marie-Rose woulda done."

She closed her eyes, sealing them wet. "You're stronger than you look, dragging me out like that."

"Well, back a my neck is bleeding and yours is, too."

Her eyes flew open. She removed her glove and put her kerchief to the wound. It came away red.

Gil said, "Don't know what kind of scratch wouldn't just scab over. You think it's got something to do with Marie-Rose?"

"Or Mother's return."

"Or maybe both."

She pressed the handkerchief back in place. "We'd best get back home, fast."

nine

NEW ORLEANS, NOW

*I*N ETHAN'S FLASHLIGHT BEAM, Madeleine could see a huge, glimmering disk of an eye—all black except for a golden ring on the outside. A hoot owl, was all. It stood perched atop the backrest of a battered couch. Ethan centered the light on it and Madeleine could see that a second owl stood there, too.

The first owl burst into flight. Madeleine reached for Ethan's shoulder as the creature disappeared through the broken window frame, and then the second owl followed with a screech. Feathers and dust bloomed like fireworks, sparkling in the intersecting beams of flashlight and sun splash. A crisscross of light.

Madeleine called into the darkness. "Homeless Outreach. Anyone here?"

Ethan followed the path of her voice with a sweep of beam. Not likely anyone was here—those owls wouldn't have tolerated human roommates. At least none that were alive. Given the recent murders, keeping an eye out for victims was an unspoken part of the search, too.

Mercifully, most of the windows were out. Odors of mold and pee were strong enough as it was but they'd have been worse if the glass had been in place. Instead, a healing cross-breeze washed in from the southern opening and out the eastern. Were it not for the great black thunderhead that had risen from the south, the apartment would be filled with daylight.

"No one here," she said, turning away.

"Hang on, let's just be sure.

She sighed through her nose.

Ethan limped forward into the living room and passed his beam over all four corners, then continued toward the back. Her eyes having adjusted, she could see well enough without the beam. Beyond, the kitchen seemed to have been stripped. Still useful enough for a hobo, though. A person could put together a serviceable meal of scraps without the benefit of running water or electricity. She'd managed it as a girl before she'd even learned her fractions.

Upholstery stuffing lined the divot where the owls had been nesting on the couch. No chairs or other furniture. Plenty of trash.

She stepped to the southern window. Couldn't see the others. The buildings across the way were glaring in brilliant sunlight, but the sky behind them was dark. The Huey P. Long Bridge split the horizon with black storm clouds above and bright white buildings below. The apartments across the street weren't blighted like this one. She saw children's toys and a broken patio chair over there. Active residents. The aluminum siding reflected the late afternoon sun enough to make her squint, with the thunderhead forming a velvet curtain above the bridge. Lightning fluttered from the direction of Pontchartrain.

With a start, she realized that Severin was here.

She could feel her presence from somewhere behind. Madeleine resisted the urge to turn. Instead she kept gazing at the bridge but focused her thoughts on the river devil behind her: *Severin, what are you doing here? It's not time yet.*

"Much much to see," she replied in her whispered child's voice, and then added, "Much for play."

Madeleine stiffened, and risked a look. *What do you mean, much for play?*

The little girl was but a faint sepia glow, a negative shadow, resting atop one of the doorless kitchen cabinets. She was grinning down at Ethan as he made his check of each corner. Of course he didn't know Severin was there. All his careful searching and he had no idea a river devil watched him. Madeleine wasn't about to let him in on it, either, in case doing so encouraged Severin to settle in.

Severin, listen to me. Did Zenon have anything to do with the murders?

"We can have a look to see."

Madeleine shook her head, eyeing Ethan for a moment, and then turned back to the window. *It's not time yet. Come back when it's time.*

She knew Severin was put out by the dismissal, but her presence faded away. Madeleine closed her eyes and tried not to think of Chloe's prediction. How the bargain with Severin wouldn't last. The fresh, ionized wind rolled over her and into the room.

She turned to face Ethan. "We should move on. One more to go."

He'd searched the kitchen and bath and was now shining the beam into the bedroom. "Just want to make a thorough check. Don't want anyone jumping out at us."

"We're doing all this for *their* safety, not ours," she said, but even in the dim light she could see his expression grow tense and she added, "You know what I mean. Of course our safety's important, too."

Too late. He flashed the light on her face.

When he spoke, his voice was angry. "I have a hard enough time as it is thinking about you constantly putting yourself at risk like this. When you talk that way it doesn't help things."

She spread her hands. "Rare situation. Besides . . ."

She let the argument fall off. No good bringing it up.

But Ethan had already picked up on her train of thought. "Pigeon games."

The wind poured over her neck and tangled hair into her face. She brushed it away.

He said, "You're playing with matches, Maddy."

"It puts me in a unique position, you have to admit. I'll never be a victim of attack because if anyone were to come after me, I can use pigeonry."

"No. It's not infallible. You haven't fully mastered it yet. And even if you had it's useless against a stray bullet."

She strode back to the front door and folded her arms, trying not to be tense. Frustration would only lure Severin back.

One more apartment to check. She just wanted to get it over with, get back to the group below and get them safely to St. Jo's.

He limped toward her. "Or a surprise attack. Your pigeon games don't work if you don't see the guy coming."

No use trying to keep still another moment. She turned into the corridor.

❧

THAT CLEANSING FLOW OF breeze vanished. No light in the corridor, either. Having adjusted to the dimness in the apartment didn't help much when the hall was black as pitch. It didn't slow her. She turned right toward the last apartment and ran her knuckle along the wall for guidance, should she encounter something horrid in the dark—a tuft of mold, a roach—touching it with her knuckle was less odious than with her fingertips. Her free hand groped for her bag, where her own flashlight had been languishing unused. Ethan was the type to switch his on long before it was absolutely necessary.

She charged forward, knowing Ethan's flashlight would illuminate the final door soon enough, or maybe she'd just find the damn thing first by sheer blind groping.

Too late, she realized the narrow hall was not empty. Someone grabbed her arm.

Madeleine's mind lurched to high alert.

Don't panic!

Because to panic would agitate the river devil. . . .

Whoever grabbed her was male. He threw her backward against the wall, and she felt something hard crack across her mouth.

Her lips lit with immediate sparks of pain. She sank to her knees.

Thwack!

A second blow, this time landing somewhere above, a stiff object colliding into the wall where her head would have been if she hadn't slid to the floor. She let fly a half-scream before swallowing it back again, forcing herself to be silent.

"Madeleine!" Ethan's voice from the apartment where she'd just been.

She hooked her mind onto the attacker and clamped. Squeezed out all panic or fury. The corridor was tilting, Ethan's flashlight now swinging as he stormed into it. She realized she was listing sideways. But she was on that attacker in her mind. On him, in him, wired to him. She funneled the force of her own concentration into that brain. Dragged him down. Down. *Set that weapon down! Get down! Down!*

And he was. Ethan's beam was shining on them, blinding her momentarily, and then she saw the guy on his knees a few feet away. Papers and empty cups littered the floor, and an oblong piece of wood was resting directly in front of him. Something he'd just laid there. An instant response to pigeonry.

Ethan tore forward. Madeleine did her best to rise to her knees, shaky as she was, and lifted her hands. "It's alright, Ethan. He's disarmed."

The flashlight swung to the guy on the floor and then up to her face. She shielded her eyes. Her lips were throbbing with increased blood flow, but they likely wouldn't be showing any bruising just yet. Not on the outside. Inside her mouth she was tasting blood. She hoped Ethan couldn't tell she'd been hit.

"Maddy, you alright?"

"Fine. Just fine." And then she added, "We just startled each other."

The flashlight beam swung mercifully away and back to the man on his knees. No, not a man. A boy. A teenager. His face was half-covered with a handkerchief, bandito-style, cinched into his afro.

From somewhere in the direction of Lake Pontchartrain, the first tremor of thunder rolled inland.

She leaned over and put her hands on her knees, trying to keep the tears from running. No emotion; just a physical reaction to the pain. "What's your name, son?"

"Ain't your son."

She could have made him answer but she didn't. His voice unsettled her. Deeper than it should have been—like an ogre's voice—and on the boy it seemed otherworldly.

Just a boy. This was just a boy.

She heard something snap from behind Ethan. He swung around and shone the beam down the corridor, and Madeleine caught her breath.

There were several other boys standing there, the nearest one with a steel rod raised over Ethan.

Down! Down! On your knees! Drop it!

The nearest boy dropped, and he released the metal rod. It made a chiming peal as it landed. The other boys looked confused. One had a knife. All wore bandanas over their faces.

"Jesus," Ethan said.

He stepped in front of Madeleine, arms spread.

Madeleine thought:

Down!

The boy with the knife dropped. Her mind contracted on him, making him put the blade on the floor. He obeyed. It seemed as if these boys had materialized from nowhere and everywhere, from between the very studs under the torn drywall. She bridled in her fear.

Street kids. They must have overheard Ethan and Madeleine searching that last apartment and hidden in the corridor to wait.

She fumbled in her bag for the flashlight as she used pigeonry to drop the rest of them, one by one. But as each boy went down, the previous one rose up again. Impossible to train her mind on all of them at the same time. She snapped on her flashlight.

The first boy, the one who'd struck her, was back on his feet. He'd been the one who'd positioned himself directly in Madeleine's path. Setting himself apart from the others right from the start. He was probably their leader.

She turned the light toward her own face. "My name is Doctor LeBlanc. Will you please tell me your name?"

Her lips stung as she spoke. Ethan was shining his beam over the others. They seemed watchful.

The boy replied in his incongruously deep voice, "Oyster."

He'd given this information on his own—she hadn't used pigeonry. A good sign.

She said, "Oyster, we need to get outside. All of us."

She angled the light so that it illuminated him without blinding him. The look in his eyes confirmed that it was right to address him as though he spoke for the rest. He seemed to contemplate her statement as the others watched.

Another roll of thunder.

From behind her, the boy who'd had the knife spoke: "We ain't goin nowhere w'you, lady."

Madeleine looked toward his voice but couldn't see much beyond Ethan. "It's not safe in—"

"Take your big ugly cripple and get out!" The boy's voice was going shrill, and Madeleine realized these kids were as frightened as she was.

"Shut your mouth, Mako." Oyster's drawn, lethargic voice again.

Madeleine said, "There'll be a shuttle down under the bridge. It'll take you to St. Jo's where they'll feed you and give you a bed and a shower."

She held back the real reason for evacuating them: that some unseen entity was on the prowl among them, causing one person to turn on the next with no provocation.

"What you say your name is?" Oyster asked.

"I'm Dr. LeBlanc. This is Dr. Manderleigh."

"Doc LB," Oyster said.

Madeleine nodded. "Yes, a lot of people at the shelter call me that. Have we met?"

Oyster was silent. Ethan remained silent as well, though his body language spoke volumes.

Madeleine asked Oyster, "Are there any others?"

He turned his face slowly toward the last door in the hall. The only one she and Ethan hadn't checked yet. Something about Oyster's movement unnerved her; the sluggish way he turned his head, leading with his chin, his forehead angled back. A walking corpse sort of manner. Madeleine felt Ethan touch her elbow. She could tell he didn't like it either.

Oyster called toward the last door in that strange, deep voice: "Del!"

Madeleine barely breathed. Thunder echoed again, a fresh rumble arriving on the heels of the previous one like the narrowing intervals between birth contractions. The last door opened.

Sunlight poured around a woman or girl who must have been the one Oyster had called Del. Because the last apartment faced away from the bridge, its windows overlooked the sun-drenched horizon, not the black thunderhead that was mounting from the causeway.

"We movin on," Oyster said to the silhouette.

"Coming back?" the girl asked, and her voice was that of a teenager.

Oyster didn't answer, so Madeleine said. "You'd better gather your things."

Del opened the door all the way and turned into the apartment with a sigh. A sleeping baby lay against her shoulder. Madeleine stepped toward the doorway and saw the same ragged disrepair as the other apartment with the owls. Unlike that place, though, she saw no furniture here other than a bare mattress, and the predominant odor was chemical. Cans of spray paint littered the floor.

Del snatched a skirt from the bedding and threw it into a black canvas bag. The baby stirred.

"Here, let me help you," Madeleine said stepping through the doorway.

"Stay out of my room," Del snapped, and Madeleine halted.

Then Del said, "Don't be messin with my stuff," and shoved the baby into Madeleine's arms.

Madeleine accepted the baby in mute surprise and held it against her chest, shoving the flashlight back into her bag and then placing her hand behind the infant's head. It tightened its face like it might cry. Instead, it clucked twice and settled right back into sleep, a limp, weighty bundle at Madeleine's shoulder.

Del shoved the rest of her things into the bag and then turned and strode past Madeleine and into the corridor without looking back.

Madeleine looked after her for a heartbeat, the baby's head still resting at her collar. She scanned the room one more time, making sure there were no other signs of people, and then joined the others in the dark hall. Her lips throbbed.

"Alright, down the stairs," Ethan was saying to the group, shining his flashlight along the corridor.

The boys and Del marched forward under Ethan's direction, and Oyster trailed behind them all, slowing his steps so that he was the last behind Madeleine. She didn't like having him at her back. Del disappeared down the stairwell ahead without retrieving her baby (son? daughter?); didn't even look back to see whether Madeleine was following. As she walked carefully through the darkness toward Ethan, Madeleine put her nose to the top of the baby's head and sniffed. Sweat, grime, and that indefinable baby smell. It was the latter that caused her to take in a second whiff and draw the child more securely into her arms.

t e n

ENON STARED AT THE ceiling. He couldn't tell whether it was morning or noon—or suppertime, for that matter. Curtains were drawn. Supper meant absolutely nothing to him, anyway. Supper didn't enter through his mouth anymore.

The only way Zenon could tell what time of day it was, was when the damned sun would send one direct damned ray straight at his face. It colored everything red. Not because of some sweet sentimental sunset bullshit, but because the afternoon sun's death-ray beam would cause the blood to rush to his eyes. Never bothered him before in his life. But now he couldn't turn his head away, or close his eyes, or even blink. Oh, his eyes closed alright. *And* they blinked. Just not when he wanted them to.

The whole thing was horseshit. He could use the stupid pigeon game on a bunch of worthless drones but not on his own damned body.

"God, you're a wallowing, self-pityin sonofabitch," Josh said.

"What's it to you? You river devils don't have real bodies so you don't know what it's like to lose one."

Josh let it go for once. "Come on, your body's worryin your pretty head so bad, why don't you step on out of it?"

"Later. I don't have the energy no more."

"You gonna miss out on Miss Chloe again."

That got Zenon's attention. He stopped trying to look at the ceiling through his eyes, and let his consciousness settle backward. Back into his own head. He could almost feel a slight rush of blood along his jaw. Blanked out his mind. And then he rose up, easy like a feather in the night, and took a look around.

Sure enough, old Chloe was there. So was Oran. He liked Oran.

❧

<h1 style="text-align:center">eleven</h1>

❧

NEW ORLEANS, NOW

ENON LOOKED AT CHLOE and Oran, then back down at his own form lying in the bed. Hardly recognized his own self. It looked like he was shriveling with every tick of the clock.

He realized then that several other river devils besides Josh had assembled. There were some that were humanlike, and others more lizardly. All different sizes. Weird how they liked to fade in with the background. The animal-type devils changed their colors and blended in with bunched-up sheets, behind plants, a tiny one on the face of a clock. The human-looking ones had seemed like hospital workers at first. They were whispering. He'd never seen so many.

It occurred to Zenon that they were gathering for Chloe. The old bat was looking at his slack body there in the hospital bed while he watched as a ghost, looking over her shoulder. She'd brought another gris-gris that she was having Oran put under the mattress.

She did that a lot. Maybe she thought it would help to resurrect him. Well, then, this ought to give her a thrill.

"Go on already," Josh said.

Zenon turned to Oran. Focused.

Oran paused as he was reaching for the mattress with the gris-gris.

Zenon smiled. Like driving a car.

"What is it?" Chloe said to Oran. "Stop dallying."

Zenon dug in until Oran threw the gris-gris on the floor. Some kind of weed fell from the bundle and a feather tufted up and danced in the air-conditioning. Chloe gave Oran a hard look.

And then Zenon had Oran take hold of Chloe's wheelchair and turn her toward the foot of Zenon's bed.

She sputtered at him. "What are you doing, Oran? Stop that."

This was just rich. Oran pushed her all the way around until Chloe was on the other side of Zenon's physical body, between his bed and the window.

"Oran! Put me back!"

"Time to get up now, Chloe," Oran said.

She whipped her head around to look at him, but her ancient shoulders didn't allow her to turn all the way. Zenon would have bet that old Oran had never before acted fresh with her. Not once in thirty years.

Oran walked around so that he was facing her and then bent over, grabbing her by the ankle and snapping the footrest up. Zenon had to chuckle. Oran's posture on bended knee looked like that of a servant, his ash-colored skin and white-orange hair washed in the overhead fluorescent light. He folded back the other footrest and returned to his post at the back of Chloe's chair. She huffed. Oran tilted the chair forward.

Oran's voice saying, "No good sitting around on your ass, Chloe, your butt'll just get harder to heave."

It was perfect. Zenon's words, Oran's voice. Even Oran's own accent.

Wheelchairs were constructed to tilt backward, not forward, but old Oran was stronger than he looked. He had to squat and lift, bearing the brunt of the weight himself with the smaller front wheels making a weak fulcrum. He managed it, though.

Chloe's legs splayed straight out and she had to grab the hand rests. Her feet touched the laminate floor as she veered forward.

She cried out in excitement, "Wait! Wait! Send him around to help me!"

Zenon thought it over a moment, and decided to indulge her.

The wheelchair went back down with a thud. Oran walked around to face her, sheened from sweat. He seized her by the wrists and pulled. She pulled back at him and rose out of the wheelchair. She seemed too excited to protest or fuss for her bones. Oran's expression showed Zenon's delight mixed with Oran's fear.

"Ma p'tite pigeon," Chloe said.

Oran shook his head. "No, he's actually my pigeon."

"Zenon!"

She searched Oran's face with fascination. Zenon watched, too, and could see how the real Oran was still struggling against this, weirded out by his own acts. And the implanted thoughts from Zenon reflected in facial expressions that weren't typical of Oran.

Chloe cast a glance back toward Zenon's physical body in the hospital bed. "Zenon, I have waited for you to return. Have you heard me talking to you all these—"

"Waiting, Chloe? You wouldn't have had to wait for me if you hadn't put me in this goddamn bed to begin with!"

Chloe frowned. "You know I had nothing to do with it."

"Ain't so sure about that. You put Madeleine up to it. Told her to use the pigeon trick against me."

"Zenon, you were going to kill her. I only suggested how she might defend herself. She was the one who pigeoned that man into attacking you. She's the reason you piss into a bag and can't even speak your own name!"

Zenon made Oran throw her wrists back and she teetered. For a moment it seemed she was going to fall. Her sluggish body managed to recover balance and she stepped to the handrails at the foot of Zenon's bed and gripped them.

She said, "I never wanted this for you! You were the only one who ever embraced the bramble. You never fell to the madness because you kept in step with the river devils."

"For what? So I could be a hired gun for you and the damn devils?"

"It is only the beginning, Zenon. You had to understand the culling so it would not get in the way. You are free now. Free to take the secrets of the briar. With my help."

Oran leaned forward to speak in her ear as she stared at Zenon. "Your help, Chloe, is what got me into this shit to begin with. Secrets of the goddamn briar, my ass. Secrets for you, they ain't for me. I showed you how to talk to the river devils. How to live for fuckin ever. And then you put Madeleine up to taking me out!"

"Listen to you, sniveling man. Is that what you spend these months thinking? You so stupid blind you see only what you want. Madeleine put you in that hospital bed, not me. Madeleine! You always grovel on your belly for Madeleine!"

Zenon twisted in on Oran. Oran lifted his hand to strike Chloe. But the river devils reared. All of them. Bearing teeth, scratching. Zenon halted. And Oran halted.

"Knock it off," Josh said.

Zenon looked at him. "What, you too? Why y'all afraid of her?"

"Not afraid. Just respectful."

Zenon waved in disgust at Josh, letting Oran go. He didn't need this crap. Let Chloe keep her feathers and weeds and her bootlicking bands of river devils.

Oran took a step backward and folded his arms across his chest. His hand went to his face, his gaze darting from Chloe to Zenon to the door.

Chloe scowled at him. He turned and leaned into the corner.

"Zenon. You still here?" Chloe said.

The river devils were watching her, watching Zenon. He reached forward and dragged a finger along the spine of the one that was wrapped around the clock. It opened its mouth, hissing.

He regarded the rest of them. The whole sordid lot. And it occurred to him: If Chloe is garnering this much loyalty from the river devils, why couldn't he? After all, he was the one who could walk the briar, not Chloe. What if Zenon could take control here? Where would that lead?

He eyed Chloe. Though he had the advantage of dwelling in the briar, she was a powerful manipulator from the outside. She'd spent a long life practicing her so-called river magic. What he needed was a way to tip the balance in his favor. What he needed was an ally.

Chloe turned and slowly looked around the room. "Listen, Zenon, come back and listen. Can you still hear me?"

He smiled. It's what Chloe had been trying to do all along. Recruit an ally. In him. In Madeleine too, probably.

The small blond nurse with VESSIE printed across her name tag entered through the doorway. She was carrying an empty cardboard box.

"Get out!" Chloe shouted at her.

Vessie stopped. "You'll need to keep your voice down, ma'am."

Chloe said, "Get out and leave us alone."

Vessie's expression hardened. "No ma'am. You're the one who's going to have to leave. Visiting hours are over. I'm done looking the other way for you people. Now you get on out before I call security."

twelve

NEW ORLEANS, NOW

HEY STRODE THROUGH BRIDGE City toward the banks where the others were waiting. Madeleine had never been so grateful for daylight and clean wind, though the daylight was quickly funneling away into a thunderhead. The retreating sun shone at their backs and made the white tee-shirts glow against the charcoal sky.

Oyster, Mako, and the other street boys no longer seemed frightened nor menacing. They kept their kerchiefs in place and probably thought they looked tough, but to Madeleine they seemed like overgrown trick-or-treaters. Del, though only an adolescent like the boys, looked of an age beyond her years. She walked bent forward with her arms flopping at her sides and her tank top clinging a size too small, and the crease between her brows gave her a tough beauty that would one day devolve into plain hardness.

And the baby lay snug in Madeleine's arms.

Though Madeleine was horrified by the casual way Del had relinquished her baby to a stranger, she savored the feeling of holding the infant. It made her think again of Marc's child, Cooper. As much as Madeleine longed to bridge that gap to her nephew, she couldn't risk bringing the river devils into his life.

Ethan was walking next to her, keeping up despite his uneven gait, and was absorbed enough in keeping a wary eye out that Madeleine was able to hide her injured side from him. She hoped she could avoid his notice until the swelling subsided. Thunder was now rolling up from Pontchartrain with the regularity of ocean waves.

"We thought you's the doomsday committee," Oyster said in that strange deep voice as he fell into step with Madeleine and Ethan. "Wouldn't a hit you if I saw you's a lady."

Ethan's eyes narrowed on the boy and then rose to Madeleine, but she quickly looked away before he could see her injured side. Lightning flashed all around, followed almost immediately by an explosion of thunder. Madeleine clutched the baby and quickened her pace.

Mako joined Oyster, his knife now tucked away somewhere out of sight. "They say they's a voodoo spell in the water. Make people go hara-kiri."

"Madeleine." Ethan was looking hard at her face.

She tried to keep her head turned but he grabbed her elbow and looked to see her swelling lip.

A huge raindrop landed on the pavement, then another on her arm. The entire pack of boys broke into a run. Madeleine wanted to run, too.

Another flash of lightning, this time further off in the distance, and the thunder was slower to follow. Ethan's injury prevented him from being able to run for the bridge with the others, and she didn't want to leave him behind. She forced herself to slow down. Rain was splashing freely now, hissing the pavement, collecting into serpents of water that writhed and rushed for the drains. The bridge shelter loomed only a minute away.

"Go on ahead," Ethan called above the rush. "Keep the baby dry."

She bent her head over the baby and ran for the bridge. It felt good, as though the wind and water were washing through her, rinsing her free. Ethan had seen the injury but he'd let it go for the moment at least. She'd hear about it from him soon enough.

The baby finally broke into an all-out bawl. Thunder ripped so hard it threatened to burst Madeleine's eardrums.

A police car was parked just outside the bridge. She hoped to see Vinny, her friend on the task force, but she didn't recognize the officer seated inside the car talking into a radio handset. Same with the one standing with the others under the bridge.

Madeleine jogged out of the rain and under the bridge with the rest of them. The concrete structure stretched high above, spackled with mud sparrow nests, graffiti painted in scribble patterns along the massive footings. Traffic sounds swelled and droned amid the pulse of thunder. In addition to the five boys plus Del, about twelve homeless people were already waiting. She knew most by sight if not by name—she saw a woman who used to be a dry cleaner before Katrina, but since had been struggling with addiction. Another younger couple had come to New Orleans after Hurricane Rita to work day labor in the reconstruction. Also addicts. She recognized another young man, couldn't think of his name, whose brows met in the middle in a single thick line. He used to wait tables but went homeless, then got back on his feet only to go homeless again. He had no chemical addictions as far as Madeleine could tell. Just a painfully shy loner.

Madeleine scanned the faces of the three other outreach volunteers. She knew them all. They'd held a brief meeting to strategize before setting off this afternoon.

No sign of the shuttle to St. Jo's. In the sinking light, everyone looked the same shade of gray. Ethan was still making his way toward the bridge on his crooked leg.

"Whatchoo got there, Miss Madeleine?"

She looked and saw Shalmut Halsey sitting near a concrete piling.

"Hey, there." Madeleine smiled, relieved to see a kind face, and hoisted the still-weeping baby so he could see.

Shalmut began to rise to his feet but made it only halfway before sitting down again.

She took a second look at his face. "You alright, Shal?"

He shook his head. "Fine, fine, just a little too much medicine."

Madeleine detected a sick odor of booze on him. "I thought you were gonna go to the shelter after they questioned you this morning."

"I thought you's gonna go home'n sleep," he slurred.

Considering what happened last night, it was no surprise Shalmut would try to drown out the head noise. He did that even when things were fine.

Maybe I'll use him next, Alice had said while she still gripped a broken bottle with freshly spilled blood on it. Madeleine's shoulders tightened.

"Where the shuttle at?" Shalmut asked. "I'm ready to go."

She looked into the rain. "They had a lot of stops to make, trying to bring everyone in."

"St. Jo's cup gonna runneth over," Shalmut said with a rheumy laugh.

"Shalmut, do you remember the little boy at the levee? The blind boy and his mother?"

"Bo Racer, yeah," Shalmut said.

"Bo Racer?"

"Yeah, kid go by name of Bo Racer. His mama name is Esther."

Madeleine thought over the strange name for a moment. "Do you know where he is?"

Shalmut shook his head, or maybe he rocked, it was more a gesture of overexerting his thought energy than answering the question.

Madeleine tried, "Are they always at the levee like that?"

"No, no, they got a home. Just get run out sometimes."

"Where's their home?"

"I don't know, baby."

"They live in an apartment?"

"Naw, an ole trailer."

"A trailer," Madeleine said, thinking. "In the country or one of the parks?"

"That damn park, the park, the Rose Bush or Rose Something."

"Rosewood Arms?"

Shal looked relieved. "That's it. Rosewood Arms."

Then he squinted like he was striving to think of something. "Wait a damn minute. They here."

"Here?" Madeleine said, looking across the darkness between steel girders.

"Yeah. On over there."

He pointed in the direction where Del and the boys were. Madeleine strained to see. On the other side of the small assemblage, sitting next to a pile of construction rubble, sat a little boy and his mother. They looked an African-Hispanic mix. The boy's smile was gaping wide, sunglasses on his face. The mother looked tired.

Several feet away, Del was now shouting and cussing for no apparent reason but to draw attention. The boys gathered around her and one of the other outreach volunteers ambled toward them, too. The baby's wailing rose.

"Don't know why, there's no sun up in the sky . . ."

Madeleine looked back at Shalmut. He was singing to the baby in her arms with that roughshod voice of his. Even drunk out of his mind it sounded like heaven. The baby quieted.

". . . Stormy weather, since my gal and I, ain't been together . . ."

She'd heard his voice so many times before. He and her father used to sing together, busking for dollars from the tourists. Daddy rarely needed the money—he just lived on the street because his turbulent mind caused him to blink in and out of mainstream society. She felt her throat go hot.

Ethan made it under the bridge and hitched his way toward her. She smiled at him. The baby was watching with wide eyes as Shalmut sang.

Ethan reached Madeleine's side and looked full into her face, frowning.

She turned her lip away from him but he gently took her chin and turned it back. "What happened to your lip, Maddy?"

She shrugged. "When I surprised Oyster in the dark. They thought we were coming to attack them."

Shalmut stopped singing. Ethan's clean-lined face was pulled taut with anger, and he was soaked to the bone.

"Them huffers," Shalmut said, and Madeleine followed his gaze to the pack of boys who had finally pulled the kerchiefs away from their faces. "Mean as snakes, them kids."

Even in the dimness beneath the bridge, she could see multicolored smears under the boys' noses where they must have been huffing spray paint.

The strange bird call echoed under the bridge.

Madeleine listened. Same as she'd heard in the predawn woods just before she found Shalmut and Alice. The sound, it came from the blind boy, Bo Racer. He'd stood and was looking around. The nervous tick-tock sound bounced up toward the cathedral height of the bridge's underside and back down again. His mother Esther stood, too.

Next to Madeleine, Ethan's gaze zeroed in on Oyster. He took a step toward him.

"Hang on, Ethan," Madeleine said.

But Ethan was heading straight for the huffers, as Shalmut had called them. Madeleine hoisted the baby higher on her hip and followed. Ahead, Del was flapping the water out of her tank top, exposing a fair share of skin in the process. The police officer watched her. A violent crack of thunder, and Del screamed with exaggerated fear. The baby started crying again. Lightning was flashing all around now, like camera strobes, and the rain cracked open to a deafening rush. Madeleine slowed, listening as the downpour intensified, growing thicker and louder and forming a solid white sheet from the top of the bridge. It stole the breath from the air. One by one, the huffers opened their mouths as if to allow in more oxygen, the same way alligators and dogs drop their jaws to cool down.

"Wait a minute, Ethan," Madeleine said, her hand on his arm.

He wheeled on her. "I told you to be careful in that corridor! You act as though you don't even care what happens to you."

Rain was now shearing the perimeter so hard it drowned out the sound of cars charging across the bridge overhead. The water looked like an opaque curtain that daylight could no longer penetrate. If she walked through that curtain she'd disappear. And if someone were standing three feet outside of the shelter, she wouldn't be able to see that, either.

Beneath the white noise came the blind boy's clicking, that ticktocking bird call. Like at the levee just before dawn.

Her heart rate jumped. The air beneath the bridge seemed to thicken. Something was wrong.

She could hear the blind kid, Bo, calling. "Mama, it's here again."

Oyster was staring at Ethan. "Hey, bent-dick, you got a problem?"

The other boys caught sight of Ethan's face and repositioned the kerchiefs over their noses.

Wrong, wrong, wrong. Ethan and the boys were squaring off, but something deeper was going on. Something briar. Madeleine looked up. Severin was crawling upside-down along the footing of the bridge, her naked form streaked and smudged. Lightning and thunder shuddered all around.

Get away, Severin. We have a bargain.

Severin grinned down from above. "The blind boy comes, you break its neck, truly, easily."

Ethan's arms were tensed at his side as he glared at Oyster. "You need to check your attitude, son, and think twice about hitting unarmed women."

"Y'all need to think twice about busting in on other people's territory," Mako shouted.

"Hey," the policeman said as he took a step toward the huffers.

Bo's mother reached for her son.

Bo turned to her. "Mom, I said it's here again."

"Gimme my baby!" Del shouted at Madeleine.

Madeleine raised the child to her, and Del stepped forward. A sense of anger electrified the underbelly of the bridge. Everywhere, in everyone, but it wasn't just the huffers' anger, or Ethan's, or Del's, it was . . .

Severin raised her head, leering down at Madeleine, and lifted a finger to her lips in a shush. Black thorns were unfolding from the piling, forming a nest beneath the devil-child.

Maybe I'll use him next, Alice had said.

Madeleine turned to look for Shalmut Halsey but he was no longer there. She spotted him standing behind the police officer. Shalmut, who only moments ago couldn't even get to his feet.

"No!" Madeleine shouted.

Shalmut's hand went to the policeman's belt and pulled his gun from the holster.

"Shal! NO!"

Del's arms were still raised toward her baby when the first bullet flew. It took her just inside the left shoulder. Madeleine jerked the baby away and Del's eyes froze to shock. The infant bawled, raising its arms to its mother. Del took two steps sideways and looked at her arm. Blood coursed from just below her collarbone. The tank top stained black-crimson. She had been standing just behind Bo, who turned and ran toward Madeleine.

"Break its neck!" Severin cried.

And Severin imparted a vision so awful, so awful. Fractions of a second before Bo reached her: Severin's vision of how Madeleine might swing her arm out, catch the thin neck, and . . .

Madeleine had to close her eyes against it, hugging the baby to her chest.

Bo kept running past her, blind boy running blind, into the wall of rain.

Click click click click, tick-tock click.

Shalmut fired again. Madeleine hadn't heard the report but she somehow heard the bullet zip past her ear. Someone was falling. *She* was falling. She sank to the ground before she even realized Ethan had knocked her over a moment before the bullet would have struck her in the head. She had a hand in the mud and the other clutching the baby's head.

Del reached for the baby again, though she herself could barely stand.

Esther was wailing and scrambling after her son.

"Get down!" Ethan yelled.

The policeman stood in shock. Shalmut shot him point-blank through the forehead.

The baby shrieked, all of the folks under the bridge shrieking, their voices blanketed in thunder and rain.

The policeman slumped to his knees.

Del fell sideways and did not use her hands to break her fall. Lying in the dirt, she pedaled out her right leg twice—same way Vessie had been bicycling Zenon's leg in his hospital bed.

Shal, drop it!

Shalmut's eyes were wide. He swung the policeman's gun and people scattered in its path. Another report rang out, the sound seeming so inconsequential. Nothing compared to the thunder. It took Mako in the back as he was running for the rain.

Severin had brought the thorns. They curled black from the sparrows' nests, from the girders, even from the graffiti, stretching forth to envelop the madness that was occurring. Madeleine saw another river devil standing just beyond Shalmut. She'd seen him before. Whereas Severin looked like a little girl, the other river devil looked like a full-grown man. Muscular arms. She saw him in silhouette only. He stepped forward as lightning flashed, and she caught sight of his face. Eyes impossibly pale like powder blue robin's eggs. His skin filthy like Severin's with that odd shadowplay of sunlight on aged copper.

Severin laughed. Musical, delicate, childlike. She glowed faintly in the darkness of the underpass. Her tiny hand stretched toward Shalmut and shed light on him, too. He and the river devils both shone in that sepia glow, washing to white with each strobe of lightning.

Madeleine tried to clamp onto Shalmut. Nothing. Slippery as Alice had been. No way to make him stop this. Madeleine was as helpless as the rest of them.

Another shot. One of the outreach volunteers went limp where he lay crouched on the ground.

People disappeared into the rain. Madeleine was on her feet again, trying desperately to get a fix on Shalmut, stumbling forward, but her pigeonry had no effect.

Shalmut turned back and looked her dead in the eye with the gun swinging in her direction. She saw now, saw through the illumination of Severin's briar light, that he was smiling.

Madeleine stopped. Shalmut wasn't smiling with his mouth, and not his cheeks. His smile was nothing more than a lift to the eyes.

Madeleine recognized that expression.

Other than the fallen, most everyone else had already disappeared into the rain or was cowering in the mud. Except Ethan.

Ethan lunged. He knocked Shalmut in the left side of the jaw, and Shalmut's head snapped sideways. The gun discharged again. The bullet landed in a wooden palette. Shalmut's head wobbled as he fell to the ground. Madeleine watched, and realized that she was still trying to clamp her pigeonry into him. Still trying to grab control. Clamping onto a spirit that was already loosening from its host.

Shalmut was sprawled in the dirt, a cloud of dust creeping from him like fog on a riverbank. He lay still.

thirteen

HAHNVILLE, 1927

WHEN PATRICE AND GILBERT returned to Terrefleurs, they did not find that Trigger had collected Marie-Rose and brought her back home. They did not find Trigger at all. Not right away. The plantation workers were settled into their Sundays, shelling peas on their porches and recuperating from a long week in the fields.

Patrice and Gil found Rosie first. After checking all the out-buildings, they'd returned to the main house and looked through the basement. There, curled atop a burlap sack of red beans, lay little Rosie.

Gil said, "But I'd checked the basement. She wasn't in here."

Rosie was wide awake, but in the briar and not responding to their prods. More disturbing were the sounds she was making. Guttural clucks. Odd little lashes of her tongue. And a queer sort of smile at her eyes. Patrice did not like that smile.

The thorns were curling their way into the cellar, beckoning Patrice into the other world. The scent of cool, rotted earth and rolling mist. She made herself calm. Refused to acknowledge the grinning river devil who watched from above in the beams crisscrossing the ceiling.

"We've got to find Trigger," Patrice said.

Gil had walked to the other side of the basement and was staring at the space beyond the coal furnace. "Well, I found him and a little somethin extra."

The look on Gilbert's face had Patrice on her feet and crossing to his side in half a heartbeat, leaving Marie-Rose alone on her bean sack. Trigger was there alright. He was standing opposite Gilbert with that same strange smile Marie-Rose was wearing.

On the floor lay a man Patrice did not know. Near death. A step stool was crushing his windpipe.

Patrice looked from him to Trigger and then back again. The stranger's mouth was open to a gray, blood-streaked tongue, and he was missing his front teeth. She thought to help him but at the same time, knew that he must be a bad man. That he had something to do with all this. A rumpled raw cotton sack lay near his knee.

In the man's hand was a knife, and it was streaked with blood.

She dared a glance at Trigger again. A black smudge across his cheek. A bloody gash down his forearm.

Trigger made a low, strangled grunt.

"Trigger?" Patrice tried, and then thinking he might answer to his given name instead: "Guy?"

But Trig was in the briar, just like Rosie. His look was so foreboding that Patrice had to remind herself that he was still her baby brother, gentle as a kitten. She reached for his hand but he stepped away, shying back without having looked directly at her. He stepped up, back onto that stool that rested over the fallen man's neck.

"Don't—" Patrice started to say.

An unearthly hollow sound emitted from somewhere in the stranger's throat.

A noise from behind made Patrice whirl. Marie-Rose was standing only three feet away and making a strange gasping cluck, her gaze leveled on Trigger, and he was looking at her, too. The expressions on their faces made Patrice back toward Gil and wrap her arms around herself.

"Their necks," Gil said, and Patrice saw that both Marie-Rose and Trigger had blood at their back collars.

"What's happened here?" Patrice said.

Gil pointed to the man on the floor. "Who *is* he?"

But the question strongest on Patrice's mind was not who he was, but how he'd come about lying there on the fruit cellar floor. Had one of the younger ones attacked him?

Gil said, "I'm goin in."

"No. Let me."

Patrice knew she was the eldest and strongest of the four. And something was off about the way the younger siblings were mired in the bramble.

She said, "Keep an eye on them. Don't let them wander."

"I will."

"And keep an eye on . . . him." She gestured to the man on the floor.

Gil nodded. "Careful, Treesey."

❧

IT TOOK NO TIME at all for the thorns to come. No sooner had Patrice receded her mind that the fruit cellar seemed to worm to life. Potatoes in the bin sprouted eyes that gave to roots that became black, lengthening thorns. So did the tiny roots along the wall.

Patrice could see Trigger facing her just as he was in the material world. He was standing atop something that was not a step stool, but a sort of iron jaw, a trap, and beneath its teeth some kind of horrible bramble devil was writhing. A black, tarry thing that looked like a man whose arms and legs were far too long and thin. Trigger looked down at it and wobbled atop the trap, making the creature squeak.

"Trig—" she started to say, but he put his fingers to his lips in a hushing sound.

He smiled beyond Patrice's shoulder, and she turned to see Marie-Rose. She was grinning at some kind of colorful, winged flying fish. A briar sylph. It looked lighter than paper and it shimmered in a colorful display in stark contrast to the black briar. Weightless on a breeze. The sylph was making those sounds, the swallowed "g" sounds, and Marie-Rose was answering back.

And then Patrice realized that the sylph had led Rosie to one particular tree that stood out from all the others. A tall black pine that seemed to reach higher than heaven. At its base were carvings. Patrice recognized them at once.

Papa.

Carving used to calm him. A way for him to bring his physical body back together with its ghost. Trigger had recently started whittling, too.

Before he'd died, Papa had carved dozens of toys for the children. Patrice alone had fourteen dolls made of tupelo gum—one for each birthday. There would be no more.

So lovely was the sylph. And so absorbing the briar. Patrice had to work hard to form a thought: She had come here for a reason.

All four of the children's river devils were there, laughing, whispering, pointing. Patrice's devil was touching the iron jaw. It somehow made Patrice want to touch it, too. Even though part of her knew that in the other world, a real man lay trapped by it.

The colorful, hovering sylph receded toward the black woods and Marie-Rose stepped out as though to follow it further.

"No," Patrice said aloud, and her two younger siblings shushed her.

Why? she wondered.

But she didn't need words to communicate with them, especially not here. So Patrice compressed her thoughts into a single feeling. She let her body assume a sensation that reflected their mother—a feeling like tension and dread and always-fleeting hope or love.

Trigger and Rosie both reacted immediately. They went rigid, their gaze on Patrice. Impish smiles vanished.

Patrice beckoned to them, and they followed her without protest. She led them away from the oil slick. It required far more concentration than she'd ever had to muster before, and the journey back seemed longer than it should have taken, but finally, they were all out.

"WHO IS HE?" GIL said, looking at the man on the floor.

Trigger almost seemed surprised. "I don't know. I found Rosie down here in the cellar. I went to get her down, and he came after me. Must have been hiding."

Patrice said, "What do you mean, *get her down?*"

"I mean just that. She was up there."

Trigger was pointing to the ceiling joists that stretched above the sack of red beans where Marie-Rose had been curled up. "If she hadn't a been makin those sounds I might not've seen her. But I looked up and there she was. Grinnin down at me like the Cheshire cat. Only she wudn't seein me. She was lookin at the sylphs."

"That explains why I didn't see her," Gil said. "Must've walked right under where she was hidin."

Trigger said, "She wudn't hidin. She'd been stashed up there."

"By him?" Patrice said, nodding toward the man on the floor.

"Looked that way. He hid Rosie up there. And then when I was trying to get Rosie, he came after me. Threw a sack over my head. But then I got out and he tried to stab me. Not sure what happened after that. Briar."

The man opened his mouth and closed it again, sending a fresh course of blood over his lips. His throat made a choking sound.

"I think he's drowning in his own blood," Gil said, and then looked to Patrice. "What should we do?"

She pulled the stool away from the man's neck. "Did my mother send you?"

The man's eyes met hers, but he gave no indication of an answer. He certainly couldn't speak. And yet it was enough: Patrice had felt what was in his heart and recognized her mother's presence in it. Her hands went cold. The intention inside this man had been to take the smallest child, and to kill another one. It's what Maman had sent him to do.

Patrice shook her head, unable to trust what she saw in him. It must be her nerves—she must be reading him wrong. As much as their mother hated them, Patrice couldn't believe she was capable of murdering one of her own children.

The stranger's mouth stretched wide and drooled red down his cheek.

Marie-Rose said, "Do something!"

Patrice shook her head. This man had come here with murder in his heart. Still, God would not abide their causing him to suffer, would He?

Gil said, "Maybe we oughtta sit him up."

Patrice shook her head. "He'll still die. It'll just keep him suffering longer."

"Didn't Mother once save that boy who couldn't breathe by cutting into his throat?"

"Yes. That was Ferrar. But I wouldn't know how to do that."

She tried to imagine herself cutting into the stranger's windpipe and found the idea impossible. And he'd likely choke her if she tried it.

Trigger reached down and took the knife from the man's hand.

"Wait," Patrice said.

But too late. Trigger thrust it into his heart.

Patrice gave a little cry, and Gil did, too, and they clutched one another. There came a horrible gurgling sound from where the man lay. Marie-Rose stood perfectly still, staring wide-eyed. Patrice grabbed her and pulled her into the huddle.

Trigger said, "There. Now he ain't sufferin no more."

Marie-Rose finally opened her mouth and let loose a sob.

Patrice rubbed her back. "Shh. Shh."

The stranger had already gone still.

Patrice took Rosie by the chin and checked her face. "It's over, now. Are you alright? Did he hurt you?"

"My neck," Rosie said.

"We all have that. But I think we're fine. Whatever was in the scratch, it must not have worked properly or that man would have got us all by now."

Gil was glaring at Trigger. "You just killed him outright!"

"Well if you'd really gone lookin for Rosie like you're supposed to!"

"I did come down here! I checked end-to-end!"

Trigger pointed at the dead man on the floor. "So why didn't he come after you the way he done me?"

Gil paused, his cheeks flaring despite the darkness in the cellar. "Maybe cuz I wasn't alone. Joseph was helping me look."

"Joseph," Trigger said, then nothing more.

The twins were staring at each other, and it seemed the slightest movement might cause them to lunge. Joseph was Gil's friend who lived in the field workers' cottages with his parents. After Mother had left Terrefleurs, Gil had started to pal around with Joseph instead of Trigger.

Patrice said, "Trigger, listen. Do you know if anyone saw you down here?"

Trigger kept glaring at his twin, nostrils flared.

Patrice touched his arm and gestured toward the man on the

floor. "I mean do you think anyone saw *him?* Does anybody on the plantation know he's down here?"

Trigger shook his head. "Naw. I mean, when it happened, I sort of got pulled into the briar so I can't be sure. But I don't think no one from Terrefleurs saw."

"Anyone."

"What are we going to do?" Marie-Rose asked.

"First we'll have to bury him where no one will find out," Patrice said.

"Mama'll find out," Rosie said. "That's what the tar was."

Trigger was nodding. "It's why we couldn't talk in the briar. She used that pool of oil to spy on us in some way. Not sure how. That thing came out of it."

Patrice picked up the sack from the floor and covered the tiny window facing the back allée. "Well, if she knows she knows. Let's hope no one else does."

"Then what?"

Patrice turned to look because she wasn't sure which of the boys had spoken. It was Trigger, his face hard, fists balled, and he looked like his own tension might cause his thin bones to bust apart.

Patrice said, "Then we leave."

"Leave?" Rosie said.

Gil was nodding. "Leave Terrefleurs. In six months. Or three. When we've saved up."

"No," Patrice said. "That plan's no good now. We have to leave immediately. Today."

"With no money?"

"Do we have a choice?"

All four children were looking at one another. Checking for signs as to whether this could truly be happening.

Gil said, "Maybe I should stay back. See if I can raise a little money, then join y'all."

Trigger said, "You stay, we all stay."

Patrice said, "Nobody's staying. We have to keep together or we might as well be dead. We leave. All four of us. Today. Pack only what you can carry. Two changes of clothes plus what you're wearing. Rosie . . ."

Patrice reached down and took Marie-Rose by the elbows. "You go on up and start packing. Not a word to anyone. Not a word! You understand?"

Marie-Rose was nodding.

Patrice released her. "Go on ahead. Boys, help me with him."

Marie-Rose ran for the stairs, pulling the dirty hem of her nightclothes to her knees as she ascended.

Patrice leaned over the dead man and closed his eyes as though she might be able to portray some kind of authority in doing a thing like this. Only, her hand was shaking. She motioned for the boys to help her wrap him in sacks and blankets. They had to tie him snug like a trussed hen.

She couldn't believe Trigger had killed this man.

She couldn't believe she'd let him.

No; she couldn't believe she'd *left it to him*. Trigger was only eleven years old. Patrice should have killed this man herself the moment she saw him lying there on the cellar floor.

She said, "We'll put him in the eastern well. It's condemned anyway."

"We gonna swing for this?" Gil asked.

Trigger said, "Why would y'all swing? I'm the one who done it."

"We're all in cahoots."

Patrice said, "Stop. No one's going to swing. We put him in the well, then we'll cover him with sticks and branches."

"How we supposed to get him in the well with no one seein us? And once he's in there he'll stink up the whole plantation! Then everyone'll know!"

Patrice folded her hands and thought on it a moment, carefully sidestepping her Christian beliefs. No point in wondering what was right in the service of God at this moment. She had to protect her siblings. And anyway she was too newly reborn in Christ to have the faintest idea what God would ordain for a fix like this.

She said, "We take him with us. It's a two-day journey to New Orleans. Somewhere along the way we're bound to find a place to put this soul to rest."

fourteen

NEW ORLEANS, NOW

THE EARLIEST MEMORY MADELEINE could squeeze into focus, the farthest, most distant star of her mind, came from when she was an infant: her first taste of envy.

She could recall that her father had placed her momentarily inside her brother Marc's crib. Marc had had a wonderful seabird mobile dangling just beyond reach. It had played a tinkling song when her father touched it just so, and the birds flashed and spun in a slow circle. She and Marc watched it and laughed together.

But when her father placed her back in her own crib, she was stuck once again with her own mobile: a bunch of grimacing cartoon animals that neither flashed nor spun nor played music. Nothing, no matter how hard Madeleine had cried or kicked at them, could make them come to life like Marc's had.

"What's the matter, kitten?" her father had said.

And she remembered very clearly that she understood his question, but she hadn't had the language yet to reply. She'd learned to listen and understand well before she'd learned to speak. This made her even more furious.

Her father had given up and left the nursery. Madeleine bellowed in frustration and looked over toward Marc in his crib. He was standing at the bars, grinning at her.

He bounced, bent at his diapered bottom, calling her name: "Ma-dee! Ma-dee!"

She stopped crying and smiled. Then, miraculously, Marc escaped his crib by crawling over the side and lowering himself to the floor before disappearing from her field of vision. That made her laugh so hard it radiated from her belly to her mouth and arms and legs all at once. Every piece of her lurching in jumping jack glee.

Even as Madeleine thought back to it, she realized the hilarity shared the same intensity as the frustration, only one felt good and the other felt bad.

She tried to immerse herself in the memory now, coaxing it to life, distant as it was. The oldest memory she owned.

"So, is this to escape?" Severin said.

"Maybe," Madeleine replied.

But the simple act of answering Severin caused images of her old nursery to flutter away. Madeleine was in the river devil's world again.

Severin said, "You use the memory to avoid me, so."

"You're out of turn, Severin. You're supposed to let me live my life. We have a bargain."

They were resting on a bed of soft green moss that had swirls of red and brown marbling. It wavered beneath them like a waterbed. From far, far above came the hint of sunlight but no actual sun. Madeleine could see only towering cypress that stretched so high she couldn't find the tops. Black trunks, black limbs, with coils and coils of black, black thorns; pale green leaves and silver falls of Spanish moss.

Something had happened. There'd been a murder, she thought,

but no; multiple murders. Under the Huey Long Bridge. The briar had turned itself inside out into the material world, as it liked to do. She tried to think of just what had transpired but it hurt to concentrate. Things were easier here, actually. A thought didn't need to have a beginning or end. Nothing seemed important. Sometimes she couldn't quite remember why she was so bent on keeping the briar away.

From the center of the wavering moss meadow, a fountain roared to life.

"What's that?" Madeleine asked in surprise.

But when Severin answered, it sounded like Ethan's voice. "You said you wanted to take a bath."

Madeleine shrank, self-conscious now. "Yes. Right. I do."

Because she wasn't really here in the river devil world, not physically. Her body was home, disconnected from her mind, and she was likely still covered in dirt and blood from that thing that had gone down under the Huey Long Bridge. She would have said she wanted a bath, yes, and now Ethan was drawing the water for her while her mind was trapped with Severin.

Was she trapped? Had she tried to leave the briar? She was ashamed to realize she didn't care to leave it just yet.

The fountain caused the moss to recede to a shimmering gap of water. Madeleine stretched for it, her bath. Steam caressed her face. Her body slipped into the water.

"Ooh, it's warm."

The fountain stopped flowing.

Severin sang, *"London Bridge is falling down . . ."*

The moss wavered along slow, expanding ripples. Madeleine was wearing a dress. A thin blue summer dress. It floated around her, weightless, like a brilliant cobweb in a breeze. Steam rose from the water and even from her skin, obscuring the cypress. She lowered her head beneath the surface and drew the warm water over her face and hair, her feet bouncing lightly against the silty floor.

When she lifted her head again, Zenon was there.

She scrambled upright.

Severin had wandered off behind the columns of steam. Madeleine could still hear her singing "London Bridge" in that small voice. Zenon was smiling. A genuine, warm, true-blue smile while he gazed at her as though they were long lost friends.

He said, "You sure make a pretty picture, Sis."

"Get away."

"Surprised to see me?"

Her breathing hitched. "You killed all those people."

"Didn't have to lift a finger. Good thing, too, seeing as I can't lift any fingers no more."

"You were going to kill me."

He snorted, and his expression hardened. "You're still alive. It's good training for you."

Her shoulders were raised just above the surface. She was treading water now, where only moments ago she'd felt the riverbed beneath her feet.

She said, "But what if I hadn't survived?"

"Well then you'd be dead."

He reached out and snatched her arms. She jerked backward, sending a wave splashing toward the islands of moss. He held both her wrists with one hand and put the other to her head, and then pushed her down. She kicked at him. The sound of splashing disappeared to a muffled roar in her ears as she fell down into the warm well. And she felt stinging, stinging, stinging.

He pushed her down further, deeper, and then he swam downward and was dragging her with him. She couldn't breathe, couldn't scream. They were moving so fast. Light disappeared to shadows. He stopped and held. Her lungs were burning. She fought with everything she had. Her vision began to tilt, then spin.

But beyond the crust of panic, it occurred to her that he was underwater, too. She forced herself to think beyond the desperation.

Stinging, maddening creatures had swarmed her spine and abdomen. She looked down. Their bodies were like curled dragonflies, with luminescent colors and long, delicate wings, but their forelegs ended in dagger-like stingers, and their faces looked near-human but for their enormous eyes. Even as she watched them, their stinging subsided.

She was so fascinated that she realized a substantial period of time had passed—could have been moments, or even an hour. And she realized she was breathing here underwater.

But of course she could breathe. This was a place of the mind. Her body was not in the bramble. Her body was at home, and Zenon's body was in the hospital. This was a dream world. Briar.

Zenon was smiling at her again. She actually smiled back.

When he spoke, he did not use his voice. "Training, baby. 'That which does not kill me' kinda shit. You just learned something about breathing underwater. You're welcome."

"I didn't ask for any training, Zenon," she replied with her mind, her smile slipping away.

She could still feel bubbles dislodge from her skin and slide along her body toward the surface. "Let go of me and leave me the hell alone."

"Why don't you wise up? I thought you finally got smart when I caught you hunting the lumen."

"The blind boy? That's crazy, Zenon! Why would I want to hunt down a little boy?"

"Crazy?" He yanked her forward. "You wanna know about crazy? The hell you think your body's doing while you're lounging around here with your river devil?"

Madeleine glared at him. But, she'd already been wondering about that very thing. She was probably acting more and more like her father. Daddy had faded in and out. She'd watched as he'd slipped away, wandering the streets, ranting and railing, sometimes even violent.

Zenon said, "Quit being a princess and figure out what you really are. A warrior. Same as me, yeah."

"Stop it. I'm nothing like you."

"Oh yes you are. There ain't but two types in the world: predator and prey. Those pigeons out there are the prey. The lumens are the prey. You were meant to be a predator, and if you keep denying it you're just gonna turn into some pee-smellin bag lady."

"You're guessing, Zenon, you don't know any more about this than I do."

"Except you know I ain't lyin."

She was listening, trying to make his words ring false in her heart. The stinging creatures were drifting around, waiting to light.

He said, "Tell you what, I'm a do you a big favor. Gonna give you a chance to get rid of that lumen. Your reward is you don't lose your mind. That's the only river devil bargain that actually sticks."

"I won't do that. I will never do that."

"Oh yes you will. But until you do you'll be spending a lot more time in this here briar hole while your boyfriend slowly gets tired of it all."

"I don't know how you pulled off that stunt under the bridge, Zenon, but you've got to stop it. You're wrong about all of this."

He shook his head, the shimmering light above casting shadows on his face. "Baby, I'm the best friend you got. Your cripple boyfriend's gonna get you killed or crazy, sure as shit. Best thing, forget the boyfriend. Forget any friends. You give a shit about something it becomes your weak spot. They can use it against you."

"Who's they, Zenon? Isn't that us? Children of the briar? Aren't we the enemy?"

"Only if we're doing it right."

He laughed with sharp delight. It almost felt contagious. Inviting her to laugh, too, and she had to force the tickle of it from forming inside of her. Everything felt so backward here.

Zenon said, "There you go. Resisting your nature. Listen. I'll make a deal with you. You kill off that lumen, the blind kid. Won't be easy. That lumen way makes'm slippery."

"I would never—"

He continued as if she hadn't spoken. "But I'll come after him, too. Give you a little challenge. You win? You get him first? Then we can work together. Maybe go after Chloe."

"Stop it, Zenon! You can just forget about—"

"But if I get to him first, if I make the kill, then I'll be coming after you next."

"Is that supposed to motivate me?"

"It don't have to. You hearin me, girl? I'm helping you to be what you're meant to be."

She closed her mind to him and drew herself inward.

A memory. Sitting on the porch swing with Daddy in Bayou Black, watching the stars. The smell of wet grass and cedar and pine. Frogs singing the bayou. Crickets. A breeze.

And in her heart she said, *I want out, let me out.*

She felt herself fading from Zenon's grasp. He couldn't stop her. Severin could but must have chosen not to.

Even under water, Madeleine could still hear her singing: " . . . *London Bridge is falling down, my fair lady."*

Madeleine looked up as she moved toward the surface in a trail of pearl bubbles. Above she saw only a ring of light at first, and then it came into focus. Not briar. Her own bathtub at home.

Ethan was there. He was staring at her. The expression on his face was frustration. Impatience, even. After all, Ethan had just been forced to kill a man. He had other things on his mind besides dealing with a crazy girlfriend.

She looked back at him. Her attention span in the briar had grown more dreamy, like the drift of a butterfly. But as she drew back into her physical self the entire weight of what happened under the bridge hit her afresh. Shalmut, the policeman, Mako, Del, a volunteer from St. Jo's. All of them shot dead save for Mako, who'd been rushed off in an ambulance. Madeleine trying desperately to answer

the investigator's questions while her mind spun down thorny rabbit holes.

And the baby. She'd held the baby the entire time, tight to her breast, while its mother, Del, was gunned down. A social worker had eventually taken the baby from Madeleine's arms and after that, Madeleine didn't know what had happened to it. She never knew its name. She never even found out whether it was a boy or a girl. Just a sweet, delicate, blank face.

Ethan reached into the water and pulled her up by the shoulders.

Garish light. Water peeling down her skin. Noise again, such different noises. The apartment was quiet but for the drone of air-conditioning, and yet it seemed so loud compared to the plush, isolated sounds of the briar.

"What exactly was that all about?" Ethan demanded.

She regarded him, blinking. Realized she ought to breathe. Her lips parted and her lungs filled. It made her cough.

He let go and sat back on the commode, wiping his hands over his hair and face. She ought to say something to him, she knew. Say something about what happened to Shalmut Halsey. Tell Ethan he had no choice. Tell him anything. That she loved him.

But what she said was, "It's the blind boy. Bo Racer."

Ethan looked exhausted. He didn't speak.

Madeleine said, "He's going to be killed if we don't do something."

"What were you doing lying there like that?" Ethan asked.

"What do you mean?"

He gestured at the bath. "Your head was underwater there in the tub. I heard a splash and came in to check on you. You were just lying there, had this strange smile. I waited but you stayed underwater."

She gazed at him, saying nothing.

He said, louder, "You can't breathe underwater, Madeleine. You had your mouth and nose beneath the surface the whole time! I watched you!"

"How long?"

He shook his head, and when he spoke again his voice had softened. "Ten minutes. Maybe even fifteen. At first I was going to pull you out but I saw clearly that you were OK. I watched you, waiting for you to come up, but you never did. I finally couldn't stand it any longer and pulled you out anyway."

And then he said, "How . . . ?"

fifteen

HAHNVILLE, 1927

*T*HE EASIEST THING WOULD be to take a horse and cart to New
Orleans. That would enable the four LeBlanc children
to tote along some possessions and still have room for
the dead man.

But, Patrice couldn't allow it. Without the cart, Terrefleurs died.
The cart provided a way to move cane, sugar, equipment, feed—and
often the very workers themselves. To take the cart would be to clip
Terrefleurs' wings and leave it to starve.

The children could just ride out on horses, but then they couldn't
really pack them in such a way that a dead man might ride incon-
spicuously. Patrice wasn't sure at which point the spirit left the body
and a dead man stopped being a man at all, but it seemed that this
point might be coming for the stranger. In abandoning its host, the
stranger's spirit would leave behind a rigid shell. Difficult enough

to drape a pliable body over a horse and hide it with blankets; an entirely different thing when that corpse had gone stiff.

The only means left was the car. They would have to take Papa's Ford, running or not, even if it meant pushing it all the way to New Orleans.

An hour had passed since Patrice and Gil had returned home from church, and Trigger and Rosie were already packed though Patrice had had to repack Rosie's bag. She'd chosen four of her prettiest dresses and bonnets and a wooden horse, and completely neglected shoes or underclothes of any stripe.

Trigger was packed in under five minutes. Gil, however, was paralyzed by the upset and completely unable to choose anything to take along. Trigger took over his brother's packing and told him to go say good-bye to Joseph.

Patrice said, "No! No good-byes."

Gil gave her a hard look, but she said, "We can't afford the risk. What if someone tells? We need time to get a head start in case Tatie Bernadette brings Mother here after the baptism."

"Come on, we'll each say good-bye to one person only," Trigger said.

"And we'll swear them to secrecy!" Marie-Rose said.

Patrice looked at her. "You don't have anyone to say good-bye to."

"Do so!"

"Who?"

"Francois!"

This gave Patrice pause. She clearly couldn't say good-bye to Tatie Bernadette, but to leave without speaking to Francois, her father's old friend and the ailing caretaker of Terrefleurs, that was hard to imagine.

"Alright. But we can't tell anyone where we're going. Or about the—you know, the stranger."

Three nods.

Patrice thought about Eunice for a moment, but then let it go. "I

waive my right to a farewell. I'll just accompany Rosie when she
goes to see Francois."

"I'll see Joseph," Gil said.

"And swear him to secrecy!" Marie-Rose said, eyes wide.

Trigger said, "I waive my right to a farewell, too. Got my brother
and sisters and that's all I need."

❧❧❧

PATRICE THOUGHT FRANCOIS LOOKED like a sack of bones. He was skinny
like the twins with their recent growth spurt, but Francois was in his
fifties and the diminished weight came from muscle and fat burning
away under pain. It inflamed his lips and left bloodstains at his seat.
He'd never quite seemed right after Papa died. Seemed tired and listless. But in the past two months he'd shrunk to paper and it had become clear that something deeper was wrong. The doctor's medicine
brought him no ease.

Patrice sat on the stool and tried not to think about the stench in
his cottage. She was at least cheered by the fact that Francois hadn't
been sleeping when the girls had knocked on his door. Rosie stood
next to Francois, hand on his arm, and it gave Patrice a pang because
it reminded her of the way Rosie and Papa used to look together.
Rosie turned and gawked at Patrice, suddenly childlike. Her eyes
begged Patrice to say something to start the discussion.

"You're lookin fine today," Patrice said, because Francois was
actually sitting up at the edge of his bed.

"I feel fine. Mighty fine today. Think I'll go fishin."

"Oh, that'll be nice!"

"Where y'all goin?" He was looking at the brown sack of a dress
Patrice was wearing.

She hesitated, but then Rosie blurted out: "We're leaving Terrefleurs, Francois. We all are. Us children."

He said not a thing. Just cut his eyes away.

The cottage was all oak, wide planks on the floor and slats making up the walls, and long sheets at the ceiling with roofing nails jammed through. It was dark.

"So, I've come to say good-bye," Rosie added when Francois kept up his silence.

He was a man of few words in French, and even fewer in English. He just sat there blinking. Patrice had to turn away. She looked instead at the enameled basin he used for washing up. Aside from that, the lantern, the bed, and the stool, there wasn't much else in the whole cottage. Patrice wondered what he did all day now that he was ailing. He never came to the main house to listen to the radio. He couldn't read. The plantation school started up only a few years ago and no adults had ever attended.

Francois cleared his throat and finally spoke. "When you . . . When you . . ."

But he didn't finish whatever he was about to ask: *When you comin back? When you leavin? When you decide to do a damn fool thing like that?*

Patrice rose and turned, seating herself next to him on the bed. There were questions spinning at the back of her mind, too, but she had no idea how to voice them. So she just sat next to him. Wondered how he'd fair. Tatie would look after him, for sure. Francois' wife had left long ago, headed up to Chicago with another man who'd been a Terrefleurs field worker under Francois' lead. That was a scandal folks never seemed to tire of talking about.

"Where you go?" he finally asked.

"We'd rather not say," Patrice said before Rosie could reply.

"Just as well, just as well. How you gwine get there?"

"We'll . . . drive?"

Dead, stone, staring silence. No one so much as blinked.

Then Francois said, "I'll help ya get the Ford goin."

And he rose, bless him, and Patrice stood, too, putting a hand to his arm. "No thank you, Francois. Let us manage it."

"No ma'am. Can't oblige that."

He took a moment to let his body adjust to being upright. And then he went down again, carefully to his knees, and retrieved something from under his mattress. Patrice was surprised to see that it was a Bible.

"Hold that." He handed it to Marie-Rose with both hands as though if he weren't careful it might take flight.

Rosie held it in the same way. The thing had a worn embossed cover and warped pages that looked like they'd often made the rounds from damp to dry and back.

"It was hers," was all Francois said, which Patrice took to mean that it had been his wife's, and then he was regaining himself to a stance.

He took a walking stick by the door and stepped outside, and Patrice and Rosie followed with the Good Book. The stick was too long to be a cane and seemed better suited for spear-chucking if you sharpened an end. It looked freshly carved from young wood.

"Where did you get the cane?" Rosie asked Francois.

But then in it occurred to Patrice that Francois was heading straight to the barn where the Ford and the dead man were waiting, only the dead man wasn't altogether hidden just yet. He was wrapped in blankets and curled in a wheelbarrow.

"I'll just run on ahead and get the door," Patrice said and stretched out her gait.

Francois inclined his head toward Rosie as Patrice scooted ahead for the barn.

Francois said, "Ole Trigger brung me this cane. Carved it himself."

Patrice glanced over her shoulder and saw that Francois was grinning. Actually grinning.

$$\approx$$

sixteen

$$\approx$$

HAHNVILLE, 1927

ANY ON THE PLANTATION believed that Francois' illness stemmed from the children's mother unleashing her wrath on Terrefleurs, though none of them knew that it was the children who'd kept her away. Patrice supposed many of the plantation dwellers had their suspicions. The believers of river magic thought the witch might claim the lives of all the Christians of the plantation. The Christians prayed for deliverance.

On it went.

Though Francois moved slowly, the walk to the barn was only a few feet and Patrice arrived just steps ahead of Rosie and Francois.

The wheelbarrow was empty. No sign of the dead man. Trigger was standing over the open hood of the Ford, hands stained and face sweaty.

"Where is he?" Patrice whispered.

"In the back," Trigger replied, pointing to the rumble seat.

She looked, and recognized the dead stranger only by the blankets they'd used to wrap him. He was strapped in with twine and the children's bags were tied down over him. Trigger must have done all that by himself.

Patrice fingered the twine and found it good and snug. She grinned at Trigger despite the macabre absurdity of it all, and he grinned back.

"Francois is coming," Patrice said, and stepped back to the barn door to open it wide for him.

Another sun break cast a sheer white light in the dust motes that swirled beneath the wide barn door's swing. Francois and Rosie approached the entry.

Francois paused, looking straight at the rumble seat, and then he gave a grunt and turned his gaze to the motor. Rosie stepped forward and peered into the convoluted pile of black metal and rust.

"Did you start it?" Francois asked.

"No sir," Trigger replied.

"Give it a crank, then," Francois said.

Trigger obeyed, using his entire back to work the crank and making quite a racket.

While Trigger was grinding away at the Ford, Francois leaned over and whispered into Patrice's ear, "Who he?" and he gave just the subtlest gesture toward the rumble seat.

Patrice blanched. Though the stranger had seemed perfectly concealed when the barn door was closed, the now-open flood of light reflected against a gap in the horse blanket covering the man's head, revealing brown hair with golden red highlights.

All three children were now staring at that hair. The Ford coughed four more times and died. Francois reached down and tugged once, hard, on the exposed hair.

"He'd come for us," Patrice blurted, and bit back the rest.

Francois threw Trigger a glare and then cocked his head in the direction of the barn door. Trigger scrambled to close it, fast as a jackrabbit.

"Throw the latch, too," Francois said, and Trigger obeyed.

Francois stared at the barn door as it closed. Just wavered there in his bone sack for a long moment. Then he hurled his cane across the barn so that it clattered against the door and fell back to the dirt. A dust cloud came up where it landed. The children looked on in awe.

Francois circled the Ford once, his weakening body seeming to have been restored. With fury.

Patrice could see the dead man's hair in the rumble seat now that she knew to look for it, but it was quite camouflaged. She took a disintegrating horse blanket from what used to be a chicken coop but now wasn't anything, and she draped it over that horrible, vulgar, splayed mop of hair and tucked it in like she was keeping biscuits warm in a basket.

Finally, Francois said to Trigger, "You put gasoline in it?"

"No sir. Just some oil."

"Show me where you put the oil."

Trigger showed him and Francois looked satisfied. Rosie watched, too, as though she might be the one to do it next time.

"Now put the gas," Francois said.

When Trigger gave him a blank look, Francois pointed to the corner behind the old coop where a barrel stood. Rosie slipped her hand in Patrice's and they watched while Francois showed Trigger how to run the hose down to fill the tank.

Patrice said, "But it doesn't run."

"Liable to be fine. Just need the gas." And then Francois climbed into the passenger's side of the Model T and released a sigh that seemed to outfox his very lung capacity.

"Tell me what happened here, girl," Francois said.

Patrice told him all of it. Every speck. Marie-Rose listened with wide eyes, having missed the details of the church service this morning. She was still gripping Francois' Bible. Trigger finished putting gas in the tank and cranked the motor car to life.

"Your mother sent a letter to me," Francois called over the rumble of the motor.

"She did?" Patrice was surprised.

He listened to the motor for a few moments, then nodded and told Trigger to turn it off.

Francois said, "Couldn't read no letter. Miss Bernadette read it for me. She'd got one, too."

"What did it say? They say?"

"She told me I got to come to New Orleans, your mama. Supposed to tell a judge that your papa married your mama, good and proper. Miss Bernadette thinks a cousin of your daddy's was trying to get Terrefleurs. Sayin your mama don't really own it, seein as your daddy wasn't in his right mind and she a colored woman."

Patrice listened, hand to her throat. Trigger's face was smudged with grease. He was leaning over the hood, watching Francois.

Francois said, "We didn't know what to do. Of course we don't want nothin to happen to Terrefleurs, and we sure don't want no wrong to come to you young'uns. But your mama, she a hard one. I remember what it was like before she came. Your mama sets things right in a lotta ways, but in others . . ."

Patrice knew what he meant. After Papa went to wandering with the sickness in the head, it was their Maman who brought Terrefleurs from near-bankruptcy back around to a thriving, sugar-producing plantation. But she was mean and murderous, trying to enlist her children's skills in the briar as a way to increase her station and wipe out her enemies.

Francois swallowed and said nothing further. Patrice waited for him to speak again but he just closed his eyes and let his body sag. Fury gone, the sickness had found him again.

She asked, "Did you write back to her?"

He opened his eyes. "Naw. Miss Bernadette and me, we just let it go quiet. Ain't no way I's going to make a trip to New Orleans, anyway, sick as I am."

He looked at Patrice full in the face for a moment, then his gaze traveled to the barn door. "She wrote another letter after that."

"What did that one say? Same thing?"

Francois shook his head. "Said she wanted to find Jesus. Miss Bernadette read that one to me, I just laughed and laughed. I figured your mama was talkin Jesus because she wanted us to go see that judge of hers. But Miss Bernadette, she wasn't laughing. She went to tears a little. I felt real bad. I oughtta have said something to y'all, I guess."

Patrice's stomach was in knots. All those years, Tatie Bernadette had been the one to sing the children to sleep at night, tend their injuries, paddle them for naughtiness. Though Mother had only returned to Terrefleurs periodically when business called for it, Tatie Bernadette was always there, ever present. That's why they called her "*tatie*" though she wasn't really their aunt.

But Tatie Bernadette, she did love God. And she would never turn away a soul who sought the Kingdom of Heaven.

Francois said, "I never did ask Bernadette to reply to the letters for me. Figured if your mama thought she's gwine to lose the deed to Terrefleurs, she'd come here herself."

Trigger's eyes met Patrice's.

The barn door rattled.

Francois nodded, and Trigger peeped through the crack, then opened it. Gil stood there with tear streaks on his face. It occurred to Patrice that he was the only one weeping over leaving Terrefleurs. Maybe that was because he was the only one who had a friend to say good-bye to.

"Let's go," Francois said. "I'm a-ride with y'all as far as Locoul."

The four children looked at him.

He said, "Get on in before ole Bernadette gets back."

And that's when Patrice finally burst into tears. Because Tatie Bernadette, she was the one they were all leaving behind.

seventeen

ADELEINE AND ETHAN LOOKED for Bo Racer in Bridge City at the Rosewood Arms mobile park. The storm had heaved the heat somewhere down the coast and left behind a pleasant breeze. People were out, smoking and chatting with one another along the chain-link or having a sip and a sit or a turn with the weed whacker. Turned out everyone knew the little boy with the click. And everyone seemed to have a little something to say about him.

A lady in pink clamdiggers named Cheryl told Madeleine how Bo had just recently mashed her cow peas when they were still just sprouting in the garden. Apparently he'd wanted to 'see if they'd growed yet.' Cheryl had smiled as she relayed the story. Bo was also known for finding lost dogs or cats, she'd said.

"He say he can hear them. You know, he's blind. Ain't got no eyes a-tall." She was leaning on the fence with her hand bowed at her forehead for shade, her gaze on the weedy asphalt as she spoke to Madeleine and Ethan. She never looked at their faces.

She said, "Even clear across the highway. Sandy's dog got out and run off. Bo found'm. Told Sandy to go looking over there. They found the dog, mm-hmm."

"Keen sense of hearing, I guess," Ethan said.

"I guess," Cheryl said with enough irony in her tone that Madeleine laughed.

"Bo Racer; I'm assuming that's not his real name?" Madeleine said.

Cheryl shook her head no. "His name is Beauregard Ramirez. His mama is Esther Ramirez. But everyone call him Bo Racer because he never stops movin."

Then Cheryl lowered her voice to a whisper and said very slowly, "There . . . he . . . go."

Madeleine and Ethan followed her gaze to a stand of devilwood that bordered the mobile park. Two kids were playing in an abandoned semi-paved drive just beyond the end. One boy was running like mad pushing another boy in a wheelchair, both shouting as they careened around the turn, and it looked like the second boy was about to bounce out onto the pavement. The wheelchair jostled over olivelike berries dropped from the devilwood.

"Bo?" Madeleine said, looking at the boy in the chair.

"Mm hmm," Cheryl said.

But as they drew closer Madeleine saw that the child in the wheelchair had sight. Then she recognized Bo as the one pushing, the one rocketing along behind. His mouth was gaping wide and his head was thrown back toward the sky.

The one in the chair was shrieking what sounded like, "Left!"

Bo's legs kicked as the two careened around the curve in the drive. Madeleine could hear Bo's clicking, too.

"Is he . . . is that other boy telling Bo when to turn?" Ethan asked.

"Yeah, that's my boy, Ray. Can't walk and he can't hear. They play like that all the time."

"Looks kind of dangerous," Ethan said.

Cheryl waved her shade hand with a roll to the eyes. "We quit trying to stop'm. Esther say Bo gonna do what he do. And he the only friend Ray ever had. They play like that til they get tired, and then they don't give us no trouble. I known that boy Bo since he was a baby. Went from crawling to running and never bothered to walk. Even though he couldn't see."

Madeleine watched, intrigued as the two barreled toward the end of the street. Bo slowed and turned though the other boy, Ray, hadn't told him they were at the end.

Bo spun Ray's wheelchair around and then picked up speed again, clicking like mad, Ray whooping and grinning as they raced by.

"Look at that rascal go," Ethan said.

Cheryl took Madeleine's hand and patted it. "Watch."

Madeleine looked at her.

Cheryl called out to the boys, "I wish that little boy from next door would come over here and talk to me."

But Bo and Ray continued rocketing down the drive, oblivious to Cheryl's call. They neared the curve and were about to disappear around the bend. Madeleine looked back at Cheryl. Cheryl winked, the first eye contact she'd made since they arrived.

And then Cheryl cast her gaze down toward her pink clamdiggers and, very softly, as though speaking to the crooked big toe curving over her sandal, whispered: "Bo Racer."

Madeleine looked over at the devilwood grove. And though he was zooming along about two hundred feet away and couldn't possibly have heard Cheryl's murmur, Bo slowed the wheelchair and stopped.

Madeleine could hear Ray shouting from the chair, "Why you stop?" and even from this distance she could tell Ray's speech was not clear; like that of a deaf child.

Bo had turned his face toward Cheryl and was clicking.

That night bird sound by the levee. The tick-tocking click from under the bridge. It made Madeleine's heart skip.

Cheryl said very quietly, gaze still on the dusty toe, "Bo Racer, come on over here and see your friend the neighbor lady. Gonna introduce you to some folks."

Then it looked like Bo said something to Ray. Their hands came together in a private kind of sign language and vocal speech combination; though the distance prevented Madeleine from hearing their words now that they weren't shouting. Bo leaned his shoulder in to the wheelchair and turned it around. And then he and Ray were racing again, this time headed for Cheryl.

❧

"MOM!" BO YELLED AS he threw wide the door.

A high, tense voice from inside called back, "Ya mama's sleeping! Close ya goddamned mouth!"

Madeleine and Ethan halted on the steps. Ray was "parked" below by the fence, scowling up at them, and Cheryl had returned to her garden.

Bo said into the dark room. "These people come here to talk to mom and me. They—" He turned toward Madeleine and Ethan. "What's y'all's names?"

Madeleine said, "This is Dr. Manderleigh. I'm Dr. LeBlanc."

"Doc LB!" Bo said.

"Shut it!" the high voice said.

"But Mare, she's Doc LB! The lady at—"

"Shut that door!"

Bo stepped inside and shut it.

Madeleine and Ethan looked at one another, awkward, surrounded by half a dozen ferns that had sprouted furry, snaking feet. Bo's and the woman's muffled voices came from inside the trailer.

In the yard were one huge dead tree and one smaller live one.

The trunk of the dead tree was wrapped in a mattress; the live one was wrapped in layers of yellow foam seamed with duct tape. Like someone had tried to pad the entire yard.

From the other side of the chain-link, Ray was giving a look of such menace that the ferns were at risk of withering.

Ethan cleared his throat and said to Ray, "Guess you and Bo are good pals."

Brows still knit, Ray replied with thick words accompanied by hand signs, "He's my best friend. I won't let anything bad happen to him."

Madeleine nodded. It had taken the boy a while to get the words out. Though he still had some dexterity to him, the speech and hand movements were slow and blunted.

Ray added, "He's going to be the first blind person to play for the Saints when he grows up."

Ethan said, "He can play football?"

The door squeaked and Madeleine looked back over her shoulder. A short woman with enormous eyes and elliptical painted brows was glaring at them, a face like Esther's only rounder and less haggard. She wore a loose gray suit and bare feet.

"What you want?" She was the high-voiced one Bo had called Mare.

Madeleine said, "We just need to talk to Bo and his mother."

The woman seemed at the end of her patience. "Oh, that right? About what?"

A pause. Madeleine averted her eyes. How to explain why Bo's life might be in danger because a hospitalized man in a vegetative state wanted to kill him?

Ethan said, "It's about what happened under the bridge last night."

Mare put her hand to her hip and gave a long sigh that held a ghost of that high voice in it, but she made no further move. Something stung Madeleine on the ankle.

Ethan opened his hands. "Look, we just want to help."

Mare said, "Y'all are doctors, huh?"

Ethan nodded. "Academic doctors, but yes."

"Academic." Mare rolled her eyes, then widened the door. "Get in. Mosquitoes'll carry us all off."

Madeleine cast a wave back toward Ray who was watching with the same mistrustful frown, then stepped through the entry after Mare, Ethan's hand on her back. The scent of cigarette smoke greeted her and beneath that, old bacon and mildewed air-conditioning.

"Doc LB," Bo whispered just as loudly as he'd been speaking earlier, and he reached for Madeleine's hand and shook it. "I heard a you."

"Pleased to meet you," Madeleine whispered.

At the boy's touch, something jumped inside Madeleine. Not bad, not good; just a feeling of sudden alertness—like she could sense the very blood and breath and the life current in her own body.

Severin appeared.

She was but a glimmer at the back of the room. Madeleine narrowed her eyes at her.

And then Bo moved on and was shaking Ethan's hand, his grin wide and pointed high. "How you doin?"

"Just fine," Ethan whispered.

Mare shoved Bo's shoulder. "You. Out."

Madeleine said, "But if you don't mind we'd prefer to—"

Mare said, "I ain't his mama, and you ain't talkin to him unless his mama wants you to. And she's asleep."

She opened the door and steered Bo by the neck. "Get on outta here, Bo."

"Bye!" he said with a wave just as the painted aluminum door slammed shut on him.

Madeleine watched through a crack in the blackout curtains as he ran down the stairs, causing the entire trailer to quake, his clicking audible through the thin walls. Hard to believe the boy had no eyes. He vaulted over the chain-link even though the gate stood five feet away. The wheelchair speedway game recommenced with Bo and Ray exchanging not a single word between them.

Severin pressed her face to the window. Madeleine watched her, biting back reproach. Then Severin pressed her face *through* it, through the glass, and crawled up toward the roofline. Her filthy ankle disappeared somewhere above.

Once again Severin was disregarding their bargain. Annoying. Ominous, even, but Madeleine could do nothing about it at the moment.

Full voice, as though the rule of whispering had vanished with Bo, Mare said, "I guess y'all wastin your time. You wanna leave your number, Esther'll call ya when she gets up."

Ethan said, "He always run like that? Like a bat outta Hell?"

"Always." Mare sighed and went to a mirror where she dabbed powder over her face, then reached for an eye pencil. "He never stops runnin, which is why this place look like a trash hole with Esther wrappin the trees with padding. Bo run into'm enough times."

Ethan said, "Those boys OK playing in the drive?"

She said, "Ain't no cars. That boy nothing but trouble. He was always in a sling or a cast since he's a baby. He's runnin before he was walkin. No joke. Didn't matter he had no eyes. They took'm out when he was just a few months old."

Ethan said, "Cancer?"

Mare nodded without taking her gaze off the mirror. She'd moved on to lip pencil.

Madeleine said, "We came here because we wanted to make sure Bo had a place to sleep tonight."

Mare shrugged. "He sleep here."

"OK, good. Things have gotten really dangerous on the street, and—"

"I said, he sleep here," Mare's eyes fixed on Madeleine's reflection in the mirror.

Mare snatched a receipt and scribbled something on the back, then thrust it into Madeleine's hand. "That's Esther's number. Call her another time. I don't know what your business is, but I know it doesn't have to be part of *my* business in *my home*."

Ethan and Madeleine looked at one another.

Mare said, "Look. Y'all need to move along cuz I'm fixin to go to work and Esther's sleepin."

Madeleine said, "I'm not trying to get in your business. I do want to caution you to keep your doors locked and keep the gate locked, too, and be careful about answering the door."

Mare looked from her to Ethan. "What the hell is going on? Is Bo causing trouble?"

Madeleine said, "No, it's nothing like that."

"He always gettin into fights at school."

Ethan said, "Bo's a fighter?"

Mare nodded. "He can't keep his mouth in check. Esther let him do whatever he wants. She used to be a junkie, cleaned up her act when Bo was born. Found God. But she uses it as an excuse to let Bo run wild and get into fights."

From the far end came a voice: "That ain't true. Bo don't get in no fights."

It was Esther, standing at the end of the hall, twisting a velvet-rayon robe to a knot at her chest. "There's a difference between getting into fights and getting picked on by bullies."

Mare pointed at Esther. "Bo done found trouble and now these people come here to tell us to check the locks! People getting shot and stabbed out there!"

Ethan said, "Hey, Bo didn't do anything—"

"How'm I supposed to live like this, huh?" Mare shoved her feet into a pair of high heels and stalked for the door.

Esther remained rigid where she stood. Mare snatched a bag from an easy chair and left with a slam. The sound of Bo and Ray filtered through the walls, high and spirited and then compressing to hollow tones as they continued past.

Esther let out a stream of breath and sank into a chair at the kitchen table. "God, I hate that woman."

Madeleine said, "I think I alarmed her."

Esther rubbed her already-ragged eyes. "Y'all are from the shelter, right? St. Joseph's volunteers?"

Madeleine nodded. "We came here to make sure you and Bo are going to be safe. I don't mean to pry, but if your friend's letting you stay here . . ."

"She ain't no friend. She's my cousin—who the good Lord sent to keep me humble I guess. And she staying with us, not the other way around."

"Oh. Didn't you and Bo spend a night on the levee?"

Esther nodded. "Was because Mare had a date, had us clear out. She don't get her way she ain't gonna pay me rent. My car actin like it wanna quit on me. We need the money."

"I see. I don't know if you're aware of this, but someone was killed not far from where you were camped on the levee."

Esther fell silent.

Ethan asked, "*Did* you know about the murder?"

"No. I heard, but I wasn't sure. Is that why you're here?"

Ethan and Madeleine exchanged glances, and Madeleine said, "Yes and no. There was a quilt left behind at your encampment. And Bo's cane. It looked like you left in a hurry, which is why we thought you might have been nearby when it happened."

And then Esther narrowed her eyes at Madeleine. "We met somewhere before?"

"I saw you that day under the bridge, but I don't think we've actually met. Unless it was at St. Jo's?" But Madeleine couldn't recall having seen Esther there.

Esther was frowning and shaking her head. "Don't think so. But I'm sure I know you."

"What's the matter with your car?" Ethan asked.

Esther shrugged. "It's old."

"Well, let's take a look."

Her expression lifted a fraction, and she rose from the table. "It's just outside."

Esther grabbed a set of keys that looked like it could double as wind chimes, and they went out to the carport. Bo and Ray were still at it, their silhouettes strobing by as they passed behind trees from the other side of the grove.

Esther unlocked a silver Buick and Ethan checked under the hood, which looked to Madeleine about as decipherable as reading tea leaves. Growing up, Madeleine had done the cooking and hunting and some of the fishing, but her brother was the tinkerer, and he eventually became an electrician.

Ethan said, "I'm no mechanic, but the engine definitely doesn't sound right. That belt needs to be replaced. Pronto. You shouldn't drive it until you can get a new one."

Esther said nothing.

Ethan wiped his hands. "I can at least do that—pick up a new belt and throw it on there."

"Really?" Esther looked relieved.

"But it still needs work. The belt's the least of its problems."

Esther nodded. She licked her lips and glanced at Ethan, then at Madeleine. It looked like she wanted to say something but felt she ought to be careful about it.

Madeleine said, "We may be able to help, you know. I'm not talking about the car."

Esther cut her gaze for a moment, then looked Madeleine in the eye. "You said before that we left that quilt and that cane there on the levee because we left in a hurry. You're right about that. But it's not like we knew what was happening. Bo, he's real sensitive. That morning he clicked on something he didn't like and told me, 'Mama, we gotta go now.' That's why we left. Over the years I learned to listen to him when he acts like that."

Madeleine said, "The thing is, though, we want to make sure y'all are going to sleep here at home for the time being."

Esther looked next door where Cheryl was still bent over her garden, the evening sun illuminating her clamdiggers and casting a pink halo along the lattice beneath her trailer. "We only do that when Mare makes a fuss. We stayed on the levee because I don't like to go into the blights. To Bo it's like camping."

"I understand. But for the time being . . ."

Madeleine paused and wet her lips. "For the time being, until the danger passes, please do keep Bo here. I don't think y'all are gonna be safe anywhere else. Definitely not the levee. Probably better stay away from St. Jo's, too."

Esther was watching her carefully. "I know who you are now. I remember seeing you on TV. That psychic from that murder trial."

Madeleine's lips parted. When she'd been a star witness at Zenon's murder trial, the prosecutor had exposed to the court how Madeleine often talked to "an invisible little friend named Severin." The story had been all over the news. Madeleine, a psychologist and witness to a murder, had looked like a complete crackpot. It was a disaster. In the wake of it, some folks thought her crazy, others called her psychic, and the judge, well, after some of the jurors proved tainted by information overload, the judge had declared a mistrial.

Madeleine said, "Not really a psychic. That was . . ."

"You see devils. They after Bo?"

A lump was forming in Madeleine's throat.

"Tell me!"

Ethan was eyeing the grove of devilwood. The boys had gone quiet.

"I'll be right back." Ethan closed the hood and started for the trees.

eighteen

ESTHER AND MADELEINE BOTH stepped down the drive. Esther was still in her robe and slippers. Through a gap in the trees, Madeleine saw Bo standing with his hands on Ray's wheel-chair. They were facing a group of boys. Four boys. Older than Bo and Ray by a few years, and filthy. And then Madeleine recognized the stains under their noses. The same group from yesterday, minus Mako and Del.

"The huffers."

"Damn bullies," Esther said.

Madeleine turned her head upward and saw Severin grinning from the roof. She was watching the boys. Ethan was already through the gate and striding toward them.

The strange thing was, although Ray was shouting at the boys, no one else said a word. The huffers weren't taunting like they'd done yesterday. Bo was clicking in an unbroken stream. Madeleine recognized Oyster's frizzy hair, and saw that he was carrying a long silver Maglite. Two of the other boys were holding objects, too— one had a beer bottle and the other held a length of white painted wood that looked like it used to be a porch spindle.

"My God, my God," Esther reached into her robe pocket and pulled out a cell phone. "They never leave him alone."

Ethan had reached them. The four boys moved as one. An initial lurch followed by more fluid, independent movement. They formed a wide box around Bo and Ray. Bo's clicking accelerated.

Madeleine heard Ethan telling the huffers to back off. She looked back at Severin. Was Zenon here? No sign of him.

Madeleine looked toward the huffers and tried: *Drop what you're holding.*

No response.

She scanned the grove and the houses nearby, letting her sight recede into itself before opening up again. Briar sight. And she saw him. Zenon. Standing with his river devil near the wild olives. Zenon looked whole and fresh and young, at the peak of his prime, just like he'd been in the briar. Nothing like the limp shell that was giving itself over to atrophy in the hospital bed.

The briar revealed, too, how Bo glowed with a light from within. It struck Madeleine with awe. His lumen glow.

The piece of wood rose in one boy's fists, and he swung it at Bo. Bo sprang away. Even though he was blind and couldn't possibly have seen it coming. He was in tilt, careening sideways with his hands locked on Ray's chair.

"Get away from my boy!" Esther cried.

Ethan knocked the spindle from the boy's hand and it went clattering to the dirt. But the boy barely even looked at Ethan. His gaze never left Bo. They all kept watching and moving toward Bo. Bo moved like a charging boar and could probably give them a run for their money, but he seemed unwilling to let go of Ray's chair.

"This way," Ethan cried.

His leg prevented him from keeping up with the chase. Ray was shouting, and Esther was shouting, and in her mind, Madeleine shouted at Zenon, "Stop it, Zenon! Get out of here!"

The neighbors had stepped from their mobile homes and were watching from their yards, clucking and calling in alarm. Even through her panic, Madeleine noticed an oddity about them all in the way they appeared through the lens of the briar. Some of them had devils. Everyone did, really, it's just that some flourished more than others. But some of the neighbors seemed to radiate something else through the briar lens. Something strange.

Esther was hollering into the cell phone, "I need the police, just send the police! Oh, God."

Bo rounded the devilwood grove with Ray's chair just like he'd been doing earlier. No way they'd be able to outrun the huffers with the wheelchair slowing them down.

A loud crack. It sounded like a shot. Esther screamed. But whatever it was none of them slowed down.

"I got Ray, just go," Ethan was calling.

Bo finally let go of the chair and ran, ran, ran. One of the boys picked up a softball-sized rock and threw it, catching Bo on the shoulder, but Bo never paused. He shot from the drive and zipped through the devilwood grove, weaving through the trees and clicking like mad. The four boys went in after him.

Ethan had scooped Ray up in his arms and was limp-running him back toward the trailer.

Can we stop it? Madeleine asked Severin, speaking only in her mind.

Severin was grinning at her from above. "Take the painted wood, maybe."

Madeleine saw the spindle that Ethan had knocked from one of the huffer's hands. She ran for it. As if borrowing her momentum, Esther went barreling down the steps after her. Somewhere along the way Esther had ditched her cell phone and picked up a hammer. Three of the huffers were spreading in a wide half-circle around Bo. They drove him straight into Oyster.

"Stop!" Madeleine cried.

Oyster raised the Maglite and whacked Bo in the head with it. Bo staggered a half step but kept moving.

Ethan called, "Madeleine, you and Esther get back inside."

The neighbors, in their strange briar appearance, were stepping from their yards and onto the drive.

Madeleine realized she was gripping the spindle. No recollection of having picked it up. She looked back at the trailer and saw that Severin's eyes were sparkling, energized. A little girl river devil with her favorite game in play.

Madeleine knew that this was wrong. Severin didn't want her to save Bo. Severin wanted Bo dead. So why was Madeleine following direction from Severin?

Chloe's words from the hospital room yesterday came to mind:

You hold a magnifying glass too long and it only serves to burn the object. You drop it, and look at the rest.

Madeleine took a flash inventory of what was happening in her mind, a jumble of the relevant and irrelevant:

The strange way the neighbors looked.
Olives spread over the drive.
The spindle in her hands.
The clicking.

And Madeleine understood that Bo was using his clicks to see.

And that the neighbors held a trace of Bo's luminescence inside them. It shone in Ethan, too, like a mirror reflecting a flame. Madeleine stepped toward the grove and the people. Cheryl was there, eyes wet. An older man wearing jeans with no shirt and bare feet— having run out without taking time to put on shoes—was striding across the stickery ground to take one of the huffer boys by the arm.

And while Madeleine watched, that luminescence spread into the huffers, too. They just seemed to slow down.

Except for Oyster. Through the bramble lens, Oyster looked darker, a sepia shadow, like the river devils. He was closing in on Bo.

"Stay away from my son!" Esther screamed, running at Oyster with the hammer raised high.

He ducked as she swung, then drove his fist into her face. Esther went sprawling.

Oyster picked up Esther's hammer and circled toward Bo in a crouch. He walked low and careful, below eye level, behind the devilwood where Bo's clicks would have a harder time finding him.

Bo seemed to be tiring. His movements were slower.

Madeleine whispered, "Bo Racer, run straight home."

Like before, he heard it. Bo turned and burst into a sprint. Straight line for the trailer.

Oyster had to leap to his feet to keep up, and in doing so Bo found him and swerved just enough to avoid the hammer crashing toward his skull. Ethan threw one fist under Oyster's bicep, forcing his arm upward, and slammed down on his wrist. The hammer went to the ground.

Bo was heading for the trailer. Madeleine stood in the drive between him and the gate.

"Swing the spindle, now!" Severin cried from behind.

And for reasons Madeleine couldn't fathom, her fingers itched to do it. In her mind she could even see herself gripping the spindle, her arms forming an arc, the hard, heavy block of wood at the base aimed for Bo as he ran clicking toward her. Aimed right for the spaces of his eyes.

That's it, now. You can see it all in your mind, can't you?

Zenon. Suddenly at her side. Whispering in her ear. Like he himself was a river devil.

She didn't move.

Bo swerved around her and kept running to his gate. He paused and turned, clicking in Madeleine's direction.

"She's one of'm, mama," he called.

Madeleine let the strangeness and fury course through and then out of her. The spindle slipped from her fingers and fell to the olive-littered earth.

From the devilwood grove, still gripping Oyster by the arm, Ethan was watching her.

Esther was staring, too. Blood coursed from her nose where Oyster had hit her.

"Get in the house!" Esther cried.

Bo turned and continued to the trailer.

Madeleine looked at her hands. Shadowed, sepia. But luminous, too. Bo's light in there.

Zenon said, "You keep hangin on, Madeleine. Fight the fight and for your prize you get to be crazy. All the same to me."

He turned and strode for the devilwood. "Don't worry. I'll be back for him."

And then he was gone.

A police cruiser entered the trailer park and was moving in their direction. Esther looked at it, hand to the blood on her face, and stumbled onto the drive.

She turned and pointed her finger at Madeleine. "Get away from here. I saw how you was lookin at my son."

Madeleine felt heat rush to her face. She could say nothing, only shake her head.

Esther said, "You stay away from Bo. You keep your devils in your own pocket. Stay away."

nineteen

HAHNVILLE, 1927

FRANCOIS WAS SHOUTING TO Patrice over the roar of the motor. "Reverse don't work. So if you need to go back, you put it in neutral and push."

Patrice gripped the steering wheel and wondered whether the motor was supposed to sound like that. It made her feel like her teeth might fall back into her spine. Would that sound continue the entire journey?

Francois was sitting in the middle between Patrice and Trigger. Trigger had demanded to drive but neither Patrice nor Francois would let him. Gil and Rosie were in the back, in the pop-up rumble seat. They had to sit on top of the luggage that was strapped over the dead man. Rosie didn't mind and Gil, well, he probably didn't realize it and that was just as well.

Francois went on with his instruction. "You mash the left pedal to switch gears, and if you just hold it forward, that's slow gear. Hold that left pedal in about halfway and that's neutral. Got it?"

Patrice nodded.

"Use neutral to coast. The middle pedal is reverse."

"And reverse don't work," Trigger shouted.

"Doesn't," Patrice mumbled, knowing they wouldn't hear.

And yet Trigger corrected himself: "Doesn't work."

She shot him a grin from across Francois.

"No it don't," Francois agreed.

"How do we go fast?" Trigger shouted.

"We don't!" Patrice and Francois replied in unison.

Patrice was beginning to feel quite faint with the exhaust filling the barn.

"Open them doors now," Francois called back to the rumble seat.

Both Gil and Rosie hopped out and swung the barn doors wide.

Francois pointed to the steering column beneath Patrice's grip, "To go, you give it gas with this lever on the side of the steering wheel stalk."

She tried it. The Ford lurched forward and Patrice's head snapped back. "Ooh!"

"Stop!" Francois cried.

But he hadn't shown her how to do that yet so they kept moving. The Ford was at least no longer lurching and it just sort of rolled out onto the drive. Gil and Rosie were standing way back against the open barn doors.

Francois shouted, "Mash the brake! The pedal on the right."

The Ford halted and the occupants pitched forward. The engine died. Trigger hopped out and went for the crank.

"Hold on, hold on," Francois said.

He took out his kerchief and mopped his head, grumbling.

At least they'd made it out of the barn and into the fresh air and sunshine where the clouds had broken apart. That seemed like progress. Steam rose from the earth.

"Close the doors please," Patrice said to Gil and Marie-Rose.

They closed the barn doors behind and reclaimed their positions atop the luggage and the stranger in the rumble seat.

Patrice couldn't help but think of Tatie Bernadette, that she'd be arriving back here soon. It had been almost two hours now since Gil and Patrice left the service. Mother would be baptized by now, abomination that it was. And after, the parishioners would lay hands on her.

If any of you, if any one person here lays hands on that woman, you are inviting devils!

It still seemed unreal. Thus far the children had managed to keep their mother away by using the briar to ward her off. But they hadn't anticipated that Maman might send a stranger or that she would get at Tatie Bernadette.

Some plantationers had assembled in the allée, drawn by the spectacle. Patrice looked toward them, pained, knowing that they were moments away from coming up and asking what they were doing and where they were headed in Papa's old automobile.

Francois must have seen them, too, because he motioned to Patrice. "Listen close before I let Trig crank this thing up again because I'm tired of shouting. You use your right foot for the brake, and your left foot for the gears."

Patrice thought it sounded simple enough.

Trigger asked, "But how do we go fast?"

"Boy, y'all are not gonna go fast, you hear?"

"We need to at least know how it works."

Francois sighed. "That left pedal, if it ain't pushed all the way and if it ain't in the middle, then you lettin it out and that's the fast gear. And you can give it gas on the lever up here to make it really go. But I mean it, y'all ain't goin fast. You gotta go slow the whole ways. Now go on ahead and crank'r up again."

Trigger cranked. The motor reared to life. Trigger hopped back in.

"Easy, easy," Francois said.

Patrice took it easy.

Francois said, "Mash that pedal and then real gentle, do the lever here on the steering wheel. Now you goin. Now you goin. Watch the road. Always watch the road. Don't never look at your feet. You go by feel."

The plantationers had circled closer in, though Patrice had barely noticed their approach. They were now backing off the road as the old Ford made lurching advances, though its movements were no longer so violent as that initial attempt. And then Patrice started to get the feel of it, and the Ford was moving smoothly but slowly forward.

Patrice could see Eunice walking ahead in a thin calico dress. There were tears in her eyes. Patrice wondered what had upset her. Did she know? Before she could stop herself, Patrice sought inside Eunice's heart. She found that Eunice was sad to see Patrice and the others go. How Eunice knew they were leaving for good, Patrice couldn't guess. Maybe all those bags in the back.

But the rest of the plantationers seemed oblivious to the significance of all of this, and had only gathered to enjoy the spectacle of seeing all four children plus Francois riding around in the automobile.

A few children were walking alongside the slow-moving Ford. Patrice itched to look over her shoulder into the rumble seat to make absolutely sure that the dead man was concealed. Maybe when Rosie and Gil were hopping in and out, they might have upset the blankets that hid the stranger. But she didn't dare tear her eyes from the road.

Eunice walked up alongside the Ford and was pulling something—a necklace, it looked like—over her head. Patrice felt like every muscle in her body had tensed to stone as she gripped the wheel and eased the lever. Eunice leaned over and slipped the necklace over Patrice's head while she drove, then kissed her cheek.

"Go on now!" Francois was shouting at everyone.

Patrice hadn't dared to so much as glance at Eunice when she'd put the necklace over her head. Even now, Patrice couldn't say whether it was made of silver or gold or string. Or whether Eunice was now still watching or was walking back to her cottage. Nothing but the steering wheel and the road, which looked like a death combination if ever there was any.

They rumbled down the allée of pecans, Francois coaxing Patrice to accelerate the gas lever a bit more, more. It felt like every leaf and frog and blade of grass in all of Terrefleurs was turning to watch them go. And yet Patrice couldn't look. She saw only the road.

Such was the way she left her home.

twenty

NEW ORLEANS, NOW

*T*HEY WERE DRIVING TOWARD the intersection of Tchoupitoulas and Napoleon, and in her mind Madeleine was turning over the situation with Bo. She took out the paper Mare had given her and punched Esther's number into her cell phone.

Ethan said, "It ain't even been half an hour since we left. Maybe y'oughtta let her cool off."

Madeleine glanced at him. The call was already giving over to voice mail. She considered hanging up but when the beep came, she stammered something out: "Please call back" and "It's an unusual situation," and she left her number. The phone felt limp in her hand.

Ethan shook his head.

Madeleine said suddenly, "We can't go home."

"We can't?"

"No, they'll find us. Please just pull off somewhere and let me think a minute."

Ethan frowned but did as she asked, pulling the Lexus down a side road.

"Who's gonna find us?" he asked.

Madeleine cut her eyes toward him and then at the road again. It had gone bumpy with potholes. "I don't know. I think we might have led them straight to Bo."

He pulled past a gated drive with a sign that read RESTRICTED ACCESS and kept going until the road ended in an industrial wharf. Freight containers crowded in on tracks along the waterfront. He parked along cyclone fencing in a spot where they could still see the river between two rusted freight cars.

"Why'd you stop here?" she asked.

"Lady says pull over, I got to oblige."

"But, *here*?"

"What, you were thinking somewhere that serves café au lait?"

Despite herself, Madeleine chuckled, pinching the bridge of her nose. "I guess it doesn't matter. I just need to think this through."

"Why?"

"Because I gotta figure it out."

"But why?"

She looked at him.

He said, "Why figure it out? What's to figure?"

"This isn't going to stop unless we do something. That little boy's life is in danger."

He pursed his lips in feigned bewilderment and for a moment it made him look like Robert Mitchum. "I don't know, baby blue, I think we just done all we can."

"Zenon's fixated on Bo!"

"True. And there's still nothing we can do about it."

She said, "I think by tracking Bo down to that trailer park, we led Zenon straight to him."

Ethan shook his head. "I don't buy that. Zenon's got his own river devil plus whatever else is crawling around in the briar with him, and he's spendin a lot more time in the briar than out of it these days. Those river devils can find anyone they want to find and you know it. Hell, you're even trying to avoid letting Severin locate Marc's kid."

He was right, of course. She felt the frown deepen around her eyes.

He took her hand and kissed it. "You think I don't care what happens to Bo Racer?"

"Of course not."

"So alright, then. This might be one of those situations where you gotta look away for a little while. Let your subconscious take over."

"You sound like Chloe."

"Well she ain't always wrong. Let the other half of your brain go to work a while. Get your mind off it, and then boom: The answer's right there."

She fell silent as she watched the stratus clouds fill with golden light.

"Look on over there," he said, pointing west toward a stack of shipping containers that rose several stories high.

Above the rail cars, Madeleine could see what looked like the top of a building, only it was gliding toward them. A ship on the Mississippi. The trains in the foreground gave it the illusion of being a kind of strange land craft—white railing and flags and a spinning sonar device all gliding along as though it were a penthouse on roller skates. Then it came into full view through the gap between the rail cars and both Ethan and Madeleine drew in. It was enormous.

"Come on," he said, and was out of the car and striding around to open her door before she'd even unclipped her seat belt.

"Ethan, what are you—"

"Just come on, baby."

He tugged her over weedy pavement until he found a section of the cyclone fence that had toppled and was lying flat, then helped her over it. She looked back where the RESTRICTED ACCESS sign had been and shook her head. For all his polish and upbringing, Ethan liked to take rules in stride.

Shipping containers were lined along the tracks and then beyond, stacked like walls of Pez candies. Security didn't seem to be a major point of concern in this corner of the wharf. She and Ethan passed an enclave beneath a rusted railcar with an empty bottle of cheap gin and a stack of magazines. A view of the river. Judging from the look of the paper, someone had been camping there as recently as the past few days. Someone who was probably at St. Jo's right now.

She said, "Ethan, what are you going to do if I really do lose my mind?"

With his gaze holding straight ahead he said, "Hook you up to my car battery with jumper cables."

"Ethan, seriously—"

"Stop. Just stop, baby. We got a beautiful sunset here and you gonna miss it."

She looked ahead. He was right. On many levels.

He squeezed her hand. "You know, there are people in Malaysia, sea nomads, who can hold their breath for a very long time. Like, seven minutes."

"That so?"

Her gaze dropped to her shoes as she stepped across the hardpan. She'd been so caught up in Bo and Zenon she'd barely given the underwater breathing phenomenon much thought.

He said, "When I saw you in that bathtub like that, I figured, 'next thing she gonna do is sprout a damned mermaid tail.'"

She laughed at the thought.

He gave her hand a tighter squeeze. "You're like that. A magical, mythical creature. Beautiful."

She looked up into his face and saw no intention of flattery. It made her smile.

He said, "Truth is, we humans don't really know what we're

capable of. A runner breaks a world record and then suddenly other runners can match that same pace. Just needed someone to prove it could be done."

"That's true," she said.

"This whole business with that briar world of yours, it just seems you get a shortcut on evolution."

They neared the river and it smelled like tar softening in the sun. The golden light in the clouds had already gone over to peach, and it reflected in shimmering stars on the Mississippi's surface. The ship was turning in toward a pier now, a horizontal skyscraper with massive bay doors on the hull big enough for semis to drive through. Ro-ro, they called them, for the kind of roll-on, roll-off cargo they carried.

"Got a kind of an industrial beauty to it," Ethan said.

"Mm-hmm."

She felt small. Everything else seemed so massive—the ship, the walls of containers, the horizontal stretch of the Misssssippi, the endless sky.

He put his arm around her and she leaned into him, and they breathed the heavy river breeze together, watching the ship dock.

He said, "I want you to marry me, Madeleine."

Her spine straightened. They both kept their eyes fixed in the direction of the ro-ro vessel, but Madeleine was no longer seeing it.

She said, "Marry?"

"Yeah, marry me. You can't tell me you haven't thought about it."

She had. Distantly, fearfully. She felt his eyes on her, but she kept watching the ship.

She said, "It feels almost like we're married already. We spend nearly every night together."

"Nearly ain't enough for me anymore. I don't want to go back and forth between my place and your place, I want our place. I want us to move in together. Now. Right away. And then, aw hell, lemme do this right."

And then to her dismay—because at that point he was practically holding her up—he let go of her and got down on his knee right there on the hardpan, and reached into a pocket for a small black box which he opened for her.

She was forced to look at him now. Couldn't keep staring at the ship. And she had to stand on her own without leaning on him. Ironic that a proposal to unite forced her to both face him and stand strong on her own.

He said, "Madeleine LeBlanc, will you marry me?"

A thousand thoughts were ricocheting through her head. Not thoughts; worries. But she did her best to push past them and answer Ethan's question.

"Yes." The word tumbled out heavy and flat.

Ethan stared at her a moment, then started to laugh. Hard.

"What?" She was beginning to feel silly.

His body was quaking so hard by now that she worried he might drop that ring.

He shoved the box into her hands and doubled over fully with his palms on the packed earth, laughing even harder, his otherwise deep voice going high pitched like a female.

"Ethan!" She grabbed him by the collar and yanked him to his feet.

He wiped his eye and said, "Good God, baby, you could give an ole boy a complex. You make it sound like you're talking to the automated system on a customer service call. 'Are you calling about your bill? Answer clearly, yes or no.'"

She grinned. "I was just trying to focus."

"Well you focused alright. 'Yes!' Lord have mercy."

She laughed with him, then grabbed him by the neck and kissed him hard enough to shut him up. He smelled like sweat. His arms pulled her in closer and he felt strong and sturdy. He made everything seem so easy. Or maybe she just made things seem difficult.

"Well, woman, you gonna put it on or what?"

She pulled the ring out of the box and slipped it, shaky, over her ring finger. It made it as far as the knuckle and then stopped.

"We'll have to get it sized," he said, and started to pull it off.

"Not so fast!"

She shoved it back to the knuckle and held it up to the light so she could admire how the evening sun glittered in the stone. It was a beautiful round diamond on a platinum band, simple and elegant, not too garish and, bless him, not too small. Looking at it made her feel girly in a way she'd never been, or hadn't seen herself as being capable of. Lots of women cared about rings and she'd never been one of them. Until now.

Ethan was telling her that he'd been planning to do this last night, over dinner, but with all that happened they never made it to dinner. So when they pulled in here he'd decided not to put it off a moment longer. She tilted the ring this way and that without listening to him, until the words "hardheaded woman" pierced through and caused her to lift her gaze.

"What?" she asked.

"You know good and well I've been trying to propose to you for a long time. You always find a way to thwart me."

She tried to tune him out again and went back to staring at the ring.

He said, "We need to get it sized, Madeleine. You just gonna lose it."

She knew it was true. Reluctantly, she slipped it off her finger and put it back in the box.

He put it in his pocket and said, "So the other thing. I want you to move in with me, sooner rather than later."

"What, just get rid of my flat above the flower shop?"

"We can live above there instead if you want."

She said, "No, not necessarily, I'm just trying to think this through. My place was never meant to be anything but a temporary home. It's an industrial zone—too loud. I was going to . . . But I can't go to your place! No pets in your building."

"We'll sneak Jasmine in."

"Ethan!"

"Come on, she ain't a pet. She's a bottle rocket disguised as a Jack Russell."

"You can't just ignore the building covenants and regulations, Ethan."

"Covenants and regulations? Honey, listen to yourself. You're getting caught up in details. We'll figure it all out later. I love you."

The thoughts tumbled inside her: What if she got to wandering more? What if her mind vanished into the briar, like so many of her family, and left only a jabbering fool behind? He'd be seeing her at her worst. But Ethan knew all that. He was walking in with eyes wide open.

A sudden, deep horn blast came from the ship, and they both jumped.

Madeleine put her head on his shoulder. "You sure you want—all this?"

"Baby blue, it ain't even a matter of want. I can't stand to be without you. You're the best part of everything."

She felt a smile that came from somewhere deep within. They turned back to face the water. A flock of gulls cried out and lifted in unison from the near bank, veering on a diagonal so that the sun projected its colors onto their underbellies like a stretching, living movie screen.

And then: boom. A distant realization; a hatching of an idea.

She could divert Zenon's attention away from Bo. Zenon, in his new isolation, wanted to groom her as a kind of warrior just like himself. Instead of standing by to protect Bo, she could find a way to make Zenon focus on her. *She* had a chance against him. She could fool him.

She leaned closer into Ethan. No point in telling him until she had a more concrete plan. They'd just decided to get married and no way was she going to ruin this moment. Bo was safe for now, at least.

"Hunter or prey," Zenon had said. "If you don't hunt, I'll kill you myself," he'd said. The thought made her mouth go dry.

She dashed away the tightness in her throat and promised herself not to worry about it until the idea had jelled on its own. Worry was a false enterprise. Like panic, it never helped.

twenty-one

BOUTTE, 1927

AS THEY TRAVELED ALONG the bumpy road, Patrice became conscious of things she wished she'd done before leaving Terrefleurs. For one, she wished she'd double-wrapped her breasts, because the car moved like a motorized pecan-tree shaker. Relentlessly. She'd gone so sore.

And she wished she'd touched the piano—just once, before she'd left, taken the ivory keys under her fingers.

She wished she could have bid farewell to Tatie Bernadette, and a proper one to dear Eunice.

She wished she'd taken at least one of the dolls Papa had carved for her—

Her thoughts stopped dead. Because it dawned on her . . .

Patrice hadn't packed a single doll. But she hadn't packed a single anything. She hadn't packed.

She hadn't packed!

All that fretting over Rosie's terrible packing job and Gil's inability to do so, but she'd never gotten around to doing it for herself.

"What're you doin?" Trigger called over the motor from the other side of Francois.

Beneath her, the Ford choked itself out and just rolled. She must have let it slow to nothing without realizing it. The silence that rushed in after the roaring motor was so tangible it felt like cotton in her ears. She squeezed the lever for gas but it was already too late.

Patrice found the brake and stopped the dead roll.

"Eh?" Francois said, waking from sleep.

"Where are we?" Marie-Rose said from the rumble seat, and next to her, Gil asked, "Why'd we stop, hon?"

Patrice said, "I forgot . . ."

And let it die. No use telling the others that she'd failed to pack her belongings because they couldn't well turn around and get them. Tatie would be home by now and she'd never let Patrice or the others leave Terrefleurs, even if it meant locking them in the cellar. Sure, the LeBlanc children may be able to fight off one of their mother's murderous thugs. But they had no chance against Tatie Bernadette when she was in a fit.

The clothes that Patrice wore were all that she had now. Nothing else.

Patrice licked her lips and pulled her hands from the steering column. "I . . . I didn't mean to let it stop."

Her fingers had gone stiff from all that gripping. Francois blinked and looked around as though he couldn't figure why he was riding around in a Ford with the four children. But then he paused, his gaze dropping to just below and behind him where the dead stranger lay buried under all the luggage plus Gil's and Rosie's buttocks.

Finally, Francois said, "Turn here."

Patrice looked to see a break in the trees that could hardly be called a turn. "Here?"

"Mm–hmm."

What if she'd stopped the car a mile ago? Or a mile beyond?

"Just . . . ? *Here* . . . ?"

"Mm–hmm."

Seemed more a cattle path than a road. But Francois was staring forward now, having provided all the information he cared to give, and Trigger had already hopped out and was cranking that wretched, oinking motor back to life. And so, when Trig hopped back in again Patrice turned the Ford down the little shadow path under the trees and prayed the Ford would behave as loyal as Sugar Pie would have if Patrice had been riding her instead.

"Why down here?" Trigger hollered.

"Time to lighten the load," Francois replied.

Patrice felt a hiccup lodge in her chest and stay there. They were about to dump the stranger in the woods.

The Ford crept over the muddy lane, into the groves and out to a meadow that looked like it wanted to break apart into marsh. In fact the road made no promise that it intended to remain solid. They rumbled along in a cloud of exhaust, the golden–green cord-grass towering higher than the Ford.

The road split in two, and Francois had Patrice keep left. After a while it happened again. Then on the third time he had her turn right, which seemed like a way to circle back to where they'd just come. It all felt very arbitrary and the path they followed showed signs of having been forged by beast, not man. But Francois seemed easy, like he planned it all this way.

Patrice was relieved that he'd come. So relieved. Whatever it was they were doing now, she never would have thought to dispose of the stranger this way.

They turned a sharp bend and found a bull standing in the path.

Patrice mashed the brake pedal, noting that she'd managed to do so without causing the Ford to stall, and they stopped just shy of the bull.

Francois waved his hat. "Get outta yanh!"

The bull turned to look at the Ford, then turned away again, bored stupid. Its bulk filled the path and left no room on either side for the automobile to go around.

"Get rid of that animal," Francois said to Trigger.

Trig hopped out and slapped the bull on the rump. Patrice held her breath. She and the boys had once been terrorized by one of the bulls in Terrefleurs. It chased them up onto the roof of the feed shed and wouldn't let them leave. They were stuck up there for what seemed like hours, until one of the field hands came by and rescued them. That was a mean bull, and Patrice was sure he would have tossed each and every one of the children if he'd had the chance.

But this bull was not mean. It simply wouldn't go.

Francois said, "Never mind. Just kill it."

"Kill the bull?" Trigger said.

"No, the engine, the damn engine."

Patrice let it die.

Francois scooted over across where Trigger had sat and got out of the Ford. The bull's hide twitched to shake off a fly.

Francois grabbed his stick and pointed at the boys. "You and you. Come with me."

Gil said, "Where we goin?"

Francois didn't answer, and the boys followed him around the other side of the bull. Suddenly, the girls were alone.

Rosie got up from the rumble seat and stretched toward the sky, throwing her voice into it.

Patrice listened until the sound of footfalls disappeared, then she got out of the Ford and leaned over the hood, lifting her breasts so that the undersides pressed against the hot metal. She'd been sore enough what with the growing stage, but this was unbearable.

"They forgot to take him," Marie-Rose said.

"Take whom?"

"The stranger. We here to dump him, ain't we?"

"Aren't we."

"Well, we are, right?"

Patrice closed her eyes.

Rosie said, "If they ain't dumpin him what they doin out there?"

"I don't know, honey. Hush up and listen."

Marie-Rose listened. "What?"

"Listen!"

The breeze filled the cordgrass with rustling whispers. After a moment, a bullfrog started with its deep, throaty call, and another more distant one answered back.

"You listenin to that old frog?" Marie-Rose asked.

"I'm listening to what we aren't hearing anymore—that horrible motor. Doesn't it make you batty?"

"I like it!"

The bugs were already humming. No bites yet but Patrice didn't give it long. She kept still in the hopes that lying flat on the hood of this Ford might somehow give her a little extra peace.

Rosie picked her way out of the vehicle and hopped down to the ground, landing in a crouch. "Yuck! It's muddy."

She climbed up onto the hood and put her face close to Patrice's. "What are you doing?"

"Nothing," Patrice said, and removed her chest from the hood, stretching her back and trying to see past the cordgrass or even the godforsaken bull. Neither cared to budge.

Sweat tickled her collarbone and when she went to wipe it, she realized she was wearing a necklace—the one Eunice had thrown around her neck as she was driving away. Patrice examined it: a simple gold cross on a braided chain.

Marie-Rose got to her feet and walked across the hood.

"Don't do that, Rosie," Patrice said, but her sister was already climbing from the hood to the back of the bull.

"Get away from that bull!" Patrice said.

Marie-Rose had already pulled up her dress and was straddling the bull and kicking him like he was a horse. "Get a move on, bull!"

Incredibly, the beast didn't so much as blink an eye. The mud smelled like bull hockey, which meant he'd probably already been there a while.

Patrice said, "Marie-Rose Etienne LeBlanc, you get away from that bull! You gonna get yourself a case of ringworm right there in the nether region!"

That got her. Rosie scrambled off the bull and back onto the hood of the Ford.

Patrice said, "Listen Rosie. You can't be a little girl anymore. You don't have anyone to look after you. It's just us children now. You understand what I'm saying?"

Rosie seemed to ponder this with a sense of wonder. "I'm to be treated like an adult?"

"Yes ma'am, and you got to act like one. There's no Maman, no Tatie, no one at all to tell you to behave."

Marie-Rose seemed to be thinking this over, trying it on for size. She slid off the hood and walked around to the rear of the Ford, circling up to the bull, and then back to the rumble seat again. She stared into it.

"We have to get him out," Rosie announced as her first adult observation.

Patrice looked at the crisscrossing twine in the rumble seat. Darned if Rosie wasn't right. It would take some doing to untie all that luggage and free the stranger from his temporary resting place. Might as well get one step ahead while they were stuck here waiting. Patrice stepped back to join her sister and see about loosening that twine.

PATRICE AND ROSIE HAD managed to drag the stranger out of the rumble seat and onto the mud all by themselves. He lay there with the blankets loose over him from all the tugging and dragging. The bull hadn't even bothered to watch them as they toiled. Patrice set about securing the luggage back in place in the rumble seat.

"What's he doin, peein?" Rosie asked.

Patrice looked over at the bull. It was standing there still and silent like a taxidermist's prized work.

But then Patrice realized that Rosie was talking about the dead stranger. The one blanket covered just his head and chest. His penis was protruding at his waistband.

"Get away from him, Rosie," Patrice said, and righted the blanket so that it covered him more completely.

How strange that the man should have an erection in death. Patrice knew very little about such things beyond that which a person learns from being around livestock. She'd once seen a bull climb up on a heifer. She remembered laughing with Eunice about how the bull had grown a second tail, and then she'd realized that something very particular and important was going on. Both the cow and the bull had been out of breath, the bull foaming at the mouth, that second tail seeking out the cow like a snake chasing a rabbit into a hollow log.

She thought about that day every now and then. She and Eunice had giggled themselves silly. They'd whispered and made all sorts of speculations.

Soon after, Patrice was forbidden to play with Eunice or any of the children at Terrefleurs. Mother had made her to go inside when other children were around. As she grew older, Patrice got the sense that other folks knew more about things like the cow and bull than she did. So many secret jokes. She could guess about those things, and it was enough.

After that, school was the only interaction the LeBlanc children had with others. They would take the boat down the bayou for studies, but you weren't allowed to talk during lessons and in the schoolyard the other children kept their distance from them. The LeBlancs had had each other, that was all.

The stranger was now wrapped like a loaf of Sunday bread and

Patrice had the luggage just about tied. This time she made Rosie help her. When Francois and the boys returned, the girls had everything secured and were pitching foxtail darts at the bull, trying to make its hide twitch.

"Where'd y'all go?" Rosie asked.

Trigger flicked her ear. "Off to find a pirogue."

He looked hot with his skin all gleaming with sweat, mud on his face and hands and dungarees. But he was grinning like a villain. What was this to a boy like Trig, but an adventure he'd only ever dreamed of? Forging into an unknown wilderness for danger and manhood. Patrice mused how that smart little boy could sometimes be dumb as dirt.

Francois gestured at the bundle of dead man lying in the mud. "Go on now, boys. Pick him on up."

Gil said, "I need to rest a spell first. That was heavy."

"What was?" Rosie asked.

Trigger went to flick her on the ear again but she ducked away and managed a kick to his knee.

"Rosie," Patrice said.

Rosie paused, her expression showing that she remembered she'd just been shown the cut-off road to adulthood. She gave Trigger a look of condescension.

No one had thought to tote along any water. Gil seemed very distressed by this despite all those bullfrogs suggesting they were pretty well surrounded by water. As for Francois, his coloring was no good. Patrice tried to think of a way to let him out of this but came up empty. They were out in the middle of nowhere, had to finish what they'd started.

"Whose bull you think that is?" Rosie asked.

Trigger said, "Francois says it's probably from Locoul seeing as that's the nearest plantation."

That seemed dubious if only because Francois would never have commented about a thing like that. The children looked to him for affirmation. Not even a shrug.

"Come on, let's get it over with," Trigger said.

Gil and Trig grabbed hold of the stranger and hauled him around to the other side of the bull after Francois. This time the girls followed, getting the sense that to traverse the bull barrier was to step beyond a secret portal. The stranger was a petrified log. Patrice watched the boys struggle with their load, both too proud to admit their skinny shoulders could hardly bear the weight. No telling which was head or feet by the number of blankets. And then, *blankets*, Patrice thought, and she nearly insisted they salvage them off the stranger in case they needed them for tonight. Or any night.

After all, once they'd laid the stranger down to his eternal peace, Patrice wasn't quite sure what to do next. They weren't so much going somewhere as getting away from somewhere. She was so worn down she'd do whatever Francois told her to do.

Francois kept them moving by making rhythmic steps and singing a slow cadence. His walking stick hit the dirt on the offbeat. They turned a bend and left the bull behind to his statuary ways, and Patrice shamed herself out of taking the dead man's blankets.

Rosie skipped ahead to walk with Francois. He looked down at her as he sang and never stopped moving, slow though he was. It made Patrice's chest feel tight—they were running poor Francois into the ground. They'd grown up knowing him as a silent man who kept to himself. But they'd loved him because he'd always been at Papa's right hand and therefore was a fixture in their lives.

Deep humidity squelched the breath from the air, and sure enough, the grass opened to a snaking channel. There, a raft lay waiting by a set-in. Gil and Trig must have excavated the raft from somewhere in the cordgrass when they'd gone off alone with Francois.

"That ain't no pirogue!" Rosie said.

It did seem awfully pitiful. Patrice realized that this must be near one of Francois' many secret fishing holes.

Francois had the boys heave the stranger onto the raft and then set it in at the shallows, then he said to Patrice without even looking at her, "Y'all can move along now. I'll take it from here."

"What?"

He and the boys were splashing up to their waists. Patrice looked down and realized she'd stepped into the shallows, too, silt tugging at her shoes.

She couldn't let him. Couldn't let Francois fuss with the dead body all by himself what with the sickness ready to take him to Jesus any minute now.

And, now that he'd come along this far, she couldn't let *him* abandon *them*. Without Francois they were really and truly alone.

She hadn't any plan. She should have been thinking of a plan!

But all she said was, "Francois?"

He took his hat off and shooed the boys away, then waved the hat at Patrice and Rosie. Gil and Trigger turned and splashed back toward shore.

"Where's he goin?" Marie-Rose asked.

Francois was using his walking stick to pole the raft through the channel. The dead man lay atop the wood in his dark cocoon. Already Francois was far enough that although she could hear him singing, Patrice couldn't make out the words.

Marie-Rose stared after them. "Is he really leavin us for good?"

"He's helped us more than he should have," Patrice said. "Taking care of the stranger like that."

Trigger said, "Aw, he'd take us the whole distance but he wants to die in peace."

"Trigger!"

"Well it's so and I don't feel bad! Look at him. He ain't got another day left in him. I felt sad when he first went sick but now he's ready to lay on down and die. Dyin ain't nothin to be afraid of. Best thing a man can hope for is a good solid passing."

"Oh, hush up," Patrice said.

Trigger liked to shock. But the look on his face said he meant his words. It unnerved Patrice. And she hoped he was wrong about Francois wandering off to die like an old hound.

The boys sat down on the banks and let their muscles sag into the mud. They looked exhausted from hauling the raft and the stranger. The girls sat, too. All four watched Francois turning smaller and darker as he poled the raft further down the bend. Francois didn't look back at them.

"So quiet," Gil said.

"You know what's so curious about that?" Trigger said.

No one indulged, but Trigger answered his own question anyway. "No river devils."

Patrice tore her gaze from Francois and looked at her brother. It was true. Of the four children, not one of them had any devils hovering about at the present. Not so much as a whisper. She touched the scratch at the back of her neck and wondered.

Gil said, "All of us here on the shore like this, you know what it reminds me of?"

"That day," Trigger said.

It was all he needed to say. They were all thinking of it: the day they'd banished their mother. It had been several months ago, when Mother had gathered them together to kill the boy with the blood-shined eye. Ferrar was his name. The children were all ready to do it, too. Drunk on their power, on the river magic. All those river devils siding with their mother, looking to spill that blood. That lumen blood. Ferrar was the opposite of what they were. Ferrar must have been touched by God. And they, they were touched by . . .

Patrice blinked. It didn't matter. God welcomed all souls. All souls.

On that awful day, Mother had seen to it that Ferrar was shot, but the bullet hadn't come from the children. They'd shaken free of evil at the last moment. Patrice had brought Ferrar back to Terrefleurs and nursed him back to health herself. Before today, it was the last time they'd seen their mother. They'd turned her own magic against her.

Patrice watched as Francois receded further. The dreary cadence he sang came only in drifts of intonation. She could no longer even recognize the tone as the same cadence he'd used to march Gil and Trig down the lane with their dead man load.

Francois disappeared around the bend. One last flash from the stick Trigger had carved for him And then he was gone.

twenty-two

NEW ORLEANS, NOW

ENON AND JOSH WATCHED through the briar as Esther pulled over to the side of the road. The car she drove was nothing special. An ageing silver Buick Century.

Josh said, "Ole Esther bought that thing a couple of years ago cuz it was the same age as her son Bo—an '04."

"Isn't that cute," Zenon said.

The car came to a halt at an awkward angle on the shoulder. Esther sat behind the steering wheel and didn't get out. Her gaze was leveled on the yellow stink hissing up from the hood.

Zenon admired Josh's handiwork on the Buick. River devils might be weak on pigeonry, but they were masters at throwing down the hard times. The messed-up car was particularly gratifying because that mooncalf Ethan Manderleigh had paid Esther a visit and put a new timing belt on the thing. He'd told her the car still had other problems, too, and that she should take it to a mechanic. And he'd told her all about how she needed to go on ahead and let Madeleine talk to her and help her out. Esther had agreed to think about it. But she hadn't called on Madeleine. Not yet. Zenon and Josh had been watching. Esther hadn't called because she'd gotten herself nice and paranoid, and that was good news for none-too-humble briar folk like Zenon. Esther wore her son's light. But paranoia dimmed it. So did fear.

Esther sat in that car looking like she wasn't sure what in the hell to do next.

Finally, she opened the door and stepped out. Traffic zipped by on Jefferson Highway.

Zenon curled his hand into a ball and spoke through it like it was a loudspeaker. "Call a tow truck!"

Josh laughed. "Yeah, call a tow truck, Esther!"

Esther sighed, and said aloud as if she'd heard them, "Ain't no money for no tow truck."

Josh nodded at Zenon. "You see that? We finally got her attention."

The more Zenon did this, the more he relished it. It was like he was the invisible man. He could see into other people's lives all he wanted. Pigeon them from the briar. That in itself was damn near intoxicating. But now he was pulling strings on the river devils, too, instead of the other way around. It made him feel godlike.

Josh put a hand on Esther's shoulder. "Aw, don't take it so hard now, Esther. But you're right. You pay for a tow truck, you pay for a mechanic, and you just throwin good money after bad. That car's had it."

Esther was shaking her head, and Zenon knew that although she couldn't hear Josh directly, his thoughts were nesting inside her mind and masquerading as her own.

Esther had her own river devil, of course. Everyone did. You just had to have your feet real deep in the briar to see other people's devils. Esther's was a scraggly, underdeveloped thing called Lin who was stunted from years of lumen exposure. Lin was about the size of a ferret and looked like an old-growth wisteria vine that had gone wooden and bare. But if Lin were to be believed, she'd had her heyday when Esther was younger, before Bo was born. She'd told Josh and Zenon all about it in her papery, whispery, river devil's voice.

According to Lin, Esther had been an average kid and got on well with most people until about high school. That's when she'd gotten into trouble and went to an abortion clinic without her mama knowing. She and her mama had got to fighting a lot. Her daddy had drifted out of her life. Somewhere during those high school days, Lin got her foothold with Esther. Esther developed a nice shape and rotten habits. Lin helped her to learn how to smoke first, and then how to drink, then different kinds of smokes and a whole lot more drinking, and then Lin led her to things Esther put straight into her blood. Esther's grades fell off and then she fell off school altogether.

Her mother threatened to kick her out unless she got a job, so Esther got one putting groceries into plastic bags.

Lin let Esther believe she was in control. Told her she shouldn't let her mama rule her life, and the worst thing Esther could possibly do was end up just like her mama, working and going to church and never really making her mark on the world.

Then one day Esther agreed to meet a boy out back behind the Winn-Dixie where she worked. Esther had actually believed he'd just wanted to kiss her, ask her out. He did kiss her. And then he offered her a bag of weed for a blow job. And Lin had told her, *This is it. This makes you different from Mama. You can break this taboo. This is what real excitement feels like.* And Lin told her that since she liked the boy it wasn't prostitution.

Esther did it. Right there behind the cardboard-box crusher. Lin told her that she'd broken from her mother's grasp. Maybe Esther's body wouldn't someday cave in on itself like those cardboard boxes did, like her mother's did. She was alive and invulnerable.

Esther listened to Lin's river devil whispers and wove them into her own thoughts and beliefs.

A year went by and Esther's habits had both intensified and grown harder to pay for. Her mother eventually kicked her out. Lin helped Esther to one-by-one let go of ideas about how a young lady ought to act: selling favors, selling party favors, taking what wasn't hers, taking beatings. Esther went through spells where she was never *not* high.

When Esther found out her mother had died of an aneurism, the first idea Lin breathed into Esther's mind was that she wouldn't have to duck her mama's calls anymore or look upon all that disappointment.

That little bug-eyed, twist tie of a devil, Lin. She'd had Esther in those days. She'd really had her.

When Esther became pregnant again, something changed. She didn't get an abortion this time around, which was fine. A mother with addictions held all kinds of possibilities for a river devil. And sure enough, Esther kept stealing, kept doing tricks, kept doing drugs. Right through the entire pregnancy. It seemed certain that she would give birth to an addicted baby, but she didn't. Instead she bore a lumen child.

That very day, Esther was stained with that lumen light.

She held that baby in her arms and later fell on her knees and prayed for forgiveness. Asked for the strength to do right by her son. Lin had actually laughed, knowing how easy it was to break those kinds of vows. But no matter what Lin did, no matter what accident she laid in Esther's path, no matter how nasty the withdrawals of the chemicals leaving Esther's system, Esther never budged. Never touched any booze or toke or anything stronger than a sweet tea after that.

And even later, when they'd removed Bo's eyes from his tiny, cancer-ridden infant body, Lin couldn't shake Esther. She'd whispered for Esther to indulge a little guilt. Esther ought to blame herself for her son's eyes, Lin had told her, because the cancer must have come from all the drugs Esther had pumped into her womb when she'd been carrying Bo. And Esther probably even believed that the guilt felt right in some way. But she let it go as quickly as Lin whispered it on her. Esther saw guilt as a conceit before God. She simply accepted what was, and the little baby Bo accepted, and that was that.

Esther reorganized her life little by little, finding respectable jobs and making a home for herself and Bo. Lin never stopped her whispers, but Esther had most certainly stopped listening.

Of course, Lin was just one river devil.

Zenon figured that any given human being might have a fifty-fifty chance against one lousy whisperer. But here were three, kind of. Two and a half: Lin, Josh, and Zenon. Zenon was not a river devil but nowadays he felt more briar than human. A river devil on growth hormone. Hell, he was more effective than a river devil.

They lingered there in that ditch on Jefferson Highway with Esther, and Zenon was feeling fine. He'd thought he'd never see the sun again, never walk the streets of the city. Look at him now. He had the sun but without the heat or bugs.

What Zenon saw here was an opportunity. The three of them could work on old Esther, and if they got to her that would not only leave the blind kid alone to fend for himself, it would prove a point: that Zenon could rally his own little organization within the briar.

Esther balled her fists and cried out, "I know what's happening!"

Zenon stopped and watched. Josh and Lin watched, too.

Esther turned in a slow circle and searched the very air around her. "I know there's a devil on my shoulder out here. I know it!"

Zenon and the others laughed. A devil. One devil. *Hell, little lady, you always got at least* one *devil.* Lin was a shriveled little thing that rode Esther's shadow like the hood on her jacket.

Esther put her fist to her forehead and squeezed her eyes, and she muttered, "My car just broke down, that's all. It's just finally pooped out like I knew it would do. This ain't the end of the world."

A car pulled over. A blue Honda. Esther stepped back and regarded it as though it were the serpent in the Garden of Eden.

The passenger's side window rolled down and a man with glasses and a thin mustache peered out at Esther. "You got car trouble?"

Esther looked at her old Buick, which had stopped hissing but kept up the stink. She said nothing.

The driver said, "I'll give you a lift if you want."

"No thank you," Esther said.

"You sure? Or I can call—"

"I got it," Esther said.

He shrugged, put the car in gear, and it started moving again. He rejoined traffic on Jefferson Highway without looking back at Esther or rolling up the passenger window. Zenon saw that as Esther watched him go she'd let a tear well over onto her cheek.

Josh said, "She thinks we'd have pigeoned that guy if he gave her a lift."

"Well, she'd be right, we would've," Zenon said.

He leered at Esther. "Aw, come on. You don't need that ole car. What do you use it for anyway?"

And Esther said aloud, "How'm I gonna get to work? How'm I gonna get Bo to the doctor? He has so many appointments."

Hearing her engage with him like that! From the material world to the briar! The power of it sent a charge through Zenon's body. A week ago, he couldn't have pigeoned Esther to put an extra sugar packet in her tea. And here, now, she was talking to his spirit self as though he was physically walking right alongside her.

Another tear spilled over her cheek. "How'm I gonna take him to special needs programs and soccer practice? Little boy figured out how to play soccer when he can't even see the ball. Made the team! How'm I s'posed to tell him he can't do that because Mama can't take him to practice?"

Josh said to her, "Listen. That kid is what's kept you in that no-end night auditor job at the Hilton. Messing with all the appointments and the soccer practice by day so you have to work at night. It's why you've spent years without sleep."

And Lin added, "It's over. You can't take care of him. You always knew it was too much."

Esther said, "I need a new car. If I could just get enough together to get a new car I could tell Mare to move along and it'd be Bo and me again."

"That's right," Lin said. "It's impossible without a new car. That's the only thing that'll get you out of this."

Josh said, "Go on ahead and leave that old Buick on the side of the road and let the city of New Orleans have it."

Esther looked long at the Buick, then turned and gazed down the ragged shoulder.

Lin said, "Go on, you can walk it."

Esther paused. She went to the trunk of the Buick and opened it. An umbrella, some tools. Bo's scooter in there. And his books, too.

Lin said, "Braille isn't easy to come by. Maybe you should carry it with you."

Esther gathered up the books and the scooter and left behind the rest to die with the car. Now, loaded down, she began to walk.

"I guess we walkin all the way to work like this," Zenon said.

Josh said, "It's gotta be three or four miles, at least."

And Lin said, "In this heat."

Esther's brow wrinkled. Oh, she was listening alright. Hadn't listened to Lin in years, but look at her now. Zenon could see it on Esther's face. How she recognized the feel of listening to a devil. She'd probably been so sure she'd become a different person.

"I know you out here," she said aloud. "You can just go on and get."

And then Esther paused as if waiting for the devils to obey.

Lin slinked up good and close. This was her Esther. She knew this woman better than anyone else.

Lin leaned over to Esther's ear and whispered, "You remember what hurt the most? Remember? That Mama hadn't lived to meet Bo."

Esther said not a word but her eyes filled afresh.

They would have liked each other, her expression seemed to say.

Lin said, "If only Mama had lived a little longer. When she died her daughter was a nothing but a junkie and a whore."

Zenon marveled at how random the thoughts seemed. Lin was just pushing all the familiar buttons at once. From this perspective, here in the briar, it sounded ridiculous and completely unrelated to the car breaking down. *But look at Esther. Just look at her!* She was listening alright. She wasn't just listening, she was letting it stick.

Esther said, "Just keep my son safe, dear God, that's all I ask."

Zenon studied her. Speaking those words was a clear indication that Esther knew she was being whispered. And yet saying them also sounded a whole lot like giving up.

They walked.

❧

TWICE MORE, PEOPLE OFFERED Esther a ride. Twice more she refused. She ignored the buses, too. Kept marching with the devils. Sure, Zenon could make pigeons of anyone on a bus or any driver that picked her up, or hell, anyone on the road could swerve and hit her. Little lady had to know walking didn't make that much difference. The effect was purely psychological. Made her feel like she was in control. Downright endearing, it was. She kept it up the whole way, carrying heavy blind kid books and that scooter in the boiling heat. Wasn't gonna lay aside her load for nothing. And that was fine, just fine. She didn't realize she was helping them along.

When Esther finally showed up for work an hour later, she got in trouble for being late. And she showed up plumb wore out and blistered. And she hadn't slept since the night of the levee.

Better yet, Zenon noted, she'd talked herself into all stripes of worries. It took that slippery element right out of her, that residual glow from her son.

No, they didn't need to round up pigeons and sic them on Esther. By that point she was ready to turn on herself.

✤

twenty-three

✤

"A LITTLE WALK, YES?" Severin said.

"Alright," Madeleine answered in her mind.

And her room was no longer her room. She kept with her physical body for a moment, lingering in the warmth of Ethan's caress. He'd already fallen asleep. She loved ending her day with him, that moment when they changed into bedclothes and slipped into the clean white sheets; they would talk or read or make love. And then they'd hold tight to one another while he drifted into sleep and she drifted into the bramble.

He'd changed the belt for Esther's car, but had since been unable to get her on the phone and no one was home this evening when he'd stopped by again. Madeleine watched his face as the division between moonlight and shadow grew deeper, the darkness blacker. In the briar, the light levels were always that of a full moon evening but without the moon itself.

She lifted her gaze and saw that Jasmine was already disappearing behind curls of thorns. The walls were going. Above, the ceiling fan remained suspended in place but the ceiling itself was receding. Those kinds of surface planes, they didn't exist in the bramble. Not walls, ground, ceilings, or even the illusion of sky stretched overhead. Planes belonged to the physical world. In the briar, there was no sky. No day or night. Only black, black trees, tall and thin and draped in thorns where the branches should be. The trees had no tops. They stretched forever. And the lightness between their ascent wasn't sky, only silver fog, and it rolled endlessly like ocean waves.

As she watched the ceiling plane go and the trees stretch to infinite heights, it occurred to her that this was her favorite part of going into the briar.

And, strange that she should have a favorite part. The river devil's world was a world of dread. Had been.

The ceiling fan, now attached to nothing at all, spun round, round, round.

It seemed the more time she spent in the briar, the more it came into focus. There were creatures in those woods—river devils of course, but other beasts, too. Brilliant winged and hooded reptiles the size of garden snakes that looked like Chinese dragons. They darted between the trees just beyond reach.

And the gravity that held her tight to Ethan, it abandoned her. She was lifting away. Her physical self still lay with him, yes, but the other parts of her were rising, stepping, turning, following off with that rolling mist. The pull of it all was just too strong.

She called for Zenon.

ZENON TESTED HER ON pigeon games. Madeleine was good at it but Zenon was masterful. Their ghosts walked the streets of New Orleans while their bodies lay in their respective beds. Madeleine manipulated rats and mice and sleeping pigeons. Zenon showed her how to manage two at a time. Together they made pigeons play leapfrog, rats hang by their clawed feet.

This is my half brother, Madeleine thought. *He's just like me.*

As much as she would ordinarily loathe any interaction with Zenon, in the briar she lost that sense of revulsion. All was intrigue. Fascination. Disconnection. It was probably why Zenon both wanted her company but would think nothing of killing her. Intrigue, fascination, disconnection.

And beneath it all she hoped that if Zenon was working with her—training her, as he liked to call it—he was leaving Bo alone.

It seemed strange. Both he and Chloe seemed so anxious to school Madeleine in the ways of the briar.

When she returned to her body she almost felt a sense of loss. One problem with the briar was that it wasn't always terrible. It had been, in the early days of Severin, but lately the river devil's world was just a time span of wanderings or fascinations, often downright pleasant. Oh, it still held perils—devils, Zenon, ghastly reflections of the physical world—but not all the time. Also, the river devil's world was plush, rich, and it sometimes invoked a kind of ecstasy. Coming back to reality was almost like giving up a whole spectrum of colors. There came a temptation to linger. Madeleine had to remind herself not to let down her guard.

Her mind and spirit having returned to her body, she lay with Ethan, a tangle of limbs colored to softness in the moonlight. His skin was so light against hers. On the other side of the room, Jasmine lay curled in her daisy bed. Madeleine watched Ethan's ribs rise and fall, rise and fall; Jasmine's rose and fell, too, twice for every one of Ethan's breaths.

Madeleine knew she should sleep. But the funny thing about sleep, it refused to be forced.

How to draw Zenon toward her, away from Bo? The very thought led her to imagine dozens of dangerous outcomes, each one ending in pain or getting herself or Bo killed, or both. No new ideas, only dread and fear. It was a perverse ecstasy, wallowing in the worries. The needless, needling worries.

She remembered the creatures who'd descended upon her when Zenon had dragged her underwater—those dragonfly-like things that had stung her and heightened the panic.

Zenon spent all his time in the briar now. For him, it had become a constant training ground. How would she ever keep up with him?

Rise and fall. Madeleine matched her breathing to Ethan's. Her hand went to his chest. She could feel his heart beating inside. The breath, the blood, the lungs, the heart, the brain. Altogether they did not equate to life. Life was something beyond this collection.

The moonlight darkened as a cloud rolled in, and then the only illumination came from streetlights beyond the window. Madeleine kissed his temple. Jasmine lay sleeping on the other side of the room.

This was part of it, she knew. Somehow, this quiet feeling was what kept the briar from seeping into her heart.

The clock switched its blue digital display to 2:43 A.M.

Raining outside now. The streetlight illuminated droplets streaming down the window and cast fractals across the wall. A flash of lightning and then thunder. The rain intensified with the electrical surge in the atmosphere, and the sound of it was divided between rushing in the trees and pelting on the roof. She drew in a breath.

Across the patter of raindrops, her cell phone rang.

Madeleine turned her head toward it. Ethan blinked awake and rose up on his elbow. The beautiful feeling vanished. But she could get it back; another quiet moment and she could feel that softness in her heart again.

She slid back from him and stepped toward the kitchenette for her phone. Didn't recognize the number that appeared on the caller ID.

"Hello?"

"Doctor LeBlanc?" Madeleine knew the woman's voice but could not place it.

"Yes?"

Ethan had followed her into the kitchen, and he passed his fingers along her shoulder as he made his way to the cupboard. He frowned at the phone. Madeleine shrugged.

"Hello, Doctor LeBlanc," the voice finally said.

Then, silence again. And Madeleine knew.

She said, "Is this Esther? Esther Ramirez?"

"Yeah." Esther's voice hung in a clench, and it sounded like she'd been crying.

"Tell me what's happened. Is Bo alright?"

Esther's words were slow and careful. "Mare says he's just fine. But I don't know what to do. I'm at Ochsner."

"You're in the hospital?"

Ethan's brow deepened as he listened to Madeleine's end of the conversation.

Esther's voice held steady. "Yeah. The night nurse was kind enough to let me use her phone. I just called Mare. She says Bo's fine, but . . ."

And then her voice broke.

Madeleine said, "It's alright, just tell me."

She could hear Esther's breath hitching. "I've done something terrible, Doctor. I can't say why. I took someone's stash and shot up yesterday. Was a coworker, he kept his paraphernalia in the laundry. I found it and used it and he beat me pretty good. I just now woke up, or . . . came down. Mare been watchin Bo for me, she says. And Doctor, there's things . . ."

When the silence stretched on, Madeleine said, "I understand."

"You do, huh? You understand. Well I'm glad for that. You came to warn me, I know, but you could've told me more about this, I think."

Madeleine pressed the palm of her hand into her forehead, listening.

Esther said, "I'm calling to ask you to go see to my boy."

Madeleine said, "Sure. I can do that."

"You and Doctor Manderleigh both, OK? Is he there with you now? Can I talk to him?"

Madeleine said, "Hang on."

She handed the phone to Ethan. "She wants us to check on Bo."

She remembered the moment when Severin had conjured the thoughts of violence against Bo as he was escaping the bullies, that flicker of savagery Madeleine felt in her heart. Esther had seen it. Smart that she was insisting Ethan go, too.

"Yeah," Ethan was saying, and then, "You mean, take him home? With us?"

Madeleine looked up, surprised. *Take* him? Ethan looked puzzled, too. He lifted his brows at Madeleine, and she nodded.

He said, "OK, we'll do it . . . Yeah . . . Hang on."

He passed the phone back. "Wants to talk to you again."

"Yes," Madeleine said into the receiver.

Esther said, "I know I'm asking a lot. But I prayed about it and I think you two might be the only ones who can actually do something here."

Madeleine swallowed. "That may be true. Have you made arrangements with Mare?"

"Gonna call her again right now. I imagine she'll be relieved. But if she ain't, I'll tell the police if I have to. I'll tell them that my boy needs to be with you, not her."

"We'll be there first thing in the morning."

But Esther said, "No ma'am. Please go now."

Madeleine looked toward the window where the rain had escalated to a steady pour. "Now?"

"I'm afraid for my boy, you understand? I just talked to Mare and she told me he was fine, but she wouldn't let me talk to him directly."

Madeleine tightened her grip on the cell phone. "You never actually got to talk to Bo?"

"Said he's sleepin. That woman don't give a care if he sleepin. She'd wake him up to complain about the weather."

Esther paused, and her voice trembled. "She didn't chew me out for never coming home from work yesterday. She didn't even ask me what happened. Do you hear what I'm saying?"

Madeleine drew in a hard breath and let it out. "We're leaving now."

twenty-four

NEW ORLEANS, NOW

THE WIPERS LEFT BEADED trails where there had been something hard and sticky on the windshield. The devilwood grove in the Rosewood Arms mobile park had a much blacker look at 3 A.M. No streetlamps. Porch lights glowed at some of the trailers, but not at Esther and Bo's place. It stood completely dark.

"Do you think they went to bed, after all?" Madeleine asked.

Ethan shook his head. "If they did, we'll just have to wake them up."

He parked at an angle and left his lights on so that they could see their way through the gauntlet of ferns up the steps. He knocked on the door and then wrapped his arm around Madeleine. They huddled together under the umbrella. No lights came on inside, and no one answered the door.

Ethan knocked again, this time pounding a little harder.

Finally, Mare answered the door. She was fully clothed and she carried a long black flashlight, unlit.

Mare had a strange-enough look about her that Madeleine decided not to bother with greetings, and she said simply, "We've come for Bo."

"Take him if you can find him." Mare turned around and disappeared into the living room, leaving the door open for them.

Madeleine followed her in while Ethan shook out the umbrella. The only light inside came from a red cigarette coal. It moved in an arc and then glowed as Mare picked it up and took a puff, though Mare herself was completely invisible in the dark.

Madeleine asked, "Is the electricity out?"

But then Ethan entered and flipped the wall switch, and the lights came on.

Mare shrugged. "Looks like they working."

"Why were you sitting here in the dark?"

Mare was still wearing what looked like her work clothes—a black flowered skirt and a suit jacket. The ashtray was spilling over with cigarette butts and it left a ring of ashes on the coffee table. Somewhere in the pile of butts a filter was burning.

Next to the ashtray lay a long, wide carving knife. Mare set the flashlight down next to it.

"What happened to Bo?" Madeleine asked.

"He run off like he do."

Ethan said, "At three in the morning? In the rain?"

Mare said nothing for a moment, holding her cigarette like a piece of chalk and staring at the burning end. Her hair was cropped in tight curls like a flapper's. The exaggerated arches of her brows and the heavy makeup gave her the look of a silent-era film star.

She said, "I do love a smoke. Never tried to give them up. Not once, no."

And in that, a switch had tripped. Same high-pitched voice, but something about the intonation was different. Her words sounded more down-country than New Orleans.

Mare brought the cigarette toward her lips. "Now look at me. Water water ever-where."

She drew in very slowly, as if thinking across each micron and particle that streamed through the inhalation.

Madeleine whispered to Ethan, "I'm going to look outside."

She could tell by Ethan's expression that he knew Mare was not alone inside her body. Mare was still in there, it seemed, but she certainly wasn't driving.

"I'll come with you," Ethan said to Madeleine.

But Mare said, "No, let Maddy go. She got a job to do."

Madeleine said to Ethan, "I'll be fine. Best to keep an eye on . . . her."

"That's right," Mare said, and then she stubbed the cigarette out on her knee.

Madeleine jerked backward at the sight. The smoke made a whisper as the coal extinguished itself somewhere between Mare's skirt and her skin. Ethan took a step toward her. Mare rose to her feet.

Ethan snatched the knife from the table and handed it back to Madeleine. "Get rid of that thing."

Mare laughed. "Go on, baby, tell him, 'Yes, mastah; anything you say, mastah.'"

Madeleine said, "Zenon, why don't you leave Mare alone? She's got nothing to do with this."

Mare smiled. "Ain't my first choice. Lumen boy's got all the neighbors tainted."

Madeleine was gripping the knife Ethan had passed to her, her knuckles tense, and she felt horrifically energized by the feel of it in her hands.

Mare said, "That's it, Sis. You want a little practice round? Go ahead. Stick it in this here pigeon. I'll make sure she holds still."

Too easily, Madeleine could see a vision off herself piercing Mare with the knife. Target practice. No Severin here to blame it on, either. The briar wanted to bloom forth like mold through old drywall.

Madeleine started to turn away. . . .

And then Mare rushed toward her. It happened so fast Madeleine didn't even know she'd raised the knife until it was too late. Ethan stepped in just as Mare was throwing herself at Madeleine. He caught Mare and pulled her so that she went to the ground. Not so much a counterattack as a deflection of Mare's path.

A thin line of blood showed on Ethan's shirt.

"I hurt you!" Madeleine said.

"Forget it, I'm fine."

Mare rose to her feet and picked up the flashlight. "I never did like you, Ethan Manderleigh."

"Yeah, Zenon? Breaks my heart. Tell you what. Someone's gonna put a stop to you, and that someone's gonna be me."

Mare said, "What, you gonna come put a pillow over my face while I'm lying helpless in my bed? That's the only way a candy ass like you could ever pull it off."

Ethan said, "You got to go after women and children to make yourself feel like a man. Take over a woman's body."

"You stupid mooncalf. You have no idea what you're messing with. This look like a game of chess to you? Well it's bigger than that. It's the whole fucking future of the human fucking race. Madeleine got a chance at leading the charge except you keep getting in the goddamned way."

Too late, Madeleine realized that the flashlight in Mare's hand didn't look the way it was supposed to. It had been tampered with. But Ethan saw it, too, and he threw himself sideways just as the thing exploded. Madeleine screamed.

That sound, like a gunshot. She'd heard it before when the huffers were chasing Bo. Oyster had been carrying a flashlight then, too.

Mare was looking at the desecrated metal in her hands. Three of her fingers were missing.

She said, "Damn these homemade zip guns. Never work worth a shit."

She took two steps to the couch and dropped onto it; pulled out another cigarette, one-handed, and lit it. She breathed in and held a moment. Then released. The smoke poured out from her lips in a full, deep stream.

Mare said, "I need to find a redneck or a cop next time. Someone who embraces the right to bear arms."

Her torn hand was draped over the armrest of the couch, blood leaking onto beige-and-blue striped velour.

"I've got to find Bo," Madeleine said.

Mare was looking off somewhere beyond the planes of space confining the trailer. "Loves that boy better than life itself, Esther does. Stupid woman. Kid's nothing but trouble. Now, look, here I gotta do without fingers. Damn that Bo."

Mare was in there, tangled together with Zenon, and she was probably so confused by now she didn't even know she'd been taken prisoner inside her own body.

She took another drag.

Ethan handed Madeleine the umbrella. "Please be careful."

She turned toward the door.

From behind, Mare said, "Kid's all yours, Sis. Predator or prey."

✦

twenty-five

✦

NEW ORLEANS, NOW

*M*ADELEINE JOGGED TOWARD THE devilwood grove and called Bo's name. Rain was sopping her jeans despite the umbrella. The lightning and thunder had long since ended but the rain held steady. She called out again.

No light at all. Madeleine realized she was still gripping the knife. She held her hand out in front of her but it was so dark she couldn't see it. She swung around slowly until the blade was backlit by a distant porch light.

Bo didn't answer. If he was out here, she knew, he'd have heard her calling.

Movement caught her eye. "Bo?"

A small figure among the trees.

"Bo," Severin parroted back.

Madeleine gave a huff. Everything was black except when Severin passed before it, then Madeleine could see a tree trunk or leaves or just a window of rain. Severin herself was barely visible as anything more than a moving lens.

Madeleine said, "What are you doing here? We have a bargain."

"A bargain, so," Severin said.

She wove through the trees, swinging an arm around each trunk like a carefree child, following a pattern similar to the way Bo had dodged the huffers two days ago. Madeleine knew if she receded into her mind a step she'd be able to see Severin better, but she didn't dare do this. Her mind needed to remain staunchly on this side of the briar or else she'd be putting Bo at an even greater risk.

"A bargain is a bargain, Severin."

"A bargain is what makes a maybe. *Here* is of interest to me now, so."

Madeleine clenched the knife in a wet fist. "I won't be following you into the briar any more if you keep intruding."

"Ah, so you will! And so I will. It is your will."

"What do you mean, my will?"

But Severin was weaving in a wider circle, ignoring and infuriating. Madeleine watched in mute loathing and could almost feel the stinging creatures bursting from the briar.

And yet it seemed that if she cracked open Severin's nonsense, she could find a kind of logic inside.

Madeleine shouted, "I don't want you here! My will is that you go!"

Severin linked her arm around a tree to spin again, but suddenly she was nose-to-nose with Madeleine. Madeleine gasped.

The river devil's eyes were brighter now. Her child's feet hovered above the ground and the creatures of the briar clouded around her hair.

"Your will is what we say," Severin said.

Hooded creatures, with strange, sharp curves, shimmered in the rain like violet-and-ruby-colored glass. Madeleine couldn't help but stare at them. Fascinations. The rain had lessened and a churning fog was now filling the grove. Light, scented, illuminated in silver.

Madeleine heard a sound from very far away: *click-click click-click*.

She turned. The creatures darted in front of her, puffing their hoods.

"No," Madeleine whispered. "I'm not in the briar. I'm here in the trailer park."

Severin leaned forward and circled her arms around Madeleine's neck.

Madeleine said again, "I'm not in the briar."

The little river devil allowed a grin to pass over her face. But then she backed away. The fog swelled in a curling wave behind her, thick, shimmering. Severin leapt down to all fours near a wide puddle. The hooded creatures disappeared into it. And then Severin crawled into the puddle, too, stepping into it as though it were a deep well, pulling herself down inside.

Madeleine turned around. The fog was gone and everything was black again. The rain returned in full deluge; it had never stopped. She was soaked through. Ethan's umbrella lay inverted and was full of water in a puddle, one of the metallic arms broken in a reverse joint. The knife, though—it had never left her grip.

She picked up the umbrella.

The clicking came from a fair distance away.

❧

SHE FOLLOWED THE SOUND all the way back to Esther's trailer, stuffing the broken umbrella in the trash can as she approached. The rain made warped streaks in front of the car's headlights.

"Bo?"

She could see Ethan's silhouette at the window, but Mare was somewhere out of sight. Madeleine looked next door, where Cheryl's trailer stood. A likely place for Bo to have gone.

But when the clicking sound came again, it didn't come from Cheryl's place. It came from the direction of Ethan's silhouette beyond the curtain sheers. Madeleine stared at it. And then she looked lower, at the darkness beneath the mobile home.

"Bo."

"Doc LB?"

Madeleine stepped toward the underside of the porch and strained her eyes into the black space beyond the mobile home's footings. She could see nothing. Not so much as a glint.

"Come on out of there, Bo."

He went quiet for a moment, and then said, "I can't."

"Why not?"

She could hear him shivering. The temperature was around 70 degrees but he was probably soaked and exhausted.

He said, "Doc LB, Mare tried to kill me. She's gonna cut me up with a knife."

Madeleine looked up toward the window. "I don't think she's herself tonight, Bo."

"Hell no she ain't herself! She always a crab, but not like this!"

Madeleine said, "Shh, you need to keep your voice down. It's not safe. Listen. You're coming to stay with us for a while. OK?"

Bo fell silent. The rain had plastered Madeleine's hair into her ear canal and made it itch. She flicked it away with her little finger.

"Come on now, Bo. We should hurry."

"Awright, I'm comin out."

She waited, her stomach tightening. She looked down at the knife in her hands, but could only see it when she turned the blade so that it caught a reflection of light. It felt obscene. And with Bo drawing nearer . . .

If Zenon was up there with Mare and Ethan, he was probably about to come looking for Madeleine or Bo any second now. No telling what Ethan was doing to keep him occupied. Madeleine could hear Bo moving toward her, clicking, shuffling. It seemed to be taking an awfully long time. Her eyes were wide and sightless. She closed them and listened.

Bo cried out.

"What's the matter?" Madeleine whispered.

"I can't get out."

"Why don't you come out the way you went in?"

"The water filled up over there and now I—I think I'm stuck."

"What do you mean, stuck?"

"I can't move! And something's cuttin on me!"

"Hang on," Madeleine said.

She turned and ran to the porch steps but stopped short, looking up at Ethan's silhouette. His posture was clearly tense. Combative, even. She turned away and rushed instead to the car and threw open the door. A thin flashlight was tucked inside the glove box. She took it and placed the knife inside, grateful to be rid of it, and slammed the glove box shut. She ran back to the trailer.

The flashlight beam was strong for such a small light. (Good old Ethan—a man of fresh batteries.) She ran it along the trailer's underbelly. There were pipes and wheels and cinder blocks, and old wooden pallets shrouded in cobwebs thick enough to crochet an afghan.

"Bo, wave your hand or something. I can't find you."

The beam reflected against the broad side of what looked like a discarded minifridge. He clicked, and then she saw him. The pads of his waving fingers caught in the beam just under the living room where Mare and Ethan were. Bo lay face down under a tangle of pipes. She couldn't tell what had snagged him but he looked extremely uncomfortable, his back bowed and his neck straining. The flashlight beam caught under the hoods of his empty eyes.

He was only ten feet away, but it was ten feet of a mouse maze. Not a place Madeleine cared to go crawling around in.

"I'm coming, sweetie." She said it as much to reassure him as to commit herself to the task.

twenty-six

NEW ORLEANS, NOW

SHE WENT DOWN ON her back and shoved herself under the trailer. Her body wriggled head-first between the mini-fridge and a wooden crate, her flashlight carving a path through the cobwebs. The older ones dislodged in weightless drifts and settled over her cheek.

"It hurts," Bo whispered.

"I'm almost there."

He click, click, clicked. She rolled over to climb across a cracked plastic step stool that didn't seem sturdy enough to support her weight, so she had to scrunch up and throw her legs wide. For all the blockages and hurtles, the distance from Bo to the edge of the trailer had easily gone from ten feet to thirty. Something skittered over her flashlight hand and she shook it wildly. In the erratic beam, she could see where the rains had pooled on the far side of where Bo lay, a French drain that allowed water

to run off away from the trailer. It must have been where he'd
come in.

No sitting up. Madeleine had to stay in a crawl on her back or
belly. She moved as fast as she could on her elbows.

"Doc LB," Bo said.

"Yeah."

"If I live don't tell my mom I said the H word, OK?"

"Shh, honey, be quiet."

And then she was at Bo's side. The belt loop of his pants was
snagged on a metal fitting. She reached for it and immediately
knocked her head, hard. She sucked air between her teeth.

Somewhere above were Ethan, Mare, and Zenon. Surely they
heard that bang beneath their feet.

Her hand went to the pain at her forehead. She could see clearly
now. The flashlight beam had been joined by a misty glow. Briar
light. It had ridden in on the sudden rush of pain in her head. Severin was rising from the drain so that just her eyes were above
water, and her hair was fanned out and floating. Water was foun-
taining from behind her.

Madeleine grabbed the belt loop and whispered, "We have to be
silent and fast, OK?"

"Yes ma'am." Bo said.

She tugged. His belt loop wouldn't unhook itself. His shirt was
torn and she could see a bloody welt along his lower back. Whenever he moved the fitting gouged his skin. She covered the wound
with his shirt, feeling him wince under her, and gave a forceful
pull. The fitting now gouged her own hand but Bo's back was protected. The belt loop snapped.

"Come on," she whispered.

She guided him toward her, but the pain at his back prevented
him from scooting the rest of the way under the pipes. She had to
go around, picking over foul-smelling dust where something had
nested, until she got to the same side of the pipes as Bo. She reached
under his arm.

Severin was laughing from the other side. "Ah, to please, a nice drowning maze!"

Madeleine turned to see her lift herself completely from the drain, and behind her came a torrent of water. Severin's nude, gray, little girl's body looked like that of a butterfly whose wings were made of water. The wake surged forward.

Madeleine launched her wrists under Bo's armpits and dragged him two feet in the direction from which she came. But no way were they going to make it low-crawling through that same convoluted path with the flood surge. Water swirled, turbulent and frothing.

Zenon's voice came from above: "Now or never, Sis."

Breathing in heavy gulps, she turned her head toward the sound.

He was overhead. His upper torso on the underside of the trailer while his legs were still in the living room. River devil style. As though he were leaning into a swimming pool.

Madeleine looked down at Bo, thrashing in her arms. His head was twisted around and he was clicking like mad. Clicking in the direction of Zenon.

The water rose. Bo was struggling against her now, trying to get a foothold. She gripped him. In her mind's eye she saw herself as a wolf spider with a cricket. Oh, the briar, it brought forth such a taste for hunting.

That's not what this is!

The flashlight had gone down and cast an underwater shard of light, illuminating the sand and silt so that it looked like dancing sprites. And then the light went out. The water was already to their necks.

If Madeleine didn't drown the boy, Severin would; and if neither of them succeeded Zenon was sure to find a way.

Madeleine clamped her arms around Bo's chest and whispered into his ear, "You've got to trust me."

He lessened his struggle, trembling in her arms.

She whispered, "One deep breath."

His face contorted into a grimace of fear but he obeyed her. He drew a great big lungful. And then Madeleine dragged him down under the water's surface.

All sounds reduced. She held tight while the water rushed around them. Objects were surging by—wood, metal, glass. Her arms encircled his narrow shoulders and her hands were fixed squarely over his heart. She felt its rapid beat. Heard her own blood rushing in her ears. His body tensed, and she could tell he was on the verge of panic.

She wished she could tell him to stay calm. She wanted to say, "You won't need to breathe for a long while if you just listen to what your body is telling you."

But she couldn't say these things. She could only grip him, and impart the gift that Zenon had imparted to her.

Madeleine reached down and grabbed his fist. She'd never learned much sign language, but she did know the alphabet. She shoved her hand inside his fist and signed, "s-t-a-y."

His body relaxed a fraction. He moved his hand around to her fist and though she found it difficult to interpret the sign by touch alone, it seemed like he was signing back, "o-k." She nodded over his shoulder.

She realized that Severin was there. Right in front of them. Though Madeleine's eyes were closed against the unclean water, she could see the river devil as plainly as though she were gazing into an ugly aquarium.

Severin said, "To kill him now, it will not sting. Not for you. Not for this lumen."

Madeleine replied only, "Go to sleep."

"You delay!"

Madeleine sang to her from the voice inside her mind:

Away, away, John Carrion Crow,
Your master hath enough.
Down in the barley he hoes, you go.
Away with you, John Carrion Crow.

Severin did not reply, but she was listening. Madeleine continued:

> *One for the pigeon,*
> *Two for the crow,*
> *Three to rot,*
> *Four is too slow,*
> *Five . . .*
> *Six . . .*
> *Seven . . .*

Severin looked sleepy. Her visage in the water dimmed.

> *Nineteen . . .*
> *Twenty . . .*

And then Severin was gone. Madeleine kept counting.

❧

THE WATER AND DEBRIS churned around them in a micro-maelstrom. The trailer creaked ominously. And then, silence again. Nothing but the blood rush in her ears. She kept counting. They remained where they were, clutched and curled, Madeleine's hand over Bo's heart to reassure herself of his stout, steady heartbeat.

When the count reached four hundred, Madeleine signed into Bo's hand, "p-l-a-y d-e-a-d."

He gave her the OK sign.

She lifted her head above the surface, her hand on Bo's shoulder to remind him to stay put. Above, the briar mist had receded. All was so very black once again.

All except Zenon, who was staring at her with a river devil's glow. "You're good and tainted by that lumen, but it'll wear off. They still carry the glow a while after they die."

She looked down at herself, but then realized Zenon was playing something of a trick: To see the lumen glow, she'd have to recede a step into the briar. That was the state of mind Zenon had probably maintained for years—carrying a river devil backdrop with him wherever he went—and it probably was the reason he kept fully, sanely cognizant.

He gave her a wan smile. "So. How does it feel?"

She clenched her jaw and didn't answer, instead looking back to where the drain had fountained with overflow runoff. All black but for the occasional glimmer. No sign of Severin.

Zenon said, "You did what you had to. Move on."

Madeleine said, "I'm fine, Zenon."

"Alright then. Welcome to Team Predator."

She looked at him, furious, her hand still on Bo's shoulder beneath the surface.

Zenon said, "Quit lookin like you been wronged. You can pretend it's all my doing, if it makes you feel better. Truth is, little sister, I'm doing you a favor. You didn't even know that lumen kid. My first kill? Was my damn stepfather. Someone I grew up knowing. A fuckload lot meaner way to pop your cherry than offing some stranger."

Madeleine wiped the water from her face. "I'm getting out of here."

Zenon said, "You do that. Rest up and suck it up. We'll start again in a few days."

She shook her head with a snort.

But he'd already gone. Nothing left but the sound of rushing water and the blackness. With any luck he'd take his sick ghost of a self all the way back to his physical body.

She wondered how she was going to figure out a better plan to keep them all safe in just a few days. And how long before Zenon would realize that Bo was still alive.

twenty-seven

BOUTTE, 1927

HE DAMN BULL HAD still been there when the LeBlanc children had made it back to the Ford. And other than lifting his tail to take some relief, the beast still had no interest in moving. The Ford had been facing the bull, which meant the only direction the Ford could go down the lane was backward. Only, as Francois had advised in his driving instructions: *Reverse don't work.* And so the children had had to push the car backward all the blessed way until they came to a fork in the road. It had taken hours just to get to the fork. Finally, they had been able to drive again, only to get stuck in the mud—twice. By the time the four LeBlanc children arrived in New Orleans they were covered in mud, thirsty, starving, and the hour was well past midnight.

Patrice had intended to find a suitable place to park, but that was not to be; driving the streets of New Orleans was much different from driving River Road. All her new skills were put to the test.

Parking had never been one of them. Francois had showed her how to *stop* the Ford, but not how to *park* it. It seemed there was a difference.

Also, despite the late hour, New Orleans had been teeming with people on foot, hoof, and wheel, and all seemed drunk or at least mischievous. The children saw things they'd never before witnessed— paved roads, hordes of strangers, shops mashed up against one another, people kissing in public, enough electricity to boggle the mind. And it smelled. Even the Ford's nauseating fumes couldn't cover it. These were not like the odors of Terrefleurs—burning sugar cane was about the most intolerable thing Patrice had ever smelled until now—here were human and animal and maritime and industrial smells condensed into one.

Finally, Trigger hopped out and waved folks out of the way so that Patrice might find a place for the Ford to rest. That place was a rail yard.

"What do we do now?" Marie-Rose asked.

Patrice didn't answer. Because she had no idea whatsoever what they were going to do, where they would sleep, or how they would eat. No idea whatsoever.

❧

THEY WERE ALL TOO stunned to sleep, which was good, seeing as the Ford offered the only place to do so.

They peeled themselves out of their seats and ironed kinks from their muscles. Patrice was vaguely aware that at some point she ought to get more gasoline but she wasn't sure how or when to do that.

From somewhere to the east came the sound of a piano. A celebration?

"What do we do now?" Marie-Rose asked again.

Patrice put her fingers to her temples. They were at the near corner of the rail yard, close to a main road that was as nameless to Patrice as any of them. (On which one of them did their mother live?)

In the absence of direction from Patrice, the boys were now shouting ideas for how to proceed.

"We should hole up in one of these rail cars—"

"Let's walk a spell—"

"—til first light, then we can—"

"I'll be right back . . ."

Patrice snapped out of her reverie. "What? Wait!"

Trigger was already striding away from the Ford but he stopped dead at Patrice's command.

She said, "We must stay together at all times. All four of us."

"I gotta go," Marie-Rose said.

"Me too," Gil said.

And Patrice did as well. She sighed, looking around. The rail yard was quiet.

"Alright, but we stay within earshot of one another."

The boys headed for a nearby tree and Patrice took Marie-Rose to a stack of crates, but as they approached, they heard a cough. Patrice paused, listening.

"Who's—" Marie-Rose started to say, but Patrice placed a hand over her mouth and pulled her back.

"Who was back there?" Marie-Rose whispered when they were walking back to the Ford.

"A vagrant, I think."

"I still gotta go!"

"You wanna go with a vagrant standing there watching?"

Marie-Rose was quiet for a moment, and Patrice said, "You'll have to go behind the tree."

"With the boys standin there?"

"Better them than a vagrant."

"What's a vagrant?"

"Someone in front of whom you ought not pee."

They walked over to the tree while the boys sat whistling and shuffling by the Ford. Marie-Rose got going on her business, but for all that talk Patrice couldn't bring herself to do so as well. She heard other sounds—human sounds—in other corners of the rail yard. Perhaps it wasn't as deserted as it had seemed. She watched the shadows while Rosie was occupied. She saw that someone had carved something on the tree trunk. Hard to see in the darkness, but it looked like a drawing of a train. After all, they were standing in a rail yard.

From somewhere in the city, a bell tolled once.

"That for church?" Rosie asked.

"No, I think it's just chiming the hour. It must be one in the morning."

And suddenly it all seemed so stark. They needed to figure out a way to hide from their mother. Truly hide. But for now, they needed food and a place to sleep. None of these things seemed possible. She had to think of something to do next. Anything!

Rosie finished and Patrice took her by the hand and led her back to the Ford.

"We have to look for Ferrar," Patrice announced to the other three.

Silence. The boys exchanged looks.

Rosie screwed up her forehead and looked confused. "Ferrar?"

"Yes. Ferrar. After he healed up from the gunshot, he said he was going to New Orleans."

Gil said, "But he's . . . with that light. I don't think the river devils will abide."

Patrice said, "No river devils around for now. Ferrar's the only person we really know here in New Orleans. We saved his life."

Trigger grimaced and adjusted his hat. "We *were gonna* kill him but didn't follow through. That ain't the same as saving his life."

"Isn't."

"How we gonna find him?" Marie-Rose asked.

"We'll just . . . ask around."

She looked in the direction of the piano sounds. "We'll ask over at that place."

"Good idea." Trigger was in motion, looking downright gleeful at the idea of following the gay music.

Patrice and Marie-Rose fell in after him.

"What about our bags?" Gil called.

Patrice stopped and turned. "Oh."

Trigger waved him off. "They'll be fine. Come on!"

"No, he's right," Patrice said, wary of the dark corners of the rail yard where she'd heard coughs and groans.

She looked at her brothers and sister. "This isn't Terrefleurs. We can't leave our belongings behind because someone might try to take them."

Gil got to untying the bags and they hauled them from the rumble seat. Patrice gave Rosie Francois' Bible and took Rosie's luggage herself. No one seemed to notice that Patrice had no bag of her own. They walked together into the street paved with big round stones, unlike the dirt or crushed shell roads back home, and it felt uneven beneath her feet.

The music was coming from a brick warehouse. They could see lights and hear laughter. But as they approached the doors, Patrice started to feel foolish.

"You do the talkin, Gil," she said, but then caught sight of Trigger and realized he was carrying a machete.

"Trig!"

The thing was long and dark and curved, and though it served as an everyday tool on Terrefleurs, it looked positively sinister in these streets.

"What in the name of Sam Hill are you doing with that?"

"Figured I'd tote it along in case I need a shave."

"Don't get fresh! You can't be tappin on doors with a machete in your hand."

"What was I supposed to do, leave it behind?"

"You were supposed to pack bare necessities only." She stepped up to the door where they heard the piano and turned to look at him.

"I know, Treesey, but I wasn't sure if we were gonna stay here in New Orleans or head out to the country. Personally, I think we'd fare better in the woods. Build ourselves a little cabin. Can't go hunting here in the city and this part of the river's liable to be overfished."

She stared at him. Aside from his valise and the machete, he was carrying a frog gig, a slingshot, and a fishing pole, all strapped together. Blood had seeped into the bandage tied around his arm where the stranger had slashed him this morning. Both he and Gil were covered in mud, and the girls weren't much cleaner.

"What a sight, what a fright." She was trying to sound disgusted though in truth she thought Trig might have a point about trying their luck in the country rather than in New Orleans. The dark building loomed over them and it looked menacing despite all the music.

They hadn't knocked but the door suddenly opened.

"What y'all want here?" a man said.

Behind him was a dim office, but the piano music and the sound of many voices were now louder. This man was tall; no, not just tall—big.

"We . . . We're . . ." she began, and then elbowed Gil.

Gil said, "We're lookin for a boy named Ferrar."

"Never heard of him."

"He's got an eye that looks like it's bleeding, only it's not."

"Ain't seen no one like that."

He moved like he was about to shut the door again, but instead took a long look at Patrice from her shoes to her hat and back down again, and then swept his gaze over the others. "What in the holy fuck of a cotton truck did y'all ride in on?"

And then he roared with laughter. Deep and earthshaking. Slapped his knee to get it all out. Trigger looked at the others and laughed, too, only Trigger is known for his peculiar laugh, so that only made the big man laugh harder. Patrice felt nine shades of stupid.

The big man shuddered it out til he got his breath back. He dragged a match up the wall and lit a cigarette roll, paused, then offered it to Patrice.

"No, thank you."

He then presented it in mock-offering to the others and Patrice had to grab Trig's wrist so he wouldn't try to take it. Not that she objected to him smoking; she just didn't want him to take one from this person.

"How much money do you make?" Marie-Rose asked him.

"Rosie!"

"I just want to know—"

"It's not polite," Patrice said through her teeth.

The big man just laughed, shaking his head, and cast a sidelong look at Patrice. "Yellow rose. Look at you. So this . . . Ferrar. He your daddy or your boyfriend?"

"I don't believe that's your business. If you don't know where he is then you can at least tell us where we might go to ask about him."

He was smiling at her in a way she didn't much care for. "How old are you, honey? Seventeen?"

Patrice waved her younger siblings away from the door. "Come on, let's go."

But Marie-Rose slipped right past and stepped up to the big man. "She's fourteen. And I'm seven. And if you don't tell us where Ferrar is my brother's going to chop you with his machete."

This sent the man into fits again, right down to the knee slap, and Patrice and Gil had to drag Marie-Rose by the arm as they headed for the street.

But as they crossed to the end of the street the man called out, "Hey, cotton truck! Hold on now. I'll ask for you."

Patrice looked over her shoulder, but the hulking form had already disappeared back into the office and was closing the door.

"Never mind him," she said without slowing stride.

"He's checkin for us," Trig said.

Gil said, "Come on, Treesey, we might as well see if anyone there knows something."

She let her younger siblings pull her back toward the doorway.

The vehicles on the street had already thinned out from when Patrice was parking Papa's automobile, so that now it seemed desolate. A fresh peal of laughter rose from inside.

"What's goin on in there, a party?" Rosie asked.

"I suppose," Patrice said.

"Someone's birthday?"

Gil said, "Naw, too big."

They listened. A lone horse clopped into the street and when it came into view, Patrice saw in the gaslight that the rider wore a uniform. A policeman. None of the children moved, suddenly uncertain which side of the law they occupied.

The door opened and the big man emerged again. "Simms is comin."

Patrice didn't ask who Simms was.

From somewhere beyond the street came a burst of hollering. Agitated, as though a fight were occurring. All the children turned toward the sound.

Patrice expected the policeman to turn on his mount and head toward the disturbance, but as she watched him there in the glow of lamplight she saw him glance backward in the direction of the sound, but only for a moment. He turned forward again and continued on atop his horse, gaze dropped, clopping past until he was gone.

Marie-Rose asked, "Ain't a policeman supposed to help if there's trouble?"

"Isn't," Patrice said.

The big man said, "They don't get involved around here."

They heard the interior door open, and with it came a rise of sound from the warehouse, then the door closed again. A man approached, small in frame and wearing a striped suit, fedora, and a pencil mustache. The suit looked like it wanted to be something expensive but was made of cheap material. He paused at the exterior door and took in the children with a long gulp of the eye. Patrice and the others stared back. Finally, he adjusted his hat at the big man but said nothing.

"Awright then, come on in," the big man said.

The children stepped forward but the big man splayed a hand. "Just her."

Meaning Patrice.

"Never mind then!" Patrice said, blood ready to boil.

Gil stopped her. "Go on in, Treesey, we'll wait right here."

"We are not splitting up. Not even for a minute."

"Y'all can wait in the office," the littler man said, his voice high and thin and his expression receding to boredom.

Trigger said, "You know, Patrice, if there's any trouble . . ."

To this, the big man started laughing again. "Oh yeah, that one there said he gonna cut me down with his machete knife."

A fine thing that he liked that, and that the little man thought it funny, too. They had no idea that the true weapon the children had at their disposal had nothing to do with a machete.

The little man stepped forward. "They call you Patrice? I'm Simms."

And then he lifted his chin toward the big man. "This here's Hutch."

She nodded at him but that was it. Didn't offer her hand or introduce the others.

Trigger gave her a private look. *It's alright, Treesey.* He took Rosie's valise from her hands.

Patrice regarded Simms and told herself that if it came to it the Lord would forgive her if she had to use pigeonry on him. Or anyone else.

Simms gestured at the door in a way that seemed so easy and confident she would follow that she *did* follow, despite herself, and the three younger children followed, too, at least as far as the office. She looked over her shoulder at them when the second door inside the office opened and the piano music and voices poured forth. Her siblings' expressions puffed up as if the sound lifted them on a rogue wave. It made them look like children to her. Not Guy, Gilbert, and Marie-Rose, but just a group of ragtag little children.

Then, with Simms' hand on her back she was passing through that door, and it closed on those little children's faces.

twenty-eight

NEW ORLEANS, 1927

S O MUCH SOUND. THE piano was near-shimmying in the corner. She'd expected full bright light, but the broad, vast warehouse was surprisingly dim, with most of the light concentrated on the piano. The player's hands darted across the keys, a cigarette at his lips and a lock of greased hair falling forward over his eyes. Folks were smoking, laughing, and shouting at one another though Patrice couldn't imagine how any single one could hear actual words from any other. A bank of smoke rested above their heads as though all their gassing kept the cloud up high rather than falling to floor.

Simms said something to her but she shook her head dumb. The only conversation she understood came from the piano. When she looked back at Simms he was gone. And so she looked at the faces of those in the near vicinity in the hopes that one of them might look like Ferrar's type of acquaintance—someone nearing twenty, black, who set his day by a rooster crow or steam whistle. But these people were nothing like that. Women were snuggled in close to their men, and the men's ties were loosened with their sleeves turned back. They all looked sleepy and jazzed at the same time. Some folks were donning their hats and leaving through the office where her siblings were waiting.

These were mostly white folks. There were a few coloreds, too, but not many.

Maman was black and Papa was white, so Patrice and her siblings were somewhere in between. A meaningless fact at Terrefleurs but outside the plantation, like at school or at the general store, Patrice got the sense that it meant something to others.

One by one, people seemed to take notice of her and once that happened, their attention didn't loosen.

She tried to look bored. Back in that office, Rosie was probably grilling Hutch. (What's your shoe size? When's your birthday? Did you refuse to go to school, and that's why you don't speak properly? What time did you get up this morning? What time did you get up yesterday?)

The little man named Simms had returned and was pressing a glass tumbler into her hands. She looked at it. Thirsty as she was, she could smell it was some kind of alcohol and that absolutely wouldn't do. She tried to give it back. Cherry bounce was the only such drink she cared for and then only once in a blue moon. Simms wouldn't take the drink back from her.

She told him, "I need to find out about Ferrar."

"What's that, honey?" She heard his words this time only because he was leaning down and putting his lips to her ear.

She cupped her hand over his ear and shouted, "It's what we came here for. I need to find out if anyone's seen Ferrar, the boy with the blood eye."

He nodded and took her hand, pulling her toward a group of men who were already staring at them as though Patrice were doing the Charleston in her undergarments. The men sat with elbows resting on stacked wooden spools and they each had tumblers like the dreadful one Patrice still held.

Simms looked at Patrice and swept his hand toward the men like he was offering her a banquet of wild game.

Oh, Gil should be the one to ask around like this!

Hands folded in front of her, she proclaimed, "I am looking for a boy—"

The nearest man bent forward with his hand winging his ear, and Patrice spoke into it: "Trying to find a boy named Ferrar."

He frowned and shook his head. Whether he didn't know the name or simply couldn't hear her, Patrice wasn't sure.

She cupped her hands around her mouth and shouted very slowly into the ear. "Looking for Ferrar! He's got a blood-shined eye!"

This time the man nodded in understanding, almost a look of wonder.

She asked, "You know him?"

He shook his head no.

A fat man tapped the first man's shoulder, and the first man hollered something that sounded like "she's looking for a boy."

At this the fat one smiled broadly and waved her over. She repeated herself. He had his hand on her back, though, his fingers moving along her spine. The third man pulled her away from the fat one and toward himself, his hand cupped to his ear, expectant.

She said, "I'm looking—" and he turned his face and kissed her, full, hard, his hands wrapped tight around her back.

She slapped him and tore herself away. Her mouth hurt where his teeth had rammed her lips, and it tasted like blood and brandy.

They were all in hysterics now. Patrice ran for the door and burst through it. Her brothers and sister were sitting on their valises talking to the big man named Hutch. They were all stretched out and gabbing like old pals, with Rosie curled under Gil's arm.

"Let's go!" Patrice said.

And then she realized Simms had followed her out, his laughter high and thin as his speaking voice. "Hide the machete! We all in trouble now!"

Trigger got to his feet, his features going dark.

But Simms said, "Come on, now, didn't mean no harm."

Patrice marched to the front door.

Simms said, "But what if we find your boy with the eye? How we s'posed to let you know?"

The children were scrambling after her, Rosie struggling with her bag. Patrice snatched the Bible and Rosie's valise and pushed through the door.

The night air felt clean even though it had seemed so foul only a little while ago. Marie-Rose was asking, "What's it like in there? What happened?" but nobody else spoke a word.

That's when they heard the motor. Distinctive among other motor sounds in this city. After today, Patrice would know that rumble-grunt anywhere.

Trigger said, "Papa's Ford!"

⁓∽⊱⊰∽⁓

ALL FOUR CHILDREN BROKE into a run. Marie-Rose tripped and fell flat almost immediately. Patrice turned to help her up but Rosie had already righted herself and was flying across those big round stones after her big brothers. Trig let go of his valise and it went tumbling down and opened in the street, but his feet never slowed; they were pumping faster than Patrice had ever seen him move. As the valise flew open she saw his toy aluminum automobile and wooden filling station burst out. She watched them bounce across the cobblestones.

"Oh!" she cried and nearly paused, but then determined that Papa's automobile was more important, so she let Trig's toys smash themselves on the stones.

Leaving home for good, packing only the barest necessities, and Trig had made room for his toys.

She rounded the bend in time to see the Ford moving out of the rail yard. Trigger was already a fair spell ahead and closing in on it.

Gil stopped dead, and Patrice knew he was using pigeonry.

"Wait," she called.

The Ford kept rolling though the uneven surface kept it from moving fast. Trigger caught up with it and threw himself at the driver. There were at least six or seven men milling around, three of which were piled into the Ford.

The driver socked Trigger good across the jaw. Trig went tumbling sideways, the machete and fishing pole and the rest of the bundle clattering and scattering along the ground.

Another man jumped out of the Ford and kicked Trig straight in the head.

At eleven years old, no matter how wild and brave his heart, Trig was no match for this man. Trig rolled back and barely avoided another kick.

"Stop!" Patrice screamed.

And she herself stopped though she was still on the side of the rail yard opposite them. She focused her mind on that awful man who was kicking her brother. The kicking stopped. The man fell still and Trig hefted himself to his feet.

The Ford was rolling again. Patrice focused her mind on the driver and it stopped.

Gil and Rosie were clearly trying and failing to work pigeonry on these men. They weren't as strong as Patrice though Rosie was pretty effective if and ever she could keep calm.

Trigger socked his attacker in the gut. The man doubled forward for a moment and then struck Trigger across the nose.

Patrice had to return her attention to him to make him stop, thus leaving the driver of the Ford alone. And there were other men, too. A whole group of them pulling a closer circle around Trig, drawn by the ruckus, emerging from the crevices of the rail yard. One of them cuffed Trig on the ear. Patrice turned her attention to him to stop him, but then the first one struck a blow.

Patrice was walking slowly so as to maintain concentration. Gil and Rosie were clearly too upset to be able to accomplish much pigeonry. Rosie gave up and sprinted for Trigger.

"Rosie, no!" Gil called.

He took a few steps forward and stopped, his fists balled.

"Leave him alone!" Rosie screamed.

One of the men scooped Rosie up as she barreled forward. She screamed, and then she was kicking and clawing at him. Trigger threw himself at the one who'd grabbed Rosie and punched him square in the face. He dropped Rosie, but now the circle had tightened. Patrice could barely see what was happening, who was punching whom, who was grabbing. Someone was laying into Trig again and someone else had backhanded Rosie.

There were just too many of them. Patrice could only pigeon one at a time. She gave up and ran forward.

The sound of her footfalls caused them to look up. Like in the warehouse, once they got a look at her, their attentions didn't easily slip.

"Let my brother go!"

Poor Trigger was sagging like a wet rag, with one of the men holding him by the collar. But the man paused to eye Patrice.

"Ho there, sweetie," one of them said.

Gil came to her side and linked her arm around his. "Just leave us alone, please."

The one who still held Trigger glanced at the Bible in Patrice's hand, then leered at her. "What are you, missionaries?"

Arrhythmic laughter, and then they were jeering.

"I heard missionaries are good eatin!"

"She looks like she'd taste real good."

"High yella pie."

One of them picked up the machete. Many of them looked

hungry—a sick kind of hunger. They were bone thin and mean and stupid, and their eyes showed they intended to take whatever they could get from the children. Patrice didn't have to search inside to know this.

The sound of horse hooves. She turned to look. The policeman they'd seen earlier?

Next to her, Gil started singing:

Holy, holy, ho-ly!
Lord, God almighty!
Early in the morning our song shall rise to Thee

The men's faces went slack, then split into grins. She could smell them—good Lord, they were so close and so foul. Black teeth and rotting from the inside. Two of them were clean, though. She recognized them from having been in the warehouse. The others must be vagrants. More of them now. At least ten.

Gil brought the Bible up so that he and Patrice were holding it together. She realized then that Gil was trying to make it look like they *were* missionaries. As though for some insane reason that might make a difference. Nevertheless, Patrice started singing, too.

Cherabim and seraphim
Fall down before Thee

The men looked like they wanted to lapse into fresh laughter or slap the song from the children's mouths, or both. But the clip-clopping hooves were now full in the street, too close to ignore. Patrice looked and recognized the same policeman they'd seen earlier. The men were looking at him, too.

But as she watched, the policeman turned his head toward them and then immediately looked forward again and kept moving. He would be gone in a moment.

Patrice and Gil kept singing, and then Rosie and Trigger joined in though Trigger botched the words. The four huddled in around one another.

Patrice focused her pigeonry on that policeman. That one man riding the horse.

The clip-clopping stopped.

Patrice heard from the street, "You there!"

Some of the men seemed uncertain. But the one with the machete looked toward the street and passed his tongue over his lower lip.

Patrice didn't dare let go of the policeman's mind. She held, hoping these wicked men would just scatter and leave them alone. She couldn't very well force the policeman to march into that machete blade.

Some of the men lost that wild look in their eyes. The ones who'd been at the warehouse and two of the truly rough-looking fellows. But the one with the machete and the ones who'd been striking blows to Trigger and Rosie looked ready for a fight.

"Go on get outta here before you get hurt," the man hanging onto Trigger said to the policeman.

And then little Marie-Rose stepped forward. She was singing that song, right along with Patrice and the twins. Patrice kept singing, too, and couldn't afford to keep Rosie in check lest she let her attention slip from the policeman.

The policeman was now approaching, still on horseback. Some of the men avoided eye contact with him. And yet no one left. They seemed unwilling to relinquish the spectacle, if not the spoils of war.

Before Patrice knew what was happening, Rosie walked right straight up to the man with Trigger's machete and reached out to him. He looked down at her, his jaw gaping and confusion in his eyes. But then he very gingerly placed the hilt into Rosie's waiting hands.

Patrice wondered if Rosie had pigeoned him to do that. Perhaps the singing had forced her into a more stable frame of mind.

And then two of the men picked up the rest of what was in Trigger's bundle—the frog gig, the fishing pole, the slingshot—and handed them to the children. The man hanging onto Trigger let go.

The children kept singing.

One by one, each of the men stepped back and drifted away. No one hurried. They certainly didn't seem the least bit intimidated by the policeman. But they did filter off, each in his own way—this one lingering as though he must check to see if he'd forgotten anything; that one shuffling off with mincing steps like in a soup line. One actually sang "Holy, Holy, Holy" in off-beat timing with the children as he shuffled away.

When they were all gone save for the policeman on horseback, the children stopped singing.

Patrice released the policeman.

❧

"TRIGGER," PATRICE SAID, AND she put her handkerchief to his face.

He moved it down under his nose and coughed, spitting between his feet. "I'm alright."

"What are y'all doin out here?" the policeman asked.

"We're lookin for a boy named Ferrar," Gil replied.

"You sure picked a damn fool time and place to do that." And then he regarded the Bible in Patrice's hands. "Sorry ma'am."

The horse watched them from behind what looked like an eye patch. Patrice could see only its eye and long lashes if it turned its head toward her.

The policeman said, "Y'all got a home?"

"Yes," Patrice replied, perhaps a bit too quickly.

The policeman paused, scrutinizing her. "You from the children's home? I'll need to take you back there."

"They're with me."

Patrice turned to see Simms walking toward them with Hutch at his side.

Simms said to the policeman, "I hired some missionaries to do some singing for me."

"That so?" the policeman said.

Patrice was too perplexed to either support or deny Simms' claim, but Gil was nodding.

Simms took Patrice by the arm and used his hat to herd the others back in the direction of the warehouse. "Come on, your parents are worried sick. Try not to get lost from now on."

The policeman called after them, "Tell them to keep their children locked up at night! Damn missionaries."

From behind them, the clip-clopping started up again as the policeman rode back toward the street.

Patrice freed her arm from Simms the moment the policeman was out of earshot. "What do you mean by this?"

Simms said, "Can y'all read sheet music?"

Patrice looked at him, too puzzled by his strange question to reply.

But Gil was nodding. "She plays the piano all the time for us back home, and we all sing along."

Simms said, "Fine. Y'all can share a room. Girls in the bed, but the boys'll have to sleep on the floor."

Patrice said, "No thank you."

Simms opened his arms in a disarming manner. "Don't worry, no monkey business. I meant what I said. I wanna hire y'all to do some singing."

"You'll pay us?" Gil said.

Simms eyed him and then his gaze fell on poor, bloody Trig. "Just the girls. Y'all lookin a little too rough."

"I don't understand," Patrice said.

"Just get some sleep and we'll talk about it in the morning."

Patrice folded her arms. "No sir, you'll tell us now or we won't be going anywhere."

Simms paused and faced her, sighed, then said to Hutch. "Tell her."

Hutch said, "Y'all sing for us out on the street corner. We give you the music to sing from. Folks pause to listen, then we sell them the sheet music. Got it?"

Patrice considered a moment. That didn't sound so terribly bad. The good Lord knew they needed the money.

She and the other children started walking again in the direction of the warehouse. *First sign of nonsense and we'll march right back out again.*

Simms chuckled. "There, that's it. You do got some sense in you."

"*Have* sense," Trig corrected from beneath the bloody handkerchief.

Patrice shot him a grin.

It would be nice to take a bit of sleep. Daylight was only a couple of hours away.

t w e n t y - n i n e

NEW ORLEANS, NOW

O COULD DO EXCELLENT impressions of crickets, frogs, and birds. Usually his clicking faded into the background the way a clock tick disappeared unless you put your attention on it. Here at the clothing store, though, he was under strict orders to keep quiet. No animal or bug calls, and absolutely no clicking. The only exception was if he sensed Zenon was nearby as he'd done under the bridge. In that case, he was to avoid speaking a single word, but he would alert Madeleine and Ethan by doing his cricket chirrup.

Ethan seemed grim and sleep-deprived, but he kept looking around like he expected the Ross to fall under siege at any moment. Madeleine kept a hand on Bo's shoulder as they moved through the racks. Her other hand was pressing her cell phone to her ear, with Bo's mother, Esther on the line.

Esther was saying, "Mare didn't tell me much about what happened. Just called me up and told me she was moving out."

"She did?" Madeleine said.

"I heard from my neighbor Cheryl that Mare blew off three fingers with a homemade gun, but your Doctor Manderleigh put all them fingers on ice for her and the doctors had gone on and reattached them. Two of them, anyway."

Madeleine chewed her lip.

"Bo's safe for now . . ." Madeleine said, her voice trailing like she meant to add something else, but she let it fall.

Her free hand still rested on Bo's shoulder as he moved through the aisles, and she knew he was listening to Madeleine's end of the conversation. He wanted to see his mother. See her in person.

Madeleine and Ethan hadn't dared let him back inside that trailer, so they needed to quickly and subtly buy some clothes for him. The fact that he was still alive hadn't been something they wanted to broadcast in case Zenon came around.

Esther continued. "I can't say I have one tear to shed for watching Mare go. But the truth of it is that without Mare's rent every month I don't know how we're going to make ends meet."

Madeleine paused. "Esther . . ."

Esther interrupted her. "That isn't . . . It doesn't . . . I'm not saying what I mean to say here, Doctor LeBlanc. You got to understand . . ."

Madeleine listened, but Esther went silent. Her breath sounded quick and shallow.

Finally, Esther said, "Bo's safe. That's the most important thing right now. The rest I just need to work out. What I mean to say to you . . ."

She paused again. "The cravings are jumping in my blood. After all these years. Whatever got into me the day I stole that fool's stash, I'm afraid it's not over. That the addiction's only part of it. Do you . . . Is this making any sense?"

"You need to stay where you are and get better, Esther. We're taking good care of your son."

"I think I might lose my job."

"I know."

"And with Mare gone and no job and no car . . ."

"Esther, listen for a minute, OK?"

"I know. One thing at a time."

"Yes."

"These cravings. I can't believe I let that back in."

Madeleine scanned the store. If Zenon had any reason to doubt that Bo was dead, he could work with his river devil to find out the truth. But he had no reason to doubt it. He'd witnessed Madeleine holding Bo beneath the water's surface and had no cause for suspicion. Unless of course he saw Bo walking around alive and healthy.

Now they were on the other side of town where nobody knew Bo. Still, a little Hispanic boy with no eyes who clicked his way around town was a pretty high profile thing.

Esther said, "I have to ask you something, Doctor LeBlanc."

"Yes?"

"It's just . . . When y'all were over at the trailer that day. When those huffer kids came and tried to chase Bo down. I saw the way you looked at my son. When he run past you. I saw it. I wasn't imagining it, was I?"

Madeleine removed her hand from Bo's shoulder and pressed her fingers over the phone. "I . . . No ma'am. I wish you were imagining it. I can't say that you were."

Madeleine stopped, and Esther remained quiet.

Then Esther said, "And so how can you tell me he's safe for now?"

Madeleine took a deep breath. It wasn't an easy question to answer.

She tried, "This is about as stable as things are going to get for him right now. If something were to happen, Ethan and I are pretty much the only ones equipped to handle it."

Esther said, "I know. I think you're telling me the truth. I've prayed for help, and maybe the answer is that God sent you."

She let a breath go by, then: "I just, I hope you understand. I need to see my son."

"It's dangerous . . ."

"I know. I have to see him. I'm his mother. Can you bring him here? Or I'll check out of this place and come to you."

"You can't check out of the hospital. From what I heard you can barely walk."

She could hear the anxiety in Esther's breathing.

Esther said, "I've got to see him."

"Let us figure this out. We'll have Bo call you as soon as we're finished here."

They ended the connection and Madeleine glanced at Ethan. He'd overheard, of course. She looked away.

Bo ran his hand along a table of folded shirts. "Do they have one in periwinkle blue? It's my favorite color."

Ethan looked at him. "How do you even know what periwinkle blue looks like?"

"I don't, but it looks good on me."

He was giving an open-mouth grin with the gaps between his upper teeth making him look like the Cheshire cat. One of Ethan's shirts poured over his shoulders and a pair of Madeleine's drawstring shorts were cinched around his waist.

Madeleine said, "We've got to get out of here. Are you sure size twelve is going to fit?"

"Yes ma'am, it's my size."

"OK, we'll skip the fitting room." She added the shirts to the shorts they'd already selected, and herded them toward checkout.

"After this are we going to see Mom?" Bo asked.

Ethan looked at Madeleine.

"I just don't think it's a good idea," Madeleine said.

Ethan gave a tired shrug. "He might as well, baby blue. Zenon's got to sleep some after last night and the longer we wait the riskier it gets."

The truth was, the thing neither of them wanted to admit in front of Bo, was that Bo may not have another chance to see his mother. Both their lives were in danger. Madeleine and Ethan had already gone over all the possibilities while Bo was sleeping. It seemed the hospital wasn't all that much riskier than home.

Also, Zenon was at the same hospital as Esther. But Zenon was on a different floor of a different wing and it might as well be a different town for his inability to move. Of all the places he'd care to project his ghost for a prowl, lowest on the list would be the same old tired institutional halls that confined him every day.

"So can we go?" Bo asked.

Madeleine looked up at Ethan, and he gave her a nod of encouragement.

She said, "Alright. But it'll have to be quick."

They stood in line behind a woman with three children. Ethan turned and walked a few steps away to a stack of boys' shirts, pulling out one that was cobalt but that Ethan undoubtedly thought was periwinkle. She looked at the family checking out in front of them, the kids both energized and bored. Recollections filterd through her mind—what Zenon had said about changing the face of humanity. What that might mean for her. And what it meant to everyone else in the world, like that family standing there.

thirty

S USUAL, PATRICE AWOKE to a rooster's crow. Then she realized she was not in her own bed, but in a room she did not recognize next to her baby sister who'd twisted the blanket around her ankles. Guy and Gilbert lay back-to-back on a thin pallet on the floor.

It came to her that she was in New Orleans. Surprising to learn that there were roosters in New Orleans. Slowly, she remembered:

Simms. The warehouse. That horrible incident in the rail yard. The Ford was long gone. So were most of Trigger's things. Though they'd recovered the machete and fishing pole and other gear, his valise and its contents had been stolen where he'd dropped them in order to give chase to the Ford.

With no change of clothes, he and Patrice were in the same fix.

She sensed movement. Her river devil was in the room, stealing glances at her as it moved about, but it didn't address Patrice directly. Strange. The devil's lips moved. Patrice couldn't understand what it was saying.

Gil had awakened, too, and was looking at Patrice. She put her hand to the back of her neck and found that the scratch had finally scabbed over.

※※※

THE SUN HAD REACHED and passed its apex but still no sign of Simms. People were filtering in and out of the warehouse, people who seemed to know what they were doing and who had real business there. They took no more notice of the children than they did of the skinny cats who darted behind the corners and stopped moving when you looked directly at them. The children had slept late and then took to idling outside near the street, asking anyone if they'd seen the boy with the blood-shined eye. No one had. Patrice was starting to get a real sense of just how big New Orleans was—a city of strangers. Patrice never saw the same person twice. The only recurrences were that distant clock that chimed the hour and the ships on the Mississippi sounding off at one another beyond the rail yard.

Patrice looked over at Trigger. He was standing near a hydrant and talking to a man in orange suspenders and a gray cap. Asking after Ferrar, Patrice thought, until the man handed Trigger his load, then carried on down the street.

Patrice started toward Trigger. "What have you got?"

Trigger grinned and presented a basket full of sausages.

"Trigger!"

Patrice looked down the street but the man had disappeared with the crowd. Calm and in control, Trigger's pigeonry skills were now much more sharp.

She took Trigger's arm. "No more pigeonry!"

"Easy!" he said, flinching.

She let go. His eye was black and swollen, and he had cuts and bruises everywhere.

Gil said, "Pigeonry or pigeon sausage, honey, something's gotta give."

That got the twins laughing, and when the twins laughed together it always sounded like a couple of hissing geese. Marie-Rose shoved a sausage in her mouth before Patrice could take them away.

Gil said, "Come on, Treesey, this isn't working. Trigger can find Ferrar in half a blink and we can get this over with."

Patrice said, "We chose to forsake the briar. Even if it's inconvenient for us. No more pigeonry! And no tracking unless it's normal tracking."

"We used the briar last night, and yesterday, too, against that stranger."

"Those were life or death situations! We'll just have to get along like other people. Today we'll earn a little money to get us going. Then we find Ferrar. The good way."

Marie-Rose said something but no one could tell what it was.

"Don't talk with your mouth full," Patrice said.

Rosie pointed to the warehouse, where a motor car was pulling up. "Simms is back."

❦

PATRICE'S DRESS WAS STILL muddy from the day before when they'd sent the stranger off with Francois. Now, they were all standing in the warehouse. It looked much different in light of day. Dingier.

Simms checked her over. "Ain't you got nothing else to wear?"

Patrice shook her head.

Hutch said, "We could get one of the girls to loan her something."

"Naw, we don't want her lookin like that."

Marie-Rose piped up. "I have a dress she can wear! It used to be hers."

"No," Patrice said. "Too small."

But Simms said, "Give it a shot."

Something about the way that man spoke, you'd think he used pigeonry to get his way because Patrice found herself going back up the stairs to the room to try on the dress. Stupid; it wasn't going to fit. She was a good foot taller than Rosie!

She pulled it over her head and looked down. Whereas the dress came to Rosie's calves, on Patrice it rested right around her thighs. At least it bloused out in such a way that it fell loose around her middle.

The door opened and Simms came in.

"I'm dressing!" Patrice said.

"You look dressed to me."

"You should have knocked."

And Simms gave her such a look as to make the blood feel cold beneath her skin. She had to turn away.

He said, "Where your cross at?"

"What?"

"Yesterday, you were wearing a cross around your neck."

She still was. Eunice's cross. She reached into the dress and pulled it out so that it rested atop the fabric.

He said, "That's fine. Now get on down the stairs. We wasted enough time already."

"In this?" Patrice said, incredulous that he would want her to wear Rosie's dress.

He nodded. "It's nice. You look like a true angel."

Strange the way he delivered that compliment. More matter-of-fact than flattery.

But then he paused at the door. "Here."

He walked toward her and she felt herself stiffen, he'd come so close. But he pulled at the dress. She realized the sash was dangling loose. He tried to tie it once, twice, stepped back and looked at her, then he yanked at it and she heard it rip. She looked down and saw that he'd torn it out where the ends were sewn into the seam. It left two-inch gaps on either side.

Furious, she looked up at him but immediately swallowed back her protest. His look was so hard. Too late now, anyway. The dress was ruined.

Without another word he turned and strode for the door. She stole a look around the room in hopes that there may be some mirror, any mirror, but found nothing.

"Let's go!"

She hurried after him.

At the bottom of the stairs, a soft-curled lady in a long dowdy skirt was painting Rosie's face. Just the lips. She was dabbing purple-red color with a brush to form a cupid's bow. Patrice was astonished at the effect. Rosie had become a living doll.

"Now her." Simms pulled Patrice forward.

"What's this for?" Patrice asked.

But the woman just said, "Don't talk sweetie. Need your lips real still."

But Rosie must have already asked this question because she said, "It's so when we sing our mouths will enchant all who wander near."

It sounded like she was quoting someone else. Patrice cut her eyes toward her sister without moving the rest of her face. The paintbrush felt like a strange creature pressing against her lips. Guy and Gilbert were looking on as though their sisters had just revealed themselves as fairies.

"The dress really does look good on you, Treese," Gil said.

Trigger was stealing glances at Simms. Patrice looked, too, wondering about him. He looked Italian or Mexican or some other sort of dark-complexioned race. He wasn't wearing the fedora today but he was in a suit. Another cheap one.

"There," the woman said.

Still no mirror. Patrice's lips felt gluey and leaden, and the paint smelled like must.

"Don't lick your lips, don't even touch them," the woman said.

Hutch pushed some papers at Patrice and waved at Rosie. "Y'all sing this one."

Patrice looked at it as she held it out for Rosie—sheet music for a song she'd never heard before. "No accompaniment?"

Hutch exchanged a look with Simms and chuckled. "Can't tote no piano out to the street corner."

Patrice glanced at Rosie, whose forehead was wrinkling like an old hound as she glared at the papers in Patrice's hands. Rosie was slow on her letters at school, let alone words, let alone musical notes.

"Sing it!" Simms thumped the paper and it made Patrice jump.

She gave it a go. With no background music and not so much as an opening note to prompt the key, Patrice did her best to guess the tone and modulated her voice to follow the rises and falls, at least as the notes seemed to appear in relation to one another. Too disorienting to add in timing; each sound came out as a dead, round whole note. Rosie moved her lips but did not sing at all.

Patrice dared a glance at Simms and he looked disgusted.

What now, was he going to renege on hiring them to sing the sheet music? Was he going to demand payment for providing them a room to sleep last night?

Her voice squeezed to a halt. She hadn't finished it. Everyone was staring.

"It's only because I've never heard it before. If I could just have the piano—"

Simms grabbed her by the throat and yanked her forward. But whatever he was about to do or say to her never happened. Trig had his pocketknife up under Simms' jawbone. Hutch moved like he was going to knock Trigger into pieces, but Patrice wrapped her mind around him and saw that he held still.

Simms let Patrice go.

Trigger did not let Simms go.

"Leave it," Patrice said to Trig.

Trig released Simms.

Simms straightened his tie and gave a long look of incredulity to Hutch. "What you doin over there, hibernating for winter?"

Hutch just stared back.

Patrice said, "Let me play the song once on the piano. Then Rosie and I will have no trouble singing it."

❧

THE PIANO SMELLED YEASTY. Patrice set the sheet music in place and settled her hands over the keys, pausing to squeeze her fingers to dispel the shaking. All those eyes staring at her at once. Something so powerful about that. Right now it was a power she didn't want—it threatened to scorch her right off the stool.

Her fingers pressed down on the keys and it began. Two, three measures, and then she stopped. One of the men sighed but she couldn't stand to look up and see which one. She read through it for a few seconds. Started again.

This time she played the song. The piano could have used some tuning, but the song itself actually sounded quite lovely, with the opening chords coming through sweet and sentimental, almost a comic sadness. The timing fell into place without Patrice having to concentrate too much. Gil turned the page for her when she came to the end of the first one, then continued turning pages as she played it through once.

When she finished she rubbed her hands together twice and started right back at the beginning again before anyone could say a word. This time she sang it.

When she was finished, she asked Rosie, "Do you have it?"

Rosie nodded.

Patrice stepped away from the piano and stood next to her sister. They sang the song together. It sounded right. Rosie kept up as best she could, though she couldn't read the music fast enough and had only heard Patrice sing it the one (and a half) times. When Patrice looked up during those last verses, she saw all had taken seats except for Trigger and Simms, who were standing at the farthest ends from one another. Simms was smoking. Big old Hutch had gone gentle-faced in the way some do when they drop self-awareness. Simms seemed to note Hutch's reaction, too, and he seemed more interested in that than the singing itself.

They came to the end of the song. Patrice and Rosie just stood there together. All were silent, except . . .

The river devil.

It had come back. It looked like a man but with female breasts and sharp teeth. It kept singing where Patrice had finished, as though it was fascinated by her. The other children's river devils were there, too, though for Patrice they were like shadow creatures. Patrice retreated into herself and tried to dispel the briar world—not possible by trying to force away thoughts. It meant she had to be calm. She had to watch and listen—to everything: the world around her, her own heartbeat, even her thoughts as disembodied objects.

She did this. She watched and listened. Her brothers and sister, from the looks on their faces, were seeing the devils, too. Patrice listened to the sounds beyond the walls to the street: hooves and wheels and voices. A dog barking. She noticed light filtering through a gap in the brick.

The river devil faded away.

From somewhere in the city, the bell sounded four times for the hour. Its tone was the same key as the song.

And Simms was talking. He was saying that they'd wasted enough time and should get a move on.

Patrice nodded, throwing her entire attention into that single interaction with Simms. "Let's go then."

Simms was narrowing his eyes at Trigger. "We may actually have a little work for the boys, too."

thirty-one

NEW ORLEANS, NOW

WHEN BO ENTERED ESTHER'S hospital room he threw his arms around his mother with no regard for tubes or machinery or bedside tables. But then again, Esther didn't show any regard for those things, either. She just hugged her boy, tears streaming. Madeleine was struck by the look of abject fear on her face.

"We'll give y'all a moment," she said, and hung back with Ethan.

Mercifully, there hadn't been anyone in the second bed. Ethan closed the door so that Esther and Bo could be alone. The lights of the hall were stark white, as was the textured linoleum, as were the walls. A horizontal stripe divided one white from the next.

Madeleine said, "Ethan, when you were talking to Zenon through Mare, and he made those threats, what did you say to him?"

"Told him he wouldn't get the chance to hurt anyone else."

And then he turned to Madeleine with a look of utter exhaustion, resignation, and fury. "Because I'm gonna kill him myself."

Madeleine took his arm. "Don't talk that way, not even for a minute!"

"I don't see as I have a choice, Madeleine. He's making threats against your life. I can't just stand by and let anything happen to you."

"I can hold my own against him. I have so far."

"So far."

"And you won't be able to help me or anyone else if you go to prison for murder."

She pulled him closer. His eyes were bloodshot and his jawline had gone to stubble. She lifted her face so she could find the scent of his skin, up in the neck where it smelled most like him.

She said, "You need rest. We'll come up with a plan after we sleep."

He nodded, pulling her in close.

❧

THE DOOR OPENED AND Bo emerged. "Mom wants to talk to y'all."

Madeleine and Ethan followed him in. Esther was sitting up in her bed with an IV in the back of her hand and a frayed paperback on the bedside table.

Her face.

Her right eye was black and folded shut, and the right side of her mouth was swollen and split. A mesh cast bound her right hand.

The left eye, the untouched one, was wide and wet and it appraised Madeleine and Ethan with a look of desperation and fear. "I wanna thank y'all for bringin him."

Madeleine said, "I'm afraid we shouldn't stay much longer. It isn't safe."

Esther turned to her son. "Bo honey, why don't you sit over there in the corner and listen to your new music box for a minute. You can show me your moves."

"Yes ma'am."

"Over here, OK?" Ethan said, nudging Bo to the far corner and drawing the curtains to Esther's bed so that Bo was hidden from the door.

Nothing but Ethan's classic rock on the iPod but Bo seemed to like it. He slipped on the earbuds and moved his head to the rhythm, the volume loud enough where the song was audible.

Esther said, "My neighbor Cheryl offered to watch him."

Madeleine and Ethan looked at one another.

Madeleine said, "I'm not sure that's safe. For Bo or for Cheryl."

Esther nodded. "That's what I thought. It's just, you hardly know him. And I don't know you."

Ethan said, "That's true, but we understand what's coming after him. Best thing for you right now is to go ahead with the rehab and let us protect him."

Esther pulled in her breath and closed her eyes for a moment. "I wasn't going to go. Couldn't risk losing my job. But they already fired me anyway. So I guess the decision's been made for me."

Madeleine put a hand to her shoulder.

Esther's lower lip was trembling. "Why him? Why my boy?"

Ethan slipped his arm around Madeleine and gave her shoulder a gentle squeeze.

Madeleine said, "He's got a special light inside. It's hard to explain, but there are dark forces that would like to extinguish that light."

"Those devils, the river devils," Esther said.

Madeleine nodded.

"But why?" Esther asked, and tears spilled over onto her cheek.

"I wish I could say. I just don't really know myself because I'm still learning. The immediate threat is from someone alive, someone like me. We're trying to stop him. The river devils, they're limited in what they can do. They whisper into your ear, tell lies."

"And I fell for it," Esther said.

Madeleine opened her hands. "There's more to it than that. You do have the power of choice with the river devils. They know how to find your weak spots, but you're still ultimately in control. But aside from them, you're up against a serious warrior."

"Warrior." Her jaw went tense as she seemed to digest the idea. "That what you mean when you say someone like you?"

Madeleine shrugged. Esther was looking at her they way a fawn might regard a bobcat.

Esther said, "That what turned those schoolyard bullies into full-on thugs? Made Mare chase Bo under the trailer with a carving knife?"

Ethan said, "He has a way of getting inside your mind and compelling you to act against your will. If you don't know what's going on, it can be confusing. Feels like your own idea."

"What exactly are we up against? Isn't there anything we can do?"

Ethan nodded. "If you suspect you're being manipulated, you have to blank out your mind. Don't fight it. Just accept and observe no matter what happens, and you'll be yourself again."

Madeleine said, "The light that's in Bo, it's gotten into the people around him, like you and Ray and your neighbor Cheryl. It makes it difficult for the bad ones to get a foothold."

"But he got a foothold on me," Esther said.

Ethan shook his head. "If you let yourself get bogged down in worry or anger or panic or guilt, it's an opening for them."

The sound of the door swinging came from the other side of the curtain. Madeleine and Ethan both looked. A nurse was coming in.

"Do you mind coming back in a few minutes?" Ethan said, striding to the door to block her entry.

Madeleine moved around the bed to position herself in front of Bo.

"It's time for her meds," the nurse was saying.

But Ethan was gently guiding her back out the door and

Madeleine could hear his tired, reassuring voice: "Just a couple of minutes is all. We'll let you know when we've gone."

Madeleine looked at Esther. The beating she'd taken after stealing her coworker's stash was a harsh one. It had happened only because Zenon wanted to isolate Bo and make him vulnerable. Madeleine thought Esther was probably safe now as long as she wasn't around Bo. Bo, however, was not safe. Especially not here. They had to go.

Madeleine turned and looked through the curtain but didn't see Ethan. Not in the room, and he wasn't standing on the other side of the wire glass window, either.

"Hang on." She walked to the door and opened it.

Ethan wasn't there.

She swallowed, looked left and right. He hadn't said anything about going anywhere.

But she already knew where he'd gone.

Madeleine turned back and went swiftly to where Bo was listening to the iPod in the far corner. "Come with me, honey. Can you be really quiet and hide in the bathroom?"

"What's the matter?" Esther asked.

"I need to check on something."

Bo had pulled out the earbuds and was following her to the bathroom. "Did Mare come back for me?"

"No, no, we're just playing safe."

Madeleine secured him inside the bathroom, then stepped back into the hall, closing the door behind her. It had only been a minute or two since the nurse had tried to enter. If she hurried, she could get to Zenon's room before Ethan did.

THE CORRIDOR WAS QUIET. Madeleine scanned ahead as she jogged toward Zenon's room, drawing curious glances from the staff. From halfway down the hall, she could see that there was no guard posted out front.

She hurried to the open door and caught her breath. Ethan was already there. Zenon was not.

She stepped inside, looking from Ethan to the bed—empty and stripped down. No quilt, no shortwave radio. The chair the guard had been using in the hall was now pulled inside and placed by the door.

"What's happened?" she asked.

Ethan said, "You shouldn't have left them alone."

"I didn't feel I had a choice! What exactly are you doing here, Ethan?"

"You know damn well what I'm doing here."

And then a voice from behind said, "Well maybe you can enlighten me."

They turned.

Standing in the doorway, arms folded, was the short blond nurse, Vessie. "I don't recall y'all having checked in at the nurse's station. You can't just wander into patients' rooms like this."

Madeleine said, "What happened to my half-brother?"

Vessie shrugged. "Gone."

"Gone where?"

"No one knows. The hospital tried to reach you."

Madeleine frowned. "Well they didn't try very hard. How do you lose a patient with a guard posted at the door?"

"From the looks of things, he up and walked out on his own."

Ethan said, "The man's been in a coma for the past several months!"

Vessie's hands went to her hips. "I don't like your tone of voice. If you have a problem you can take it up with the administrator, but for now you better get off my wing before I call security."

Madeleine stepped toward her, teeth clenched. "No, my dear, you are going to tell us exactly what happened."

And she found that little catch inside Vessie's mind, and she pulled. Hard.

Vessie sat down abruptly. "I took him out."

Madeleine exchanged a frown with Ethan and then looked at Vessie again. "Go on."

"That's it. I took him out on a stretcher. Covered him with a sheet."

"What about the damn guard!" Ethan said.

Vessie looked at him. "He helped. We went in the early hours when no one else was around. I know where the blind spots are in the security cameras. It was easy. There been all kinda investigators come askin questions."

Madeleine said, "Just tell us where he is now."

"I don't know. Me and the guard, we took him down to patient transport. There was a man waiting there for us. No one I know. Loaded him up and took him away. Bye-bye."

thirty-two

ADELEINE AND ETHAN FOUND Bo waiting safely in Esther's bathroom. Esther looked anxious.

"We've got to go now," Madeleine said.

Esther reached for Madeleine's hand. "I have one more thing to ask you. And I'm sorry. You've done so much."

"What is it?" Ethan asked.

Esther took a deep breath and looked at Ethan. "Doctor Manderleigh, I want to ask you to personally watch over my boy. And Doctor LeBlanc, I want to ask that you not be alone with him."

Silence settled over the room. Esther was still holding Madeleine's hand, her fingers cold and moist.

Bo said, "But Mom!"

Ethan started to say, "Do you realize—"

But Madeleine shook her head. "No, it's OK. I understand."

Because Esther was right. Esther had looked at Madeleine and seen shadows of the monster inside. A relief, actually, that the truth was out there. She squeezed Esther's hand and did not look at Ethan.

⁓⁂⁓

SEVERIN WAS RUNNING. SHE clearly wanted Madeleine to chase after her but Madeleine didn't want to go any deeper. She looked back and saw only the black trees with their coils of thorns and the curling mist. Already she wasn't sure where the entry point was. Beneath her feet the spongy, pale green duckweed rolled with the water's surface. She could slip into that water or she could run across it. Water in the briar wasn't like water in the material world.

"Severin!" she called.

Rustling of leaves. The child's laughter echoed back to her, echoed among the trees, and did not seem to come from any direction in particular. Irritating.

The dragonfly beasts sprang up from the duckweed. But before they could sting her she turned and stared them down. They hovered, watching. She let her fury course through and away from her so as not to indulge them.

She sang softly against her frustration, "Three blind mice, three blind mice . . ."

The dragonflies receded. They could be lulled like Severin.

Or was Madeleine just lulling herself, she wondered. And the other creatures were reacting in kind?

She heard the rustling again, and wondered if Severin was making the noise. Everything around her was silver and black or faint green or red. Leaves fluttered everywhere but she couldn't pinpoint the origin of the sound.

She felt . . .

Something out here. An airless, cold void. The chill came not so much from an active source as from an absence of warmth. Of life. Blackness, thickening the shadows. She wondered if Severin had caused it.

She watched.

Emerging from the trees came the colorful flying lizards: sylphs. They formed around her, their hues shimmering, their backs gleaming, their collars puffed. Madeleine could not help but feel awe. The void was still there, but now less important to her. The sylphs circled around her like the wind patterns of a tropical storm, then trailed off into the woods on a stream of mist.

Deeper into the briar like Severin. She didn't follow them, either.

She wasn't going to fall for these tricks—chasing deep into the woods, where the trees might fall away to tunnels of thorns. Where she might lose her bearings.

She had no intention of staying here for days, weeks, months, the way her father had been known to do. She was going to return to the material world tonight.

At the base of one of the great trees, a shelf of lichen had formed a sturdy half-ring. She went to the shelf and lay down. It felt soft as any feather bed. The mist settled over her face in a crisp, cool mesh. She closed her eyes.

"Ah, so as to sleep? Should you sleep it does not count for our bargain."

Madeleine opened her eyes and saw Severin crouched on a limb above where she lay.

"What bargain, Severin? You only honor it when it suits you."

The little river devil's face formed a sly frown that became a grin. "You blame me. You should blame yourself. I come at your will."

"Why do you keep saying that? You show up uninvited and I tell you to go away!"

"What you say with words is not all that I hear from you."

The rustling sound came from the trees again. So it wasn't Severin making it. Madeleine looked, and saw that Severin was watching for the origin of the sound, too.

"What is it," Madeleine asked. "What's out there?"

"It is there and wishes to be everywhere. It is what makes us."

Madeleine sat up on the shelf of lichen. "Severin, I need to find where Zenon is hiding."

"He is here in the bramble. Call to him—"

"No! I need to find his physical body. Where is he hiding?"

"Let us take a look to see."

Severin climbed down from her branch and settled in next to Madeleine on the shelf of lichen, pushing herself up under Madeleine's arm. Madeleine waited. The sensation began only as a matter of equilibrium, a sudden feeling of weightlessness. Her mind went dizzy. The platform of duckweed suspended over the water's surface—though only inches beneath the lichen shelf—seemed to wobble in such a way that Madeleine thought they might fall in. And then the duckweed was disappearing to whirlpools. Madeleine held on to Severin. The world around them fell away, and she couldn't tell if they were lifting or falling. Everything shifted to black.

Then, Madeleine saw a gleam. Far down below. A long, shimmering dendrite shape that stretched as far as she could see. And then she saw that it led to a strange spread of light: a circuit board with lighted parallels. It bent itself in a crescent moon shape around a bend in the glassy dendrite. A city. Her city. New Orleans.

But before she could even steal more than a glance, it went dark.

Everything was dark. And then there was a patch of duckweed just a few feet away from her. And trees were stretching up from the duckweed, black and thorny, stretching impossibly high.

"What happened?"

"No, we cannot," Severin said.

"What do you mean 'we cannnot?'"

"He is not there where we can find him."

Madeleine pulled away from Severin. "Why not? Is he . . . dead?"

Severin shrugged, growing bored. "He found a trick of hiding, is what he's done, surely."

"Is there any way to find him?"

And then Zenon's voice came from across the duckweed. "Who you looking for?"

Madeleine jumped.

He was watching her from between two wide tree trunks, looking satisfied with himself. "Look at you, pretty as you please, stretched out like a bayou fairy."

She rose from the lichen shelf. "How long have you been standing there, Zenon?"

He strode toward her, walking over the duckweed. "Honey, you don't need to go to no special lengths to find me. Just call. I'll come every time. Hell I'll come even when you ain't callin.'"

"You really have become a damned river devil."

He laughed. "And you, baby, are still good and stained."

She looked down at herself, her blood pulsing with phosphorescence beneath her skin. Bo's light.

"Stay away from me, Zenon. I'm done with you."

"Honey, you ain't never gonna be done with me. We connected just as sure as our river devils are bound to us. It's in our blood and our genes. Ain't nothin gonna change that. Besides."

He sat down on the lichen shelf and reached into his pocket for a cigarette. "Weren't for you I wouldn't have any friends 'sides that bastard, Josh. You're fresher company."

"We'll never be friends again."

"Sibs then." He struck a match and flared the end of his cigarette.

Severin stretched out on her back in the duckweed and floated across the surface, the tiny pads clinging to her, making a garland in her hair.

Zenon took a drag from his cigarette and pointed it at Severin. "Your devil's underdeveloped, baby. You need to work to get her bigger, more coherent."

Madeleine would sooner nurture a patch of poison ivy, but she asked, "How do you do that?"

"You get your hands dirty. Right now she just antagonizing. Am I right?"

Madeleine nodded.

"All that's good for is putting you in the insane asylum. You don't have to go nuts. What you do is make your kills, but you control your mind when you do it. Don't go postal. Can't be rage or nothin. Like you did with the little blind boy, that was fine. Calmly drownin him under that trailer like he's a sack of kittens. More of that and you train for the briar."

"You sound like Chloe. Trying to school me on the briar."

His expression changed. The easy, cocky smirk left him and was replaced by a more sober demeanor.

"Look, we on the same team now so quit bein difficult. You ready for some more training?"

"What, you gonna try to teach me firearm and bayonet drills?"

He shook his head, stone serious. "We can if you want. But you can do that anywhere. Right now we got bigger fish to fry."

He was on his feet and face-to-face with her before she had time to react, his hands wrapped around the base of her skull. She tried to jerk away but he had her clean.

Severin flipped over in the water and surged toward them. "Ah, so lovely!"

It's not that Madeleine felt the change itself. Not like she could sense that something was draining out of her or that something else was filling her up. But as Zenon held on she did know that any quiet inside her had been replaced by noise. It felt exciting and exhausting all at once, the way she might sometimes listen to music that pushed her limits. It both energized and depleted her.

The cigarette was still burning in his right hand. Casting its scent into her hair.

He released her and put it to his lips, speaking through it. "There now. See what your big brother done for you."

She stared at him, unsure what any of it meant. "What was that?"

He waved the cigarette at her. "Stain removal."

She looked down. All traces of that phosphorescence were gone. If anything, she saw hints of the strange sepia anti-shadow, like the way the river devils and Zenon looked when they walked the material world.

"Much better," Severin said.

Madeleine lifted her gaze to the massive black trees. "There's something out there."

He nodded. "That's it, baby. I just gave a little piece of it to you."

"But what is it?"

"It's going to come in real handy."

"It's cold."

She tried to pinpoint the sensation. Cold, not in such a way that made her feel a chill, but perhaps more the way a cold-water fish might exist. Not desirous of warmth. Cold on the inside.

He said, "You know how long it took me to get to that phase? And here I give it to you in just a few seconds."

"I didn't ask for it."

He laughed. "You're fuckin welcome."

"So you can just pass these abilities on to anybody?"

"No, you probably gotta have the briar in your blood. Everyone else is just pigeon meat."

She wrapped her hands around herself, thinking. He was wrong. She'd passed the stop-breathing technique to Bo, to save his life.

"But . . . so the lumens?"

He shrugged and took a drag from his cigarette. "They're different. They can steal any of these little tricks from us, too. And they stain the people around them so alla sudden we ain't nothin special. You gettin me?"

"Yes. No. Not really."

"It's why they gotta go, babe. I come to believe that people like you and me, we get to be the hominids that come after homo sapiens. Or—"

He gestured behind him. "Or—the lumens do. They like a virus. Evolutionary competition. Look at your science books. Sometimes a species'll split off into parallel sub-species. But only one of'm wins out in the end."

He said, "So you're ready for the next phase. You got one lumen down, the little blind kid. But he was all over the place. Stained up everyone who's around him. His mama, some school kids, people that lived nearby."

Madeleine stared at him. "And?"

"So you gotta clean house."

"You mean . . ."

"To send them through," Severin said.

And Zenon said, "Yeah. Get rid of'm all."

"You can't be serious."

"Oh, I'm serious alright. Kill'm all. Wipe'm out. Eradicate."

Intellectually, she knew she ought to find the idea shocking. Ludicrous. Unthinkable. Zenon was a madman.

And yet.

Inside, she felt differently. The cold void that now permeated through her had deadened her sense of vitality. In its absence, the new excitement was what replaced the feeling of being alive.

thirty-three

NEW ORLEANS, NOW

ADELEINE SAT UPRIGHT ON the couch. She looked toward the stamped tin ceiling above just to make sure it was there. No black thorns. And no Zenon or Severin. She was fully back. But that coldness, it still lingered inside her.

Ethan had been sleeping with his arm wrapped around her but he awoke with a start. Bo lifted his head at the change in their breathing sounds, his hand over the Braille copy of *The Cay*.

"What is it?" Ethan said.

Madeleine was staring at Bo, trying to find that sense of protectiveness she'd felt for him before. But: nothing.

"We've got to get out of here," she said.

Ethan rose up on his elbow, rubbing his eyes. "What? Now? Baby, I'm tired."

Madeleine watched Bo as he returned to his book. "You sleep. I'll take Bo out for a little bit."

Something inside her was objecting to this idea. Where would she take Bo? How safe would he be in her company, now that the void had emptied her? The truth was, she wanted him out of her home. Felt absurdly territorial.

Ethan blinked the sleep from his eyes. "No. Let's stick together. Let me just brush my teeth and change my shirt."

Madeleine swallowed and nodded.

"How's your book?" she said to Bo, eyeing Ethan as he left the room.

"It's good. There's a blind kid in it. He wasn't blind starting out, though."

She stood, breathing in carefully.

Because the urge that filled her right now . . .

Madeleine closed her eyes. She had to stop this. Whatever she felt, she needed to make her conscious mind override the other thing, or the lack of something, that begged to be filled. Make pain to prove its existence.

Bo was clicking at her. "Doc LB?"

In her mind, she counted, breathing in and out carefully. Because she knew Severin would appear at any moment unless she found a way to still this thing.

Ethan emerged from the bedroom wearing a fresh tee-shirt and walked to the bathroom. The sound of running water.

"It's back," Bo whispered.

Madeleine swallowed. "You can tell that from clicking?"

"Yes ma'am."

"Well that's good. But it's not really back. You're picking up on something in me."

Bo was quiet for a moment. "You gonna kill me, Doc LB?"

The statement sent a frenzy of emotions through her and none of them were sympathetic. Her stomach rolled. She wasn't sure how long she could keep this up before going mad. She closed her eyes again and counted aloud, distantly aware that she hadn't answered his question.

But as she counted, she felt a touch on her arm. She opened her eyes. Bo was there, his hands reaching for her, and then his arms went around her neck in a gentle hug.

"Don't worry Doc LB. You gonna be OK."

And that quickly, it changed. The void was replaced by warmth.

⁕

MADELEINE KNEW THAT IF they stayed home and Zenon came looking for her, he'd find out Bo was alive. Better to disappear into a crowd for a while. So they walked along the waterfront in the Quarter near Pirate's Alley. That way if Madeleine sensed Zenon might be nearby, Ethan could take Bo and blend in with the hordes of tourists. Security by obscurity.

How she was going to explain to Zenon why the phosphorescent "stain" had returned, though, she wasn't sure.

They streamed through people and felt the kind of invisibility you can only get in a tourist-saturated area. Bo was awake enough but Madeleine and Ethan moved like the living dead.

"We're going to have to sleep sometime," she said.

"Yeah," was all Ethan managed.

The steam calliope on the *Natchez* played whistling carnival music. Bo was listening and grinning in the direction of the thing, and Madeleine could tell he was dying to click at it.

Madeleine said, "Watching him may be difficult. You have to go to work."

Ethan shrugged. "I think I can bring him with me into the lab, at least for a little while. Things are loose right now with the students on summer vacation."

Madeleine looked out over the water. "I guess we just need to concentrate on getting through today."

"Yeah, well that one's easy."

"Why?"

Ethan gave her a sideways grin. "Ice cream."

Madeleine looked, and saw that he'd spotted the Sucre Gelato van. He took Bo by the shoulder and steered him in that direction. Tourists queued up to buy treats from a woman in a blue bouffant wig.

All these people. Zenon could make them his pigeons in the blink of an eye. He was so much farther advanced than she was. He would have eventually closed in on Bo if he hadn't wanted Madeleine to make the kill. It didn't matter where they went—they were sitting ducks.

A few days ago Chloe had offered up advice in finding the truth by distracting the conscious mind. Ethan had said virtually the same thing when they'd stood together in the rail yard. But Chloe was the one who knew the full spectrum. She was the one who'd spent a lifetime observing the ways of the briar.

Madeleine watched while Ethan read aloud each of the flavors on the menu to Bo. Bo went for a strawberry gelato sundae, and Ethan picked out a café au lait for himself and a chocolate gelato with chocolate fudge topping for Madeleine. The man knew her well. Regardless of circumstances, she always found an appetite for chocolate.

She dipped her spoon in and let the icy sweetness settle over her tongue, deliberately facing into the sweltering sunlight.

Ethan said, "Feeling better?"

She nodded. "Loads. And I have an idea."

"What."

"I need to go see Chloe."

He scooped a behemoth spoonful into his mouth and swallowed in a single gulp. "Ain't that like drinking strychnine after swallowing a spider?"

She shrugged. "If anyone knows how to get out of that trap, it's her. Yeah, she'll probably try to twist things on me. But I'll be on guard."

"Alright. We'll go see Chloe."

Madeleine shook her head. "Chloe hates the lumens just like the river devils do. I don't think it's wise to bring Bo around her."

Ethan paused for a moment, then threw his ice cream in the trash. "I don't like the idea of us splitting up. What if Zenon shows?"

"Quite frankly, if he shows, he'll be looking for me. He thinks Bo's dead so he won't go seeking him out. So if he does come looking it's better if Bo's not around. Who knows . . ."

She looked at Bo, who'd forgotten himself and was now clicking toward the gelato van. "Maybe Chloe knows a way to evade Zenon. Or better yet, neutralize him. Now he thinks he can convince me to kill off Bo's neighbors in that Bridge City trailer park. I can't keep faking him out much longer."

Ethan was breathing through his nose, hand to his hip, the grimness around his eyes having returned in full.

Madeleine said, "Let me just call and see if she's around."

She dialed Chloe's number into her cell phone and got Oran. She talked to him a few moments while Bo kept after his sundae and Ethan frowned behind his sunglasses.

"They said come on by now," Madeleine said as she ended the call.

"How long you think you'll be?"

"A couple of hours, probably. You can go on ahead and take Bo to your place and get some rest. When I'm done with her, I'll come join y'all."

He shook his head. "I don't like it."

"I don't either. But I don't know what else to do."

❧❦❧

ORAN HAD GONE TO fetch Chloe. Madeleine waited on a settee in the drawing room, pulling at her hands like they were sugar taffy.

She felt a pang as she looked out toward the grand hall of

Chloe's mansion. So much like her old house, which her father had burned to the ground before he'd died. Good old Daddy. Madeleine had rebuilt the old place but had had to sell it, which is why she now lived in a warehouse on Magazine. Another family heirloom.

Both this house and Madeleine's old place had been in the family for generations, and there were similarities—some of the old wall fabric, the cane motif in the frieze, even the china. But Chloe's house had a particularly strange quality about it, as though the wood in the framing was slowly reverting back to the trees they once were.

"Briar waiting to happen," Madeleine muttered to herself as she waited in the drawing room.

Madeleine had abandoned the settee and was looking out the window by the time Oran returned with Chloe.

"You are distressed," Chloe said, but her expression was more reproach than concern.

"You could say that."

"It is because you are worried for someone. That will not serve you any favor."

Madeleine shrugged. She hadn't come here to talk about that. Oran filled two crystal glasses with sherry and handed one to each of the ladies.

"No thank you," Madeleine said.

But Chloe barked, "Take it."

Madeleine looked at her, puzzled by her sharp tone, but she took the sherry.

"Now drink it," Chloe said, and then added, "won't you *please*."

Madeleine lifted a brow. It smelled like roasted sweet walnuts and alcohol. She sipped. Not a taste she cared much for but she could see why some drink it.

"So now, let's hear what you have to say," Chloe said.

Madeleine set the crystal on the tray and folded her arms. "I've come about Zenon."

"Mm." Chloe's expression didn't change.

"What's your relationship with him, Chloe?"

"He is my great-grandson. Just as you are my great-granddaughter."

"Stop it. You know what I mean."

Chloe said nothing for a moment, looking at Madeleine, and then: "It's a complex thing, a relationship, business or personal. Would you say that my relationship with you is complex?"

"Of course."

"And so it is with Zenon."

Madeleine said, "'And so it is.' Not, 'so it was.'"

Chloe opened her hands. "Why don't you ask what you came here to ask?"

Madeleine hugged herself and looked at her feet. "Actually, I've come to ask for help."

Chloe nodded. "Of course you have."

"Zenon, he's been coming after me. Hunting people. Figured out how to project his consciousness from his body. I think he might try to hurt me and . . . others."

Chloe looked at her for a long moment, each facial feature occupying its own fold of skin. She turned toward Oran and gestured to the Persian rug. Oran disappeared into the hall.

Madeleine said, "I want to know if there's a way to obscure myself so he can't find me."

Chloe nodded. "I can hide you."

"I mean in a briar sense, not so much physically."

"I know what you mean. You want my help but you don't want to engage with me. Cannot dirty yourself with the truth of what is to be done."

"Listen, Chloe I—"

"Get on your knees."

"What?"

Chloe gripped the armrests of her wheelchair and rose to her feet, her lips quaking. "You, Madeleine, are no different from any of them. Only your own self and your one tiny little life. No care for the wider existence. You come here for my trick of protection, then so be it. Get on your knees. I give you what you ask."

Oran had somehow reentered the room beneath Madeleine's notice. He had an armful of bleached towels which he was spreading over the Persian rug.

Chloe's hand was on Madeleine's arm, pulling her toward the towels. Madeleine found herself going to her knees as ordered. Like with the sherry, she was reacting more from stunned curiosity than obedience.

Severin had said Zenon had found a trick of hiding. Maybe that's what Chloe was doing for Madeleine now.

Chloe dipped her fingers in Madeleine's sherry and sprinkled it into her hair.

Madeleine said, "Chloe, what is this? I was thinking there was a way through the briar—"

"Shush!" Chloe took her roughly by the chin. Madeleine was on the verge of getting to her feet and walking out, but this was too important. Lives were at stake.

"*You* are the one with the gifts, Madeleine. You have what I have always wanted and yet you waste it. *You* are a child of the briar but *I* am not. And yet you come here, to me, and *you* want *me* to help *you*, but only under *your* conditions with nothing to offer in exchange."

Chloe released her and took short, slippered steps to the credenza. "I can guide you but I cannot do what you can do."

Chloe seemed so unsteady she might lose her balance.

The old woman pulled open a drawer and retrieved a stamped tin box. "I cannot benefit from the gifts you squander, unless you deign to hand me your scraps. For me it is the old ways of the river. Crude tricks. But it will work. It will hide you."

Madeleine watched in awe. Chloe stepped back to where Madeleine stood kneeling on the towels and pushed Madeleine's head down. She stroked Madeleine's hair forward, muttering, "to hide this girl, to hide, to hide, to hide her hide . . ."

She was sprinkling something down the back of Madeleine's

neck. Musty herbs. And then more sherry. Madeleine didn't know what to make of it.

And then, a slicing pain along the skin at her neck.

Madeleine jerked her hand to the spot and got to her feet. Chloe was watching her.

"What was that?" Madeleine said.

She looked at her fingers. Blood where she'd touched the back of her neck.

"Cruder magic," Chloe said.

Madeleine looked at Oran, who'd now shrunk back down the hall though his reflection was visible in the mirror.

Chloe said, "It is all you need. You must now be surrounded by water. You will be hidden."

Madeleine looked at Chloe with incredulity. "That's it? And Zenon can't find me?"

Chloe nodded.

Madeleine frowned. It didn't feel like it could be so simple. "But what if I want to hide someone else, too?"

"Who you hide, girl? Your brother's child?"

Madeleine felt an internal jump. "What are you talking about?"

"There is nothing to hide but yourself from yourself. This is all you ever do."

Madeleine felt a strange tickling on her nose, and she scratched it with the back of her hand. She needed to hide Bo, too. Hiding herself wasn't nearly enough. But she didn't dare tell Chloe about that.

The tickling progressed from her nose to her lips. Madeleine rubbed. But in doing so a shimmer of light caught her eye. When her hand moved through the rays of sun that were spilling through a gap in the curtains, she saw a faint reflective thread, invisible but for the sunlight that bounced from it. No, there were several threads.

Madeleine gasped. Spiders. Tiny ones that could fit on the head of a pin. Spinning over her hands. Her arms. All over.

She tried to shake them off. Slapped at her legs.

"Get back down, Madeleine," Chloe said.

"The spiders! What did you do?"

"Then it has caught hold already. This is good. What you see is an illusion."

The spiders were wrapping her in their silk, so thin and faint she could only see it when the light shined on it. But then one of the spiders bit her on the forearm. She gave a start. In the pinprick of blood that welled up, the creature burrowed into her skin. Madeleine screamed.

"Go to your knees, girl. River magic isn't for pretty."

The spiders were wrapping, wrapping, burrowing into her skin. She sank to her knees. The ghastly things were wrapping her from the inside now. Around her throat so that she could no longer speak above a whisper.

"Chloe," was all she could choke out.

Her feet and hands were numb. Her knees had gone cold. She felt the spiders in her spine, in her joints, in her neck. A curtain of white with a single blood speck covered her left eye, and she realized that she was now on her side, staring into the towels. She was wheezing.

She managed to squeeze out the words, "The blood is real."

A single spider darted over her eye carrying its silken thread. It itched. She watched it move across her field of vision with another silken layer.

And though she could no longer see Chloe, Madeleine could hear her voice from somewhere above. "Yes, Madeleine, your blood is real. And now you belong to me."

⤬

thirty-four

⤬

NEW ORLEANS, 1927

WHAT SURPRISED PATRICE WAS that Simms and Hutch went off somewhere with Guy and Gilbert, leaving the girls alone with the soft-curled woman who'd painted their lips. She was holding a satchel full of sheet music.

Patrice realized she'd never introduced herself to this woman and didn't know her name. But as Patrice was about to remedy this she stopped herself, thinking it could somehow make it easier for Maman to find them if the woman knew their names. Names were powerful.

People crushed in all around them. Patrice couldn't believe how many people were on the streets. No wonder no one they'd asked had seen Ferrar. How could any single person remember seeing another in this madness?

How were they even going to find Ferrar?

And were the children, also, just as anonymous? Perhaps with all these crowds, Maman would be less likely to locate them.

"Well, get on with it," the woman said.

Patrice looked down at the sheet music in Rosie's hand but paused when she looked back up at the soft-curled woman's face.

"Go *on!*" the woman said. "Ain't got all day!"

But suddenly, the manner in which she was speaking—she wasn't of her own way. She was being whispered.

"Allons! Rapidement!" She said it with wide vowels like the country French common at Terrefleurs.

Her voice had changed and her face contorted. Patrice felt Rosie rear up beside her.

"Careful, Rosie."

Rosie was holding the sheet music and it was crumpling in her hands. Patrice gripped Francois' Bible.

"Don't look at it," Patrice whispered to Rosie.

Patrice rarely had to look upon other people's river devils. Usually it was just her own, or the ones who taunted her siblings. Everyone had a river devil but few knew it, and the devils liked to stay hidden. The fact that they'd become so apparent to Patrice now meant that the briar was folding over them in a very uncontrolled way. They shouldn't be out on the streets like this. They should be home in bed, tied down or at least watched over by someone. Walking their physical bodies while their spirits drifted was a dangerous thing. It meant you had to pay attention to both worlds at once.

Patrice knew that there were two things above all else that inflamed a devil—being subdued or being recognized for what it was. And she recognized the creature on this woman. It snaked around her and infused itself into her skin. It saw Patrice.

The woman made a sound resembling that of a cat facing down a coyote.

Patrice swallowed in hopes of bringing moisture back to her mouth. She understood that some of this was unfolding in the material world, but not all of it.

Relax, listen to the birds—

But there were no birds here on this street. No wind in the trees, no quiet bayou. That's where she was used to focusing her attention.

Patrice could see Hutch and Simms now. They were looking at them from down the block. Looking so as not to be noticed. Spying. Their devils, too, had become visible. Everyone's had. All the people on the street wore them like capes. The devils twitched when they saw the children. Or rather, when they saw the children seeing them. Some of the devils looked like humans. Others looked part-animal. They were baring teeth at the girls.

Next to Patrice, Rosie started singing. Loud. *Very* loud, and gloriously off-key.

But Patrice realized her sister was right to do this, and Patrice started singing, too. The girls sang full voice, bringing attention inside to the song, and in focusing attention the effect was like stealing oxygen from the river devils' flames. At least as far as the girls were concerned. There were enough folks on the street who were feeding their own river devils with their mind chatter, their worries, their fears—all of which the creatures inhaled and spat out as chaos. Chaos that might erupt in the form of tempers flaring, or it might simmer for later release on their families, friends, enemies.

Patrice and Rosie were singing. Awfully. They tried to find the proper key but their voices were seesawing in erratic directions. The soft-curled woman, though her river devil had relinquished interest in the girls for the moment, was sneering at their tone.

Then, somewhere nearby—much nearer than at the warehouse—the clock tolled once for the half-hour. Full and round. Patrice moved her attention to the sound and matched its key, the same as the song, and she sang out from the bottom of her belly. Rosie fell in after her and was finally on key, too. The sound was lovely and innocent even to Patrice's own ears. The song was pretty.

And its effect was immediate. People slowed in the streets, and their devils seemed drowsy.

"Look, how sweet!" someone was saying.

"If you tilt them do their eyes close?"

Laughter.

The soft-curled woman settled down, too, and shooed the girls forward so they might stroll while singing, caroler-style.

Patrice stepped forward and felt like she was walking among a pack of wild dogs that she hoped wouldn't catch her scent. To slip attention would be to draw the chaos from all those river devils. So very many of them. She glanced at her sister. Rosie had an expression that hung somewhere between fear and outrage, a very Marie-Rose kind of quality that made her intimidating beyond her size to just about anyone but her siblings. Her painted cupid's bow lips were now pouring out that song as though they could blow brimstone to ice.

Hutch was now moving through the crowd, looking theatrically interested in the girls' song. But that wasn't right. Patrice had seen his face when he'd listened the first time, when he was truly curious. This was different—he was grinning and gesturing at the girls. His devil was whispering.

Someone was buying a sheet of music from the soft-curled lady.

Someone else was moving through the crowd. One of the men from the warehouse—that fat one who'd run his fingers up Patrice's spine when she'd inquired about Ferrar. He was watching Patrice and Rosie but again, his attention was elsewhere.

Where?

The soft-curled woman led the girls forward. They'd now gone through the song three times. The plan was that they would sing it five times, then move down several blocks and begin again.

It disturbed Patrice that Hutch and the other man from the warehouse were following along. Also, the soft-curled woman had only sold three copies of the sheet music. Were they going to be able to sell enough to pay the girls and still make a profit?

With all these thoughts, her attention was wavering. The river devils seemed to grow restless. And the thorns arose, too.

Patrice looked to her left and saw water was now coursing down the cobbled streets. She caught her breath in mid-phrase, and her voice stumbled back to the melody.

That water wasn't real.

This was the thorn world overlaying God's world. This was the shadow river, coming to swallow her into the briar.

And on the other side of the river, a pool of tar, and a tar creature watching. It moved as though anxious to get to Patrice and Rosie but it couldn't seem to cross the water.

Patrice focused her attention back to the song. Each note as an individual piece, the feel of it in her throat, the lyrics as separate words with separate meanings.

But it wasn't working.

She intensified her focus. So much so that each fraction of a second seemed to pass with the slightest hesitation between them. It should have helped keep the briar away, but it did not. Not this time.

Rosie was gripping the music so that it steamed limp in her hands. Patrice knew she must be experiencing the same thing.

The briar river coursed by at no more than six inches deep. Patrice could still see the cobblestones in distorted glimpses beneath the flow. The water made a lapping, rushing sound, and another sound came, too. A song. Different from the one the girls sang, and it made it near impossible to cling to the refrain of one and listen to the other.

But she had to listen. She heard the other song in her bones.

What she heard was Francois' song. And Francois was singing it.

⁂

PATRICE COULDN'T SAY WHEN the girls had stopped singing. It might have been Rosie who first let the song fall off so she could listen to Francois' voice. Or maybe Patrice had been the first. The soft-curled woman was railing at them though to Patrice she was now just a distant finch. The briar had filled in so quickly that it seemed impossible to keep track of anything from the material world. But now that they were immersed in the briar, at least the devils were no longer outraged by them. They counted them as among their own here.

Patrice forced herself to try to follow what was happening. Keeping focus was suddenly so difficult.

Trigger had emerged from some side street and his hand was in someone else's pocket.

Gil had shown up, too, and was reaching toward a man leaning against a lamppost.

The man turned to look at him. "You want to find that hick with the blood-shined eye? You go on over to the bridge. That's where alla them end up."

The sound of Francois' voice grew stronger.

Rosie gawked at a shimmering fairylike creature. A sylph.

Patrice was suddenly aware of the soft-curled woman grabbing her by the arm.

"You leave her alone!" Rosie said, and the soft-curled woman let go.

"All of you, leave us alone." This time it was Trigger talking.

Patrice looked and saw that Hutch and Simms were turning and striding away. So was the fat man from the warehouse, and the soft-curled woman. Trig and Rosie and Gil were frowning as they watched them go.

The four LeBlanc children weren't as upset as they were last night, and their pigeonry was more effective.

And on the heels of that thought Patrice remembered that this was a sin.

"Don't do pigeonry," she said to them.

What a dull, naïve idea to which she'd clung. She decided to let it go. Now, here. Setting the resolution adrift.

And then she was immediately distracted by the river that now flowed past her ankles. And then by Francois' singing. Her attention leapt from one thing to the next. The sylph was most compelling. It spread its wings and flirted with the children like it wanted to be chased. Marie-Rose stepped forward.

"Don't follow it, Rosie! You'll get lost! You can't tell what's briar and what's not."

Patrice's river devil moved toward her from the shadows, walking slowly. "It goes to see your Francois. To hear his song. Don't you long to hear it, too?"

Rosie looked back at the devil. "Francois?"

"Don't talk to it," Patrice said.

Rosie said, "But Francois. If he's here we should go see him."

"He isn't really here. You'll only see echoes of him. He left us to attend to the stranger, remember?"

"Even so, we ought to check on him."

"Only if we all stay together. No one wander, you hear?"

She could still see people everywhere, only now *they* were the shadows and *the devils* were the flesh.

"Trigger!" Patrice called.

He was striding after the sylph. He paused and looked back.

"Come on," Rosie said.

Patrice looked for Gil. He was moving in her direction but looking back at the man who'd been leaning against the pole. Rosie was trying to catch up with Trigger and the sylph.

"Alright, we can follow it!" Patrice said to no one because no one was listening.

Why was it so compelling to follow that ridiculous sylph? Like sitting in church and realizing your soul might be teetering between hellfire and salvation, but really all you care about is that right now you have to pee.

Concentration was so exhausting. Gil caught up to her and they fell into step together without a word. They followed along and allowed the sylph to do the concentrating for them. For all of them. Patrice's shoes splashed in the street that was now the river.

They turned the corner and saw him.

Francois, lying on his back on the raft. The dead stranger lay at his side. The raft drifted down the shadow river, turning gently. It ground against the cobblestones for a moment and then coasted forward. Something else, too, a shining black shape about the size of a dog that at first Patrice thought might be a river devil. Maybe that tar creature.

Next to Francois, the dead stranger lay with deep streaked cavities where his eyes had been. The black shape moved over him, and Patrice finally saw the long, crooked neck—a vulture.

Shops and hotels and homes lined the streets. Shadow people and their river devils were looking down from their curling wrought-iron balconies. Patrice couldn't tell the thorns from the metal.

"Francois!" Marie-Rose called.

Francois turned his head to the side to look at Rosie. He was still singing in his deep, slow voice.

"Francois!" Rosie cried again, and she splashed into the river toward him, going slower as the river dragged deeper, her dress bunched in her fists.

Trigger splashed in, too. He overtook Rosie and went surging toward the raft.

The vulture raised its beak from the dead stranger. And then it leaned over Francois. Bending to his face. Craning its neck.

"Stop!" Patrice shrieked.

Trigger took off his hat and flung it at the bird. It turned its filthy beak and stared at Trigger, canting its head to the side as though it might be half-blind. Trigger made it to the raft just as the vulture stretched its wings and took to the air.

Francois had his hand over his eye. Patrice and Gil splashed toward the raft.

"Francois! What's happened?" Rosie cried.

Francois turned his head back to face the sky. He lay on his back, knees bent, the left one swaying a little. Hand to eye. Hand over the eye where that filthy bird had bent over him. He went back to singing that slow, mournful song he'd been singing yesterday when the children had bade him farewell in that remote bayou.

Patrice covered her mouth, horrified.

"He's gone daft," Trigger said.

The sylph dipped and turned around, drawing their gazes, beckoning them to follow. And strangely, Patrice nearly did just that, so fickle was her attention now. Gil was taking a few steps toward it.

Patrice gathered her wits. "We have to get Francois off this raft."

They each pulled on Francois but could not make him move. Francois remained on his back. The raft kept floating. They could not slow it much; just make it turn a little, or rock. Francois kept singing. His hand was over his eye and a black stream ran down his cheek.

"It's cuz he ain't here, he's not really," Trigger said.

Gil looked at him. "You're right. He must still be out on that damn bayou. He's not really here and we're not really there."

"But that vulture, you swatted it away," Patrice said.

Trigger shook his head. "I scared it. Just because it saw me doesn't mean I was there. It flew off on its own."

"A whisper!"

Patrice's river devil. She looked to see it moving toward them through the water.

A sense of futility swept over Patrice. She wasn't sure if it came from her own being or whether the river devil had somehow caused it. The children stopped walking with the raft and it drifted down the dark, mottled river over the cobblestones, Francois still singing that awful song.

"We've got to get back to him," Patrice said.

"How?"

No one replied.

If they didn't find their way to Francois soon, get him off that bayou, he would surely die. Patrice looked and saw that her river devil had moved through the water and was by her side, its lips peeled back to a sneer.

"You think yourself different from me. Here you're the same. Really, always you are the same."

Patrice refused to look at the hated thing but she could see Guy and Gilbert were stealing glances. Hard to blame them. Ignoring these creatures seemed pointless. In the real world, to look upon a devil was to inflame it and undermine it. But once the briar set in, the devil demanded attention.

Patrice straightened. "Where's Rosie?"

Guy and Gilbert turned.

Patrice looked to either side, then spun in a circle. "Rosie? Rosie!"

The buildings cast their silhouettes over the water. River devils were creeping up walls of thorns, or bending around their human counterparts. The sun curled away behind a cloud. Marie-Rose was not there.

꧁ ꧂

thirty-five

꧁ ꧂

*T*RIG TOUCHED PATRICE'S SHOULDER. "I'll track Rosie and bring'er back, don't worry."

Patrice liked to believe it, that he could find Rosie. He'd learned tracking from the hunters at Terrefleurs and could find a footprint beneath a crush of pine needles or a tuft of rabbit fur hidden in the cotton bolls. He'd once tracked a jay to its nest because Tatie Bernadette claimed it had stolen a needle. The nest held a coin, a piece of glass, an acorn cap, and lots of dried vine, but no needle—Tatie later found that when she stepped on it on the gallery. Trig knew the droppings of all the animals, wild or domestic. But in the briar, Trigger's talent took on a new quality. He could divide the scent of briar must from that of a river devil or even his siblings. And then, once he located what he wanted, he could bend the space between the here and there to take a closer look.

River devils could find things in a similar way.

Patrice stumbled after Trig as he moved from the river's center to its outer edge, which was lined with buildings. To the children's eyes the flow splashed up and into shops and residences. But in daylight reality they knew there was no water there.

The river devil ran her clawlike nails lightly down Patrice's scalp, and Patrice resisted the urge to wheel around and swat it away. That would have been the same as talking to it. Patrice steeled herself and kept after Trig, feeling graceless and numb with panic. Her feet were stuttering on the cobbled street beneath the river. She kept thinking how Marie-Rose wouldn't have chased the sylph with Francois lying there like that.

Something was stinging her leg—tiny winged briar insects clinging to her stockings. She slapped her thigh but more of them surged up from the rushing water.

"Easy," Gil said, taking her arm and helping her over the submerged cobblestones and toward the water's edge.

As soon as he said it she knew he was speaking the truth: Easy. She had to keep her mind and heart easy. The children might be trapped in the briar for now, but all the skills they'd learned that kept them from getting lost in it still applied—that peaceful core she'd seen in Ferrar one day several months ago. That's where the power was.

The insects drifted away.

Gil said, "Trig'll find her, Treese."

She raised her head and looked him in the eye. "I saw you talking to that man on the street. Earlier, when Rosie and I were singing."

Gil's face clouded.

Patrice said, "You knew him?"

Gil shook his head and tried to stride forward but Patrice took his arm. "And I saw Trigger with his hand in someone else's pocket!"

Gil scowled at her. "Well if you already saw and you already know then what are you asking!"

"You were pickpocketing!"

"What! You think Simms makes money from the dang sheet

music? Come on, Treese! You still tryin to make a hundred dollars from sellin eggs!"

She stared at him.

Gil said, "You were their sylphs, you and Rosie. Sweet baby dolls to distract the folks while we—"

"Stop it. Just stop."

She put her hands to her head and tried to squeeze away the thoughts. The insects returned to her legs, arching their long, slender abdomens to insert their stingers. Useless to slap them. That just attracted more.

She said, "How could you do a thing like that? We left Terrefleurs to get away from evil like—"

"We are evil, Treese! We walk with devils! Bible says God saves man from them, but He never protected us. We are not man."

She shook her head. It hurt to hear him speak that way, the hopelessness in it.

He jammed a finger in the direction of Patrice's river devil. "That thing was right. We are them."

"We're more than that! And we don't have to listen to their sickness unless we want to."

"Is that so? Well here's God's own truth: If Trig and I don't make enough money for Simms he's gonna sell off you and Rosie by the hour."

"Sell off . . . ?"

"It's why we sent them away. Pigeoned all of'm. At first, when he told us we had to pick some pockets to earn our keep, we were so mad we couldn't pigeon'm. Then after y'all started singing it got easier."

She couldn't conceive of what he meant by "sell off." Slavery? But the awareness was already there, even though it hadn't yet formed its shape—something to do with the way Simms had sized her up in Rosie's gown, the fellow in the warehouse who'd kissed her and made her mouth bleed. They'd all been laughing at her and leering at the same time. She felt stupid and naïve, aware they had something particular in mind that she ought to understand, and yet she was still unsure.

"Gil, I don't know what you're talking about. Simms can't sell us to anyone. Not for an hour, not for a second. We'd never stand for it."

"Oh, yeah? What about last night when they stole Papa's automobile? We weren't going to stand for it then. Only reason we escaped with our necks is because we got lucky."

"God stepped in."

Gil looked miserable. "How can you believe that, Treese? How do you know? Just because Tatie Bernadette believes? And the reverend?"

"Because I feel it."

She swallowed, groping in her mind for a stronger argument to back up this statement, but there was nothing more compelling to say than that. She did feel it. What else was there?

Gil softened his tone. "You say we can't use pigeonry because it's the devil's work, but that's exactly what we resort to every time we're in a fix."

"I know."

She took his hand and folded it beneath her fingers. "I'm doing the best I can."

"We are, too."

"Please don't steal again."

"Honey."

"Even when Trigger pigeoned that man for sausages, that was stealing."

Gil shook his head. "I'll tell you a secret. After we got rid of Mother, Trigger made a deal with me. He said if there has to be sin, he and I were gonna be the sinners. He said you should stay clean of it. And I agreed."

"Gil, that's ridiculous!"

"You're the only one who has a chance—"

"Stop it!"

"Well, we got Rosie covered, too, for now. But I think in the end she's gonna be more like us."

"Stop!" Patrice cried.

Gil stopped. His gaze went to the Bible folded across Patrice's chest, then over to his twin. Trigger was staring at a green-painted wall. Patrice could tell by the way he was looking that he had found Rosie.

Bring her here! Patrice thought.

And she knew she could do more than that. She could see what Trigger saw if she would allow the briar to unfold in that way. Tracking was a special skill, like pigeon games. It was the kind of skill Maman was always trying to acquire, but could only get at by proxy through her children or by using crude spells that were never reliable. Skills like tracking, pigeonry, and breathlessness came only through focused exploration. One thing to be lost in the briar; another to explore it. A sin to explore it. To explore was to condone.

But she had to get Rosie and she couldn't just let her brothers continue to carry out her sins by proxy.

She left Gil and moved toward Trig. The muscles in his thin back were tense. All his talk, all his posturing, and yet Trigger was just a little boy. Never was that so obvious than times like now, when he was straining to be something bigger than himself. He alone was supposed to bring back Marie-Rose.

Patrice fixed her gaze on the painted green wall and let it open up the way Trig might look at it. Let it show reflections of their sister— not like some magic mirror, but in an all-encompassing kind of inner knowledge. The thorns moved. They stretched and turned, growing, writhing. They formed the outline of Marie-Rose. But the shape of her was only a small piece of it. The thorns brought the truth of what was happening. Not the sights, smells, sounds. They brought the feeling.

Marie-Rose was far away. A mile or two already, even though

she'd been right here by Patrice's side minutes ago when they'd seen Francois on the raft. Patrice's stomach knotted at this realization. That this time Marie-Rose hadn't just wandered. That this time—

Rosie was in an automobile.

She was with Maman.

That horrible creature made of tar was there, too. Maman was speaking to it. She addressed it with words from her mouth and words from her mind. It had left smudges on Rosie's dress.

Patrice could see beyond her mother and straight into her mother's intentions. Maman had a whole life that she'd built up in New Orleans. She had people who worked for her, bad men. These men would do anything Maman asked of them.

Patrice saw a flash into Rosie's fear. A sudden pain down the back of the neck. A sense of outrage.

Rosie was lashing out. But she was fading from view. The sense of her disappearing behind a cobweb. Patrice focused with everything she could muster. A window splintered into a thousand crystals beneath Rosie's foot. Blood. Pain. Rage. Another cobweb. And another.

And Rosie was gone.

❧

thirty-six

❧

LOUISIANA, NOW

MADELEINE OPENED HER EYES. Her vision was still obscured, trying to see through the silken web. She was nowhere that she recognized. She could make out a cot beneath her, walls of decaying wood, sunlight piercing through knotholes and gaps between boards. No windows. A door, though; she thought she could see a door.

She could barely move. Parts of her body hurt.

No one else was there. Not a soul. That was the first day.

thirty-seven

LOUISIANA, NOW

OMETIME DURING THE NIGHT Madeleine roused. Her bladder, that's what woke her.

She managed to sit up all the way. Her hands were bound behind her back. Not bound by the webs—though they still seemed intact—her hands were bound by actual twine.

But her feet and legs were free, which meant she could stand up and walk about the room. This room, though, wasn't just a room; it seemed to be the entire structure. Some kind of one-room shanty. Black as pitch but for two distinct shards of moonlight. She crept from the cot and kneel-crawled to those shards and they illuminated her jeans, if only a few inches at a time.

"I can't see anything," she said aloud, and her voice sounded froggy.

The effort of crawling that small distance wore her out and she wanted to lie down right there, curl around her moonlight, and go back to sleep. Except she did need to pee.

"Severin," she said.

And she waited. But Severin didn't come.

Wouldn't you know.

The air was fetid and thick and her mouth had a horrible taste. She needed water, too. Water in and water out. Night creatures were making up for the poor visibility by replacing it with sound. Crickets and frogs and birds. Their calls were so rhythmic that in her blindness she could almost see their sound patterns.

What had happened to Ethan and Bo, she wondered. Had Zenon discovered Bo was still alive?

She had to get the hell out of this place.

She remembered there had been a door. Had seen it when she'd opened her eyes during the daylight hours. She mustered her strength and veered toward the wall where the moonlight was coming through, and then backed along it with her fingers feeling her way. She turned a corner filled with cobwebs and kept moving. There.

Her bound hands searched in light hops along the outline of a crossbar until she found a latch. She pulled it and the door squeaked open. Something splashed.

She pushed through. The doorway wasn't full height so she had to lean over, which was fine because she had no energy to stand up straight. The fresh air tasted like heaven.

She ventured the thought: *I'm free.*

But it didn't feel the least bit true.

The shanty was floating. Beneath her feet, the boards formed a raft. It seemed to be anchored because she could see no tether line. A bucket stood just by the door. Her latrine, apparently.

She called, "HELP!" and then listened to her voice disappear into a vast nothing.

Water all around. A very broad expanse, and it reflected stars.

They crawled across the surface in a wake sent by some unseen thing that had just jumped in and was now swimming away. Along a distant shoreline, fragrant trees stood bathed in moon-light.

thirty-eight

HLOE HAD PUT HER out here, of course, though Madeleine couldn't say why. Her mind was so foggy she was having difficulty thinking through any reasoning in it or, for that matter, how to escape. And she couldn't make herself stay awake for long. Pain was usually what roused her. Pain where she was bound or injured or bitten by insects. They swarmed her like she was an abandoned picnic spread—ants, mosquitoes, spiders, flies, beetles— all creeping and buzzing and sampling her. Incessantly.

When she awoke outside the floating shanty at sunrise she found jugs of clean water. They were suspended beneath the surface on trap lines tied to the raft. She needed only to hoist one up and drink from it, though having her hands tied behind her back made it a distinct pain. She used her feet and knees and teeth and bound hands. The sunrise drink of water seemed immediately followed by a sunset, and nothing but sleep and unbearable heat in between.

And then the sunrise-heat-sunset pattern started over again, and again, and Madeleine realized she ought to have kept count. There couldn't have been more than three or four days, or . . . five.

Her body was hurting. The scratch on the back of her neck seemed to reopen itself again and again. Sometimes she awoke to fresh pain there. The inability to move her arms had gone from discomfort to soreness to excruciating pain that went back down to dull again.

The first jug of water was already empty and it now floated above the surface like a fishing bob.

No food.

But after that came the day when it rained, and that's when things started to change.

A THUNDER CLAP DESPITE burning sunlight. The shanty was suffocatingly hot and she'd left the door open to allow in the breeze. Still no thorns, no silver mist. There had been no sign of Severin or any bramble since she'd been wrapped by the spiders.

White sunlight from the doorway threw a coffin shape on the flooring, the glare so bright that everything else had turned black except for the ceiling. There, dancing hoops of sunlight reflected up from the water. She stared at the patterns, and then realized that there was a person up there. Up above.

She sat up with a start.

He was high in the corner where the walls met the ceiling, his arms and legs spread like a tree frog. He began to move when she sat up, creeping along the ceiling toward the center of the roof. His features were obscured in the dark. All she could see were his wide, light eyes and an unruly beard.

"What do you want?" she said.

That's when she saw the blade in his hand.

She threw herself off the cot and back-scooted to the wall but he dropped down in front of her, blocking the door. He raised the blade.

She screamed. She braced herself against the wall and kicked at his hand. The blade sliced into her ankle and she screamed again.

She tried to get a fix on his mind. Tried to pigeon him. Nothing—slippery as a lumen though she saw no light.

But he was pausing. The glaring sun behind him, he was only a silhouette. Shirtless and barefoot with hair that looked like he'd cut it with that same knife, wearing just a pair of trousers that had been torn to the knees.

He raised the blade again. But as Madeleine braced herself to try another kick, the metal caught the sunlight and reflected back into her eyes. They teared over. She blinked and turned her head away. He moved the blade ever so slightly, keeping the glare trained on her eyes. On her face.

She moved along the wall until she had jammed herself into the corner, heedless of the cobwebs that stuck to her hair and the wounds on the back of her neck. Of which, she was certain now, there were more than one.

His posture had settled. He no longer seemed about to spring at her. Instead he sank to a crouch, and he'd let the hand with the blade rest across his knees. He turned his head and looked out over the water. Ripples of light reflected on his face and she saw that he was very young. Perhaps a teenage boy. Skinny as a whip.

And then he was gone. She was barely aware of him moving, she just felt the raft tilt and heard the splash.

thirty-nine

LOUISIANA, NOW

SHE SLEPT. OR PERHAPS, lost consciousness. Rain was pouring down outside the shanty and through various points in the roof. The slice in her ankle felt hot.

She needed rather urgently to use the latrine. She hoisted herself up from the corner and made her way out of her jeans, then stumbled out into the rain. A sudden cramp hit her before she could manage to position herself over the bucket. She went down, falling sideways on the raft, and her bladder released involuntarily, a fierce pain in its wake. She shuddered as it squeezed and then subsided. A urinary tract infection.

She closed her eyes and let the downpour wash her. Tears welled up and flushed away. Her body was a series of fevers—on her ankle, in her bladder, in the cuts at the back of her neck—and she was also beginning to feel a sinister kind of tickle in her ear.

If Chloe wanted her dead she wouldn't have gone to all this

trouble to stash her away on this raft. Yet that strange boy had clearly intended to kill her, and then for whatever reason, had changed his mind. It made no sense.

And why, at the one time when she actually wanted it, was she unable to evoke the briar?

Even if she were to brave an escape off this raft, knowing that she could now hold her breath for extended periods of time, she could never muster enough strength to make it to shore with her hands bound. Nor would she know where to turn once she got there.

Madeleine realized she was sobbing now as the rain washed over her. But what terrified her the most were the thoughts of Ethan and Bo. Without her help—her bird's eye view from the briar and her skills in the pigeon exercises—Ethan and Bo had no defense against Zenon.

Having vowed to look after Bo, Ethan would protect him to the death. This was the thought she could not bear.

forty

NEW ORLEANS, 1927

ACK IN 1925, WORKERS had driven pilings into the Mississippi River floor to begin construction for a great bridge. The local authority had had no budget and no real belief that they could actually build it. This had simply been a way to convert a dream to some kind of material stage.

But, in driving those pilings, they established the right through the current congressional authority to initiate real construction.

Each time the ferry crossed the river, its passengers would comment on the pilings that waited to support a "someday bridge"—even after the workers faded away and the job site had gone quiet for months, a skeleton of something that had never been born.

No wonder that, two years later, the project had halted. There was no money for this bridge. But now the people and the politicians shared a common idea—even though some doubted it could ever be a sound one—the point was that the idea existed for all to share.

Patrice shared it. She and her siblings had heard the commentators through the radio back at Terrefleurs. Some had been inspired, speaking of an innovative modern age. Others had criticized the effort as a frivolity that had no real hope of manifestation. Especially now, after the floods of this past spring of 1927, when the Mississippi River had roused and shaken like a dog, tossing away man-made adornments. It had taken their father's life, among so many others.

The bridge site had attracted men who came looking for work, even though it was common knowledge that construction had stalled. There was of course no work available now. But those who needed laborers knew they could come to the bridge site to hire hands, and so a kind of work camp had emerged of its own.

ROSIE'S TRAIL HAD GONE cold. Even Trigger couldn't find her anymore.

Patrice didn't ask the thing that she feared most: *Did Mother kill her?*

There was no one to ask.

But Rosie wasn't dead. She couldn't be. There remained a well of stillness inside Patrice's heart, one that kept reason despite the panic. If Marie-Rose were dead, then they'd be able to find her body. Their mother had concealed her somehow. It had to do with that scratch down the nape.

In many ways, Maman was no match for them. The children inherited the ability to walk the briar from Papa. This had always frustrated Maman. Maybe the jealousy she felt for her own children was what embittered her toward them. But though Maman might not be able to direct the briar the way her children could, she did have tricks.

"We gotta go after her," Gil said.

Trigger said, "Where? All I know is where I saw her when she disappeared."

"So that's where we go!"

"She was in an automobile, driving, and I don't know where she's goin."

"So find her! You're the tracker!"

Trigger hesitated.

Patrice raised her hands to her cheeks and shook her head. "Even if we could find her, we wouldn't be able to get her back. Maman was there with a mess of crooks at her beck and call. If we go after Rosie now it'll be like last night, only it'll end badly. We can't face off against all of them. We're not even in their world right now. Our bodies are, but we're . . . here. In the briar."

Trigger nodded. "I think Maman's laid a trap to try to get us all one by one."

Gil's face had gone completely ashen, and he stared first at Trigger and then Patrice as though waiting for one of them to say something that would resolve it all. The cunning plan.

Patrice returned her brother's stare and then had to drop her gaze. Her throat had gone stiff. She didn't dare think of Rosie's face.

"Find Ferrar," was all she could get out.

Trigger needed no further prompt. He turned to the wall and began the same method he'd used when he went looking for Rosie.

Gil said, "Criminy, Treese, what's Ferrar gonna do for us?"

"He'll help us. We need it. Especially now that we're stuck in the briar. He's the only one who'll understand what's happened to us. He can be our ears and eyes."

"Treese! He's a lumen and we're surrounded by river devils! Don't you think there might be trouble?"

"We have to take that chance! Ferrar can help us get Rosie back and go hide. He knows all the little islands and coves along the entire Gulf from when he was running liquor for Maman."

"Meanwhile we're just leaving Rosie behind! With Maman!"

"It isn't as though I want to! I'm all ears, Gil! Let's hear your better idea!"

His cheeks went dark and he turned away.

Trigger turned back to them and said, "I found Ferrar. A few miles away."

Gil snorted. Patrice dearly wished they were not in the briar now that they knew where Ferrar was. She should have let Trigger do this right from the start instead of trying to walk some ridiculous line of morality.

Trig said, "He's at the bridge. Just like that man told Gil. Only, there's no bridge there."

Patrice shook her head. "It's under construction. That's what they said on the radio."

"Alright then. We just head in the direction of the Mississippi and then follow her curve for a few miles."

"And how do we manage that?" Gil said. He had a pinch to his lip, and he looked like he was about to collapse from pure nerves.

"We walk!"

"Which? Our bodies or our minds? Remember last night? All those people trying to get at us? It'll be like that, only worse, because we're here in the briar and our stupid bodies are off on some dang daisy walk!"

Trigger took off his hat and rubbed his head. Patrice let loose her breath. Because Gil had a point—the physical world was holding solid for them only in glimpses. They couldn't traverse the distance because the briar held their ghosts, and their bodies would be walking blind and mad. Who knew what sorts of criminals might be lurking along that road? The children couldn't go after Rosie, and they couldn't travel to Ferrar. They were trapped.

The briar mist had curled away any sense of direct sunlight. Time was so difficult to track that there was no telling whether minutes had passed since Patrice and Rosie had been singing in the street—and it really only felt like ten minutes—or it might have been hours. Nighttime or day? There was only briar light now. River devils and other creatures milled about. The city had receded so far behind the thorns and the black pines and cypress and the mist, and that relentless river's flow—it seemed like the once-vibrant New Orleans boulevard had become like a long-abandoned antebellum home down a wooded lane.

Gil said, "I got it."

"What?"

"We'll be missionaries again."

Trigger lifted his head.

"I don't understand," Patrice said.

Gil flung his arm toward the street. "We'll just do like in the rail yard. Hold the Bible and sing Christian songs the entire way to the bridge. They're all afraid of church people round here."

"You make it sound like superstition!" Patrice said.

Trig and Gil said nothing.

Patrice said, "Using those songs to fool people into thinking we're doing the Lord's work, it's akin to using His name in vain."

"Aw, come on, Treese. It *is* the Lord's work. Think of it like sa-yin a prayer, over and over. Put your heart into it and God won't pay mind to a little lagniappe."

Trigger said, "We might as well try. People see our bodies walkin the road, they'll leave us alone."

"But our bodies will just get lost." Patrice said.

Gil shook his head. "We only have to concentrate on both worlds enough to keep our bodies following along the road. Don't strain too hard beyond that. We can move along a road, at least."

How could she argue? With Rosie snatched from them and Ferrar the only one who could help, she would do anything to get to that bridge.

PATRICE RECALLED A LEGEND told about a family friend, Jacob Chapman, who'd been mauled by an alligator long ago at Terrefleurs, and as a result his hand had had to be amputated. The country doctor hadn't been carrying any anesthetic in his bag. And so, legend had it that

Jacob Chapman and Papa liquored themselves up and sang through the entire procedure.

This supposedly happened before Patrice was born, and Patrice wasn't sure she believed it. How could you keep singing during a thing like that?

But there was something to it. There was the off-handed kind of singing like when Patrice was trying to make chores seem less odious. And then there was the kind of singing where she was careful with every note, the quality of tone, exaggerating the formation of her lips, and taking deliberate shape of a sustained intonation that ended in vibrato. It didn't matter whether she was a good singer or not—it was the consciousness of the act. This was what transformed singing into a peaceful, powerful experience.

Maybe not enough to distract a man from having his gangrenous hand sawn off.

But to sing in the right way was to engage in the kind of place that Ferrar had once shown her. A pure, still lake. It dissipated chaos. Patrice was able to see beyond worry—a river devil's enterprise—and beyond her thoughts and the infinite distractions.

The three children walked for miles, singing hymns and holding Francois' Bible, which was now their only possession aside from the clothes they wore.

forty-one

*I*T WAS PROBABLY NIGHT. Patrice guessed this because when she forced her concentration on the physical world she could smell campfire smoke. To concentrate in this way was like trying to swim while very, very tired. A few moments and then you had to stop and take a breath.

At the bridge site, near where the ferry ran, Patrice smoothed her hand over a post that held fresh carvings. They looked similar to those that she'd often seen in the briar.

Papa?

"It's how they find their way out on the road," Trigger said.

Patrice looked again at the symbol. An open rectangle. She wondered what it meant, but then realized that Trig had said "they," and she looked toward the clearing where the smoke originated. A smattering of camps with men cooking hoecake and soup.

"Ferrar," she said.

Because he was probably out there among them. This thought was confirmed by the way the river devils looked: the tension, the predatory crouch. Patrice felt a coupled sense of thrill and dread.

It occurred to her how shocking she must look. She stepped out of her shoes and turned toward the ferry dock, splashing into the river.

"Treesey, hold up!" Gil said.

But he and Trig were already stepping out of their own shoes and following after her. The water brought her physical senses to life—the smell of mud and reeds, the feel of the Mississippi River crushing against her skin. She washed her face as best she could with bare hands, and then she rubbed herself from her neck down her arms, at her underarms, around her breasts and down her belly, between her legs, down her legs, finishing with her feet. She tilted her face toward the sky and scrubbed her hair in backward sweeps that both cleaned and smoothed. And she bobbed above and below the surface, in and out of the briar, in and out of the physical world. Until she saw Ferrar.

He was up on the dock. She recognized him in an instant though he was just a wavering shadow that might be a dream. But he came closer and in doing so grew larger, went down on his knee, reached straight toward her.

She reached up. They clasped their hands together and held, neither of them saying a word.

In the briar light, that lumen quality of his made him look like an angel, even with that scarred eye. It felt like he had one eye looking at her and another that was made of stars. His expression showed surprise and delight. His eyes were wide, pupils dilated.

She took a breath to speak but then stopped. Because anything she said would break this spell. It felt like something had opened up all around her. As though a light had poured through the lens of her body to the lens of her mind and converged to illuminate the spirit. Neither briar nor physical world. Just a vast, eternal something that she couldn't define.

"Hello there, old socks!" Trigger called.

It brought Patrice back to her surroundings. Or at least closer to them. She smiled at Ferrar and he grinned back.

Gil said, "We came a long way to find you!"

But Ferrar never took his gaze from Patrice, and never loosened his grip. He pulled her up from the Mississippi's waters and onto the ferry dock.

HE FED THEM SOMETHING he called "bullets" but were actually just beans. Patrice kept stealing glances at him: black skin like hers, blood-shined eye, the crisscross over the throat. His appearance had frightened her when she'd first met him. Now it made him seem invincible. Everything about him was fascinating. She even loved the way he spoke: a French accent—not so thick as their mother's—laced with a soft, familiar, River Road twang.

The children ate every last bite and Patrice was mortified when Ferrar solicited some of the men from other campfires for more food. Despite the fact that they were camping by the river, no one along these banks seemed desperate. They were simply here to work where wages were competitive. Every day, farmers and foremen from three separate parishes crossed on the ferry or came up from the road to seek labor.

There were river devils everywhere. Everywhere.

Patrice tried to ignore them but they were agitated by Ferrar's presence. It took all of Patrice's concentration just to stay in conversation with Ferrar. She knew she wouldn't be able to sustain for long. And so she poured out their story, told him all about Maman's return and Rosie's disappearance. She told him about the stranger Trig had killed.

"What did he look like?" Ferrar asked.

Patrice told him. She remembered the blood on the man's lips and the gurgling he'd made when Trig crushed his windpipe with a stool. But mostly she remembered that hair. Not as she saw him in the fruit cellar. She remembered the patch that showed from beneath the horse blanket when Gil had opened the barn door. The brown hair tinged with red and gold in a single ray of sunlight.

Ferrar said, "I know him. Had to run hooch with him a few times. He's the one who did the collecting when folks owed your mother money."

The children looked at one another. They'd already suspected that the stranger had worked for Maman.

Ferrar said, "Name's Bruce Dempsey. I never liked to turn my back to him. They called him The Brute."

"But why would he have come for us?" Gil asked.

"To bring you to your mother, I imagine. Alls I can say beyond that is if he was the one comin for you it wasn't gonna be for kindness."

They were quiet for a moment. It sounded like the Mississippi was rushing past the banks but it had to be the wind in the trees making that shushing noise. The Mississippi usually went easy. Easy.

Easy, Patrice thought, because the river devils were whispering at their hosts. The devils were much more vivid than the humans, who were just shadows. Why was it so difficult to keep the briar away? She was concentrating so hard that surely her physical body was in a sweat.

Trigger cocked his head and squinted upriver.

Patrice said, "We came looking for you because we didn't know where else to go. But, our being here makes it dangerous for you."

"I'll do whatever I can to help y'all."

"We've got to get Rosie back."

Gil and Trig were already slipping, the way their gazes kept darting from one point to the next. Patrice tried her best to listen and look past the briar to Ferrar in the physical world.

And she was aware that his knee was touching hers. Such a small thing. A circle of skin no larger than a Mercury dime. She was still

wearing that idiotic dress of Rosie's. She looked at Ferrar, and he
smiled and lowered his gaze to the fire, going shy.

She said, "We've got to hide. At least until we get our wits back.
Then we can find her and go get her. I never wanted my brothers to
improve their pigeon games but I've got to work with them if we're
ever going to find Rosie."

"Why didn't you? Why wouldn't you want them to improve their
pigeon games?"

Patrice frowned, and the briar surged around her. She resisted
the urge to fight it and instead focused on Ferrar's face and the firelight, letting the briar come forth and then recede again of its own.
There, she saw him again in clear focus.

She hadn't answered his question, but he said, "How do you
know these things aren't from God?"

She was surprised to hear it. "You of all people should know. The
day we met you we nearly killed you. Because Maman was trying to
make a point."

"But you didn't kill me. You used the skill instead to drive your
mother out."

"Treesey," Gil said, but his voice was so soft it barely registered.

Ferrar said, "What can I do now, tonight, to help you?"

"We need to find someplace safe to wait out this time in the briar.
And then we must go get my sister back."

Ferrar was thoughtful. Patrice knew she couldn't keep this up
much longer. She put her hand to her throat, regretting the amount
of time it had taken her to get her story out.

She looked at Ferrar. *Just tell me someplace where we can go!*

Ferrar said, "Bayou Bouillon."

She closed her eyes and relaxed a hitch.

He said, "You remember."

"Mm, you told me about Bayou Bouillon once before. Good
place to hide."

"The best, but . . ."

"Can you get us there?"

Ferrar's face had taken on a strange expression. "You sure you haven't been there? It's so full of ghosts."

"Patrice!" Gil said.

He and Trigger both were on their feet now, staring toward another camp.

Patrice said, "Please, how do we get there? We're running out of time."

"It's far. The only way to get there is by boat. I have only shoes." He pointed at the thick leather soles.

But Patrice rose to her feet with her fists balled. The briar was pulling her down to it. Gil was calling her. Trig.

She said, "Ferrar, just show me where this Bayou Bouillon is."

He frowned and rose to join her. "About fifty miles that way. But you can't get to it by—"

"*Think* of this place. As though you're there!"

He looked confused, but he listened. She knew because she saw Bayou Bouillon now inside him.

Oh, this briar! Easier now to search inside a man's heart than to say hello.

A very secluded village where people existed outside of any law. Bayou Bouillon. Full of ghosts. This was a place where the water boiled cold. She saw the gentlest, finest bubbles, the swirling eddies. A boardwalk and floating one-room shanties with roofs made of accordion tin.

Was she holding Ferrar's hands? She wished he could pull her through to him the way he'd pulled her up from the water beneath the ferry dock. She strove for that one last glimpse of him and of the physical world. She just couldn't force her way through again. Her focus collapsed.

Too soon. Far too soon. Because the river devils, each and every one of them, had been occupying themselves with the men of the camps. Whispering. All this time, whispering to all those men.

Gil looked at Patrice and was shaking his head. "We shouldn't have come. We're going to get him killed."

The devils hated Ferrar. They saw to it that their hosts hated him, too. Wished him dead. Patrice remembered how Rosie's river devil had hated him. Ferrar was a lumen. He opposed chaos just by existing.

"Patrice, you hear it?" Gil said.

Yes. Patrice turned her ear toward the river. Francois.

Every night.

He sang out one line and went quiet.

She listened for him. Listened so carefully she could hear the heartbeat pounding in her own body.

When the sun goes in.

There, Francois sang out again. Just the one line.

Patrice looked toward the Mississippi, gone now, and in its place only the shadow river that coursed through the briar. She saw the raft. It drifted toward them.

Trigger sprang toward the riverbanks.

"It's no use!" Patrice called after him.

A hand on her physical body. Someone was clutching her wrist.

She said, "Ferrar, is that you? If you can hear me, look around you. They hate you. They want you dead. I'm so sorry."

The river devils were hesitating. Patrice had seen them react to Ferrar before. She knew how his lumen quality could replicate itself inside of her and the others, and dispel whatever whispers or sickness the river devils tried to spread. She opened her heart and waited for that sense of peace to come.

Every night.

Trigger was now splashing into the river. "Francois! Ho there, Francois! Hear me?"

Patrice dared a look at the raft where she knew she'd see that awful vulture. She wanted the thing to look at her. She just wished he'd stop looking at Francois.

When the sun goes in.

The dead stranger—Bruce Dempsey, as Ferrar had called him— still lay in a heap of blankets now torn to rags by the vulture.

The river devils erupted into fury all around them. Those who were wanderers were in the trees. Those with human hosts were shoving, goading. And she knew what they wanted. They would keep at their hosts until someone attacked Ferrar.

I hang down my head.

The vulture leaned over Francois. He finally stopped singing and simply wept. He did not lift a hand against the thing. He probably couldn't. Trigger was swimming toward the raft.

Something else. The creature that looked like it was covered in tar. She sensed it before she saw it. She turned. It was folding its horrible, filthy arms around Gil.

"No!"

Gil bucked and tried to wrench away from the thing. But it had him. Was dragging him down into the slick of oil or tar or whatever muck it had come from. It had the feel of Maman in it somehow. Like she was spying. This was her crude, brute magic, but her beast had taken Rosie and now it had Gil.

"Gil!"

But he was gone already.

Just like that.

Gone.

Patrice dug her nails into her scalp and screamed.

Thornflies were swarming her. They came up from the river, that dark, coursing bramble flow. Trigger had reached the raft and was looking back. He probably didn't even know his twin had been taken. Patrice had no idea what was happening to Ferrar somewhere in the physical world. With all those river devils focusing their fury on him he could very well be dead.

The vulture raised its head from Francois and turned its gaze to Patrice.

Let the river swallow you! she called to it from within her mind.

She stepped toward it. Someone was pulling her physical body backward. Ferrar? Or some other fool who'd been listening to river devil whispers?

Or the creature made of tar.

The river formed a wake that rolled down its center instead of outward toward the shore.

Yes. Let the river swallow us all.

The river's wake rolled on itself and then folded again, turning in a circle. The raft turned. The water coursed afresh with a higher flow. She felt her physical body kicking, but whoever had her was not letting go. Not the tar creature. Someone in the physical world. The tar creature was long gone now, and so was Gil.

The water was surging at her ankles. It had reared up from banks and was sweeping over the campsites. Fickle river devils abandoned their goading, chiding and danced in the chaos of the water. They called for panic among their hosts.

The raft was turning in a wide circle. Trigger was on it, now, his hands on Francois' shoulder.

Patrice felt her physical body go slack, and she knew that the water had knocked her off her feet. She let it pull her toward the center. Toward the raft, which had tilted toward the sky and then disappeared.

forty-two

*I*N A STRANGE KIND of way, Madeleine's urinary tract infection made itself useful. The frequent need for the latrine forced her to rise up from her cot and walk outside. She also made herself drink water every hour to keep her system flushing. Movement was good, she thought. It made her breathe deeply, caused the blood to circulate. The breath, the blood, the water; all in constant, cleansing flow.

The early evening rain subsided to a fresh drizzle. Daylight diffused through the clouds and lit the inside of the shanty in soft tones of gray.

She felt the raft rock beneath her, and she sat up. The strange boy was standing there, dripping wet, in the doorway.

She said, "Go away!"

He blinked at her. He looked like he was about to say something.

But then he turned and slipped back into the water and was gone. Like a ghost.

Madeleine was striving to stay alert now. The lack of food had left her weak and sluggish, and her injuries kept her in a constant state of pain. She listened for signs of the boy returning but heard nothing but the usual evening dissonance. The sun gave her a scarlet sunset as it sank over the bayou, underlighting the remaining clouds with deep vermillion and sending a fan of crepuscular rays heavenward. She watched it all. The sun finally disappeared and the daylight trailed off behind it, leaving complete darkness. No moonrise yet. The clouds blocked the stars.

She realized she was kneeling beside her cot. No recollection as to when or why she'd positioned herself there, or for how long. Her knees were so stiff she realized hours must have somehow fled by. Her hands were raw behind her back, and the mosquitoes fed relentlessly. The sounds that carried across from the shore—the chirruping of frogs and crickets, and the night birds' calls—they all converged together into a single rhythm. Pulses of unified sound with silence in between. She listened, fascinated. Her mouth had gone slack. The shanty itself seemed to twitch with that sound. She realized she was not alone.

"Who's here?" she asked aloud.

No reply. Just the pulsing dissonance. Madeleine's breathing grew shallow, because she knew what had come. Not the boy. The coldness. The void that had filled her in the briar, a disembodied thing that had become embodied in her, until Bo had wrapped his arms around her and pushed it out again.

She felt something move over her jeans where she knelt. A slow, dragging motion. She crawled backward to the wall and pushed herself against it. She couldn't hear it move. It found her again. It wound its way up to her waist, light flicks of a serpentine tongue at the skin of her arms.

A voice, neither male nor female, said, "Almost."

She cried out, terrified, as it moved up over her shoulder. The thing was not the void but it had traveled in on its coldness. She felt it bite the back of her neck and she screamed. She drew in her breath and screamed again, quaking, letting her fear travel with that long, drawn scream over the bayou, ending in a sob.

But the thing had made its bite, and its body was now unraveling from her.

A sense of déjà vu. Had this happened on previous nights?

"What do you want?" she shrieked.

A silence, and she gulped back tears.

Then, the voice came again. "You are given a chance. You may live if you choose."

Madeleine felt her throat go numb in dread, but the familiar sleep was stealing over her.

The thing said, "Tell us where to find the infant."

Madeleine cried, "What infant?"

The chirps of the bayou creatures continued their pulsing, louder now.

This time, another voice came in reply: "Your brother's child. Tell us, or you die here, alone."

"Oh God, Chloe? Are you doing this? I'm your blood!"

But she knew it wasn't Chloe she was talking to. And it wasn't a bayou serpent, or the cold void. She was talking to all of these. They had somehow come together the way a great fungus can permeate beneath the soil and taint several fields of crops at once.

She heard, "If you choose to live, you will see all and know all, and you will be elevated above all men."

"If I find out where the baby is for you, what will you do to him?"

She listened for the answer. The spiders were at their wrapping again. No further reply came. Only the distant pulse of the night creatures, still unnaturally aligned. The silence between each call was the most dreadful thing Madeleine had ever known.

THE NEXT SUNRISE, SHE awoke on the floor again. The pains of her body were such that she was retching before she'd opened her eyes. A relief, at least, to be able to see if only in the gray shimmer of dawn. She looked at it rolling beyond the doorway and saw turtles sitting at the end of the raft. They slipped over the side and into the bayou even as she watched.

And then the immediate need for the latrine had her lurching forward, fighting her way to the door, determined not to wet her jeans. For some reason it seemed a matter of life and death that she preserve that single dignity.

The breeze outside was fresh on her face. In the diffused light of morning fog, she could see a crusted brown line that ran forward from the back of her neck around to her chest. She managed to get out of her jeans and over the bucket, and then it was done. She braced herself for the painful squeeze that came after.

The fog was so heavy this morning that there was no visible shoreline. It felt cool, though, and smelled light.

She pulled her jeans back up using her thumbs as a combined hook where her hands were tied, and then began the labor of wrestling the water jug from the trap line. Ignoring the pains. Forcing her stiffened body to move.

But then something stopped inside her. And she couldn't. Just couldn't.

The trap line slipped through her fingers and the jug floated backward on some unseen current below. She was shaking. Her body wouldn't stop. She couldn't make it stop.

"Help me!" she called out over the bayou. "Please! Boy! Please come back!"

She lay down on the raft. She wasn't going to pull that jug out of the water again. Because she couldn't. Her breaths were coming in shudders. She had so little strength.

The coldness that stole in on her last night, it was madness. And it—they—wanted her brother's baby. Little Cooper, the last child of the briar after herself and Zenon. She realized, then, why she'd been kept in such a state. Starved, sickened, injured. She was probably much more compliant now than she might have been when it all began.

She knew she had to leave.

She was going into that damn bayou. She had to chance it. See how far she could swim while holding her breath. She should have done it on the first day, the very first sunrise. She would have had more strength then than she had now.

She positioned herself at the edge. Took a long breath. And then she tilted forward.

⚘

THE WATER ACCEPTED HER with a whisper. Her legs were kicking sideways like a frog's but with her hands still tied she had so little control, and it took all her strength just to keep upright as she went down, down. Not forward. Not forward at all. Her body sank at an astonishing speed.

She looked up and saw the surface disappearing, the light above shrinking so that it resembled the opening to a rabbit hole, and all around was speckled green and gold and brown. Bubbles rose in lazy drifts.

This wouldn't do. She had to move forward, not down. Even with her ability to hold a very long breath she would eventually run out of air. But the more she kicked and tried to propel herself, the faster her reserves drained away.

She steeled herself, making herself quit the frog-flails, and she kicked in rhythmic propulsion. Her body was dropping fast but she was at least falling at an angle now, not straight down.

Only, she'd lost track of which way was shore.

Ridiculous! What was she going to do, walk the entire aimless distance along the bayou floor?

Her head thrown back, she was tempted to scream, that hole of light above seemed so very far away.

She didn't even see him coming. The boy. His face flickering in bends of light. He seized her bicep and she let out the scream that had been locked inside. It flew muted in a volley of bubbles. That knife was between his teeth, his hair and beard waving on end toward the surface.

The scream had forced the air from her lungs and she now began to convulse, feeling the bayou wash into her air passages. He had the knife out of his mouth and was cutting the twine that bound her wrists. Her body lurched upward. He had her by the armpit. She kicked her legs and together they surged toward the surface, her hands clawing for the sky.

They broke free to fresh air. She gagged and spat and he watched her as though she were some kind wild animal.

She wanted to say thank you to him, but all she could do was gasp each single breath one at a time. She pulled her arms forward, her arms that had been forced behind her back for days on end, and she put her hands over her eyes, weeping.

But even as she labored through the ragged breaths she realized something odd about it. Each shudder came at a specific cadence. She stopped. Forced herself to be quiet, listening. Because she'd been breathing along with the sounds of the bayou. The night creatures. It wasn't morning at all. It was still dead of night. And this fog had come from the briar.

forty-three

O N THE DISTANT SHORE, Madeleine could hear Severin singing, though she couldn't hear precisely what she was singing. Only that her voice came in pulses with the night creatures. The boy took Madeleine's arms and pulled them over his shoulders, and he swam with her across the fog-spun surface. The duckweed had encroached, which might have seemed a natural part of the bayou but for their telltale swirls of red among the green. The briar's duckweed. She was seeing the river devil world layered over the material world, which often made things confusing. She didn't know how Zenon could stand it.

Madeleine could not feel her arms nor make a fist and she wasn't entirely sure how she was hanging on to this boy, but she was. And he bore her load. He brought her to a sandy bank where they rested, silent, looking across the distance to where the shanty winked in and out of sight through the fog. Severin's voice sounded closer now. Still pulsing with the frogs and crickets, singing:

One
Pigeon
Two
Crow
Three
Rot
Four
Slow

The boy turned to Madeleine and said, "You can walk?"

It surprised her to hear him speak. She wasn't sure what she might have expected but his voice sounded like that of any other teenage boy, except his words lacked enunciation.

"Yes, I can walk. Let's go." But the second she rose to her feet she was down again.

He grabbed her by the arm. "Well, ma'am, I can see you're a big fat liar."

She looked at him and saw satisfaction on his face. He positioned himself at the side of her cut ankle and slung her arm over his shoulder, lifting her at the armpit so that he could help bear her weight as she walked.

She eyed his skinny frame. "You can't just drag me along like this. We'll never make it very far."

"Well, you talkin true that time at least. But we ain't got far to go, don't have far."

It took her a moment to process the peculiar way he spoke. "We don't?"

"No ma'am. We here."

"Here?"

But there was nothing here. Only massive cypress trees— not giants like in the true briar, but these were very tall and wide. No cabin, no shanty. And no ground for that matter. The bank where they'd been resting made a thin arm that wound into the woods, but the boy was leading her away from that and towards a flooded expanse of swamp. The water meandered between each tree with the roots rising up in knees like moons orbiting a planet.

"I must not be seeing right," she mumbled, thinking the briar was hiding the material world.

"You seein just fine. Dead of night and ain't no moon, moon isn't out, but you can see. We in a *cyprière*. This here's my tree." He patted the huge gray cypress behind him.

"You can see out here, too?"

"How much seein you need to do to swim across a lake and climb an old tree?"

She shook her head, looking out toward the shanty where it floated in the lake. "It's not going to work. We're too close to that shanty out there. Chloe'll—I mean, *they* will be able to find me."

He released her arm and leaned her against the tree like she was a bicycle. "You worried that old witch Chloe gonna find you if you stay here?"

She nodded. "She can and she will."

"So where you gonna hide that she can't find you?"

Madeleine stared at him.

He said, "Even if you walked seven leagues and buried yourself in a cold empty grave she gonna find you."

Madeleine turned and looked back at the floating shanty. The fog kept shifting around it. Now only the roof was visible, now it disappeared completely.

She said, "You know Chloe."

He gave a huff. "Much to my detriment. Alright, little lady, now I can't carry you up there. You just gonna have to figure out how to climb it on your own."

She was already leaning on the tree but as she turned, she paused.

He said, "What now?"

"Nothing, just . . . I'm Madeleine."

"Enchanted. I'm Gaston." He took her hand in both of his and gave a half bow, a near-ludicrous gesture given his age and their mutual state of dishevelment. "Now kindly get moving, Miss Madeleine."

She turned back to the tree and lifted her foot onto the lowest protrusion. The roots and limbs made it easy to manage. She used her hands to brace herself but she might as well have been leaning on baguettes, her arms felt so useless. They also felt like they were crawling with ants right down to the bone marrow.

She stumbled, and Gaston helped, and then they were up the tree. Actually, it wasn't so much a matter of climbing it as circling it. The tree was hollow at the bottom. There was a wide triangular groove at water level, and just above that was a more deliberately hollowed-out space with a level floor. She climbed up into that and Gaston followed.

She said, "What now?"

He shrugged. "Sleep if you like. I'll get you somethin to eat."

She looked around. The hollow was almost as big as the shanty. The other trees were fairly close, probably hopping distance for Gaston, and they were draped in Spanish moss.

She looked, and saw movement. A figure in the trees. She nudged Gaston.

He looked in the direction she was staring. "You just now catching sight of him?"

But as Madeleine stared, the figure seemed to blend into the Spanish moss.

Gaston said, "Can't say he relishes your being here. He ain't gonna bother you too much, though, he won't bother you. That one's attached to me."

And then he gestured down below where Madeleine now saw Severin scooping duckweed and swimming toward the shaded *cyprière*. "Besides, looks like you got your own."

She regarded him. "You can see the river devils?"

"I can see mine. Yours I can only partly see if I don't look at it directly. Unless I'm in a state. I'll be back with some food."

And then he was moving down the tree like a daddy longlegs, and he was gone.

❧

SHE HAD FALLEN ASLEEP again by the time he returned. The smell of food woke her. Outside was full daylight. He brought corn mash and duck soup, and she got the impression that the duck had just been shot or trapped or wrastled, or whatever it was a half-naked hermit boy did when he wanted to procure a duck.

The insects were incessant with their hovering but Madeleine had grown used to that over the past several days, and she was so relieved to have actual food that nothing else mattered.

"Go easy," Gaston said.

She knew he was right. The rich duck was golden on the palate but lead in the belly.

Her hands had been tied behind her back so long that she all but couldn't use them, and she had to hug the bowl with her arms in order to drink from it.

She looked at Gaston and for the first time, truly examined his face. It struck her that this boy was about the same age as the huffers who had been harassing Bo. Oyster had that posturing, self-conscious teenage way about him, although there was still quite a lot of awkwardness in his expression and in the way he carried his not-yet-full-grown body. In Gaston, there was nothing awkward. And certainly no self-consciousness. She pondered a thousand questions about him, questions she would not ask because she couldn't bring herself to slow down on the soup and corn mash. She knew the moment she set down the polished tupelo bowl she would fall right back to sleep.

And Severin, after not being around for a week or so, why was she not demanding attention?

Gaston pointed at a great willow tree beyond the opening. "There's your privy, OK Miss Madeleine? You just walk along that branch and there's a place to sit. Far sight better than the old one, which was just a goat-smellin stump."

She stared at it, and then nodded. Her bowl was empty.

"You fallin asleep again."

She opened her eyes, surprised to find that they'd closed.

He said, "That ole witch put the scratch poisons on ya. Nothin to do but sleep it off. Gonna have enough to face up to when you wake up."

"She's going to come find me. With that snake and . . . I've got to get home."

"Ain't no snake, it isn't."

"Can you help me get home?"

"Help ya?" He wiped the back of his neck, looking at her as though she had brought a fine new pox into his home. "I'll help you stay alive, that's all. Trouble is that's precisely what she wants!"

Madeleine straightened. "What she wants?"

"Why else would they stick you out there on my fishin float? She knew I wudn't gonna sit pretty and watch you die."

He looked down, his expression furious, and then he threw his bowl through the opening. It hit a branch and fell with a splash.

Madeleine said, "I don't understand."

"Miss Madeleine, what do you think is gonna happen to you once them scratch poisons wear off, those poisons?"

Her mind was so fogged. But she concentrated as best she could.

"I . . . I'll have a withdrawal reaction, I think. Won't I?"

He cocked his head. "I have no idea what that is, but if it means you ain't gonna be sleepin, you won't. You'll be awake for days. And your river devil down there is in a fine froth by now to drag you off somewhere far away. You think you wanna go home? You ain't gonna have any idea where home is. That ole witch wants somethin from that briar and she been spending the past week communing with the river devils to make sure she gets it."

The truth of his words hit hard. Madeleine could say nothing, only stare.

He said, "She been communing with mine, too. Been takin everything I got to keep the thorns out of my head."

"But why?" Madeleine asked. "Why would she want you and your river devil involved?"

"Because now I'm keepin you alive. They can't send no one else to bring you food or you'd pigeon'm, not anyone else. But then if we both fall into the briar traps, then what happens to our bodies? Anything they want. Your ghost wanders off, then your body is a cart with no horse on a downhill slope. It'll get lost or even hijacked. I know this place, it don't matter if I wander off. But if you wander off you'll get lost and die. Unless they save you."

"Which means they have all the power."

"And whatever hidey spell she got on you, it's up to her whether she keeps that up, too."

Madeleine clutched her belly, suddenly unsure whether she was going to be able to hold down her meal. Her head was swimming. Sweat dripped from her face.

Gaston's expression relented some. "What is it she said, or was it they?"

"They."

"What did *they* say they want?"

"They want me to find a baby." Her throat closed on that final word, but she went on. "My brother fathered a child before he died. A little boy named Cooper. What will they do to him?"

Gaston frowned at her but did not reply. The answer to her question was obvious. They were out in this bayou, far from any other human, completely at Chloe's mercy.

She said, "But if I refuse to tell them I can just . . ."

"They will kill you, Miss Madeleine. They will kill you, they will kill you, they will kill you."

She let out her breath. Everything he'd said sounded true.

He said, "Only reason you alive now is because they want that briar baby."

"But *why* do they want him? What do they gain?"

"Access. To the briar. Maybe they tried to get it through you and you ain't been accommodatin, you haven't been."

"Have they tried it with you?"

Gaston gave her a half-hearted smile. "Tried and succeeded. These days, though, I've had a change of heart."

Outside, a blue heron called out from somewhere over the bayou.

Shocked as she was, Madeleine's brain was trying to shut down and go to sleep. The wood that surrounded them seemed to be wavering like a wall of water.

Gaston lifted his bone-thin arm and set his chin on his palm. "Put it in the pot. Let it have a rot."

"What did you say?"

"Gonna have to let it alone for now. You gonna fall asleep whether you want to or not. Me, I don't know. I may have an idea how to work this."

forty-four

NEW ORLEANS, NOW

THAN SAT WITH HIS hands on the steering wheel, thinking of that early morning not so long ago when Madeleine's wanderings had led them to the levee. But instead of Madeleine, Bo was now asleep in the passenger's seat. Kid slept with his eyelids open.

The street was dark but for the gaslight flickering on the porches. No stars tonight, and no moon. Just a sparse drizzle.

Ethan had at first considered whether Madeleine had gone on the wander. Maybe when she'd gone to see Chloe she'd gotten sucked in by Severin and was now somewhere at large. At this point it would mean relief to him. He'd searched everywhere, of course—St. Jo's, the levees, downtown, even went back to the mobile park. Cheryl had promised to call if she heard anything. But she hadn't heard anything. No one had heard anything.

And he knew why. Because Madeleine hadn't wandered off.

And Zenon hadn't gotten to her, either. It was Chloe. Chloe had disappeared at the same time Madeleine had.

He'd filed a missing person's report for Madeleine, and then filed one for Chloe. The police were accommodating but lacking in any real results. Privately, Ethan had approached Vincent, a friend on the task force, and asked if he could find out whether Chloe had made any credit card or bank card transactions. Or maybe there were recent phone records.

"I ain't exactly assigned to the case," Vin had said. "I can't just dig out information on people just cuz I'm a cop. But they got everyone lookin, man. They takin it serious."

And Ethan believed it. Though it would be nice to think that NOPD always worked diligently on cases such as these, this one had gone high profile the moment the missing person's report had been filed. Madeleine was already notorious from the whole mess with Zenon's murder trial last year. E-mails to the Web site had come flooding in. Reporters were calling, and Ethan answered their questions in the hopes that public interest would keep the pressure on the search. But public interest was fickle. Now many days had gone by.

Ethan had already broken into Chloe's old house once. He found nothing, of course. He hired a private detective who had made some calls and also found nothing. Ethan had him turn his attention instead to Emily Hammond and baby Cooper up in Nova Scotia.

Now, Ethan was staked out in front of Chloe's place for the third night in a row. The old bat knew where Madeleine was and he was going to see that she gave it up.

A car approached. Ethan slouched and watched. It slowed in front of Chloe's but did not stop. And despite the darkness, Ethan recognized at once that the driver was Oran—the African features on albino skin tones, the yellow-orange hair. Oran pulled past and down to the end of the block, then turned. Ethan was about to switch on the ignition and follow when he realized from the pattern of headlights around the corner that Oran was pulling over. He was probably parking around the corner so as not to be discovered.

Ethan gingerly opened the door.

"Where we goin?" It was Bo.

"Wait here," Ethan whispered.

"I gotta come with you."

"It's too dangerous."

"But what if the devil come to get me?"

The kid was right. Zenon was much deadlier than Oran. Ethan hadn't let Bo go to school since the night Mare had gotten pigeoned, and it was probably more risky to leave Bo alone than to bring him along.

"Alright, come on. But no sound, and definitely no clicking."

"But . . ."

"And stay out of sight."

"How I know I'm staying out of sight if I can't click?"

"Just . . . keep the clicking to a minimum . . . and hold my hand."

They got out of the Lexus without making any noise, then ran hand-in-hand across the street to Chloe's drive. Ethan could hear Oran's car door slam around the corner. They slipped down the side and in through the back gate. The gardens here were overgrown, the path uneven. Ethan led Bo carefully around to the back. An old fountain stood in the center of the enclosure, cracked and dry. He pulled Bo behind it and sat him in a crouch.

"Don't move, and no sound," he whispered.

Bo slipped his hand in Ethan's and signed, "OK."

Kid's a natural at this, Ethan thought, wishing the same could be said for himself.

Because here he was, a scientist and an academic, lying in wait to shake someone down for information. He wasn't even sure what he was going to do when Oran showed up.

Already he could see movement at the bottom of the drive where the mailbox stood. Oran's hair was visible above the fence, looking like an orange tabby in the darkness. Ethan moved as silently as he could, edging sideways toward the gate, and obscured himself among the vines at the corner fence line.

The gate opened and Oran stepped through. He had his head down, looking at a bundle of envelopes. The gate clicked closed behind him. Ethan lunged forward and grabbed Oran by the shirt, slamming him against the clapboard siding.

Oran made a garbled cry, the mail fluttering from his hands to the ivy below.

Ethan gripped his shirt and leaned in, nose-to-nose. "Where is she?"

Oran gaped at him, eyes wide.

"You tell me where Madeleine is, or so help me . . ."

"I don't know!"

"You're lying."

"No, sir."

Ethan yanked him back toward the gate and threw it wide. "No? Fine. Then you can explain that to the police."

"Wait!"

Oran put his hand on the gate. "I'm telling you the truth. I've seen her. I helped . . . hide her. But even so I don't know where she is."

"What are you talking about?"

"She has been blessed with a hex that will hide and protect her from the person she wished to avoid. But it deliberately confuses things so that even though I saw where she is, I have no idea how to get there."

Oran gave a pleading look. "You must understand, if I could find her, anyone could. Madame Chloe only gave what she asked."

"You gonna have to do better than that."

"All I know is that she is surrounded by water. It helps her to hide."

"Oh, yeah? Well then where's Chloe?"

Oran stared at him a moment, his jaw tense, his eyes rolled like a spooked horse.

Ethan shook him. "Tell me where Chloe is!"

Oran said, "Madame Chloe is dying."

There came a chirruping sound from the patio. A cricket. Ethan looked, remembering that he and Madeleine had once told Bo to use the cricket call if he sensed "that devil" was nearby.

But in that moment of distraction, Oran clocked Ethan across the jaw, and Ethan went down to all fours. He heard the gate slam and knew that Oran was gone. He rubbed his jaw. Oran certainly didn't look like he had it in him, but he threw one powerful punch.

The mail was scattered in the ivy around him. Ethan grabbed a handful of envelopes and ran back to the cracked fountain. That damn limp, times like this he could really do without it.

"The devil comin!" Bo whispered much too loudly.

Ethan scooped him up like a sack of beans and ran for the Lexus.

forty-five

LOUISIANA, NOW

IME FLIPPED BY FOR Madeleine in snapshots. Sleep. Gaston carving on a bit of wood. Sleep. A gecko crawling by. Sleep. Severin's voice, a little closer now. The smell of meat smoke.

Between the sleeping and the briar light she lost all sense of whether minutes were passing, or hours or days. Gaston muttered to himself incessantly and when he wasn't muttering he was addressing his river devil, railing or even shouting. A wonder she'd ever thought him mute. She played possum and let him rail. Didn't want to reveal that she was awake because she didn't want to commit to *being* awake, which was a state of appalling agony from the ankle, the bladder, the ear. The pain invaded her sleep, too—she dreamed a moth had flown into her ear canal.

Twice the bladder infection forced her to awake and attend. She made it across the way to the outhouse the first time but on the second, she found she was too weak.

"Don't think nothing of it, Miss Madeleine, not anything. I got two sisters." And he helped her over and across the limbs.

"Where are your sisters?"

"Not far from here really but it might as well be a million miles."

He positioned her so that she could manage the rest on her own. "Holler when you ready for me."

She was grateful to him for his help and his discretion. Grateful, too, that her hands were free and she could get in and out of her jeans without turning it into a yoga session. Her fingers were flexing more easily now. The latrine itself was a low hanging limb that had been somehow notched and braided so that it formed an oval opening over which she could comfortably sit.

In fact, though her body had weakened, her mind was now brighter, and the willow tree outhouse seemed pretty darn genius. She'd assumed he'd just outfitted something that had been growing there naturally. But the willow was growing from a hollowed cypress stump that had been filled with dirt. A deliberate planting. The place where she sat had been carefully notched and woven in such a way that it formed a sturdy bench. The trunk had been trained into a C shape so that the bench was positioned directly over the wide, hollow stump-planter. The waste fell roughly three feet below to open-air soil, not in the bayou, and yet there was no odor. The umbrella shape of the willow's limbs formed a cool, sun-dappled green privacy tent for her.

She looked at the trunk. A spirit face had been carved into the tree, and its nose was a sucker limb with sprouts of fresh green leaves at the end. The face looked ridiculously joyful. Madeleine laughed despite the painful contraction her bladder made at the end of its release.

But then she realized the strangest part of all—that this tree must have taken years, maybe even decades to mature. The bench itself would have to have been trained in the early life of the tree, which was now a full-sized willow. Gaston didn't look a day over seventeen.

She redid her jeans and attempted to make her way back, but that just wasn't happening. In fact she was almost tempted to lie down and sleep right then and there.

"I'm ready," she called instead.

The limbs parted and Gaston sprung through them and was by her side, not so much lifting her as yanking her along. "Alright then. We'll eat again and then we got to get."

"Get where? You said yourself we can't hide from her."

"No, but some places we go she can't follow so easy. Not even with her river magic."

"How far is it?"

"Far, as the crow flies."

"And we aren't exactly crows."

He pulled her over to his hollow cypress and she staggered inside, so exhausted and in pain she wanted to curl in and cry herself back to sleep. "I don't think I can make it, Gaston. The poison must still be in my system."

"Miss Madeleine, when the scratch poisons work their way out it'll be too late. Your river devil will be waiting."

She couldn't imagine making a journey. She looked at her ankle, hot and empurpled.

Gaston handed her a bowl of something that looked like it had feet sticking out. She knew frog legs when she saw them. Choked them down out of desperation many a time when she was a kid, and she'd sworn to never eat them again. But her stomach rumbled, and she accepted the bowl with gratitude.

Gaston had grilled them with leftover duck fat while she was sleeping, and he served them to her with swamp mushrooms and some kind of fry bread. A dish she might not ordinarily touch but now she ate each as though her life depended on it.

"You eat like this all the time?"

He shrugged. "I guess this is a little special, you bein a guest and all."

"What do you usually eat?"

"Fish, crab. Just about ever day."

She smiled, swirling her bowl. "Fish and crab are good."

He looked up. "You don't like frog legs?"

She felt sheepish, ungrateful. But Lord, those feet hanging out! And then he burst with a gurgling sound that sounded like *kee-he-he*. It took her a moment to realize he was laughing. She laughed, too, more out of shock at him, and he slapped his leg.

She asked, "Where you do your cooking, is it . . ."

And then they both said simultaneously, "Another tree."

She looked through the opening toward the woods, unsure which of them would be his kitchen tree, and smiled. The sunlight had turned rosy red. The mists of the briar were still present, but weak. And then she noticed a carving just above the opening to the doorway, very similar to the one in the willow tree.

"Did you do that?" she asked him.

He looked. "Yup. Did most of them."

She realized, then, that much of the inside of the tree had been whittled upon somehow. She couldn't believe she hadn't noticed it before. Perhaps the sunset had lighted it for her just so. She slumped against the inner wall, her eyes so heavy she had to fight to keep them open, and gazed at them—images of spirits, words like "Pointe au Chien."

She said, "I wonder if I'm related to you, somehow."

He nodded. "I's figurin on the same thing."

"My father's name was Gaston."

"That right?"

She nodded.

"Well mine wasn't."

She looked at the images again and smiled. Daddy Blank—the

name most folks knew Madeleine's father by—wasn't a carver. She had wondered if Gaston was yet another long-lost half-brother like Zenon had turned out to be.

"No you don't," Gaston said.

She'd fallen asleep again. Some of the contents of her bowl had spilled onto her jeans.

"Come on, time to go."

"What, now? Honestly Gaston, I don't think I can make it."

"Well little lady you gonna have to. Here, this is for you."

He took her hand and placed a kind of necklace in it. A long leather thong, with a click beetle carved into tupelo wood hanging as a pendant. The big false eyes stared like a voodoo doll. Strange, yes, but strangely beautiful.

"Gaston, I don't know what to say."

"Here, let me tie it for you."

He put it around her throat and pulled it snug, cutting away the leather tails. "You can't take it off while you're there."

She looked at him, puzzled. "Why not?"

"It's tricky over there. Look, I got one, too. Cut the ends off for me."

He produced another necklace just like the one he'd given her and tied it around his own throat in a permanent knot. She accepted the knife and fumbled to cut off the crude leather tails.

He looked at her then, gazing at her for a long moment, then he swallowed and nodded as if answering a question.

"Right. Now we gotta get."

❧

WHAT MADELEINE WASN'T EXPECTING, what she couldn't possibly have conceived, was that Gaston would not take her outside to some boat or byway or high ground trail. Instead he led her down, straight down, deep into the trunk of the cypress.

He lifted a cutout of wood that had blended in as the floor of the tree hollow, and he slipped down into a kind of chamber below. Briar mist rolled up to her, silver and cool.

She realized Gaston must use this little chamber for storage to keep the animals out of his stash of food. It smelled like salted herring in there, which might have repulsed her at any other time but under the circumstances, having been in starvation mode for so long, she felt the urge to leap down in there and hoard the salted fish to herself.

"Well come on," Gaston said.

She hesitated above the hole; roots and bits of rotted wood pointed downward to a shimmer of reflection deep below where bayou water had leaked in—like the inside of a bog pitcher plant.

He must have seen the expression on her face, because he said, "Yes, this here's a trap alright. But not for you."

"For what?"

"It's like I done said, where we goin ain't so much gonna hide us as make it tough to follow."

She took a deep breath. Gaston seemed trustworthy. And he'd pretty much saved her life. Still, she had little defense left if he turned rogue. She looked at him and swallowed. There seemed no choice but to follow, and so she climbed in and he replaced the hidden hatch.

Now the only light came from the briar. She felt strangely exhilarated, as though while her body was feeling all the more dragged down with each moment, her spirit was shedding a dead weight and was anxious to run free. Like above, the inside of the chamber was covered in carvings, many so old that they'd weathered into the wood, which made them difficult to decipher without careful inspection. There were also wooden crates and chests, one of which must have contained the salted fish.

They had to slide-climb down on their backs, the opening growing narrower as they descended. A sudden change of temperature indicated they were below water level. The air tasted like river bottom. Now there was only enough room to admit one person at a time, and Gaston was sliding down just ahead. Sounds of his body going into water. She got the sense that going down was much easier than climbing back up.

"Ah, to see a nice hidey slide," came Severin's voice.

She was creeping down from above, and the thorns had curled in to form a tunnel along the inside shaft of the tree. Severin moved face-first, climbing hand over hand along the thorns like a funnel spider.

Madeleine's body was going slack; her grip insufficient to stabilize her descent. So hard to keep alert. Loose, rotted wood dislodged beneath her feet and showered down in a series of splashes.

"Take it easy!" Gaston said.

"We—we won't be able to get back up!"

And with those words, the stinging thornflies emerged from below. They seemed to have sprung from the water.

But the thornflies were supposed to exist in the briar only. Had she transcended?

Gaston gripped her hand and yanked her down into the pool. "I said, take it easy."

Madeleine's feet hit a slippery bottom and she would have fallen altogether were it not for Gaston's grip. He was out of breath, not from exertion—it seemed more from anticipation. Water sloshed up and around them, the basin so narrow that the combined body displacement caused the level to rise to their chests. He had one hand around her wrist and the other atop her head. A child preacher about to baptize a new servant of God. The circumference of space had grown so narrow Madeleine could no longer raise her elbows to full expanse. A drowning chamber.

Severin said, "Asleep, to sleep, beneath the brine."

"We ain't got no choice, not any," Gaston was saying. "Your river devil here?"

Madeleine nodded beneath his hand.

Gaston gripped her tighter. "Mine, too. Not much time. You gonna have to hold your breath a good long while, alright?"

Fear clenched her chest, but she nodded again, unable to speak.

He lowered his voice as though someone were listening. "On the other side, don't talk to a soul. Don't look directly at'm. We ghosts over there, you understand? We ghosts now."

"No!"

Madeleine jerked from him, but he was already pushing her head down. Down into the water. Where before her feet had caught hold on a slope, they were now sliding down, her legs pumping in a reverse bicycle motion. Gaston held her tight and was pushing and pulling her deeper than seemed possible on the inside of a tree trunk. Down into the black, waterlogged soil.

forty-six

BAYOU BOUILLON, 1927

ATRICE WAS IN THE water for a very long time. She could feel her lungs contort. The shadow river must have somehow merged with the Mississippi and taken them all. She had a distant sense that she had told it to do so.

But when she broke the water's surface she was nowhere near the ferry dock. Not physically, or through the bramble. She didn't know where she was. She realized she was not in the briar because it was dark—no briar light. An actual sky existed somewhere above. But there were no stars, only the wink of torchères somewhere to her right. Her shoes were gone and the water felt soothing against her bare feet.

She realized she was clutching something to her bosom— Francois' Bible. It seemed such an absurd and frivolous possession after having lost so much.

Arms around her waist pulling her through the water. She could see only a flash of black skin over her shoulder before he was saying, "Hold onto this," and placing her hand on a raft.

"Ferrar?" she said, relieved at the sound of his voice.

That she could actually hear him. That he was there.

She walked her elbows along the wooden surface and swung her leg up and onto it. Francois' raft. But Francois wasn't there. Nor was Trigger. Nor the dead man nor the vulture. Just the raft.

"Hey give me a hand, will ya?" Trigger's voice somewhere nearby in the darkness.

"Stay put," Ferrar said to her, and swam away in the direction of Trigger's voice.

Patrice looked over her shoulder to where the flames of those torchères wavered above water, a halo of insects buzzing in the light. She could see little else.

And she thought, *That's what has become important, that space between that firelight.*

She stared at the dark gaps in between. There came a strange, detached sense of seeing herself, as though a different part of her was watching Patrice look at the vacant spaces instead of looking at the safe torchlight.

They were in Bayou Bouillon, of course. It seemed odd that she had been trying to pretend she didn't know where she was.

Ferrar and Trigger were swimming back to the raft, and between them, a listless body she could not see.

"Oh, Francois!" She reached down and helped pull him onto the raft while Trigger and Ferrar pushed him from behind.

Francois still had a measure of strength left in him. He made his arms push against the raft instead of slumping in a heap.

"You really are alive," Patrice said, her hands cradling Francois' head.

Even in the darkness she could see that his face was all wrong. That disgusting bird had been real, not just briar. Francois said not a word and she couldn't tell the extent of his consciousness. She held onto him while Trigger and Ferrar swam the raft in the direction of the torchères.

❧

THEY SPENT THE NIGHT in a one-room shack floating over the bayou. The shack didn't rock but it did turn from side to side in lazy arcs. Patrice tended Francois by wrapping his eye in strips of woven cotton that Ferrar brought her. The room was illuminated by candlelight, a kindness on Patrice because dear Francois' face had undergone such brutality. His eye and part of his lip were missing. Cuts and sores and dry, salt-burned skin. It seemed she had his wounds cleaned and wrapped all too soon, because afterward she could do nothing further but allow him to sleep. There had been no needle and thread to sew him. Just wrappings.

Ferrar had left them alone in the shack for the night.

Trigger was leaning against the wall near the door with his eyes closed. She could tell he wasn't sleeping and wasn't going to sleep. Neither would she.

❧

THE SUN HAD YET to rise, but the bird chatter on a distant shore told Patrice that dawn was near. She wanted to go out, find a water closet or at least a place where she could improvise one. She opened the door and found Ferrar sleeping just outside on the boardwalk.

He leapt to his feet though his eyes were still half-closed. "Where you goin?"

"I need to . . . walk around some."

She wasn't sure why she didn't just tell him what she really needed to do. Never thought anything of saying so around her sister or her brothers or anyone at Terrefleurs. But she couldn't say it in front of Ferrar. Of course he knew she peed just like everyone else. But she didn't want him thinking of her peeing.

He'd caught on all the same. "Come on, little girl, I'll show you where."

Her back went rigid on the "little girl" part.

From behind her in the shack, Trigger said, "Me, too."

They walked along the boardwalk in silence, and when Patrice started to comment on the rows of shanties, Ferrar put a finger over his lips and shushed her. She looked around, uneasy, thinking of the moment in the briar when Trigger and Rosie had shushed because they knew mother was watching somehow. She wondered for whose benefit—or against whose awareness—Ferrar was shushing her right now.

The entire cluster of boardwalk and shanties was floating over water. It seemed like such a precarious place, especially with the past year's floods and the storms that must have blown through over the years. Patrice recalled the day Ferrar had told her of this place. He was lying there wounded, shot by their mother, and he told Patrice and the other children of the places he'd gone to hide along the coast, living like a pirate, running hooch for Maman to sell in New Orleans. It hadn't occurred to Patrice that these hidden coves might harbor other pirates, too.

The horizon had already gone from black to gray. She saw that land was nearby, but it formed a ring around the tiny settlement that was otherwise completely surrounded in water, save for one tiny island just large enough to support a willow tree. That's where Ferrar was leading them now, to that willow. He stopped just shy of it but waved Patrice on. She looked over her shoulder at Ferrar and Trig as she stepped off the boardwalk onto the island. The willow roots snaked into a dome formation atop the soil so that it appeared the tree was clutching the island into existence lest it disintegrate into the water.

She found a suitable place and relieved herself.

After her, Trigger visited the willow, and Patrice stood in silence next to Ferrar.

Little girl, he'd called her.

❧

PATRICE AND FERRAR AND Trig were back in that floating shack, standing around the pallet where Francois lay. There was nowhere to sit besides the floor and they were all too stiff after last night to do anything but stand. No one brought up the question of how they might have gotten to Bayou Bouillon from the outskirts of New Orleans, and that was just fine.

"Did you see the thing that took Gil away?" Trigger asked Ferrar.

Patrice looked up. Was it possible that Ferrar might have seen the tar creature?

But Ferrar said, "The thing? It was only a man. Lotta men lookin for trouble just after y'all came. But the one who got your brother, I've seen him before. Missin a hand."

"Missing a hand. Jacob Chapman? Did he hurt him?" Patrice asked.

"No, just grabbed him and carried him off. I couldn't stop him."

"Just a flesh-and-blood man," Patrice said, and looked at Trig.

Trigger was nodding. "It's what I thought. When we first saw the tar devil it had come for Rosie there at Terrefleurs. But the stranger had, too. The Brute. I thought at the time that they were kinda the same. Figured the tar thing was just the stranger's river devil."

"You're saying they're not related?"

"Well I imagine they're related, but it don't mean they're the same."

"Doesn't."

"Lord almighty. It *doesn't*. Just not sure how it figures together."

Patrice thought about this. "Mother knows if she sends a man after us we can defend ourselves with pigeonry."

"You can," Trig said. "For the rest of us it's hit and miss."

"And now she figured out a way to follow us into the briar."

Ferrar said, "So she follows y'all in both worlds, at the same time."

Patrice nodded. "Yes, maybe."

Trigger said, "And she's getting better at it. I had no trouble whuppin that tar devil that came after Rosie the first time. The second time it was so stealthy I never saw it until it was too late.

"And then when it came for Gil, it was monstrous."

Patrice thought of all those years of practice. That was probably why she was so much better at pigeonry than her siblings—she'd been doing it for longer because she was older. Now in these months since they'd banished Maman from Terrefleurs, Maman had been perfecting some skills of her own.

They stood in silence for a moment, thinking, and then they heard a voice outside. A man's voice, deep, and . . . familiar. He sang:

Every night
When the sun goes in
Every night
When the sun goes in

Trigger said what Patrice was thinking: "Francois?"

But Francois was lying on the pallet at their feet.

Every night
When the sun goes in
I hang down my head
And mournful cry

They all three moved for the door at once but Ferrar got there first. He didn't open it. Instead, he blocked it.

He said, "I told you, this place is full of ghosts."

"What's going on out there?" Trigger asked.

"It's not easy to explain."

"Let us out," Patrice said.

She stared at Ferrar, ready to use pigeonry. But his face showed no opposition. No resistance of any kind. He was not holding them there to harm them.

"I ask you to stay inside for a while. People here must keep to themselves. You'll see what I mean in time."

"What time? How do you know we'll stay here at all? We're not in the briar now so there's no reason. We can go after Rosie and Gil."

Ferrar looked pained. "I thought you'd been here before because I thought I saw you. There are . . . reflections."

"I don't understand."

"You will. I know this for a fact, *ma chère*. You'll probably understand it better than I do. But right now shouldn't we think of a way to find young Gilbert and Marie-Rose?"

The mention of her siblings caused a fresh burst of pain in her heart. Trigger's posture relented, too. Patrice hesitated but then stepped back from the door. She looked down at Francois on the pallet. He was sleeping. The other voice outside—the one that sounded like Francois, that sang his very song—had moved down the boardwalk and faded.

"Rosie's hidden from us, but we haven't tried looking for Gil," Patrice said.

Trigger shook his head. "I did. Last night. They're both plumb gone."

"What about Maman?" Patrice asked. "If we find Maman we'll find Gil and Rosie."

"I looked for her, too."

He was quiet for a moment, staring past a gap in the wall where sunlight now penetrated, his jaw muscle tense. "I can think of one other way."

"What?"

"I can let that tar devil take me to wherever the hell it goes."

Patrice stared at him, unable to believe he would even suggest it. "No."

"Just hear me—"

"*No!*"

Ferrar's hand went to her shoulder. Patrice filled with fury so fast her body quaked. She had to get that idea out of Trigger's head, right now, because once Trig got an idea like that—

"Treesey, we don't have a choice. Gil and Rosie might very well disappear forever. Forever. Are you hearin' me? You think Maman gonna let'm go if she believes she has a prayer's chance in hell of gettin briar skills out of them?"

"Stop it!"

Francois shifted in his sleep, bringing his knees up, and Patrice looked toward the door and thought of Marie-Rose hidden somewhere alone. Did she even know that Gil was there, too? Or did Maman have him taken somewhere else?

Trigger was wearing a look that said he'd already made up his mind. "My flesh-and-blood body stays here the whole time. You can look after me. I'll let the tar thing bring me to where the others are in the briar. Then I'll find a way to get their minds out. You know I can do it."

Ferrar said to Trigger, "Your papa used to get lost in that place, if I recall. Sometimes for years on end."

"Yes," Patrice said.

But Trigger ignored them. "Once we get their minds out we'll know where their bodies are. And then we'll go get'm."

Ferrar kept his hand on Patrice's shoulder, and it felt that if he were to remove it she might just sink to her knees. She couldn't guess what was to become of Gil and Rosie. Couldn't bear to lose Trigger, too.

Ferrar said, "And how do you know this—tar devil—will come?"

Trigger's face went grim, his gaze steady on the flooring, and his voice retreating to barely above a whisper. "It's here now."

PATRICE WHEELED, HER HEART in her throat. She saw nothing. No creature made of tar.

But she was not in the briar. Not since they'd arrived at this place. Quick as she could, she receded.

"Wait, Trig," she pleaded, but Trigger's ghost was already loosening from his body and stepping forward.

She shut her eyes and dared the thorns to surge around her. The black coils, the eternal briar light.

Her river devil was there, grinning.

It took Patrice a moment, but then she saw the oil slick seeping upward between the floorboards. It smelled like sulphur. Trigger was facing it with his fists clenched. The black oil spread from the cracks to a wider circle, and to Patrice's eye it sullied the pallet where Francois lay. That's when the creature came into view. It entered in the same way the oil did, up from the floorboards as though rising from the bayou.

"Get back, Treese." Trigger said.

"We have to stay together."

"Get away from it!"

But Patrice moved fast. She threw herself into it. And then it had her.

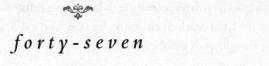

forty-seven

DESPITE THE BRIAR LIGHT, Madeleine could no longer see very well. She resisted Gaston as he dragged her deeper into the swamped-out tree hollow, and she paid dearly in thorn-flies for her struggles. Her body went rigid and felt the sting, sting, stinging.

Gaston was pulling her down to the bottommost trough, which was deeper than it had at first seemed because the narrow gap widened as they slid down the slope to a great underground pool. She slackened and allowed him to pull her along.

He's not trying to kill me, she told herself. *Otherwise he wouldn't have told me to hold my breath.*

Now she was moving with him, not fighting and not being dragged.

He turned upward and they swam in the direction of the surface before making another hard turn into some kind of underwater tunnel. The walls still felt like the wood of the great cypress tree. She swam best she could along with him. The thornflies were following like sucker fish but they did not sting now. In fact, it occurred to her that she could see again. Briar light in the tunnel. Her fit of panic was what had made her vision go.

The path was narrowing again, and Madeleine's strength was waning. How long had they been traveling in this direction? She should have been counting. There were limits to how long she could hold her breath even with the new ability. She should have taken a deep breath before going in.

Sting.

She tensed on the feel of it, and then let the pain pass through her. Her mind emptied itself of the thoughts. She needed to keep swimming, nothing else.

The tunnel opened wider.

Bones. Human remains. Before she knew what was happening she and Gaston were passing through them. *Passing through them.* Not over, not under; through. An ongoing expanse that littered the bottom of this section.

And Madeleine realized she was no longer able to move.

She drifted forward from pure momentum and then stopped. It might have been the lingering effects of the scratch poisons or maybe just good old-fashioned exhaustion, but she couldn't so much as make a grip on the wood that surrounded her. Bubbles crawled from behind her ear and up her cheek. She waited, refusing to let panic grip her, even as she watched Gaston's feet disappear ahead.

But the wood. She looked carefully above where the bones were piled. A relief pattern stood out, what looked like a plus sign with a circle in the upper right corner, and the circle had three dots in it. She recognized it as a hobo symbol but had no idea what it meant. Adjacent, there were carvings of four trees, and at the bottom right a circle with an arrow, which she did recognize as meaning "go this way."

She looked behind her. More carvings. Even down here. They likely lined the entire passage.

Something hit her shoulder and she jumped. Gaston. He was unable to turn around but he moved his foot toward her hand, and she realized he wanted her to grab hold. She tried unsuccessfully to grasp his ankle, then used both her arms to clamp on and was able to form a strong enough grip. He moved forward down the passage again, dragging Madeleine behind him.

And then they were out, free of the wood without any sense of some kind of opening having been there. Just suddenly in open water. She couldn't tell how far away the surface was. No light above.

The water swirled and pulled them in an unexpected current. Once again, Madeleine saw piles of bones. This time they were bones of all manner of creatures—man, gar, salamander, even molted shells of crustaceans—and unlike inside the tree, these were all cloaked in algae that wavered in the mild current. It covered the bones so completely they wouldn't be discernible at all except for their skulls.

There were curtains of bubbles and she could tell by the way they moved that they were at the base of some kind of whirlpool. Not a strong one—no such thing existed in the rivers and bayous— but a persistent one. The bubbles swirled like thousands of tiny suns in a spiral galaxy.

Gaston had her hooked beneath the armpits now and was pulling her away from the vortex to where the current ran more gently, and then he pulled her up toward the surface.

❧

MADELEINE OPENED HER MOUTH and took her first breath since having left Gaston's tree. Above were stars and a waning crescent moon. She squinted at them, though her vision was lacking focus. Night sounds. It had been full daylight when they left Gaston's cypress.

She remembered the sun dappling the willow outhouse. The journey hadn't been that long.

Gaston jerked her upward in the water and slapped her face.
"Stay awake!"

She tried to cough but what came out was mostly liquid, and it
coursed through both her mouth and nose. She felt it sting her
sinuses. Seemed impossible that she might have fallen asleep. Her
chest contorted and spewed again, then made an actual cough.
Her lungs burned.

"Lady, you still full capable of drowning even with briar gills,"
Gaston said.

She looked at him but saw him only through ghosting spots of
darkness. She was too weak, too tired. Behind him was what looked
like some kind of a barge. She fought to keep her eyes open.

He pulled on her elbow. "Come on, now, I can drag you a little
in the water but I can't get you up out of it."

She made herself cough, and in that way she stayed awake as
Gaston dragged her toward the structure. Several rafts and pirogues
were tethered along with the barge that was actually, upon closer
inspection, a floating pier. Her jaw was shaking, shivering, as was
her spine.

He took her arms and lifted them onto a wooden raft. "You got
that? Hold onto it now. You got only one more heave-ho then you
done. On a count a three, swing ya leg."

Her body felt like it was made of lead. This was not leftover sleep
from scratch poisons. She was ill. Seriously ill. Feverish.

"OK now, one . . ."

Gaston had his arm over the floating pier. He reached down and
pulled her by the belt loop so that her legs were surface-level.

". . . two . . ."

She closed her eyes and forced herself to concentrate on the one
single movement she had to make.

". . . three!"

She jerked her hips as hard as she could but she only managed a small lift. Gaston grabbed her leg and continued her momentum to force it up. She caught the lip of the raft with her foot.

"You got it, you got it. Lift yaself up."

Madeleine squeezed with all her might, but she could go no further.

"Hold on." Gaston pulled himself up onto the raft and grabbed her leg.

The raft started to tilt from the back and he had to lie flat to prevent it from flipping. This meant he could use only his upper body to pull her the rest of the way out, his hand hooked over her knee.

"Again. One, two, three."

This time the rest of her body lurched out of the water. She lay flat, heaving, and he caught his breath, too, sitting with his elbows over his knees.

"God almighty, Miss Madeleine, y'ain't makin it easy on me." He made the *kee-he-he* sound, and despite herself, Madeleine smiled.

Her body was now shivering hard even though she was also sweating. She realized, too, that there were tears of exertion, not just water, rolling from her eyes. And yet she felt strangely giddy.

He said, "Awright, yer majesty, you just lie there on your puffy pillows while I drive this here carriage."

She wanted to sass back but even if she could think of something witty her teeth were chattering too hard to speak. The raft was moving. Gaston propelled it with a pole.

Swamp trees ringed an area the size of a football field, and they were at the goal end where the pier jutted out. On the inside of the ring was a group of structures. Dozens of them. Most looked like houses up high on stilts. But then Gaston turned down between two of the houses and Madeleine could see storefronts deeper inside, where the passage between the houses formed an aquatic alley. It seemed to be an entire floating village.

Severin was seated on a rooftop near the entrance to the alley.

Gaston whispered, "Remember, we're like ghosts."

forty-eight

*I*N THE EARLY MORNING light, the room at the Motel 6 looked gray. Ethan hadn't slept. Bo and Jasmine, however, slept with enthusiasm. Ethan had dared to swing back by Madeleine's after the incident with Oran to collect Jasmine and get Bo's clothes. The Motel 6 seemed an anonymous enough place. No frills, but it was cheap and clean and it allowed dogs, and for a few extra bucks he could get online. And that's what he was doing now.

The Internet wasn't helping, though, at least not directly. Looking up voodoo for Chloe's hiding spell was a waste of time. Oh, there were plenty of spells out there. Each one either looked made up on the spot, or the same thing was copied and pasted from one source to the next. This was true of all the spells he came across—hiding, healing, revenge, wealth, seduction. Reading them only made Ethan feel all the more foolish.

Except.

There was something about the act of going about the rituals themselves. Things like collecting objects and tying them together into a gris-gris, or making a concoction to drink. Each individual step included methodical, focused attention. Any psychologist alive would consider that to be excellent therapy. This was a kind of active meditation.

There were countless studies that showed how regular prayer or meditation made for an excellent basis to regulate the brain's electrical and chemical balances, and in doing so it reduced stress responses. Same with self-hypnosis. But most people didn't have the patience or the control of attention to keep it up for long. Maybe a minute or two.

But this.

Doing these spells was like a kind of meditation that involved active body movement—kinesis—which of course would boost the neurological effect. And also it engaged the senses—the taste of a potion, the scent of herbs or even animals, sometimes the feel of a pinprick. Any repeated activity that engages all five senses is going to form super neurons. People looking to gain wealth may not know how to achieve it, but with this kind of neurotherapy, they would at least achieve a Jack Russell tenacity for it. And it created a new belief system. People who see themselves as incapable may change their thinking if they believe they have access to some kind of mystic power outside themselves.

He wondered if people like Madeleine somehow harnessed that kind of practice into a natural, ingrained adaptability. It helped to understand a little, but he needed much more than that if he was going to find her.

Jasmine sprang awake with a woof and ran to the door, sticking her nose in the jamb.

Ethan frowned and rose from the desk. "Whatcha got, girl?"

He stepped to the window, keeping himself hidden, and parted the curtains just enough to get a look.

Outside, parked next to the Lexus, was Oran's car.

Someone was in the driver's seat. Someone who was not Oran.

THE CAR WAS IDLING. No telling how long it had been there. The driver had a disarray of gray hair and Ethan thought at first that it might be Chloe.

No. Not her. He backed away from the window.

"Bo," he whispered, his hand on the boy's shoulder.

Bo's face went from slack to pinched, and he rolled away.

"Do you sense anything?" Ethan asked.

Bo gasped and bolted upright, suddenly wide awake, clicking.

Ethan clamped his hand over the boy's mouth and whispered, "Don't click!"

"It's OK, it ain't here," Bo said, plain voice through Ethan's fingers.

Ethan let go and exhaled. "Alright. Stay here. I'll be right back."

"Where you—"

"Just gonna be outside. You can holler if there's an emergency, but only then, OK?"

"OK."

"And you got Jazz here with you."

Bo whistled, and Jazz hopped up on the bed and turned around, her back to the boy and facing the door.

Ethan stepped outside, reprimanding himself for not having a concealed-carry permit by now.

The driver looked vaguely familiar. She wore a dirty LSU tee-shirt and was staring off into nowhere. When Ethan approached she followed him with her eyes. And when he tapped on her window, she rolled it down. That's when he recognized her.

"Alice."

"The good doctor. Last time I saw you's down by the river. Called the po-lice on me."

"What are you doing here, Alice?"

"Truth, honey?" And she laughed, a sticky, toothless exhalation.

"Yes, the truth please."

"You might oughtta sit down."

Ethan looked back at the motel room, hands in pockets, resigning himself. He walked around to the passenger side and got in. It smelled like long-unwashed clothes with a backdrop of mothballs, the fusion of Alice's world and Chloe's.

"It's a long story," Alice said.

"What is?"

"All of it."

"Why don't you start by telling me what you're doing here?"

"I came to kill you, Doc."

And she turned and looked at him, like a parishioner who'd chosen to open the confession booth screen and face the father eye-to-eye. She was searching his face as though his opinion might lay out her entire future for her.

Ethan said, "Do you still intend to do that?"

"No sir?" A comforting reply but for the way she spoke it like a question.

"So why did you change your mind?"

"Just suddenly seemed like a stupid idea."

"Well, that's refreshing. And do you remember why you thought it was a good idea in the first place?"

"Yeah."

She said nothing else for a moment. Ethan rolled down his window and the cross breeze carried through the vehicle. The faint odor of car exhaust came with it but it still felt refreshing.

She said, "I wanted you out of the way. You were in my goddamn way. Truth is, Doc, you piss me off."

"I do?"

She frowned. "No. I don't fuckin know."

"I think I know. You wanna tell me how you got out of jail?"

She laughed again, a wet chuckle that ended in a cough. "They let me out."

"The judge dismissed your case?"

"What? No. Ain't even had a judge. The driver and the other

guy, they just let me go. I's bein transported in the van with all the deadbeats. And then the driver pulled over. And the other guard's like, 'what the fuck are you doin?'"

Another laugh, and this time she turned and spat out the window before continuing. "And the driver's all, 'I'm gonna put this one free.' And I's sittin there in handcuffs and leg cuffs. I couldn't hardly believe it. But then the other guard's all, 'OK.' And he unlocks me and off I went."

Her arms were dirty, her hands were dirty, her fingernails were black.

Ethan said, "OK. Tell me about the car."

She looked at him, her mouth slack. "What car?"

"You know good and well, what car. This car!" He struck the dashboard with his fist, startling them both.

Her mouth was open, the sparse teeth gleaming, and her shoulders began to shake. He wasn't sure if she was laughing or crying. But then she let out a long, wailing sob.

"Just tell me, Alice."

She spoke through puckered lips, her voice having gone higher and tighter. "I's lookin for the other doctor. Doc LB, from St. Jo's."

"Why?"

"Cuz I . . . I thought . . . If I'm gonna be in charge, I needed her on my side. She gets stronger and I get way stronger. We gotta get rid of them rats, like the little blind boy."

Her eyes had gone wild, and she fixed them in Ethan's direction. "I do that and I can get all them devils following me. They forget about the old witch. They be following me! You know what that means?"

"No, tell me."

But her expression had frozen, and then it crumpled, and she began to sob again. "It means I'm crazy, don't it? I don't know why I was thinkin that way. You gotta bring me back to the jail, Doc. Please, I . . . tell'm to keep me in there!"

"Where is Oran? The person who owns this car?"

She was shaking her head, her grimy hand over her eyes, tears staining her cheeks.

Ethan asked her, "Is he alive?"

"I think so."

"Alice, listen to me. You gotta answer the question. There's more to this you don't know about, OK? Something bad's got a hold of your head."

"You mean it wasn't me?"

"Not entirely. Something about you makes you an easy target. I think that may be why he keeps coming back for you."

"It's because I turned my back on Jesus, ain't it? Oh, look what I become!"

He shook his head. "I don't think that's it. I have no idea why."

"I only slept on the streets a little while. I tried to get back on my feet an go get a job. Went in for an interview, then afterward I looked in the mirror an there was dirt on my face. No one told me! I went and did the whole interview like that."

"Oran, Alice. Just tell me about Oran and how you came to be drivin this car!"

She took a gulp of air. "I never done anything like this before. My old man and I used to brawl but that was fair, and we just hittin. That night down by the river, I don't know why I did that. And now I . . ."

"Alice!"

She said, "I thought for sure he knew where the doc was. Couldn't get in his head, had to make him talk the old-fashioned way."

She gave in to sobbing again, but still managed to squeeze out the truth. "I cut on him! He really didn't know where she was! But, I kept them, just in case, they're in there."

She was pointing at the glove box. Ethan swallowed, and opened it. Three fingers inside. Oran's fingers.

He slammed the thing shut. "What is it with Zenon and the damn fingers?"

"What?"

"Where is he now, Alice? Where is Oran?"

She gestured a shaky hand back over her shoulder. "He's in the trunk."

"Jesus! Give over the keys!"

She handed them to him and he scrambled out of the car and opened the trunk. Oran was in there, shaking and bleeding. He didn't react to the sight of Ethan or the trunk being opened. Looked like he might be in shock.

Ethan yanked out his cell and dialed 911.

forty-nine

BAYOU BOUILLON, 1927

*I*N A WAY IT brought relief. No more wondering when the river devils might appear, or the thorns. They were already there. No more groping for the quiet mind, trying to conjure the kind of stillness Ferrar wore so effortlessly. She could follow where the sylphs led her. There was so much to explore: learning to breathe underwater, looking inside yesterday and tomorrow, pinching time to shape the hour.

"Patrice."

She looked and saw Trigger, and just the sight of him made her laugh. "How long have you been standing there?"

"Look."

He gestured behind him. Marie-Rose and Gilbert.

"Rosie?"

Patrice felt numb. She'd forgotten. Unbelievable, that she could let her attention lapse to such an extent that she would forget about her siblings, whom she loved most in the world.

She made to encircle them with her arms but Trigger stopped her. "Think first, Treesey, Think on it. You don't want to do that."

Patrice listened to him. Yes. It had happened before. She'd touched Rosie and the tar devil had attacked her. It had struck her so hard she'd fallen over. Even though her physical body didn't exist in this world, the illusions made it seem like she truly had been hit and had even been bleeding. What happened after that, she couldn't recall.

Rosie was making the swallowed "g-g-g" noises in her throat. The tar devil kept forcing her and Gil forward. They were in a ravine of black briar pines where a sheer cliff reached toward the sky. The shadow river coursed along behind them.

Trigger said, "You touch them, the tar devils come after you, and then you're lost for a good long while. You and I have both done it. More than one time, I think. It's hard to tell. This last time, once I got my senses back, I've just been watching them and trying to figure this out."

Patrice ached to touch Gil and Rosie, but she knew what Trigger said was true. Memories flared and winked out.

Trigger said, "It's because Maman got to both their minds and their bodies. It took me a while to find them again. Every time they start to leave the briar, she scratches them with a bird's foot dipped in poison. They go through that whole cycle of sleep, then awake, then briar. I don't know how long each part of it lasts."

"But why not us? Why hasn't a tar devil been after us?"

Trigger gave her a sideways look. "One has. You don't remember? In Bayou Bouillon, it got to you because you damn-fool threw yourself in front of the thing when it shoulda come after me. But I think you need the scratch poison in your system or else it doesn't last. Not unless you go near one of their tar pools, then they'll drag you in. After the tar devil goes away, you're just lost in the briar."

"But we were scratched! That day we left Terrefleurs."

"I don't think Maman perfected it yet then. I think once she got hold of Rosie she practiced on her, with the poisons and the tar devil. Now she's mastered it."

The tar devil stood bent and swaying on lizard-like limbs. It shoved Rosie forward and she took a step, then stopped. It made a screeching sound and shoved at a pine tree, then struck Rosie on the back of the head. She staggered forward again.

A pine needle drifted down and landed in Rosie's hair, near her ear. She wiped it away and it fell to the ground, now shining black. Patrice stepped a little closer. Rosie had tar smeared over her eyes, mouth, and ears. Gil did, too.

The tar devil kept pushing them from behind, and they kept staggering forward until they came to the rock face. Another shove from behind, and Gil started climbing up, hand over hand.

Patrice racked her mind, thinking, trying to figure out how they might free their siblings from this.

"Do you know where their bodies are?" she asked Trig.

He nodded, saying nothing, and walked over to where Gil and Rosie had just been. Patrice followed. He picked up the pine needle that had lodged in Rosie's hair. It had tar on it.

"Come here." He took Patrice by the wrist, leading her to a pool that formed at the edge of the shadow river.

He placed the pine needle on the surface and then brought Patrice's hand into the water. "Now look."

They both leaned forward. There, reflecting on the surface, they saw Rosie peering back at them. Not the way she was over there with the tar devil. This had to be her physical self. She was wrapped in what looked like white thread, so tangled she could barely move. She was looking down from somewhere high above. Crossed wooden beams. Roofing joists.

From over by the rocky rise, she heard Rosie say, "Patrice?" and the Rosie staring across from within the pool said it, too.

"I'm here, baby!" She didn't know which side of the pool to address.

RHODI HAWK

But Trigger put his finger over his lips and shook his head. Over by the ledge, the tar devil gave a cry and boxed Rosie's ears.

Patrice looked back to the pool and saw Rosie's physical self reel to the side as though she'd been struck in the physical world, not in the briar. It looked for a moment like she might fall from those rafters. But she steadied herself and went back to moving again, climbing across a wooden beam with the same tired, jaunty motion she used while walking in the briar.

Trigger said, "Maman's holding them up in the attic of some old building. Their bodies concentrate on keeping balance. I think it keeps them occupied somehow. Their minds are here, in the briar, but the tar devil keeps them lost."

Patrice stared at her sister's reflection. Hard to imagine that the girl from the pool was the real, physical Marie-Rose, and that this sleepwalker at the base of the cliff was the illusion. The physical girl had sunken eyes and her hands and feet gripped the beams in such a way that barely seemed human.

But beneath the spider threads that bound her, her hair was brushed and neatly tied. She wore clean bloomers.

"Who is looking after them?" Patrice asked.

Trigger replied, "Tatie Bernadette."

Patrice caught her breath. "How could she?"

"How couldn't she? Maman forced it on her. Told her she could look after the children if she wanted but she's not allowed to leave the building or speak to anyone. Tatie makes sure they eat and go to the toilet. And she helps them bathe and dress. When she's not doin that, she sits and cries and prays."

Rosie crawled along a beam at the ceiling and angled her body so that she could get a better look back through the pool toward Patrice and Trigger, and in doing so she crept into a ray of sunlight. Her face looked so different. Her lips fuller. And as she turned, a tiny lump showed the beginning formation of a breast—the first stages of puberty. At seven years old?

"What?" Patrice said, but then she saw Gil.

He crawled into view, moving along the ceiling joists to join Rosie. His eyes were vacant like Papa's used to look when he was so, so lost, wandering Terrefleurs as a madman. As he moved, he worked his way through sticky, crisscrossing threads, just like Rosie. One of the threads was knotted around his neck like a leash, like a noose. Rosie had one, too.

Patrice stared. Gil's body was long. Not the boy Patrice lost yesterday. He was tall. Stubble at his chin.

"How long have we been in here?" Patrice cried.

Trigger shook his head. "I don't know. It's hard to tell."

"Then guess!"

Trigger was silent, his face grim. Patrice knew that if she gave over to panic the thornflies would come to sting her, to amplify her distress, and she would be no use to Gil or Rosie.

"Where's Maman?"

"She's down the stairs from where they are."

Trigger leaned back and rose to his feet, stepping forward into the water. "You can go on in if you want. They just—you know, no one'll see you."

Patrice watched him. He at least still looked like an eleven-year-old boy. But so did the briar version of Gil, climbing that ledge with those awful smears of tar across his eyes and mouth. And Rosie was still so small. Their physical counterparts had changed so much and yet their briar selves were the same.

Patrice stepped into the pool after Trigger and watched the reflections of her sister and brother ripple away. She pulled herself deep under the surface, down until she felt a strange euphoric upset of balance. And then she was standing inside a great chamber where her brother and sister were moving about twelve feet above her. Their gazes followed her as she moved. But it seemed automatic, the way insects respond to light.

The ropes around their necks provided enough slack that they could move freely about the rafters. But not so much that they could come down from them. The ropes each looped through a pulley and down along the wall to a steel arm, and then wound around that arm in several crisscrossing loops.

Trigger said, "Maman lets Tatie Bernadette unwind the cord to feed them or put them to the toilet or bathe them. Then after that she has to send them up and tie the cord again. It's the only time they come down to the floor: eat, bathe, dress, toilet. Rest of the time, they're up there. Even when they sleep."

A ladder lay across the raw wooden floor. She tried to move it, knowing that for her it was only an illusion.

"That's a waste of time," Trigger said.

"Alright. I'll see what I can do with Maman."

Trigger nodded. "I'll do my best to get them down. But even if I do, I still don't know how we'll physically get to them."

Patrice turned and followed through a doorway to a narrow, steep stairwell. She descended to the bottom landing, then passed through a locked door as though it were open.

Sitting near a window, reading a folded newspaper, was Maman.

⁂

THE ROOM WAS ORNATELY decorated with a vast ceiling and wood molding that sculpted every inch of the walls from crown to base. A white-painted radiator stood beneath the window like a set of teeth. Patrice looked back to the door she'd just passed through. No doorknob or visible hinges; it was a hidden passage to the attic. It looked like one of the painted wood panels lining the wall.

A mirror hung over the fireplace. Patrice cast no reflection in it.

Aside from Maman sitting in the chair, there was a man in the room. He lay stretched on the bed, one foot on the floor and a hat covering his face, his hand tucked behind his neck.

Patrice stared at her mother. Skinny, with that zipper scar that ran down the back of her shoulder. She had the newspaper folded down to a rectangle just large enough for the article she was reading, and nothing more. Patrice could probably walk up and peer over her shoulder and still not be able to tell whether it was *The Times-Picayune* or *The States*. Even such a simple thing as reading the paper had to be a clandestine act.

And yet the absurdity seemed to be in the plain fact that she would be sitting there reading like that. Such an everyday thing.

"Shouldn't you be getting to the warehouse?" Maman said to the man on the bed, her French accent lengthening her words.

He stirred but otherwise ignored her. That's when Patrice realized that he had no hand. Jacob Chapman.

She remembered the old Terrefleurs legend of the amputation performed with no better anesthesia than liquor and song. Jacob had come around the plantation often over the years, helping Maman with sugar business and looking in on Papa.

"Ah," she heard her mother say.

Patrice saw that Maman had looked up from the paper and was staring directly at her.

Maman said, "Is this my boy, Guy? Have you finally come looking for your brother and sister?"

Maman set the paper on the side table and rose to her feet. Patrice stepped toward her. She could try pigeoning her. It likely wouldn't work.

"Or, is it . . . Patrice?"

A knock at the door, and then it opened. Patrice recognized the woman who entered the room but couldn't quite place her. It wasn't until she was passing Maman that Patrice realized this was her own Tatie Bernadette. She'd lost considerable weight. She held a basket topped with a white linen cloth.

"Bernadette. Where are you going?" Maman said.

Tatie paused and looked over her shoulder at Maman. "It's time for their supper."

"Come back later."

Tatie stood motionless, her gaze returning to that panel that led to Rosie and Gil.

"Aw, let her feed'm." Mr. Chapman said from the bed.

He was now sitting up with his hat resting on his head instead of over his face, and he lit a cigarette.

Maman ran her gaze across the room until it landed again on Patrice. She looked like a blind person who could not look eye-to-eye, only stare in the direction of a voice.

She said, "My child. Would you like that, eh? See how we feed your brother and sister like dogs. All because you won't come out from hiding."

Mr. Chapman's hand froze where he held his cigarette to his lips. He looked from Maman to the vague direction of where Patrice stood, his eyes darting from mother to daughter. Patrice doubted he could see her. He rose carefully to his feet, placing the cigarette in the ashtray as though it were fragile as an egg.

Tatie Bernadette turned, too, following Maman's gaze.

Maman said, "Go ahead then, Bernadette, feed them. Feed the mongrels."

Tatie Bernadette burst into tears and started pleading to Maman. "Which one is here? Is it little Trigger or Patrice? You can't keep treating those babies like this. You've got to stop—"

Maman backhanded Tatie. "Go in there and feed them, or leave them behind forever."

Maman hadn't even raised her voice. Just a strike and an order.

Tears streaming, Tatie cupped her hand to her face and pushed through to the panel, muttering, "I'm sorry children. I'm sorry."

Maman said to her, "And reset their tethers when you're done. You remember what happened to them the last time?"

Tatie was shaking where she stood in the doorway.

"Bernadette, did you hear me ask you a question?"

"Yes, ma'am."

"Good. Then tell us. I want everyone present to hear."

Tatie shuddered. Tears were streaming down her cheeks. Patrice had never seen her *tatie* this way before.

"Speak, Bernadette!"

"You took off their pinky toes. Took off little Rosie's first. Then Gilbert's. They were unsteady in the rafters after that."

"More liable to fall," Maman said.

Tatie hesitated, then, "Yes, ma'am."

Maman nodded. "So I advise you to put the tether back in its place when you're through feeding them."

"Yes, ma'am." A whisper this time.

"Alright then. Go on."

The panel closed behind Tatie, and they could hear her footfalls going up the steps. Patrice found it hard to believe that that terrified, cowering woman had really been her darling *tatie*.

Mr. Chapman strode for the opposite door. Patrice felt rage well up inside her at the sight of him, his mother's accomplice. She threw her focus into him.

He stopped just as he was reaching for the handle. The cigarette was still burning unchecked in the ashtray. Chapman stood still as an oak, beads of sweat already forming at his brow.

Mother looked satisfied. "There. Good idea. Use him."

Patrice turned Mr. Chapman around to face Maman. His movements were wooden.

But on Patrice's command he said, "What do you want from us?"

"Who is this? Patrice or Guy?" Maman asked.

"Patrice."

"Ah. *Ma p'tite Patrice.* You should send Guy to talk to me. You have nothing I want."

"Let them go."

"No, child. They will stay with me forever. Or until that silly Bernadette dies and they rot away to dust up there. I let her look after them only to get your attention. Now that I've got it, I should let them die."

Patrice listened, shock pulsing through her. Until now, Patrice's worst fear was that Maman would gain control of them. Make them into slaves. But these things Maman was saying—Patrice didn't know whether to believe it. That she was truly capable of letting Rosie and Gil die up there in that attic space. Maman had never been warm with them, but . . . this? Had she changed so much when they banished her from Terrefleurs? Or was this always her true nature?

Patrice spoke again through Mr. Chapman. "How could you hurt them like that? Why would you?"

Maman shook her head, never looking at Mr. Chapman though he was the one delivering the words. She kept her gaze on Patrice. "For the years I wasted on all of you. On your father. He would go into that spirit world and bring back so little. I saved his plantation for him. I bore his children. He had no responsibility. If Marie-Rose and Gilbert could learn to bring back real talents, then it would be worthwhile to keep them alive. But they don't. They were always terrible students. They never learned."

"I did. I learned."

"Yes you did. Yes you did."

The sound of floorboards creaking above. A soft thud.

Maman said, "Does it pain you to know that if you obeyed me all those years, you might be able to save those two? Does it? You can do nothing for them now. Because you were the one, Patrice, who defied me. You had the greatest skills. But you defied me and you turned your brothers and sister against me."

"What do you want!"

"What do I want? I want you to do what you were born to do. Unlock secrets from the briar and bring them into the world."

"You've got to let them go."

"And then? Are you offering an exchange, *ma p'tite?* You for them? It is not impossible. All along, I've wished for you to be my ambassador to the river devils."

If Patrice were speaking, she would have spoken her next words through clenched teeth. Instead they came from Mr. Chapman in a dull monotone: "Why would you ever want to commune with river devils?"

Maman simply smiled and shook her head. "My dear, if you

would have honored me instead of turning on me, you would understand. To commune with devils is to control the chaos. To control chaos is to control everything."

"I'll take those bandits you keep around, and I'll turn them on you."

"Try that, and your brother and sister hang dead from the rafters before anyone can so much as touch me. It is only by my enchantments that they don't fall."

Patrice looked to the attic above. The cords around their necks.

Maman was shaking her head. "If only I could trust you. If I had you in my attic, you would let yourself die before you obeyed me. And Guy, his skills are duller than yours, but he can find things, yanh? He could find you. Maybe even get you free. Already, he was the one who found the other two and brought us to this."

Maman looked thoughtful and said, "Maybe because we speak their names. Easier to find when we speak their names aloud."

Maman shrugged. "It is no use to hide them from you. You must be compelled of your own heart. You must step to me; I cannot pull you. But the only offerings I have for one of my children are the lives of my other children."

And as Patrice listened, she knew there was only one alternative. Take this man Jacob Chapman and make him strike her mother down. Kill her in defense of Rosie and Gil and Trigger. Killing Maman was the only way Patrice could make sure her siblings survived. If Patrice were quick, Rosie and Gil would be safe because Tatie Bernadette was still feeding them up in that attic. For the present at least, they weren't in the rafters.

But Maman seemed to have guessed what she was thinking because she seized something from the table and raked Mr. Chapman across the face.

Patrice watched, reaching for him though she knew it futile, and she felt her pigeonry sieve away from him. He sank to his knees, then all fours, and then he lay on his belly and closed his eyes.

In Maman's hand was some kind of bird's talon—a large one,

from a raptor like a hawk or owl. "He is not dead. Just sleeping. I do not have your abilities, *chère*, so I must resort to common poisons and enchantments."

Patrice could say nothing more to her now that Mr. Chapman had fallen.

Maman said, "Yes. It is clear I cannot trust you. You will not listen unless I spill blood. A good thing you have three siblings. Sacrifice one, and the other two might still be around to keep you interested."

"You will sacrifice no one! No one! Do you hear me?"

But of course she didn't hear her. Mr. Chapman had fallen and Maman's sensitivities weren't keen enough to hear Patrice in the briar.

Maman said, "And even if you were to surrender to me, Patrice, my second son, Guy, would eventually find you and free you. Wouldn't he? He finds things. What is it you call him now? Trigger? He is your weapon. The one whose soul you sacrifice from your God so he can work the sins for you. I had a man like that. Bruce Dempsey. I sent him to bring my children to me, but Guy killed him, didn't he? Your Trigger."

Patrice couldn't bear to listen. The thornflies were stinging her, but she barely cared. She just wished her mother would hush. If only Patrice could simply walk away from here with Trigger and Gil and Rosie, and never look back. Never see their mother again.

Maman said, "So now you must choose. You may come to offer yourself to me, and if I feel I can trust you, I will let the other two go. You trade one for two. That is a good bargain. But if you do not make this bargain with me, the other two die."

Patrice listened, sick. It was monstrous.

Maman said, "From this day, I give Gilbert and Marie-Rose a poison. And then later I will give them something to tame it. You don't know when they receive the poison or the relief. If you find a way to kill me, you risk that they die from the poison. You fail to come to me in two days' time, I will let them die from the poison."

Patrice felt a numbness that penetrated her soul. It would have been easier if Maman had asked her to lay down her life. Then at least it would have been over soon. That at least would have been an escape.

Maman turned her back to her then, the way she'd done so many times before. She settled into her chair and picked the newspaper up. Patrice didn't move.

Mother looked up again, listening, watching, and then said, "Are you still there? Go back to your body. The tar devils will let all of you alone now. You come at sunset the day after tomorrow. Go to the ferry dock where we found you with the lumen, there by the new bridge. Then you may have Marie-Rose and Gilbert back."

Patrice looked up toward the attic.

There in the ceiling, Trigger was suspended between the floor above and below. Leaning down as though from a tree limb. Listening. His expression was grave but when he saw Patrice looking at him, he gave her a wink.

❧❧❧

fifty

❧❧❧

ADELEINE HEARD SEVERIN'S LAUGH. She was doing somersaults in the air, jumping as though on a trampoline, and Madeleine watched from a bed of duckweed. It felt so good to escape that agony-ridden body. The infections, the overall heaviness.

She looked around. If she stared at any one thing—a tree trunk, a thorny vine—it would reveal itself to be crawling with life. Tiny beasts, creeping or flying, tasting nectar, hunting one another. Many of them had human-looking limbs or animal faces. They blended in with their surroundings and only came into view when Madeleine stopped and stared. Too easy to do that, stop and stare. Everything here absorbed her. A thousand distractions to keep her attention from the material world.

"There you are." She saw Gaston emerge from the black woods.

Madeleine looked at him, remembering, and struggled to her feet on the duckweed turf. "Where are our bodies?"

"They safe for now in the village."

"No Chloe?"

He shook his head. "Believe me, she ain't got a prayer of finding her way to that place, doesn't have one. But that other one? The one she was hiding you from with the spiderwebs?"

"Zenon."

"Yeah, him. You ain't wearin the spiderwebs no more, you're not anymore. If he's briar he can find you."

Madeleine sagged. "Great."

"Well, Miss Madeleine, he find you he'll be findin me, too."

Madeleine swallowed through a smile, taking his hand and squeezing it. So young. Loyal in the way a teenager swears an oath to his country before going off to war.

Severin pointed at Gaston. "This is not for you to attend."

"I'm comin all the same y'overgrown spider."

"Wait, where are we going?" Madeleine said.

Severin turned her scowl toward Madeleine. "To see the last child of the briar!"

Madeleine shook her head, feeling her heart grow cold. Chloe's last attempt to get to Cooper.

"No way. We are not going anywhere near them."

"Ah, but now you do as I say," Severin said.

Gaston squeezed Madeleine's hand again, his voice gentle. "You ain't in control here, Madeleine, not here and now. Chloe got you so messed up that both your body and your mind is failin."

Madeleine looked at him, and it was true she felt very strange.

Gaston said, "Ya ain't got enough to face off against your river devil. She want you to go somewhere in here she'll just drag you along."

Gaston turned to Severin. "An I bet you just crawled up into Chloe's lap and purred!"

Severin glared at him. "It is a better thing that we do not bring them!"

"Them?" Madeleine said.

"She means me and Armand," Gaston said, gesturing just beyond Madeleine's shoulder.

Madeleine turned. Gaston's river devil was standing there. Right there behind her. She stifled a gasp. Something in his manner, watching her with a predatory stare, she could tell that if she had screamed it would have somehow enticed him. She forced her shoulders and spine to her tallest posture and stared back. His breath held an odor of sourness like rotting teeth.

Armand said something to her in a deep whisper. It was French, old Louisiana river French, and she was slow following it. But she did catch the word *vache*.

She said, "Better a cow who can walk with humans than a river devil who can only whisper."

His face peeled back in a sneer, exposing decay, and Madeleine turned her back on him. Gaston was looking on with galvanized interest.

But then, Severin began to move.

Against her will, Madeline was moving with her. She dug in, certain she was standing still, and yet she advanced along with Severin as she'd done back in Nova Scotia. Hands and feet and bodies in general were only illusions here. And she and Severin were bound together so when one moved in the briar, the other moved, too.

Madeleine threw a desperate glance at Gaston, who was keeping pace even though each step traversed miles. It almost seemed as though they were all standing still and the world was moving beneath them.

"Wait," Madeleine said.

Severin paused and glanced back at her.

"I'll go with you . . ." Madeleine began.

Severin laughed. "Of course you go! You have no choice!"

"But first we have to go to New Orleans. I need to see if everyone's OK."

Gaston looked doubtful. "Your man Zenon's gonna be payin you a call any minute now. You sure you want him to see who you lookin in on in New Orleans?"

He was right. Madeleine wanted to see Ethan so badly she was almost tempted to risk it. Just to make sure he was alive. The not knowing was killing her.

But of course she couldn't risk seeing him. If Ethan and Bo had managed to stay hidden from Zenon thus far, she wasn't going to ruin it.

"Nothing to see, then, in New Orleans," Severin said, and she turned back to the same path.

Madeleine said quickly, "No, there is. I want to see the baby. The orphan."

"Ah, this is only to delay!"

"What's it to you? Don't we have all the time in the world? The longer I'm in here, the harder it is for me to leave the briar. Isn't that true?"

Severin was scowling but she said nothing.

Gaston took Madeleine's arm, whispering, "You playin with fire. It's true, you get lost in here you may not find your way out. She ain't gonna lead you free."

Madeleine shook him off. "You remember, Severin. That baby? From that day under the bridge when Zenon used Shalmut Halsey as his pigeon. Shot all those people, including Del, and now that baby's got no mother."

Severin's expression grew excited. "Yes, such as that. A lovely dance of chaos, truly."

Madeleine's eyes lifted to the sylphs that now drew in around them. Graceful, gorgeous. It seemed she could smell the skin beneath the satiny, brilliant-colored down. She couldn't resist reaching up to pet one. It flew just out of reach.

Armand pointed at the sylphs and said something to Severin in
French, and Madeleine realized that the sylphs had drawn her attention so that she'd already forgotten what she was doing. The material
world suddenly seemed like a charming old legend. She shook off the
sensation.

Madeleine said to Gaston, "I don't like it. Why does Severin
want to see Cooper? We already know where he is."

"I wager it's cuz this time the old witch is watching. She workin
her spells so she see into the briar."

"She can see us?"

"Just guessing. But probably."

His gaze lifted to the trees, and Madeleine looked, too. And by
looking she observed something she ought to have realized earlier—
the coldness, the void. Always present in the briar but now it felt
like it was slowly draining the very blood from her.

Madeleine said to Gaston, voice low, "But why would Severin
even care what Chloe wants?"

"The old bat been spending the last eighty years figurin out how
to get them devils to do her work, those river devils. She know how
to charm'em. Got her own brand a devil, too—the ones that're oily
and wild. Start out workin for her but over time they just go feral."

And then Armand had turned his attention back to Madeleine.
He stood far too close, sour and seething, his gaze boring into her.

"*Qu 'est-ce que tu veut? Pourquois l'enfant?*"

Madeleine shook her head. "Just want to take a look, is all."

Because she didn't know what else to do. She couldn't let Chloe
find her nephew, little Cooper, and his mother Emily. If Gaston's
existence was an example of what happened when Chloe got her
hands on a child of the briar, Madeleine would do whatever it took
to prevent it. She'd blurted out an interest in Del's baby only as a
means of distraction from Cooper.

The river devil was pointing at her, and when he spoke again he
used English. "Who you follow? Zenon, or Chloe?"

Madeleine was taken aback. "What? Neither!"

"You follow Madeleine! Ha!" He grinned at Severin and gestured to the sylphs.

"*Vas-y!*"

Severin gave Madeleine a queer look but then resumed the journey. This time, Madeleine was sure they were not heading to Wolfville, Nova Scotia, where Cooper and Emily Hammond lived in hiding. This time they were headed back to New Orleans.

❦

MADELEINE HAD EXPECTED TO find a foster home or even an orphanage. Considering the fact that baby Declan had been homeless even when his mother Del was still alive, it seemed implausible that he had any relatives that could care for him. But this place was too given over to squalor to be a foster home. The woman who was looking after him had to be a relative. Probably Del's mother. Natural that the child would be placed in the care of a grandparent after Del died that day in the shooting under the Huey P. Long Bridge.

There were coupon circulars and bills on the coffee table, all addressed with the name Cassel Whalen, and so Madeleine took it as the name of this woman. And Cassel didn't resemble Del much but she did look like baby Declan—sort of. It seemed Cassel was missing most of her teeth which highlighted the fact that the shape of her mouth and chin were exactly like Declan's. A distinctive pie wedge point to the jaw line. She was smoking something hand-rolled in front of the TV and sipping from a plastic tumbler of what looked like pink wine on ice.

Madeleine moved across the living room to where the baby lay in a car seat atop the kitchen table. He was crying, and his diapers were sagging and bunched, a bloom of red sores just below his navel.

Madeleine threw a fierce look at Cassel. "Change his diaper!"

Cassel looked over toward Declan's car seat and then back at the television. Madeleine could tell the idea had registered but she seemed sluggish to heed it. Probably had had this idea on her own before but had gotten into the habit of ignoring it.

Madeleine grit her teeth and walked over to where Cassel sat on the sofa. She trained her mind on Cassel's hand as she raised the tumbler and poured iced wine down her shirt.

Blinking at her hand as though it were possessed, which of course it was, Cassel said slowly, "Fuck . . . my . . . life."

Madeleine tried again, and this time Cassel rose from the sofa and slipper-shuffled to the kitchen table where little Declan lay. "Whatcha cryin for, sweet baby?"

She picked him up and patted his diapered bottom as she gazed out the window, humming.

And then a surprised look crossed her face. "Ooh, you wet."

She laid him bare on the kitchen table and revealed that he was more than wet. Madeleine's head was swimming. The room was breathing with black briar. Thornflies crept along the hardened stems, waiting for a sign of panic or anxiety or fury. She watched as one of them stretched its wings and combed it back, using its hooked forearm to clean itself from head to wing to stinger.

Gaston stood at Madeleine's elbow, shaking his head. "I don't get it. Whatchyoo doin exactly?"

She blinked, trying to remember where she was or why she was there. She saw the pointy-chinned woman changing the pointy-chinned baby and remembered she'd pigeoned that.

"I wanted to see what happened to this child," she said.

"I mean, what are you doin? You come here knowin the babe's gonna have it hard. Why you gotta see on that?"

"Because I'm human and I care."

"You care because you got the stain. It ain't doin you no good, it isn't, not any. Let me clear it for you."

Madeleine stepped back.

"I already done that."

They looked. Zenon was standing near where Cassel was changing the baby, and his river devil, Josh, was there, too. Madeleine had never seen much of him beyond shadows and glimpses.

Zenon said, "Where you been, little sister? Hangin out with lumens by the stain in ya. I showed you how to get it out."

Gaston said, "She ain't know where she been and she don't even know where her body is now, she doesn't. The old witch got to her."

"Chloe?"

And then Zenon looked from Madeleine to Gaston and gave a low whistle. "Holy blue moon Jesus. I ain't seen this many briar folk in one place, ever."

And to Gaston, Zenon said, "You look like a hairy skink."

He and Gaston were staring at one another. Recognition in both their eyes, though Madeleine could tell it was their first meeting.

"How do I know you?" Zenon asked.

Gaston said, "We still lookin to figure that one out."

"What do you want, Zenon?" Madeleine said.

"Got some unfinished business, ain't we?"

Madeleine narrowed her eyes. "What does that mean?"

"You remember. Gotta get rid of the rest of them lumens."

Cassel had finished changing Declan and raised her head. Madeleine followed her gaze and saw someone walking up the drive. Cassel's man, Madeleine thought; but then she realized there was something gawky in the posture. Just a boy. Gaston's age, maybe.

He opened the screen door and Madeleine gave a start. That frizzed hair, the narrow eyes. Oyster. Of all the times she saw him he usually wore that silly bandana that covered the paint stains on his nose and mouth. Now, without it, she saw the distinctive pie shape to the chin. Just like Cassel. Just like Declan.

How stupid Madeleine had been. Of course Cassel wasn't Del's mother. She was Oyster's.

"Hey mama," Oyster said in that strange deep voice that indicated he was still huffing.

"Hey baby." Cassel handed little Declan over and Oyster took the infant with all the familiarity of a dad, laying him on his shoulder.

Zenon put a hand on Madeleine's arm, and she wanted to shake him off. He leaned in as though she'd whispered something he wanted to hear.

He said, "Check you out, sis. You ain't in your right mind."

"She gone briar to the bone," Josh said, his teeth clenched on a stick.

Zenon laughed. "I like that. Briar to the bone. Lord, I can read your intentions right now just as easy as if you were a pigeon. Only reason you come here is so your river devil wouldn't drag you on over to see our little nephew, is that it? Keep him safe from mean old Chloe?"

Severin scowled. "We go now!"

"Aw, keep your panties on. We can make good use out of these fine folks." Zenon pointed at Oyster. "I used that little punk plenty of times. He's willing, just ain't resourceful."

Madeleine peeled Zenon's hand from her shoulder and tried to think. Her mind was in such tumult that if Zenon hadn't reminded her what she was doing here she would have forgotten. Again.

Oyster set Declan down on the couch. "You got any money, Ma?"

"Naw, hell no. You know I ain't got nothin to give you," Cassel said.

Oyster pouted for a moment and it made him look so childlike. Zenon was staring at him, same way he'd been staring at Madeleine earlier. Madeleine recognized what he was doing. Reading Oyster's intentions. She followed suit. Oyster's intentions didn't stretch beyond the next few hours: Get some money. Go to the Sonic for some food. Find his friends and drink and huff the night away. Somewhere in there, he actually had a fleeting notion to take Declan to a cousin's who had a baby of the same age. Last time he saw her she gave Declan a rattle that looked like plastic keys. His cousin was a nice girl, married to a man who was hardworking but who pretty much hated Oyster. The idea of taking Declan to see her vanished. The

idea to go hang out with his friends strengthened. And then something else pushed to the forefront:

Now where can I get my hands on a gun?

It startled Madeleine. She'd never before witnessed pigeonry
from this point of view—seeing Oyster's drifting, passing intentions suddenly broken by a hardened idea.

"Zenon, leave these people alone. Oyster's just a kid."

"He's a punk. Relax. It'll keep your river devil happy. That
right, Severin?"

Severin looked smug. She peered at him sideways the way a cat
might size someone up.

Madeleine had no idea why Zenon would implant that thought
and she didn't dare ask.

Oyster went to the pantry by the refrigerator and took down a
box of saltines, one-handed, then set them on the counter.

Cassel said, "Lord, whatchyoo doin with that?"

"I'll bring it back, Mama."

"Oh, lord."

He reached into the saltine box and pulled out a white plastic
Family Dollar bag, something heavy inside. Black metal.

Severin grinned and slipped her fingers into Madeleine's palm.
"A good idea to come here, so surely."

fifty-one

BAYOU BOUILLON, 1933

WHEN PATRICE OPENED HER eyes she was occupying her own body. She saw it. Felt it. The sensation had become foreign to her.

Her body was not reclining as was so often the case—returning from the briar usually meant going to sleep, straight from the world of thorns to the world of dreams. Letting one bleed into the next. But not now. She was standing on bare feet, hands pressed against wood. The walls of a shack.

She had no memory of before or anticipation of yet to come. The disorientation would pass soon, she knew, and there was nothing to do but relish this weightlessness of spirit.

She smiled, pressed her finger against a splinter just to feel a sense of pain, and then pulled away before it broke skin. Her finger was alive, her hand and arm alive, her lungs filled and released in waves. She swore she could sense the pulse points mirroring her heartbeat.

Her lips pressed and released in a voiceless *ma ma ma*, then *ba ba ba*.

Behind her, a whisper: "Look. She's back."

She turned. Confusion was lingering. She must have been in the briar a long time because there was a lady here who must have been watching over her. That meant Patrice had been in long enough for her physical body to need assistance eating, bathing, dressing, and so forth. The lady was talking to Ferrar. But although the lady looked strikingly familiar, Patrice couln't think of her name.

Patrice stared. The lady was wearing a necklace: a leather strap looped through a carved sphere with something inside. But then Patrice realized that this lady looked just like her. Exactly so. To the very mole on her neck. And below the mole and the necklace, this lady was wearing the cross Eunice had given Patrice several days ago when she'd left Terrefleurs.

Patrice looked down. She saw that she was still wearing Eunice's cross, too. As well as another necklace with a pendant, just like the one the lady wore, only this pendant was a tiny carved oak leaf, not a sphere.

The lady whispered something to Ferrar and then they both slipped out through the door.

Patrice said, "Wait!"

And she heard the door latch from the outside.

"Wait!" She tried the door and found it locked.

On the other side of the wall, footsteps were retreating down the boardwalk. Patrice pounded at the door but they were already gone.

❧

PATRICE HAD BEEN WAITING alone in the shack when the door finally opened again. The sun backlit him to a silhouette, but she recognized his posture immediately.

"Francois!"

He put his arm over her shoulder and patted. "*Bonsoir*, honey, *bonsoir*."

And then he took both of her hands in his and said, "If we go outside you must promise not to run off. You have to stay here with me."

A strange request, but: "Of course."

He turned toward the door, and as she followed him, she said, "I've got to get back to New Orleans immediately."

"Too dangerous."

"But, Gil and Rosie. I've got to meet mother under the bridge or she'll kill them."

Francois paused, his back to her. "Maybe tomorrow."

She didn't like it. It pushed things too close.

He must have taken off his bandages, but the sunlight pouring in made it difficult to get a good look at him. Something was strange, though. He was bald, and much more healthy-looking than he ought to be. His clothes were not sagging on him.

On some level she already knew. Remembered. But . . .

He gestured to her to follow him out the door. The sunlight blinded her, and she paused with her hand over her eyes.

"Right here," Francois was saying.

He waved her to a crate that rested against the shanty wall. "Have a seat."

Someone else was sitting on the next crate. She looked at him as she sat down.

"Treese?" An adolescent boy slightly older than she was gaping at her.

"You been sleepin a long time," Francois began.

She squinted, her eyes still adjusting, and she saw that the boy sitting next to her was long-legged, peach fuzz on his chin, black-skinned and blue-eyed.

It dawned on her with a strange, ringing numbness. Trigger: Still a boy. But a much older boy.

It was coming back to her, how much Gil and Rosie had aged in the rafters beneath that roof.

Francois said, "Y'all gonna have to make some adjustments."

Patrice was weeping now, and Trigger put his arms around her. He held her tight.

"I just woke up, too," he mumbled into her hair.

Francois put his hands in his pockets and turned to the side, clearly unsure what to say.

"You remember it?" Trigger asked her.

"Only the last. The part with Maman. I'll gladly go with her for Gil and Rosie's sake but what's to keep her from going after y'all again?"

"Don't worry, she ain't gonna keep none of us."

Patrice smiled through her tears and said, "Won't. Any."

Trigger said, "Gosh, you're so pretty. You look like an honest-to-goodness lady."

"I can't believe how tall you are."

She looked up at Francois. He still had his back turned, but from his profile she could now see an eye patch and the healed scarring where a portion of his lip was missing.

"How long, exactly, were we in the briar?" she asked.

Francois looked back toward them. He started to speak but then paused.

He took a breath and let it out before answering; then: "About six years, *p'tite*."

She froze, Trigger still holding onto her. He went still, too. Six years. Six years. That meant she was twenty. Guy and Gilbert were sixteen. Rosie: thirteen. The time in the briar had seemed endless, true enough, but also beginningless.

"Lotta things happened," Francois said.

Patrice nodded though she was still absorbing this. Gil and Rosie, living like that. Up in the rafters of that horrible place where Maman kept them. Six years seemed like an eternity to Patrice at

fourteen—actually, twenty—she couldn't imagine what it meant
to them.

Francois said, "Listen. Lotta pirates around. Some of' m workin
for your mother. They tried to come after y'all lotta times over the
years. You stay away from pirates."

Patrice nodded again.

"Another thing, they ghosts around, too. And the thing about'm
is, they're your ghosts."

Patrice and Trigger looked at one another. "We're . . . dead?"

"Hell, I don't know. Don't think so."

He looked pained by the conversation. He turned his head to look
down the boardwalk, and Patrice thought he was going to walk off
right then and there.

Instead he said, "In a way, y'all come back to this place out of
order. Ain't like regular folks. They just leave and come back. But
y'all, you leave today and come back yesterday. Understand?"

Flatly, no. Patrice had no idea what he was trying to say. "Where's
Ferrar?"

"Ain't here."

"I just saw him!"

"No, you saw a . . . who was he with?"

Patrice didn't answer, thinking of the lady who looked exactly
like her, and lowered her gaze to the new carved necklace. It occurred to her that Francois was wearing one just like it—including
the oak leaf. Trigger, too.

Francois nodded. "That's it. Only way you can tell who's what.
You and me and Trigger here got the leaf. That means we're on
straight time. You don't talk to no one with other necklaces. You
got it?"

"What do you mean, 'straight time'?"

"It means you ain't doubled back yet. And don't go by your real
names. Just use your middle names. If you have to leave and come
back, you pick a different name and a different necklace."

"Change our names? Why?"

Francois was looking across the bayou and showed no indication he cared to discuss it further.

Trigger said only, "Jeez, Francois, we all thought you's gonna die."

Patrice elbowed him for his rudeness. But without taking his gaze from the bayou, Francois nodded as though he'd believed the same thing.

Finally, he gestured toward Patrice. "You healed me."

Patrice gaped at him. She remembered wrapping him in bandages, that was all.

But then Francois added, "Meanin, you goin to someday."

WHEN THEY NEEDED TO visit the willow tree the first time, Francois escorted them through the floating village and only allowed them to advance when no one else was around. Then, later, when it was time to go again, he told them to use a bucket in the shack. Trigger had no problem with that (or peeing into the bayou, for that matter), but Patrice decided to wait until Francois was willing to escort her to the tree. Using a bucket like that, it seemed like the kind of thing people had to do long ago. Outhouses and makeshift facilities that smelled horrid and bred diseases. The Terrefleurs outhouse still stood, though the main house was plumbed and there were central facilities for the workers.

Terrefleurs seemed so far behind her now. A world away. With no LeBlanc to run the place, and no Francois or even Tatie Bernadette, what had happened to it over these lost years? All that cane in the fields, but who'd seen to it that it got sold and made into sugar? Who paid the workers? What had become of sweet Eunice and her mother?

All the other shacks on this spoke of the boardwalk stood vacant. Patrice spent the afternoon with Trigger, trying to sort out what had occurred over the past six years. They sat on the crates or went inside the shack. Even with so much happening the central concern remained the same: Get Gil and Rosie back. They weren't precisely sure how they were going to do that though she and Trig were coming up with one plan after another, and immediately discarding each one for too many flaws. One day left to figure it out.

The sky had gone pink. Sunset today. Everything would change by sunset tomorrow.

Trigger said, "Francois don't seem too overjoyed about helping us get to New Orleans."

"We'll have to figure it out on our own."

Trigger pointed down the boardwalk. "Hey, look! It's—"

But Patrice managed to clamp her hand over her brother's mouth before he finished the sentence: *It's Ferrar.*

"No names!" Patrice said.

"He'll help us out!"

Ferrar was coming toward them with his head up and a smile visible even from a distance. Patrice sprang to her feet, so delighted she wanted to run down the boardwalk and throw her arms around him. But then she paused.

Wouldn't that be childish?

Little girl, he'd called her the last time they'd spoken. Yesterday for her. Six years ago for him.

Her hand went to her hair. She had no idea what she looked like. How odd, though she hadn't been able to take her eyes off of Trigger and his transformation from boy to teenager, it hadn't occurred to her to find a way to take a look at herself.

No mirror of course. Her hair had been brushed, her body washed, and she was wearing clean clothes. Someone had done those things for her the way Tatie Bernadette had been caring for Gil and Rosie. Perhaps the ghost version of herself? The future version? What a strange thing for her to look forward to.

Ferrar was now just several feet away, but she turned from him and looked into the bayou, hoping to see her reflection. There. But this bayou liked to boil cold, and the effervescence distorted her face and body in swirls and whorls. The only thing she did notice—from looking down, not looking into the bayou—was that her hips looked different. Less straight. More of an angle between her waist and hip bones.

Ferrar scooped her up and spun her around.

It startled her, and she threw back her head and laughed, squeezing him tight. A thrill ran from her belly up her spine. She'd really only met Ferrar twice, and both times she'd nearly gotten him killed. Amazing that he would be as happy to see her as she was him.

He set her down slowly, smiling at her, and held her there a moment longer than she expected. It made her feel awkward and hot at the neck.

She felt relieved when he finally turned to Trigger, patting him on the shoulder and shaking his hand. Her legs were wobbly. She sat down on a crate to keep steady and tried to tell herself that the reason why she was dizzy was because she'd just been spun.

Trigger grinned at Ferrar, now nearly the same height. "You told us there were ghosts in this place but you could have gone into a bit more detail, Old Socks."

"I never knew it was so haunted as this! Or that I might wind up a ghost, too."

That lovely mixed accent of his—country and French, twangy and soft. He was wearing an oak leaf carving just like the ones Trigger and Patrice wore. That morning, Patrice had seen the other Ferrar wearing a carved sphere.

She realized he was watching her watching him, and the intensity of his gaze made her grateful she was still sitting down.

"Have you been here the whole time?" she asked, if only to interrupt the stare.

Ferrar shook his head. "Off and on. After that first spell, I had to go find work in the city. I came back here once a month to look in on y'all and bring supplies. But it's gotten so dangerous lately that I've had to come back more often."

"Dangerous?"

Ferrar nodded. "Word has gotten out that Bayou Bouillon is enchanted. Bootleggers comin in from all over—no one is so superstitious as a criminal. Except maybe a gambler."

Trigger grinned, breathing through his mouth and wearing an expression that seemed far better suited to his previous, eleven-year-old self. "Superstitious on what? What're they trying to get out of it?"

Ferrar's expression tightened just a bit. "They've been told if any man can trap a ghost and bring him to the witch in New Orleans, she will reward him."

"A ghost? Meaning . . . ?"

"No one here is safe."

Patrice thought of how her body had been left behind unoccupied while her mind was in the briar. "How did we . . . not get taken, then?"

"This place is easy to defend. The boardwalks are laid out like spokes on a wheel. We moved you to a different one from time to time. We prevent anyone from coming down your boardwalk. Francois is the commodore here, and he oversees everything. This is where the outlaws come to trade."

Patrice looked down toward the end of the boardwalk, toward the center of the village. She could hear voices there now. See the torchlights flaring in anticipation of sundown.

Ferrar said, "And the village itself is very difficult to get to. We watch the channels carefully. When anyone approaches we see them long before they get here. Unless . . ."

"What?"

He shrugged. "Unless it's a ghost. They come up through the boil."

That stunned her. She tried to imagine an older version of herself, fresh from some other world, swimming to the surface.

Patrice looked out over the water. It appeared like any other bayou at sunset, reflecting the persimmon sky and throwing dancing cables of light across the shacks. The fine bubbles at the surface were masked by late season hatches and the fish that were feeding on them.

"We have to get Gil and Rosie back," Patrice said.

"That's what you said the last time you spoke to me. All these years, I thought I might be able to find them and bring them to you before you fell back to your body."

Such weight in his voice. She looked at him, wondering, and grew quiet to the skin.

When her father used to go lost in the briar, he looked different— less human, more animal. His facial expressions lacked self-awareness. Even people who did not know him and did not speak to him could tell something was wrong. That they should be cautious.

"What did I look like? All those years. I must have been . . . so . . . wild."

"I don't know. Francois wouldn't let me near you."

That surprised her. "Why not?"

Ferrar shrugged. "A young lady, vulnerable. He was protective. Francois has spent the past six years guarding you two and the village itself. People who live here have had to fight for it. Every attempt by outlaws to enter the village has failed, because unless they give the signal, no one can get through the channel."

"What's the signal?"

"It changes. Sometimes it's three bells sometimes it's light flashes. He allows only the regulars."

Ferrar paused, lifting his fingers to graze her jaw for just a fleeting moment. "You, he kept hidden from everyone. I saw you only by looking at your ghosts from a distance."

Something about his expression. He was hiding some secret knowledge. Knowledge about her. She didn't like that.

She said suddenly, "We have to go. Gotta leave here and meet our mother by sunset tomorrow."

He frowned. "You do that, her men will kill you. Either that or take you away."

Patrice and Trigger explained their mother's ransom. As they relayed the details, Patrice started feeling sick all over again. How were they going to escape this without one or all of them getting hurt or killed? She finally believed it now, that mother was capable of killing them. She hated them that much. She hated that they refused to be what she wanted them to be.

Ferrar said, "I think it's a bad idea. You don't know how many times she's sent bad men here to kidnap you. But that was in the early days. Now, when they come, they come to kill you."

"We have to go," Trigger said.

Ferrar turned to look at Trigger and was very quiet for a long moment. "What you don't know, is many have tried to get your brother and sister. I have tried. Always, she sets a trap, and there's bloodshed."

"What exactly are you saying?" Patrice asked.

"I don't think they can be helped."

It landed on her like a punch to the belly. Patrice wrapped her hands around herself.

Trigger said, "Well you think wrong."

Patrice turned to look at her brother and caught her breath. His face had gone so dark. She wasn't sure if it was because he was older now or that he'd gone too cold in the briar, but he looked hard. Her Trigger.

He said, "We're gonna get rid of our ma and get away safe, all four of us: Rosie, Gil, me and Patrice. This time we're gonna pull it off and nobody's gonna say any different, you get me? Old Socks?"

The way Trigger's chin was set. The look of determination on his face. It gave Patrice a chill. Maybe a little too determined. It felt reckless.

Suddenly Patrice wondered if she was about to face the worst possibility of all: losing all three of her siblings.

Trigger was staring at Ferrar like he wanted to throw a punch. "You think I'm gonna leave them to rot you got another thing comin."

"Easy," Patrice said.

"Well how do we know he ain't makin this up? He could be working for her, too!"

She had grown so accustomed to thornflies stinging her at the first hint of panic that she half-expected them to rise from the bayou and swarm her now. She tried to tamp down the anxiety. Trigger's temper was about to boil over.

But Ferrar, he said nothing. He did not try to calm Trigger down. His face showed no expression of anger or chagrin or apology or even sympathy—only a distinct . . . *listening*. Patrice stopped herself from arguing with Trigger, even though she knew Ferrar was the best ally they had right now, and that he was the last person Trigger should be antagonizing. Ferrar was listening. Patrice listened, too.

Trigger stared at Ferrar for a few moments longer, and then slumped where he sat. "I'm sorry."

She reached out and put an arm around her brother. His shirt was damp with sweat. The world on his shoulders. The sparse hairs on his face made him seem like an eleven-year-old playing dress up.

Eyes wet, he said, "We just gotta get them back."

Ferrar nodded. "I understand. I will take you to New Orleans come first light."

The sun was sinking, and the floating village was alive with voices though all Patrice could see were floating shanties and boardwalk and the winking flames of the torches.

❧

fifty-two

❧

ADELEINE WAS HAVING A hard time hanging on. Her thoughts were random and easily stolen by the sylphs. She caught swatches of conversation from the others:

"What's wrong with her?"

"Body failin"

"Where Chloe at?"

"I think she failin too."

And for one single moment, the situation became clear. Something was wrong with Chloe. She hadn't come after them as aggressively as Madeleine might have expected. Madeleine guessed it had something to do with Chloe's determination to find baby Cooper. Somehow, Chloe believed that baby could keep her alive.

And Madeleine was going to die unless she could get her hands on some antibiotics.

So she was now the beetle trying to bore its way out of the pitcher plant. Either Madeleine died and left Chloe to waste away to her death, or Chloe died and left Madeleine to waste away to hers.

And the sylphs were flying. And the briar world moved. And nothing seemed to matter. Ethan, Bo, and Madeleine's own life were nothing more than old bayou tales told by firelight. She was heading somewhere new. A place where Daddy and her brother Marc had gone.

And then she saw Ethan.

⁕

CATCHING SIGHT OF ETHAN felt like ice water on her fevered body. Everything snapped back into perspective. That she couldn't lose him. That she couldn't lose her own life. She remembered now.

He looked so tired.

They were in his lab at Tulane. Madeleine forced herself into full cognizance, separating two worlds. Her view of the laboratory was nested in deep coils of thorns. Tunnels of them. Creatures shifted out of view within the hollows.

Zenon and Josh. Gaston and Armand. Madeleine and Severin. They were all in the briar layer.

Ethan was in the physical world. Cheryl, too—Bo's next door neighbor and the mother of his wheelchair-bound friend, Ray. And . . . Bo?

There. All but hidden. His feet were showing, but the rest of him was hidden inside a chamber that Madeleine knew was used for reading neural activity. She wouldn't have spotted him herself if she hadn't been looking. She could see only his sneakers just inside the chamber doorway beyond Ethan's shoulder. And not just Bo's sneakers—a second pair indicated another child was with him. Ray. His wheelchair rested against a wall near where his mother, Cheryl, stood.

And they were all watching, the river devils and the children of the briar. But had they noticed Bo and Ray? Gaston and Zenon were talking and were paying only half attention to what was going on in the lab.

"What, you sworn loyalty to the old lady?" Zenon said.

"Sworn loyalty? What is this, a black hand gang?" Gaston said.

"I'll take that as a yes."

"Hell no, it ain't a yes, it isn't. I can't stand that old bat."

"So you're open to a new way of doing things."

Gaston lifted his hand toward Zenon as if blocking a glare from his eyes. "Son, I'm too old to be foolin with anything of the like."

Madeleine looked at him, puzzled, but of course he must be trying to be ironic. "Too old" in his teens. She looked back toward those little boys' sneakers and tried to swallow back her anxiety. Bo's lumen glow was centered around his heart and belly and was therefore not visible. Ray, too, was well-hidden. One word from either of them and they would be discovered.

Madeleine whispered very quietly so that the others wouldn't hear her, "Bo Racer. Keep still."

To Madeleine's dismay, Bo immediately started clicking. But he made only two clicks and then fell silent as he likely processed what was happening.

Madeleine held her breath, watching the others. There were enough ticks and whirs coming from the equipment in Ethan's lab that Bo's sound might have blended in. Gaston and Zenon and the river devils were now arguing, with Severin—Severin!—coming to Chloe's defense.

"She alone knows the ways of bringing the thorns through to the other world!" Severin was saying.

Madeleine saw Bo's feet draw up and disappear inside the chamber. He must have somehow heard and understood the warning. Madeleine imagined his hands moving in quick cuts of sign language to Ray, warning him to be silent. But Ray couldn't move his legs out of view.

Zenon said, "We'll talk about it later. Right now we got some scrubbin to do."

He and Gaston and the river devils turned their attention back to the lab, where Ethan and Cheryl stood front and center. Both wore that residual lumen glow. The glow looked different on a non-lumen. Whereas inside Bo, the light seemed to be emitting from within, on the others it looked like reflections of light. A mirror to a flame.

"What are we doing here?" Madeleine said to the others in hopes of drawing away attention.

"Look who's up and at 'em," Zenon said.

Gaston stepped toward her. "Hang in there, Miss Madeleine. Keep your mind bright and your body might follow."

Zenon grinned. "She's fine. This'll wake her up."

In the lab, Ethan was saying to Cheryl, "Thanks for bringin his schoolwork."

Cheryl said, "Like I had a choice? You know my boy ain't gonna stand for bein away from him too long."

Madeleine raised her voice. "Come on, let's get out of here."

But they were ignoring her now. Fixated on Cheryl and Ethan. If Madeleine could somehow shut those two up she surely would. She was too weak, and their lumen stain made pigeoning difficult. But this made it difficult for Zenon to pigeon them, too.

Cheryl and Ethan had stopped talking. They were both looking at the doorway. In it stood Oyster.

Madeleine gasped at the sight of him. He was standing with his kerchief around his throat and the paint stains mottling his mouth and nostrils like bruises. In his hand was the white plastic dollar-store bag he'd taken from the box of saltines in his mother's kitchen. He reached inside it and withdrew a gun. Not a flashlight. An actual gun. The plastic bag drifted to the vinyl tiled flooring.

Madeleine funneled her mind on Oyster: "Put the gun down!"

But Zenon was also leaning on him. Had already had him in a long hold.

Oyster raised the weapon.

"No!" Madeleine cried.

Time slowed. With it came the sting of the thornflies. They swarmed her as she watched. Their sting carried a paralysis with it.

Ethan lunged forward.

The gun fired. A sudden cracking sound and a flash of light.

Gaston was at Madeleine's side, and she realized she'd been screaming.

Gaston spoke to her in a gentle voice. "It's alright, Miss Madeleine. Let'm do what they need to do. They stained. Been around lumens. They got to go."

"It's Ethan!" Madeleine screamed.

Gaston looked back at them. "Your sweetheart?"

Ethan had hurled himself at Oyster and knocked his arm down. The bullet went astray, burning through the vinyl tile to the floor below.

Madeleine cried, "Leave them alone!"

Zenon was watching Oyster and Ethan.

Ethan pried the gun from Oyster's fingers and was shouting at him. "This ain't you, kid! This is someone else taking hold of your thoughts! You want to be a slave to some fool?"

Ethan handed the gun back to Cheryl and kept both hands on Oyster, trying to shake some sense into him. Cheryl had gone ashen and like Madeleine, was covered in thornflies. Only Cheryl couldn't see them. She probably couldn't feel their stinging. Madeleine understood that the thornflies must be heightening Cheryl's anxiety without her even knowing they existed. Something else, too—a humanlike creature that must be Cheryl's river devil, hovering over her shoulder. The gun was shaking in Cheryl's hand. Panic and dismay. Chaos. All that chaos. It sucked Bo's light right out of her.

Zenon's lip curled back in a hateful smile.

Gaston had his arms around Madeleine and was talking to Zenon. "Alright. Leave the sweetheart alone, yeah? We figure out what to do about that another time."

Cheryl's expression changed. The fear left her. She raised the gun and pointed it at the back of Ethan's head.

"No!" Madeleine screamed.

The thornflies rendered her useless. She ought to be able to take hold of Cheryl now that the light inside her was gone. But Madeleine couldn't function through her own panic. The drain of her sick, weak body dragged at her very consciousness.

Gaston was staring hard at Cheryl. Cheryl's grip on the weapon faltered. And then she turned it to her own cheek in a salute—and fired.

So fast. It was over in a second.

Ethan turned. Cheryl's body lengthened, and then crumpled. The hole at her temple was nothing more than an anthill. But then it wept blood, and Cheryl was on the ground.

Madeleine's eyes turned toward the chamber where Bo and Ray were still hidden, Ray's sneakers still dangling within view. He likely had no idea his mother had just shot herself. That his life was about to change forever.

Cheryl's devil watched her body for a moment, then raised its eyes to Armand. Armand stared back, mouth open. The other devil turned and receded into the tunnels of thorns.

"You killed her," Madeleine said.

Gaston was holding her arm. "It was her or your sweetheart, honey. We can't let them lumens take over. She's stained."

"The light had already left her!" Madeleine said.

"Once stained, it comes back all too easy. Just like you make someone a pigeon once, you don't have to try all that hard to do it again."

Madeleine was straining to see beyond into the laboratory, but for some reason she could see nothing. She looked at Gaston, right beside her, and couldn't see his face at all.

"Madeleine leaves us now," Severin said.

Zenon said, "What? Keep her alive for chrissake!"

"How do you suggest I do that?" Gaston said.

"I don't know! Get back to your bodies!"

Severin's voice: "But Chloe wishes for—"

Zenon said, "Chloe ain't one of us! Madeleine dies, you gonna be just another cockroach in here. You know what's good for you, take'r back to her body and let the hairy skink boy fix her up."

But their voices were mere sound fractals and made little sense to her. Madeleine was striving to find out whether Ethan and the boys were OK. If she really was going to die, let it be knowing that they at least were OK.

fifty-three

BAYOU BOUILLON, 1933

*P*ATRICE HAD TO VISIT the willow tree and that was all there was
to it. She wished to high heaven she'd just listened to Francois when he'd told her to use the bucket. Now she had to
go urgently, and couldn't bear the thought of using the bucket with
Ferrar around even if he waited outside the shack. It just seemed it
would make her low.

Ferrar agreed to walk with them to the tree and back. She was
relieved to get going and walked quickly so that they had to keep up.
She didn't want Francois to find out they were using the willow instead of the bucket. How could she possibly explain why, and even if
she did, he wouldn't understand.

Trigger was happy to walk to the willow again, too, if only for
an excuse to move. Their bodies wanted to stretch forth, to run, to
swim, to move in uninhibited strides—luxuries denied them for six
straight years. They would run down the boardwalk just to feel the

physical burst of sensation if circumstances were different. The deep twilight provided plenty of camouflage from anyone who might be looking for them. The light level was at that in-between stage that made things more difficult to see even than in full darkness, when torchlight highlighted movement. Now, everything looked black and white like a photograph. They walked silently, listening to the voices of traders and bootleggers all around. Patrice and Trig paused just before the center of the spoke, the heart of the village, while Ferrar advanced and waved them across when no one was looking their way. As she crossed to the other side, Patrice saw Francois seated on a barrel in front of what appeared to be a shop. He was looking the other way, toward a group of men.

Patrice and Trigger followed Ferrar's lead and strode toward the willow, their footfalls silent, the floating boardwalk swaying beneath them.

"Let me check first," Ferrar whispered as they neared the willow island.

But Patrice shook her head. "No one's out there."

He looked down at her in surprise, and then seemed to guess that she had a way of knowing whether someone was nearby, just like she could check someone's intentions. This was a new talent that had come from the six years she'd just spent in the briar. She only remembered it now.

She wondered about the younger ones, Gil and Rosie, because Maman would have her believe that their skills hadn't improved at all over the years. Odd, because they'd been in the briar the whole time. But they were under the control of a tar devil. Patrice had been dragged in by one, but not for the entire period because her mother could not administer scratch poisons to her physical body.

Patrice glanced at Trigger. He'd experienced six unencumbered years of briar, too. She resolved to ask him later whether he'd noticed his skills had evolved.

They reached the willow. Ferrar and Trigger waited while Patrice went first, stepping off the wooden boardwalk and onto the island.

The sand felt good beneath her shoes, crunching with stones and calcifications, but she tried to walk on the great tree's roots so as to avoid making any sound. She stepped beneath the canopy and it spread over her like a gazebo, lacey and gracious. In a strange way it reminded her of the briar. Sometimes even that could be a beautiful place.

Unlike the bucket, the tree did not smell bad. Patrice finished and returned to the boardwalk, letting Trigger go in after her.

She was now alone with Ferrar. He smiled at her and then looked away. Clearly uncomfortable. She thought about this a moment. Her very existence was a threat to him because of the river devils.

She said, "I'm sorry. I know we put you in danger. Again."

"I'm used to it by now," he said.

She nodded. Six years like this for him, going back and forth between New Orleans and this lost little waterlogged village.

It seemed a thousand creatures were speaking from the soft land beyond the floating shanties and the bayou that formed a ring around them. Patrice was grateful for the animal voices. Like putting on a record when a visitor comes calling because you don't know what to say.

She thought about the willow, and asked, "With all those people mooring here tonight, you'd think the willow would be busier."

"No, there's more than one. This is the commodore's willow. Francois. No one else is allowed to use it. Except for you of course. But no one is supposed to know about you."

"But they know anyway."

He shrugged.

"What do you do? I mean, what kind of work do you do when you go to New Orleans"

"I work on the bridge. Same place where you found me."

"I thought they'd stopped building it."

"They had. But we've been working on it again for a year now. It's going together fast."

"What's it like?"

"It's different from farm life. Everything is loud. On the bridge, they run the machinery day and night. The whole thing is made of steel and we hold it together with rivets. All day long, the sound of riveting. People don't talk to each other, they shout. But I love it. I'm high up in the air and I can see all the way up the river. The way it moves along, it's slow and easy."

"Mmm," she said, thinking she would like that.

"They say it'll support trains and cars, both."

Trigger was heading back up the path along the tiny willow island. They fell silent.

Ferrar turned to lead them down the boardwalk, and as he did, for just a single moment, his fingertips touched hers. Just a flash. It might have been an accident or he could have deliberately reached for her hand, then changed his mind. Patrice couldn't tell.

Ferrar strode out a few steps ahead to lead the way, and Patrice buried her smile into her chest. She suddenly felt so electrified that she reached for Trigger's hand and squeezed it tight, just like she used to do when he and Gil were little boys and she'd pretended that she was the one who was their Maman, not Chloe. Trigger grinned at her and squeezed her back. In the last waning glimmer of light, he looked like an even older version of himself, and she caught a sense of what a handsome young man he would soon become.

Ferrar stopped short ahead.

Patrice and Trigger nearly collided with him from behind, and Patrice's fingers slipped from Trig's.

An odd thing. She'd held her brother's hand, and then she'd let go. But maybe because of the darkness, maybe because of another kind of darkness, she wanted to reach for him again.

Francois was standing in the path, glaring at them with the one furious eye. Patrice paused with her brother and Ferrar, thinking at first that Francois was angry that they'd used the willow instead of the bucket. But when she checked in the briar way she sensed others nearby. Off in the direction where they were headed.

Francois whispered something to Ferrar and waved them away

from the boardwalk spoke where their shanty stood, pointing instead down another spoke. Ferrar looked hesitant but he gestured for Patrice and Trigger to go with him. This time he put his hand very deliberately at the small of Patrice's back. More a protective gesture than a tender one. Patrice straightened.

"What's happened?" Trigger whispered.

Ferrar whispered back, "Someone's gone down to the shanties where we were. If we ain't gone to the willow they would have found you."

"Should we be worried?" Patrice asked.

"Hard to tell yet. Could be mischief. Or just be a drunkard getting lost. Happens."

Behind them, toward the village center and down some of the far spokes, she could hear voices going loud. Some were laughing. They were drinking, too, no doubt. Patrice continued forward with Ferrar and Trigger. The shacks along this boardwalk were not kept as well as the ones where they'd been staying. Patrice sensed something strange ahead. Then she realized: This was the ghosts' boardwalk.

She stole a glimpse of Ferrar. He was looking over his shoulder to see if anyone was behind them, but this boardwalk was quiet.

From somewhere near the town center she heard singing.

Once I built a railroad, now it's done . . .
Buddy, can you spare a dime?

And she wondered, would she find the ghost version of herself here? And that of Ferrar? Because when she'd seen them before, something about the way they had stood together had escaped her notice. But now, with Ferrar's hand on her back and seeing the way he looked at her, she thought perhaps she understood. It made her feel very strange. Very happy.

She heard them up the way. They were quieter than the revelers. Sober. Female voices, some male, too. Ghosts.

What happened next, happened fast.

From behind, Patrice heard a thwack. A very wrong sound. Very sick.

Had she been walking with true awareness things might have been different.

She looked in time to see Ferrar topple sideways, holding his head. He staggered and then fell into the bayou before Patrice had even registered what was happening.

She should have been paying more attention instead of letting the thoughts run amok. She could have stopped it.

Someone had grabbed her, someone holding a thick length of wood that he'd just used to strike Ferrar down. This, she also had barely registered, because even as she felt her arms getting pinned to her sides, her eyes were locked with Trigger's.

A second man plunged a long knife into Trigger's belly. Just above his navel. And then the man ripped the blade upward between Trigger's ribs.

Patrice thought, *This is not so. It can't be so.*

Trigger's eyes looked wild for a single clean moment.

In that wildness, there is life. It must mean that he's not hurt that badly. He's hurt but he's not going to . . .

The man who was holding him fell away. Patrice wasn't fully aware that she'd reared up and kicked him in the face. But yes, she'd done that. Must have done that.

Trigger looked down. And when he looked up again, his eyes held an apology.

An apology.

He said, "Gil and Rosie . . ."

The one she'd kicked came up again and butted his shoulder against Trigger. Trigger went into the water.

She was screaming. A vague, peripheral thing. Her sense of sound had momentarily shut itself off. She knew she was screaming because her throat felt it.

The one behind her was still holding her by the arms though she was bucking wildly.

"Get the damn body! One live, one dead, you dumb sonofabitch!"

"No!"

She had to get to him.

"Trigger!"

She had no idea how she got there, but she realized that she was
in the water now, too.

"Trigger! Trigger!"

Torchlight illuminated nothing here. The water was black.

"Guy!"

He was gone.

fifty-four

LOUISIANA, NOW

ASTON SAID, "YOU HOLD tight. I'm gonna try to get help."
Madeleine was in her body and shaking like mad.
"Water."
Her tongue felt like sun-scorched sand. But he was already gone.
No Severin, either. And yet Madeleine was not alone. She felt the
chill first. Despite the fever burning through her body, the icy void
filled her lungs. The serpent was there.

Like when she'd been in the shack, she could see nothing. But
this time it stemmed more from sickness and delirium than from a
dark room.

"Get away," she croaked, but she made almost no sound.

She heard it whisper as it eased up along her leg. "Too late for
you, Madeleine. You chose death."

"No. I just chose not to sacrifice that baby."

"Yes. Instead you wasted time on some meaningless child. You distracted everyone."

Everyone. Yes. The river devils, and Zenon and Gaston. For once she was the one leading others down rabbit holes. But to what end? Anguish. More chaos.

She felt the creature wind up around her, encircling her—impossible, because she was lying down—but it wrapped around her chest and her neck, its coldness chilling only her spirit and not her flesh. Squeezing the breath from her.

Unable to speak, Madeleine was answering in her mind now. "So kill me, if that's what you've come to do."

"You know I cannot kill you here. You've killed yourself."

"Chloe? Are you going to die, too?"

"Already quite far gone."

"What are you?"

"I am tomorrow."

Someone gripped her hand and pulled her up.

"Gaston?"

She held fast and let herself be lifted, and as she rose she broke from the serpent. She could hear it hiss and whisper away. It hadn't bitten her this time. Probably was unable to. She blinked, and was able to see again, though dimly.

He was gripping her hand, blue eyes smiling.

"Daddy?"

She was so startled she didn't know whether to cry or squeeze him or slap him upside the head for haunting her from beyond the grave. Feelings not so different from when he was alive.

He said, "You sure you wanna come with me, kitten?"

And the tears won out. She let them flow.

"Is it really you?" she managed to say.

"No, honey. It ain't me. There is no me now. Not sure there ever was."

"If you're not my father, then who are you?"

"It's just drawin water from the barrel, honey."

He stood and reached into a rain barrel in the corner, and he pulled out a ladle. Light danced on the wet alloy where moonbeams filtered through cracks in the wall.

He said, "And then holding it in the dram for a while. Pouring it back in. That's all we are. Any one of us."

She said, "I need you to come back. I don't know how to do this."

But when he turned, he wasn't her father any more. He was her brother Marc.

"Oh," she said, and the tears ran afresh.

"You keep my son safe, Maddy, now won't you?"

"Have you seen Cooper?"

"Of course. I need you to look after him. He's special, gonna make all the difference."

"You mean between the lumens and the briar. Don't tell me you're a crusader, too."

"You have to understand, honey, our evolution can go one way or th'other. And if it goes the wrong way everyone'll be wiped out."

"You mean if the lumens survive?"

"No. I mean we ain't supposed to eradicate them. We supposed to serve them."

Madeleine stopped, searching his face. "Then it really is like what Zenon and Chloe are saying. That we become slaves."

Marc was smiling at her with those blue eyes like Daddy's. Like Zenon's. Like her own.

"Not slaves, honey. Protectors."

She heard an insect buzzing and realized it was the sound of her own wheezing. When had she gotten sick that way? Her lungs were filling with fluid.

Madeleine said, "If Chloe survives she's going to get to Cooper."

"If she doesn't, then Zenon will. You gotta survive, honey."

She gave a tearful laugh. "You're preaching to the choir, sweetie, I'm all about pulling through this alive."

"Then pull your body out of this."

"How?"

"You saw it in the halfway, didn't you?"

"The halfway?"

She shook her head, frowning, but then remembered the symbol deep within Gaston's tree. The hobo scrawl.

Marc turned and stepped away from her.

"Wait! Marc, honey, stay on with me a little longer. Please."

He turned. "You ain't got a little longer, baby. You dyin. But if you get fixed you can find us again. Now that you figured out the bridge."

And then his face crumpled into laughter, a deep, good-old-Marc hilarity. "Too bad you had to let your body and mind go to pot in order to figure out the rest. Only you, baby!"

She laughed, too, just because he was doing it, though it really didn't seem funny at all. In fact it seemed pretty damned morose. She could still hear her own wheezing and looked down at herself. But she didn't see her own body. Not at first anyway. It was somewhere below. Far below. She was down there lying in some kind of bed. Other people in the room with her.

"Get on, now!" Marc said with a wave, and she felt herself falling. Fast.

fifty-five

BAYOU BOUILLON, 1933

LL WAS BLACK FOR Patrice. True black. If there were any chance Trigger might be alive somewhere down in that water she would have found him by now. But it was too late.

She dove after her brother again and again though she knew he was gone. She could see nothing in that night water. But she could sense much. She sensed a ghost's presence. But Trigger, there was no sign of him. She sensed only the absence of Trigger. Could hardly believe he was dead. Her heart denied it. Assigned it as false.

But.

A piece of her accepted the truth of what she'd seen. Trigger was torn from belly to sternum. His body had slid into the bayou and was lost. Even if she recovered his body, her brother was gone. Gone, gone.

Up above on the boardwalk, she sensed the hearts of those who had come to take them to her mother: one dead body, one alive. That's what they were supposed to bring to the witch in New Orleans.

Patrice's mind functioned in waves: twenty seconds of searing anguish, twenty seconds of paralysis, and then twenty seconds of vengeance.

In the latter, she pigeoned each of those despicable men on that boardwalk above and brought them tumbling over the side into the cold boil with her.

This pigeon exercise required complete calm. She executed it with that calm. Cold boil calm. Brought them down and bade them fill their lungs with bayou.

Twenty seconds of searing anguish. Twenty seconds of paralysis. Twenty seconds of death.

There had been seven of them. It had continued until she'd claimed each one. The last two had been difficult—they went into the water and swam without drowning. And so she turned those two on one another so that they fought, strangled, crushed, drowned together.

By the time Ferrar pulled Patrice out she'd nearly drowned herself, her body no longer able to stay afloat.

The ghosts were gone.

❧

<h1 style="text-align:center">fifty-six</h1>

❧

BAYOU BOUILLON, NOW

ADELEINE AWOKE ON A pallet in a floating room. The sound of creaking wood came from beneath, and also a gentle rocking, so very slow. Daylight poured in from a sizable gap in the corrugated roof. Gaston was chewing on a hangnail there in the corner by the door, the click beetle necklace around his neck. A beautiful girl with golden-bronze skin was wringing out a washrag and wiping it over Madeleine's forehead. Madeleine was naked and wrapped in a blanket.

She said to Gaston, "Are we still supposed to be ghosts?"

The girl's eyes flashed. She swallowed and seemed to be holding her breath, and very slowly looked over her shoulder at Gaston. Gaston turned and faced the wall.

Madeleine clamped her mouth shut. The effort of speech was excruciating anyway. There were fire ants nesting in her lungs.

The girl took Madeleine's hand and fit it around a jar of warm liquid. Madeleine tried to lift her head to drink but she couldn't. She couldn't lift any limbs. Could lift her fingers but not her hand. Her gaze swiveled up to the ceiling and beyond it, where Marc and Daddy both were watching. Marc waved her on.

She nodded more with her heart than her head. The girl had lifted the jar to Madeleine's lips and she found she could drink. Probably, the stuff tasted awful. Everything looked to be moving in waves. Even the gingham pattern of the girl's dress seemed to move like charmed serpents.

Madeleine was going to fall back asleep if she didn't hurry.

"Severin," she called in her mind.

And Severin appeared, crawling up from somewhere beneath the bed, maybe even beneath the floorboards, and she kept low. For once she wasn't wearing a grin.

Severin put her tiny, filthy finger to her lips in a shushing gesture.

"Just us, yes?" she whispered.

Madeleine nodded in her mind. And then, mercifully, she felt herself being dislodged from that wretched thing that had become her body. Briar mist cool and quiet, all around.

◆

THEY DESCENDED AT ONCE from the forest into the fractured tunnels below, Severin whispering, "A secret in your heart, a thing to find, yes."

Madeleine nodded in reply. Severin was dragging her along, Madeleine's weakened mind unable to do anything but focus on the fissure she'd seen in the symbols, and she saw it in her mind now. Saw it clearly though she'd never been there before. The compulsion came not from her mind but from somewhere else deep within her, a part of her she'd felt when she was talking to Marc and Daddy.

And she knew Severin was taking her to that fissure. Uncharacteristically obedient. Probably because Severin held her own stake in Madeleine's survival.

"Are Zenon or Gaston anywhere nearby? Or their river devils?" Madeleine asked.

Severin halted and gave Madeleine a fierce look. "Hush that! Why invoke them?"

"Invoke? I was just asking."

"To say a name is to pray it. And the feeling in your heart wraps around the name, too, fury or love or death, so surely."

Madeleine, listened, bewildered. They were in an underground grotto, roots dangling above and water washing along beneath them. A smell of mildew and rot.

She felt so drowsy. Losing consciousness now would be deadly.

Madeleine said, "Alright, fine. Is *anyone* nearby we should know about?"

"Not as of this moment. And luck, that. What you seek is a secret."

"OK, so let's go."

Severin said, "You know the way, not I. You've stopped looking at it so now I cannot find it."

"Me?"

Madeleine thought backward, trying to figure out where the fissure was, her mind flitting over the places she'd been inside the briar. But she'd never before been to this particular place.

Severin glared at her. "What are you doing? You wish to take us on some lengthy voyage?"

"I . . . don't know how to find it."

"Just do as before!"

Madeleine swallowed, erasing all thoughts, then pictured the carving she'd seen in the root system of Gaston's tree. The plus sign with a circle and dots. The long-tailed triangle.

The sense returned. The coarse groove that she'd seen in that wood became a new, living dimension, a cleft in stone.

They were moving again, this time with the seven-league steps Severin took when covering long distances, and suddenly they were there.

❧

FOUR TREES, JUST AS in the carving. And there was the crevasse.

Madeleine and Severin were standing at a bend in the river that had gone black with shadows—unnatural shadows, those that had never been framed by light. An immediate sense of danger swept over Madeleine.

Where the water turned, an eddy had formed. Only, the water did not look like water. It swirled black and thick. A vestigial body like an appendix that once served to filter sludge but now only acquired the worst toxins of its environment, storing them in a pool that could never empty itself.

Madeleine narrowed her eyes at the odors emitting from the eddy, and watched as the water moved . . . strangely, as if a creature made of tar were stretching along the surface. An unsettling sight. There were many traps in the briar. Most caused you to lose your way so that you might wander for weeks, even years. Some caused physical pain or loathing. As Madeleine gave a nervous glance toward that shape that seemed made of tar, she noticed thornflies crawling along the roots dangling above.

The fissure was shaped much like the triangle in the carving, with the longest end being on top, and the point of the triangle falling below and to the right. The mouth was covered in moss, mottled with green and rust colors like the duckweed at the briar's surface. A breeze came from within. It smelled sweet like a meadow just before a rainstorm is about to break.

"Inside, now," Severin was saying, and her eyes were bright.

But this fissure was tiny. About the size of the glove box in Madeleine's truck. They couldn't exactly crawl inside. Madeleine looked at Severin, puzzled.

"In!" Severin said.

Madeleine peered inside but saw only darkness. And movement. She steeled herself and reached inside. Felt something covering her arm. She pulled her arm out again and saw it covered with thorn-flies. They poured out of the opening.

Madeleine kept her breathing steady, refusing to give in to alarm. The thornflies had their stingers curled and waiting, crawling up her arm and following to her neck and body. She felt a wave course through her, one that ought to be panic but she let it pass through her like a shadow and it did not catch.

Everything was slipping away from her. Like a giant fan slowly turning its blades over her vision, she knew she was about slip into unconsciousness. Death.

"Go on! Stupid thing!" Severin cried.

Madeleine went tense, and felt the first few stings of the thornflies.

Severin said, "You are going to die here, right here. In this mo-ment. A breath away."

The stings throbbed, but Madeleine released a slow sigh and let the pain happen. The thornflies stopped.

Madeleine looked again into the crevasse, and suddenly realized what she needed to do.

A clear mind. An open heart. Her spirit lifted.

And she was inside. She alone, not Severin.

❦

SHE LAY PRONE ON something soft. Without Severin's will to pull her along she found she could not move. Not an inch. Much like being back in her body.

The fan blades turned. Madeleine counted each turn. Such com-fort in counting. It took the last reserves of her consciousness. And then consciousness slipped, too.

❦

SHE FELT HER BODY churning. Her awareness was bogged down in something like sleep, only heavier. More resistant. But after a span of time her mind broke through the blackness into something she couldn't attach to briar or material world. If anything, it felt like a dream: In her ear, she felt a cocoon had formed, then hatched. Both agony and relief to feel it seize and move. She wanted it to eject itself from her. She felt bending delirium to the point of vertigo. Her body wanted to writhe, too, like that anxious, fervent thing in her ear.

All the little cuts on and throughout her body formed over clean, and they ejected the heat and puss and scab into tiny itchy balls that fell away from her like dry rice, leaving behind only smooth pink sensation. Her ankle where Gaston had cut her, her knees and hands. Her kidneys, even, and her bladder—she felt them knitting over with coolness where there had been heat and pain. Her lungs planed themselves clean and filled with a substance that, it seemed, had she not found the skill of subsistence without breath, might have drowned her.

She was aware of rolling over onto her belly to cough it out, and this time her consciousness rose even higher from the dream state. She retched.

The creature in her ear was working, working. She felt a strange sort of wrenching. It pulled the pain away with it. The heaviness. She placed her hand to her ear. Inside the ear canal, the creature went *flap flap flap flap*. Then it was vibrating, soft and furtive. It emerged, spread its wings, and flew away. She watched it go. A moth, but with briar enchantments. Had she created that? A thing that she learned from the soft, cool, mossy retreat. In its absence her ear was clean and her hearing sharp.

No real awareness of where she was, as all her sight had gone inward. She collapsed back down onto the feel of soft, spongy moss and let her body plunge back into real sleep.

This time it was restful.

❧❀❧

SHE AWOKE IN THIS same fissure. And when she opened her eyes her mind was immediately brighter though she could see only in fractals.

This was a good place. An anomaly of the briar. She could feel a kind of ambient tension, a delicious sense, sort of like the way her muscles felt when she was treading water very slowly. Drawing warmth into her body. Exploring her own strength. The scent of impending rain was strong though she knew it would not rain.

She rested there, keeping her mind easy. A strange kind of euphoria filled her, light and beautiful.

Slowly, her surroundings came into focus. Spongy moss above and below her, lining the walls of the cave. Somewhere far away Severin was speaking. Madeleine could not discern the words and didn't try, because this was not a river devil's place.

She heard, "Oh."

Madeleine looked.

Cooper.

Sitting in a corner of the fissure, his toy blocks spread out before him. He was smiling. A gorgeous thing. Eyes bright and round and set wide above his cheeks. He cooed at her.

Madeleine felt a rush of delight. "Oh, little baby. I've been wanting to meet you."

He reached his hands toward her.

She scooted over to him and pulled him up into her arms, and he nestled into her lap. He slapped at his knees and inspected first her face, then her hands, and then reached toward his blocks. She picked one up and handed it to him. They sat like that for a very long time.

But even as she held him, she felt dismay. Somewhere, on the brink of death, Chloe was watching.

fifty-seven

H E WAS SUCH A little thing. Ghastly to imagine an infant in the briar. Madeleine hadn't known this place existed before last year, and she was in her late twenties.

Little Cooper was falling asleep. She held him close, drinking in that baby smell.

She whispered, "Marc, I don't know how to protect him."

She felt a lump forming in her throat. Had she just somehow given baby Cooper over to Chloe? This was what Chloe had wanted. That Madeleine come find him in the briar.

The return to sharp-mindedness fueled a new determination. She wasn't going to try to hide anymore, it wasn't working anyway—not for Cooper and Emily, or for herself, or even for Bo.

Cooper was fast asleep now. And then suddenly he was gone. Madeleine's arms fell empty to her sides.

She closed her eyes and drew in her breath. No anxiety, no

sadness or fury, just a solid plan. Take the necessary actions. Commit to the death.

❧❧

SEVERIN WAS WAITING OUTSIDE the crevasse, ranting, frustrated that she couldn't get inside. Madeleine heard it now, though the river devil had likely been railing the entire time. And as she heard it and resisted the anger, she felt herself slipping from one form of awareness to the next, as though trying to hold onto a dream. And then suddenly she was out of the crevasse and facing Severin again.

Severin regarded her with gleaming eyes. "Such the better. Whole again."

"Take me back," Madeleine said.

"Now is not when. You owe a long debt of time in my play. Here you must while. Here with me."

"Not now. Take us back to my body!"

Severin narrowed her eyes. "A fine thing to believe that you can demand service of me."

Madeleine felt strange. Almost euphoric. And she was deeper into the briar than she'd ever dared venture. Had she died? The thought was chilling, that she might be damned to this briar world instead of in that cool, quiet place where she'd seen Daddy and Marc.

But in her heart she knew better. She was very much alive. More so than she'd been before she'd rested inside the mossy cave.

She looked to her left and recognized the broad, oily pool within a grotto of thorns. Greenish-gray light. Movement at the far side—a whirlpool. No sign of the thing she'd seen stirring at the surface before.

Severin was looking at her with a gloating smile. Madeleine's instinct was to reprimand her for not bringing them back. To unleash some fury.

But no, she wouldn't be unleashing fury. She'd be cultivating it. She knew better than to try to manhandle Severin.

And suddenly she sensed the creature. Its nearness was apparent before she even saw it. She turned to look.

The same creature she'd seen before on the eddy's surface, but now it stood just behind her. A devil who had the body of a man but whose four limbs were long like those of a spider. A devil with tar in its body and soul. She knew that it wanted to claim her and that if she allowed that to happen her life would never be the same.

It folded its cagelike arms around her. It happened so fast.

She turned her attention away from it. Inward. And she was gone. Gone. Slipped away from the creature's grasp.

Daddy and Marc were standing opposite her. The same sensation she'd used to get inside the fissure.

Without a word, Marc, Daddy, and Madeleine looked down. Madeleine's body lay on a pallet in the room below.

The sense of falling, and then Madeleine was back inside, hacking desperately against fluid inside her lungs.

fifty-eight

❧

BAYOU BOUILLON, NOW

*P*ATRICE SAT IN FERRAR'S pirogue as he navigated by electric lantern through the snaking waterways. It had an outboard motor, but the going was still slow. Even if it were light out it would have probably been slow because of the endless twisting passages. The motor hummed beneath her, vibrating her bones, making her body numb. Her mind felt numb, too. She faced away from Ferrar's beam of light and looked out over blackness. The Bible sat on her knees.

They'd left Francois behind in the floating village at Bayou Bouillon. He was badly hurt, having been attacked probably just prior to when Trigger was killed. Patrice and Ferrar found Francois lying on his side with a wound to his right lung where he'd been stabbed in the back.

"Leave me to the ghost. Take the Bible. Leave me to the ghosts." It's all he got out.

And they did. Patrice and Ferrar obeyed and left him bleeding there in the boardwalk while village dwellers hovered around him. Patrice wondered about him now. He could be cold and dead, like the seven she'd drowned. Like her brother. She ought to grieve at the thought of Francois lying there that way, but Trigger had consumed all her anguish and left nothing but a cauterized numbness in her soul.

She was going to kill her mother. She would offer herself up in exchange for Marie-Rose and Gilbert, wait until the younger ones were safe, and then she would kill her.

The motor throttled back and the boat slowed. Patrice looked over her shoulder. They were close to a stretch of land and Ferrar was shining his light along the shoreline. Gray shapes showed in the beam. Green grass or redbud, it all looked gray in the thin artificial light—all color and life squeezed out, leaving only a combination of black and white, absence and presence.

Ferrar gunned the motor and then cut it dead, tilting it up. The pirogue shot forward like a silent arrow across the water and slid up onto soft sand. Though the motor had stopped, it seemed she could still feel the echoes of its vibrations.

"Are we here already? The mainland?" she asked.

"No. This is a portage point. One of two. We have to cross overland and then set in again."

"Oh."

"Wait inside the pirogue, I'll push it up all the way."

But she was already out and in the water. She felt her dress balloon up around her like a jellyfish. The silt felt soft beneath her toes.

No shoes. Where were her shoes?

Somewhere in Bayou Bouillon.

They hauled the pirogue up onto shore, and then Ferrar lifted it onto a dolly that was waiting in the weeds. The dolly's spoked metal wheels were enormous and it reminded her of an old Civil War cannon she'd once seen. The wheels seemed reluctant to turn but Ferrar knew how to coax them.

They walked in relative darkness. The moon was out but daw-dling, and Patrice found her way more by feel of bare feet than any-thing else. She must not have been wearing shoes much those past six years because her soles were good and rough. Ferrar was bare-foot, too. She saw the occasional flash of his soles catching moon-light as he hauled the pirogue ahead of her.

After about twenty minutes they were setting in again. This time Ferrar had to use a pole that was waiting at the set-in side to navi-gate through the windings.

"Too shallow for a motor," he explained.

He used no electric light to guide them this time, just the thin moonlight and his own familiarity with these waters. Patrice looked out over a calico expanse of cut grass and water. No bird or cricket or frog sounds. Just the splash of the pole stirring the marsh and Ferrar slapping mosquitoes. Bayou Bouillon was behind them to the south and west, with Terrefleurs somewhere far to the north and New Or-leans with its bridge waiting to the east.

Patrice and Ferrar traveled without conversation. She was glad he wasn't trying to fill the silence, that he wasn't trying to console her over Trigger.

ABOUT AN HOUR HAD gone by in the winding flats with Ferrar guiding the pirogue with pole or paddle, depending on which was necessary, and then they were pulling onto another rise of land.

"This is . . ."

"The second crossing," Patrice said, remembering that they had to make two overland crossings before the final waterway to the mainland.

"Yes."

They pulled together and hauled the pirogue up onto the soft, grass-matted banks. The grass helped give the vessel a little slide.

"A break," Ferrar said.

He sat down on the trampled foliage. Patrice paused and then sat next to him. In truth she wanted to press on. Find her mother. Execute whatever transaction she must in order to get Gil and Rosie to safety. Seek vengeance for Trig. Maybe even meet her own death. But she realized she was treating poor Ferrar like a pack mule. He hadn't rested once since they'd left Bayou Bouillon.

The moon passed from behind a cloud and the banks seemed to bloom in its pale light. She looked at Ferrar and saw a black trickle running just beyond his brow.

She gasped and reached for his face but then paused, afraid to touch the wound. "You're bleeding."

He bent his head to the crook of his arm and blotted the blood. From the looks of his shirt, he'd probably been doing that the entire way.

She said, "I'm sorry. You're really hurt."

He waved a dismissive hand but said, "We have a choice now. We can keep going or stay here until dawn."

"Let's keep going."

"Please, listen first. After the last set-in, once we make it to land, we need a way to get to New Orleans."

"How do you usually get there?"

"I wait at the highway crossing. I know someone who drives a truck through there. He goes to the farms at sunrise and then he carries his load to New Orleans. He will take us, but not until midmorning. We will be exposed while we wait for him—no one out there but farmers and the bootleggers and pirates from the Gulf. So we can wait here or wait there. Here it is safe."

She listened, thinking very little of safety concerns. Trigger was gone, and she herself was doomed. But it wasn't fair to put Ferrar in any more danger, and she had to keep herself safe, too, if she was going to get Gil and Rosie out of her mother's hands.

"Alright, then. How long do we wait?"

"We can leave about an hour after sunrise. Then by the time we get to the crossroads where the truck picks us up, we'll only have to wait by the road a little while."

She nodded. Looked around. The moon was already disappearing behind the clouds again and the darkness folded over the beachfront.

And she thought, *No, no, no, no, no. I have to keep moving.*

She scrambled to her feet. Ferrar must have taken this as a sign that she was ready to set up camp because he rose and pulled on the boat. Two good yanks and it was up a fair distance from the water. He slapped his neck where a mosquito must have landed.

Patrice folded her arms across her chest and tried not to think of the look in Trigger's eyes when the knife slid into his belly.

"I have this, at least," Ferrar said.

He was pulling a canvas tarp from the boat and unfolding it over the grass. "You lie down there. If you get chilled, fold it over yourself. I'll be in the woods."

"No."

He paused. A vanishing silhouette. She couldn't speak another word for the tightness in her throat. The moon had fully receded behind the clouds and she was glad for it. She didn't want him to see her. She put her hands to her face and covered her eyes.

"Patrice?"

He'd stepped toward her. She was certain he couldn't see that she was crying but maybe he knew anyway. She stood like that for breath after breath, elbows clamped over her chest and hands to her eyes.

He said, "I know it hurts."

She nodded though he couldn't see her in the darkness, but she was still unable to make herself speak. Her tears flowed in silence. A minute passed, and then another, and the whole while he just stood there, not saying another single word. She cried and shivered. And then finally, she reached out for him. He opened his arms and let her press her head into his chest. He patted her gently on the shoulder. She kept weeping for Trigger. For Gil and Rosie in that horrible imprisoned state.

❧

HE HADN'T KISSED HER. Hadn't touched her beyond the comforting way he patted her shoulder. They'd finally settled themselves on the canvas tarp and fallen asleep beneath the dark clouds. He hadn't even so much as draped an arm over her although, when Patrice awoke to find him lying there with her, she wished he had. She didn't fall back to sleep.

When the birds began their predawn restlessness she realized he wasn't sleeping either.

And so she said, "You're awake."

"Yes. We should both be sleeping."

She was glad he wasn't.

"The mosquitoes were bad all night long. We should have at least built a fire for the sake of the smoke."

"I'll build one now if you want."

"No." Patrice reached out and took his hand.

His breathing paused. She squeezed his fingers. Such a big hand. Dawn would come soon.

She said, "How many times have you made this voyage, between New Orleans and Bayou Bouillon?"

"I don't know. Maybe a hundred."

"It's a good thing you've got a pirogue like that, with the motor."

He gave a small laugh, and it was a nice sound. "Not at first. I didn't get the motor until 'bout a year later. Before that it's all poling or paddling."

"That must have taken forever."

"It did. But then when I got the motor, I had to get the boat dollies. It got too heavy to haul the boat overland without them."

"You'd been dragging them across without a dolly?"

"Yeah. First pirogue I had was light as a cloud. Carried her on my head when she wasn't in the water. Too light to do with a motor, though—she liked to tip. So I got a bigger pirogue that was heavy enough to tote the motor, but then I had to tote the boat."

Patrice smiled.

Ferrar went on, and this time he moved his fingers so that they were tracing Patrice's. "So I found the dollies and had them dropped on the islands."

"You're not worried someone'll steal them?"

"Who'd steal a boat dolly out here? It would take more heartache to steal them than what they worth. I got'm both for free in tradin for the old boat 'cuz they both broken."

Patrice had no idea who would steal a boat dolly, but then again she knew nothing about the pirates and bootleggers that came through this part of the Gulf.

"What's it like? Runnin hooch?"

Ferrar was quiet a moment. She could see the outline of his ear now, just enough light forming beyond the beachhead.

He said, "Lonesome. Hard. Dangerous."

"Mm. I s'pose it's better working on the bridge."

"It is. But that's also lonesome. And hard."

"And dangerous?"

"And dangerous."

She thought of the waters that surrounded the landmass where they lay. Waters that had taken Trigger away, waters fed by the very river that moved under Ferrar's bridge.

Enough light to see the outline of his face now. The sun would keep following until it broke the horizon and then it would rise, and by nothing but just being there, without even trying, it would turn darkness into daylight.

She wondered if she was going to die on this day. She would get Gil and Rosie out, and then she would face her mother down. If she failed, she would be folding herself into darkness as her mother's captive. If she succeeded, she would kill her mother and lay down her soul to eternal damnation. Somewhere in between failure and success was a third possibility: her own death. Any one of these things was about to be. In that little pinch of something between sunup and sundown.

Even as she lay there touching fingers to Ferrar and listening to the birds, the shadows were receding. How long before those shadows would come back? Fourteen hours?

She said, "Those people in Bayou Bouillon, they call them ghosts. Does that mean they're from the dead? Does it mean we are dead?"

Ferrar shook his head. "I've wondered that a long time. No one seems to know. I don't think the ghosts even know."

She turned to her side and kissed Ferrar on the mouth. It felt like the most daring thing she'd done in her life. Her heart raced, waiting to know what Ferrar would do now that she'd kissed him.

He lay very still and did not kiss her back.

She said, "You don't love me?"

He didn't reply, not for a long moment, and she could hear him breathing. The kind of breathing that sounded like he had something to say but wasn't saying it, so he just lay there huffing.

Finally: "I do love you, Patrice. I've loved you a long time."

She leaned forward to kiss him again but he pushed her back, rising to a sit. She pulled herself up to her knees and smoothed her hair.

He said, "All these years, I haven't been able to see you. Not even for a minute. Except for once. Just the once. I came down the boardwalk and you were in the water, with . . . her."

Her. Patrice thought about what he meant. "My ghost?"

"Yeah. She saw me and just turned her back. You already had your back to me. I knew the best you was off somewhere else, and it was just the pretty you in the water. All I saw was the back of your head. Francois caught me lookin and liked to feed me to the gar."

Patrice listened.

"But that was it. Six years and three months. It's all I saw of you. But I saw the other you, and I saw the other me. And I guessed by the way they did, that they loved each other. Never saw them hold hands or nothin. I just knew it. Which meant you and I was goin' to love each other someday. And that's when I realized I already did love you."

She didn't know what to say to this. It occurred to her that having seen that in him, having recognized that he loved her, she ought to have figured out whether she loved him back before forcing him to speak of it. In this she was lacking gentleness. Her thoughts and emotions had tangled together so much that she could only allow them to lead her to the next step, whatever that may be. Right now she wanted only for him to put his arms around her. She wanted to feel alive. She wanted to be brave enough.

"If you do love me, Ferrar, kiss me."

"Don't. You're naïve, Patrice, you don't understand."

"I do."

"I will come calling on you and make it proper. After all this."

"No sir, you don't seem to understand. There may not be any 'after all this.'"

He fell silent. The water beyond the beachhead was forming silver ripples that winked in and out.

"I don't believe that's true anymore," he said.

"That I'm about to die?"

"That there is such a thing. After these last years in Bayou Bouillon, I see that time don't work the way I thought it did. It's a good thing to know. Because then you can always do what's right with your heart."

She was frustrated, weeping again, the tears apparently hadn't played themselves out yet.

But then she realized: "You believe you're going to die today, too."

Somehow that changed everything. It snapped her to a different level of attention. He said nothing, and he didn't even look at her.

She said, "But that's pointless. Just get me to the bridge, that's all I ask. I'll deal with my mother on my own."

But of course he wouldn't do that. She knew even as she was saying it that once they arrived at the bridge, he would not leave her. Even if she used pigeonry on him—Ferrar, with his constant light, was nearly impossible to pigeon.

He said, "Something continues on, that's all I know. I think you and I continue on."

"I think that's true, too. But we're not going to continue on because of any afterlife. It'll be because we go over there and get Gil and Rosie back, and we all walk away safe, mind and body." Patrice heard herself speaking these words as though they were coming from someone else.

Hadn't she just determined only three possibilities that waited between sunup and sundown? Lifelong darkness, eternal damnation, or death?

But for some reason she was thinking differently now. She was not in the briar, didn't dare approach it in Ferrar's company, but if she were she wondered if she would see if his strange and beautiful illumination might be spreading from him. Maybe seeping onto her.

He turned to look at her, and then he reached out and pressed her hand close into his own. She nodded though he hadn't said anything. She'd found that space inside, somewhere deep within her. She wasn't thinking from a place of hope or determination. Only understanding. The pain over Trigger was still there, and even the frustration and fear, but there was space around those feelings. They were volatile inside her, and something more solid and permanent was at her core. A subtle difference but one that changed everything.

Even as she experienced this awareness, he leaned over and kissed her.

A full, true, powerful feeling. Her heart surged. She dared not move lest he stop. But he did not stop that kiss. He held her so close, so sweetly. It strengthened the sense that things were alright. Even in the worst possible situation things were still somehow alright.

She held onto him, held onto that kiss, let it fill her heart with its sweetness, his arms so strong around her. She felt like she might blow away with the morning fog were it not for his arms.

"I would do anything for you," he said.

She put her mouth over his to shush him, but he spoke again: "I would die for you. It could go either way, and either way I'm ready."

"Hush now."

She fit her lips to his. She fit her body against him and marveled at how her skin craved his skin. His lips felt firm and large, just like his hands. She sensed the change happening below his waistband, and the knowledge caused her to heat up inside. So much mystery. Had the last six years been different, she might understand more about what was happening. Girls her age got married. They had mothers and sisters and friends who knew.

Strangely, the answer was to shush her mind, let her body take over.

fifty-nine

ADELEINE WASN'T BREATHING. THAT was the first realization that swept over her. Her body convulsed
in the effort. Thornflies, too, were there, and a
furious Severin who seemed determined to take her right back to
the briar. Madeleine sat up in bed, her hands going to her throat.

And she remembered she could hold her breath for a very, very
long time.

She stopped fighting for air. Her lungs and stomach continued
to convulse but she waited until it passed.

The girl who'd been in the room earlier was there. She was staring at Madeleine with wide eyes. Gaston was at the foot of the bed
but had turned his back to her when she'd sat up, probably because
the blankets had fallen away and left her exposed. But she was no
longer naked. Someone must have dressed her—probably this girl.
The garment was a stained white cotton chemise, soaked through

with Madeleine's sweat, and matching bloomers from her hips to her knees. The click beetle necklace was still in place.

Madeleine climbed out of the bed and strode past both the girl and Gaston, through the door, and outside. She paused as a faint breeze tickled across her skin.

She had expected to walk out into a hall, not the great outdoors. The room where she'd been convalescing was a floating one-room shack, and she was now standing on a boardwalk that adjoined several such shacks. Entire rows of them stretched like floating neighborhood blocks.

Madeleine still hadn't taken a breath and wasn't really sure what to do, but the moment she saw the water beaming back the afternoon sunlight she stepped off the boardwalk and let herself sink.

The water felt like heaven. Cool, cleansing, inside and out. She plunged down feet-first and then she swam to the surface.

The retching started again, and the convulsions in her chest, and she let her body heave. She coughed out what seemed to be both solid and liquid. Spat it all straight into the bayou. Immediate relief of air entering her lungs. Her stomach emptied, too, though it hadn't held much.

No pain in her ear. None in her ankle. She reached down, feeling for the place where Gaston's knife had cut her. No hot, weeping gouge. No scab. Nothing.

She turned around while treading the surface. Gaston was now watching her. She felt fury at the sight of him, remembering how Cheryl had turned the gun on herself.

He said, "That some kind of primal thing, like a dog wandering off to die?"

"I'm not dying."

"Then do you mind comin on outta there?"

"I'm going back."

He put his hands to his hips and sighed. "Can't. Not til the moon's up high, when the tide's on our side."

Madeleine frowned, but she turned around toward the board-walk.

He gestured back toward the shack. "Look, I went ahead and talked to her, OK? It's alright to talk to her, but no one else here. Don't even let anyone else see you."

He knelt on the wood and reached his hand toward her but she ignored it, struggling instead to hoist herself up onto the boardwalk. The result was a fine seam of splinters down her leg.

"I know you don't like what happened in that briar patch," Gaston said.

"Don't like it? Gaston, are you the one who pigeoned Cheryl?"

"Cheryl?"

"The woman who shot herself!"

"Honey, she was stained."

"I'm stained!"

"You happen to be one of us. She wasn't."

Madeleine sagged, leaning against the wall of the shack. There were several others like it in a row, but this one was distinctive in that it had a canted tin roof that made it look like the north side of the structure was sinking.

Madeleine said in as calm a voice as she could muster, "She was the mother of an eight-year-old boy who is deaf and paralyzed."

Gaston was quiet for a moment. "I know it's hard. If you'd just let me help you get the stain out of you it'll make it so much easier. Now that is the truth."

She pushed past him through the door but he blocked her from slamming it behind her. "You hell bent on goin back and you think you're well enough, then fine. I'll come back for you when the tide's high. Meantime, stay inside."

She narrowed her eyes at him, and he gave a shrug before releasing the door. "Ghosts."

He lifted his gaze to the girl who was still in the room. *"Allons."*

But the girl shook her head. *"À plus tard."*

Madeleine closed the door on him, but not before she caught his look of puzzled anxiety as he stared at the girl. Madeleine turned to her.

The girl said, "You need rest. You been on death's doorstep. Best get on some dry clothes and get back in bed."

And then the girl said, "Oh."

Madeleine followed her gaze down to her own leg. Blood was seeping from her inner thigh down to her ankle. Torn skin where she'd been stubborn on Gaston's offer of help and hoisted herself up onto the rough boardwalk. Dozens of splinters. They were painful and hot. Some had gone right through the wet cotton fabric.

The girl sat Madeleine on the stool and examined the leg, using her fingernails to pull out the largest sliver.

Madeleine closed her eyes and drew her attention to her body. The heat and pain. She could hear the sound of the wind stirring the water outside, feel the creak of the boardwalk. She wanted to wonder about all those other houses out there but refused to give in to meandering thoughts. Kept herself safe in this room.

She heard, "What's happening?"

Madeleine opened her eyes and saw the girl was staring at her. They both regarded her leg, now untouched by any wounds. Some of the splinters lay harmlessly atop her skin. Some blood was still there but was no longer flowing.

"I'm sorry about the pajamas," Madeleine said.

"You've got to take them off. They're wet and you're . . . so sick."

Madeleine gave her a look but said nothing as she pulled off the chemise. In truth she felt tremendous. Bulletproof. Not a single ache in her body. Enough energy to haul a train.

The girl took the wet clothes and Madeleine reached for her old ones.

Then girl said, "You can call me Jane."

"Madeleine."

"I know."

Madeleine gave her a backward glance as she buttoned her jeans and then pulled her shirt over her head. It smelled fresh like it'd been laundered and hung to dry in the sunshine. Jane had put the white pajamas into a washbasin along with the cup from the broth she'd fed her earlier, setting both by the door. But she was watching Madeleine from the corner of her eye, obviously perplexed by how energetic Madeleine must have seemed.

Jane said, "Are you . . . are you even sick? We were certain you were about to die."

"All due respect, who is we?"

"I did. And my . . . people. And him." She waved her hand at the door where Gaston had been.

Madeleine frowned. "And your people are . . . ?"

"We wear these." Jane touched her own necklace, which was yet another carving. Tupelo gum whittled into a tiny round cage, inside of which a pea-sized bit of wood rolled freely.

Madeleine couldn't help but look down at her own necklace. "What are these really for?"

"It's a way of keepin track. Things get mixed up over here. Sometimes you lose your memory altogether and can't keep one day from the next. I really ought not to be talkin to you at all but you were . . . dyin . . . I thought."

This place was starting to give her the profound creeps. Now that her body felt healed, she was going to find her way back to Ethan if it meant she had to ride back on an alligator. She certainly felt fit to wrestle one.

"Yeah. I'm not dying anymore." Madeleine headed for the door but Jane stopped her.

"You mustn't. Please just wait here. I'll bring you something to read. I have books."

Madeleine nearly shoved her out of the way but stopped, sighing, and looked at the young thing. Her posture made her taller than her measuring height, and Madeleine wouldn't have known she towered over the girl were they not standing eye to eye. Brilliant blue eyes and bronze skin, black hair tied into a clean knot at her neck. Couldn't be a day over eighteen.

Madeleine squeezed her hand. "Thank you, Jane. You might have saved my life."

And then Madeleine opened the door and was striding down the boardwalk along rows upon rows of floating houses.

sixty

HUEY P. LONG BRIDGE, 1933

WHEN PATRICE SAW THE bridge, the time passage finally felt real. One thing to be told that six years had gone by; yet another to see an 8000-foot bridge standing where it felt like only days ago there was almost nothing.

She saw the structure miles before arriving at the site. The cantilever formation was incomplete but she could see all the tangled threads of steel reaching for one another, waiting for workers like Ferrar to finish weaving them into a whole. He explained that construction had started fast and then come to a halt because it was a high water year. Patrice nodded, then had to reorganize her thoughts, because 1927 had been a high water year, too.

"The workers are on strike now, so construction's held up again." Ferrar said.

"You're on strike?"

"Yeah. Made it easier to come out to Bayou Bouillon, at least."

He was holding her hand as they sat atop pecan sacks in the back of a Chevrolet truck driven by Ferrar's friend. The road was high and bumpy and the land had gone from farmland to swamp to farmland again, much of which was growing cane like at Terrefleurs.

He reached over and gave her a quick squeeze around her waist, and they both grinned, looking up at the cab's rear window as though Ferrar's friend might be able to see them while he was driving. Like he had eyes in the back of his head. She felt brazen and secretive all at once.

It had hurt when they'd made love. Though Ferrar had been careful, she herself had been overwhelmed with the actions of her body. She hadn't been able to stop pushing herself against him even though she was tearing. The heat and damp and an unfamiliar urgent sensation had won out over pain. The exigency later subsided but was not quite satisfied. She didn't know why.

But despite the pain, despite the frustration of having missed something, the worse thing about it was that it was over. They'd rested there together on that canvas tarp for a good long while. She'd been the one to finally insist they untangle themselves and wash in the shallows and continue their journey to New Orleans. But oh, how she yearned for different circumstances. She imagined what it would be like to spend the whole day lying in his arms there on the banks, listening to the sleepy cicada rattles, walking her fingers against his like in the "Itsy Bitsy Spider" song she used to sing with her classmates. What if she and Ferrar could just do that all day? What if Gil and Rosie and Trigger were all safe and sound back home at Terrefleurs, and she and Ferrar had just run off together?

sixty-one

BAYOU BOUILLON, NOW

HE VILLAGE WAS THE strangest one Madeleine had ever seen. Everything was floating atop the bayou, every inch and pinch of it. Most of the houses were painted though all seemed weathered. There were no cars, of course, because there was no solid ground aside from the boardwalk that ran through it and even that was dicey in places.

Jane followed at her elbow, quietly insisting that she return to the shanty.

Madeleine kept walking. "Where are we, Jane, what is this place?"

"It hasn't got a name. It's meant for hiding. You're here to hide, aren't you?"

"Not anymore."

No roads visible anywhere along the tree line. Madeleine could only catch glimpses of it through the boardwalk alley, but the area seemed extremely remote. Not the towering cypress swamp like where Gaston lived—the shoreline here was comprised mostly of bulrushes and short, scrubby trees. Swamp gas bubbled up so that it looked like some kind of invisible rain was falling across the surface.

"It's called Bayou Bouillon," Jane said.

Madeleine regarded her without breaking stride. "I thought you said it doesn't have a name."

"Please, the less you know the better."

"Not in my experience."

They were at the center now, where one of the structures looked like it might be a storefront. There were men seated on a bench by the door, and a woman walked out carrying a burlap sack of beans or rice or some other kind of grain. All were wearing clothes that seemed worn and faded. No one looked at Madeleine. Not one of them. She could tell by the way they lowered their voices that they'd noticed her, though.

There were many things that were strange about this place, but something about the appearance of the men caught Madeleine's attention. One of them wore an eye patch, and his shoes were half worn away at the soles. It reminded Madeleine of the man Alice had killed along the levee.

The second man was barefoot. She could see the bottoms of his feet, black and callused so that a splinter would probably have to bore in a half inch before it drew blood.

And then it hit her. The kind of suspenders he was wearing. An undershirt and suspenders. And that cap.

Madeleine finally slowed, her lips parting—and Jane slapped her across the face.

MADELEINE WENT RIGID. HER ears were ringing and her senses clouded. Jane was standing with her hands clasped and her gaze elsewhere, out over the bayou, her back straight as straw. The sun was dipping below the tree line now and the water reflected wavering pink and golden rays into Jane's face.

Madeleine's hand had gone to her cheek.

Suddenly Jane broke her stillness and thrust Madeleine into movement, her arm around her waist and her hand stretched across both of Madeleine's. Madeleine was too stunned to do anything but comply.

"Will I be able to get back?" Madeleine whispered.

Jane replied through tight lips. "When the tide's high. Just as you were told."

"What . . . year is it?"

"No more questions like that."

Jane released her then, and the two walked together in silence past the rows and rows of floating houses, back to the one with the canted tin roof where Madeleine had convalesced.

When they were back inside with the door closed behind them, Jane spoke again. "If you find it so odious to wait quietly, I can put you to work. Anyone who stays here may contribute to the upkeep."

Madeleine said, "Yes, please. I'd like to work."

Jane nodded. "Then wait here. You speak to no one, and I mean no one!"

"Understood."

MADELEINE AND JANE WORKED alongside one another in silence for the first hour. Their tasks were mainly carpentry-related. They began with covering the gap in the roof. Jane crawled up atop the shack and had Madeleine hand her first a square of tin that looked like it had been borrowed from another roof, then a hammer and tacks. Jane had it mended in no time. Then they got to knocking out rotted slats from the boardwalk and replacing them with new ones. This was hard work. Madeleine and Jane each worked her own section, pulling up rotted or damaged wood with a pickax, then replacing it with fresh wood.

Though Jane was a good ten years younger and half a foot shorter, Madeleine found herself reverent in her presence, like a first-grader before a school marm.

Jane could work, too. She hacked at the rotted wood with no sign of fatigue. Madeleine's hands had blistered within the first fifteen minutes, her fingers and back going stiff. She fixed her body the same way she had before with the splinters and the infections. Even her muscles lost their stiffness and were ready afresh.

Back to work. The evening light had gone from a sunset spectrum to violet gray, and now was full dark. The moon was high and radiant though, and neither woman suggested they stop.

With the darkness, the village came to life. It seemed the cloak of shadows gave freedom to all in a place where no one dared look at one another. There were voices all around. Sound carried across the water and gave the illusion that someone was speaking just over Madeleine's shoulder even though Jane was the only other person nearby. Doors slammed. The boardwalk moved as people walked along it down the way. Madeleine could hear others sawing and hammering, too. No electric lights but the occasional lantern or torchère would appear, turning people into drifting silhouettes.

An hour later Madeleine was in need of rejuvenation again. She paused after a water break and closed her eyes, let the memory of the quiet, cool fissure of rock fill her. The scent of impending rain. The spongy moss. Healing waves filtered through her body, freshening her muscles, new skin cells building up from her palms and pushing away the raw flesh.

"What is this?" Jane said.

Madeleine opened her eyes just as Jane grabbed her palm and held it at an angle to catch the moonlight. Madeleine's hands were sticky with blood and sweat, but the sores themselves had vanished by now.

"So that's why you made such a miraculous recovery. You heal."

Madeleine nodded. "I do now."

"What else can you do?"

Madeleine shrugged. "Hold my breath a long time. Control thoughts."

"Other people's thoughts."

"Yes."

Jane shook her head in disgust. "You must have done some kind of evil for your river devil if you've been rewarded that way."

"No, I didn't."

"You're lying."

Madeleine regarded her. "You can hear them, too? The river devils?"

"I was raised to hear them. And I know how doing what they want leads to their so-called rewards, which only makes you a more useful tool for evil. Fight back and you go mad."

"Jane, listen. The things we've been told are not true. You're believing what your devil wants you to believe. They just want to keep us in a state of anguish. They are not so powerful. We can be stronger."

"No, we can't."

"We can regulate them."

Jane was whispering through gritted teeth now. "Who do you think you're kidding? We can't control them. No more'n an arsonist can control a fire once he sets it."

"Not control. Stabilize. And not fight. Learn. Instead of thinking of ways to survive around them, maybe we ought to think of how they can be useful."

"They are useful in killing lumens, Madeleine, that's all." Gaston's voice.

Madeleine turned to see he'd come up the boardwalk beneath her notice. Beyond, she could see a group of silhouettes. From the sound of things some of them were drinking. A sway in Gaston's step indicated that he might have been drinking, himself.

Jane averted her eyes from him, her face showing disgust.

Gaston paused next to her, lifted his hands as if to touch her shoulders, but then dropped them again.

He turned to Madeleine. "Back inside now. Both y'all. Gone dangerous out here."

Madeleine said, "Alright. But you're going to have to answer some questions."

"Anything you care to know."

"Wait," Jane said, and the irritation had vanished from her face.

She was staring down the boardwalk toward the silhouettes. The voices had gone exuberant.

"Get inside!" Gaston said.

Madeleine heard someone singing, *"Once I built a railroad, now it's done . . ."*

Another voice joined in: *"Buddy, can you spare a dime?"*

Jane's expression had gone to pure shock. Her lips opened. She looked at Gaston, then back at the silhouettes.

Gaston reached for her elbow but she tore away from him and broke into a run toward the group.

"Patrice!" Gaston called.

Madeleine started after Jane but Gaston took her by the arms. "Not this time, Madeleine!"

A splash. A woman screaming. Jane was calling out, too, but because her back was toward Madeleine the words were unclear.

And then, in the moonlight, Madeleine could see that one of the men had grabbed another from behind, pulling his arms backward and exposing his midsection while a third man jabbed a blade into his gut.

Madeleine gasped. There were shouts from the group. The one who was stabbed fell into the water. Jane threw herself at one of the attackers but he shrugged her off like she was a doll.

Madeleine tried to make for Jane again but Gaston was lifting Madeleine and dragging her to the shanty. He shoved her in and slammed the door.

Madeleine stared sightlessly at it. Black as pitch in here now that the roof was repaired. Beyond the walls, women were screaming, Jane among them. Madeleine was heaving, stunned.

She tried the handle. It wouldn't move.

She pounded against the wood. "Gaston! Please just get Jane!"

"Stay out of it!

She pounded again. The brutal image of that man getting stabbed screamed through her mind. And yet Gaston's throwing her into the shack like this, it seemed like it wasn't just for her safety. Something else was going on.

She turned around in a blind circle, said aloud, "Alright," and then felt her way to the pallet.

Zenon knew how to project his ghost to wreak havoc. Madeleine had done it with Severin, too, several times now. Seemed like Madeleine ought to be able to project her ghost fifty damn feet and see what the hell was going on out there.

sixty-two

HUEY P. LONG BRIDGE, 1933

I NASMUCH AS IT HAD been startling to see the partially constructed bridge looming over the Mississippi River, the work camp in its shadow was the biggest shock. Patrice did recognize it from before—an open space beyond the ferry dock, bordered on one side by a levee berm with woods surrounding the rest. But this time there was no smell of beans or johnnycakes at the campfires. Folks were huddled in groups of one to six around modest possessions, and the outer perimeter gave off an unpleasant odor. Before, there had been only a handful of workers. Now, they were so numerous that they filled the entire clearing. They looked scant of muscle and fat, and their clothes were overworn. Many looked too feeble to work. There were women and children this time, too. Not as many as the men. No one smiled.

"All these men work on the bridge?" Patrice asked.

Ferrar shook his head. "They want to. They all come here look-ing to get on the work crew."

"But why so many?"

"Things have changed since you've been sleeping."

He paused, his expression grim. "It's hard times. Real hard."

She looked across at the faces, afraid to make eye contact be-cause it felt like she was peeping into their homes somehow, into their private troubles and desperation, just by looking at them. But somewhere among them she might find Mother. And so she looked, searched the faces, scanned deeper into hearts and intentions. No sign of her mother.

The sun was sinking low in the sky. Not sunset yet, but close.

Ferrar said, "Now with the strike, some of these folks is hoping to get on as scabs. Workers don't like it. There's been fighting."

Patrice could guess which were the striking workers by the sim-ple fact that they were muscular and looked like they'd had steady meals, about half the men in the perimeter.

She swept a quick look over the crowd, and her gaze fell on a familiar face: Hutch.

He was bigger than most anyone there, and then Patrice realized Simms was with him, too. She'd looked right past him. Were it not for Hutch, she would have missed him altogether. They were both sitting on a blackened log about forty feet away.

"I know those two," she said.

"Simms and Hutch," Ferrar said.

"You know them?"

"Yeah, from way back when I used to run hooch for your mother."

Patrice gave him a sharp look. "When we first came to New Orleans looking for you, Simms said he didn't know you."

"I didn't know Hutch until recently, but I've known Simms for about ten years. I think they both workin for your mother now."

She didn't like it. Too much of a coincidence that they were here. But her mother was nowhere to be seen, and maybe she'd sent these two as liaisons.

The white sunlight was just beginning to turn golden. Finally, Simms looked her way and his posture immediately changed. He clearly recognized her despite the fact they'd only met the one time six years ago. She could tell by his expression that he'd been expecting her.

"I imagine we'd better talk to them," Ferrar said.

Simms and Hutch rose as Patrice and Ferrar walked toward them. She noted how different the two looked in comparison to the others in the camp. They wore the same types of clothes—caps, white cotton shirts, trousers with suspenders—but Simms' and Hutch's clothes were new and freshly laundered. Their hands were clean as a banker's. They lacked the muscle definition of the workers or the hollow cheeks of the hobos.

Simms called out to Patrice as she and Ferrar stepped within earshot. "My, my, my. You have grown up to be quite a doll. Quite a doll."

"What do y'all want," Ferrar said.

Simms ignored him and said to Patrice, "I see you finally found the boy with the blood-shined eye. Where your brothers and sister at?"

Patrice replied slowly and quietly, "Don't play with me."

He went quiet and looked away, obviously trying to affect an air of nonchalance, but Patrice could tell she made him nervous. Hutch wouldn't even look at her.

Patrice said, "I need to speak with my mother."

"Alright young lady, your mother sent us to talk to you instead. This ain't no place for a woman like her. Ain't really even a place for men like us, we gotta try to blend in."

"Where are Gilbert and Marie-Rose?"

"You'll get to see them. That's not a problem. Your brother Guy, is he here with you?"

Patrice took a heavy breath to ward off her fury, and she felt Ferrar touch her elbow. Simms knew good and well what happened to Trigger. She saw the intent inside him, saw the knowledge, even the nerves.

But her anger seemed to encourage Simms because he said, "Look, honey, you make it out of this alive, you oughtta come work for me. You could make a lot of dough."

Ferrar leaned forward. "You better just tell us what you doin here."

"Or what? You gettin sore at me? She gonna throw everyone in the water again, drown us all?"

Hutch finally spoke, "Come on boss, take it easy."

Simms and Hutch were scared out of their sense. Patrice might have probed deeper into their intentions but all she wanted to do was sweep them aside and get to her mother.

Simms said, "Look, I could have helped y'all out all those years ago. Y'all didn't show me no respect. So I decided to help your mother instead. She and me, we always make money together."

Patrice said, "I will discuss this with my mother only."

Simms cut his eyes toward the woods and then looked at Patrice again. "You figure you can have your way, don't you? I figure you're right. I seen how y'all do. I seen lotta voodoo in my day, but, damn! You people take the absolute cake! You do! You ain't tryin to take money to tell no fortune, you the real McCoy!"

Simms chuckled, and Hutch started laughing, too, though he kept his eyes nervous.

"Get to the point," Ferrar said.

Simms stopped laughing and eyed him, then looked at Patrice. "The point is, I heard about what happened yesterday in Bayou Bouillon. I want you to think very carefully before you go throwing people in the water here. Your mother got people right here in this camp—you won't even know who they are til it's too late. You might be able to face off against some of them but probably not all.

You turn them against one another, well that'll just look like a good old fashioned rumble out here. People here so sour they take any excuse to lay into one another."

Ferrar rubbed his thumb against her skin. "It's true. One hint of a fight around here and all the strikers and the scabs'll go at it."

Simms looked at him and nodded. "That's right, Blood-shine." He regarded Patrice again. "Now maybe you care about that or maybe you don't, workers and scabs tearing each other apart. Me, I personally don't see any reason to cause trouble here."

Hutch had his hands in his pockets and was staring at his shoes.

Simms continued but his manner of speech slowed, became more careful. "You might like to know that your mother, Miss Chloe, wanted me to go after y'all out at Bayou Bouillon. I told her that wasn't a good idea. That old man with the eye patch knows how to hold down the fort. She told me to kill him, and she wanted me to kill one a y'all and bring the other one back. Said it's the only way you'd listen, know she's serious. But see, that ain't me. I'm a businessman. I didn't do any of that."

"Someone did."

"Well, Miss Chloe, see, she gets things done one way or another. Found some deadbeat owed her money who knew the signal in Bayou Bouillon. He brought in a boatload of her people to go after y'all."

Patrice's throat was clamped shut. She wanted Simms to hush it, to stop talking about what happened, because her mind kept bringing back that look in Trigger's eyes. That awful look. But she herself was unable to speak and so she said nothing.

"Why are you telling us this?" Ferrar said.

Simms opened his hands wide. "Because. I want you to know, I'm on your side. You can tell if I'm lyin, can't you, honey? Am I lyin?"

Patrice could not reply. She just kept swallowing. Ferrar was holding onto her and she was gripping him back. But it was true. Simms was telling her the truth and she didn't need to seek inside him to know it—if he'd been one of the thugs who'd come after them in Bayou Bouillon he'd be dead by now. She could go deeper, learn more, but that would put her at risk of entering the briar and stirring the river devils. And they would certainly attack Ferrar.

"So now you understand. I ain't here to hurt you. I just come to pass along the message from your mama."

"Which is?"

Simms adjusted his posture so that his feet were spread and his hand was gesturing out in front of him, four fingers splayed. "Four LeBlanc children. One is old enough to know. One is dead. Two are in hiding. Your mother says you take a little walk with Hutch and me at sunset, she let the other two go. She say if you don't, they die. Those're her words."

"So you're here to take me to her," Patrice said.

"Well yes and no. I'm here on good will, little lady, so I'm gonna do you one better. I just gave you the message your mama wants you to hear. Now I'm gonna pass along the message she *don't* want you to hear."

Ferrar said, "Spit it out!"

Simms didn't reply. He looked at Ferrar, then looked at Hutch. And then he nodded at Hutch.

"No, please, Boss." Hutch's face had crumpled to fear.

"What is this?" Patrice said.

Simms glanced at her and then took Hutch by the shoulder, gently pushing him down to the black log where earlier they'd been sitting. The evening sun was just turning peach behind the bend. Not full sunset yet.

Hutch pursed his lips together like he was about to give someone a kiss and then started to cry. Openly—tears streaming, sobbing low in the throat.

Patrice frowned.

"I don't want to," Hutch mewed.

"What's he doing?" Ferrar asked.

Hutch started coughing, soft little puffs, then he was hacking and finally, gagging. His massive body heaved like he was going to vomit on the grass down between his knees. But he didn't. Instead he went to salivating, clear ribbons of spit dangling toward the dirt, his lips and tongue working as though there were an invisible hard-boiled egg in his mouth that he wished to eject.

Patrice took a step closer. If she dared, she would have helped him do this, but she knew she couldn't. Could only wait and listen.

Hutch's tongue was clucking. It sounded like it started at the back of the throat as a g-g-g and clucked its way across the roof of his mouth to his teeth, where it stayed, hitching, then reversed the passage of air so that it made a T sound, over and over again.

Patrice caught her breath, listened.

Hutch moaned out a syllable that did not form beyond the throat.

He gagged, spat a cascade of something that looked like frothed corn oil, and then tried again, leading up to it with the same hitching clucks:

"T-t-t-t-t-Treese."

sixty-three

*B*RIAR LIGHT FILLED THE room. Madeleine could see rusted chips of tin from where they'd mended the roofing. Sprouts bloomed from the pile of debris, black thorns, curling around and up, stretching beyond the ceiling. Towering black trees hovered above the gap where the roof ought to be.

Severin was sitting on a bough, hunched over, filthy and naked. "How did you escape me so easily?"

Madeleine didn't reply. Her spirit stood and walked through the door, past Gaston, who was looking at the mêlée with watery eyes. Severin jumped down and followed.

The briar light illuminated things much brighter than the moon had. The water looked like liquid mercury. Madeleine could see Jane, standing with balled fists and tears in her eyes. Another girl was there, too, shrieking and bucking as someone tried to hang on to her. This girl—she looked so much like Jane she could be a twin, except that Jane was a bit older. The girl and the man who was holding her fell over the side of the boardwalk and into the bayou.

Madeleine went into the water, looking for the boy who'd been stabbed. She sensed he was already deep below. Down, down, all the way down, Madeleine and Severin followed.

Splashing above. Some of the others must have jumped into the water. But they were near the surface and couldn't possibly have seen what Madeleine saw in the briar light.

The wounded boy was below, face turned upward, eyes open. Her heart fluttered at the sight of his face. Something about his eyes. But his mouth was open in a horrific grimace. She thought he might already be dead until she saw his arms were moving, scraping toward the surface.

She caught up with him and realized why he'd been moving downward so fast. He'd been rolled right into the current. It had dragged him down to the bottom and was now pulling him toward the whirlpool.

Madeleine gave him the ability to survive without breathing first. It seemed to take so agonizingly long. He was bleeding to death. She tried to drag him out of the current but of course she couldn't. This was not her physical body. He couldn't see her. Couldn't know what was happening beyond the fact that he was dying.

But she felt him go still, and knew that he was either doing without breath or he'd died. She looked into his face and saw blinking, confused eyes.

And she knew him. Gaston.

No beard, and his necklace was not a click beetle necklace, but these were his eyes. This was his jawline.

He was still falling backward toward the whirlpool, too weak from his wounds to swim out of the current. He wasn't going to drown, at least.

She wrapped her briar self around him and tended his wounds. Drawing from the fissure, the cool moss, the rainy scent. She could feel him healing beneath her grasp.

Gaston had been guarding the door up above on that boardwalk, she was certain of it. This boy looked the same age. Same exactly. He had a twin and Jane did, too?

He kept slipping back. The whirlpool was drawing him back. And then he was caught up in it, kicking, fighting. A good sign, though, that his strength had returned. Madeleine hung on as best she could. But then he was gone.

"In the hidey hole," Severin said.

Madeleine looked, saw a rent in the bayou floor where Gaston must have disappeared. Madeleine went to it and felt it pulling her in. But that was impossible. She was not a physical being.

"To play for a small time or lifetime," Severin said.

And that's when Madeleine saw the creature. The thing that looked like a man covered in oil, but with those impossibly long limbs. Its arms were open and reaching for her.

She withdrew. And for the second time, she escaped the briar of her own free will. Against Severin's will. A simple reach inside for something that was neither body nor mind.

❧

HER PHYSICAL BODY GASPED. The door was open and moonlight was spilling through it. She was once again on the pallet in the boardwalk shack.

Gaston was kneeling beside her, head in his hands. "Oh, Madeleine. What've you done?"

She pulled herself up and looked at him. "I don't understand."

"I locked you up. Thought I could change it this time. Oh, you should have just let me die."

sixty-four

HUEY P. LONG BRIDGE, 1933

FERRAR HAD HIS ARMS around Patrice's waist and was lifting her up. She was barely aware that she'd slid to the earth when Hutch had said her name like that.

"Poor girl's starving," someone nearby said.

And she heard Simms say, "Beat it, you. Everyone's starving."

She reached for Hutch. "Trigger? Trigger, honey?"

"No brawr, no bri-arr," was all Hutch would say.

She had him by the jowls and was staring into his face. His skin felt like putty and his cheeks were wet with tears and saliva.

But Hutch had little to do with it. If Trigger were here, he wouldn't be inside Hutch. He'd be standing here using Hutch the way a hunter throws his voice into a hollow.

Patrice closed her eyes and beckoned the inner world.

"No Briar!" She felt herself being shaken and she opened her eyes. "Not yet, little lady."

Simms was shaking her arm and Ferrar was pushing Simms away from her. Simms licked his lips, looking like he was about to square off with Ferrar. Hutch continued quivering and spitting.

"Just tell us what we need to know," Ferrar said.

Simms pointed at Patrice. "She ain't supposed to do none a that voodoo here. Not now. Said she was gonna want to. Said she had to wait until they's all safe."

"Who said?"

Simms pointed at Hutch. "Him. It. You ain't gonna get much more out of him than that."

Hutch wiped his chin with his shirtsleeve and looked doe-eyed up at Simms. "You gotta take me back to the hospital."

She could tell by the way he sagged that Trigger had let him go for now. It made her want to recede to the briar something fierce. To think, Trigger wasn't gone; he was here, *right here.*

"Tell us what happened," Ferrar said.

Simms waved at Hutch. "Started last night. He's actin all crazy at the club. Finally took him to the hospital."

Hutch said, "Med school at Tu-lane. But they ain't got no beds there. Kingfish done took'm away on account a Tulane ain't never give him no law degree way back when."

"Kingfish?" Patrice asked.

"Huey P.," Hutch said, and when Patrice didn't react, he added, "Huey Long, girl!"

Simms shook his head. "Forget it. This ain't about no hospital bed. He couldn't stay at Tulane so I took him to Charity Hospital."

"He just left me there," Hutch said.

"They took good care of him."

"Like a sack a laundry."

"Dammit, shut up. You weren't sick that way. Oughtta taken you to a priest instead."

Simms turned to Patrice. "Listen, you can sit here and watch him sweat this out, but it'll take all damn night and to tomorrow."

"Ooh!"

"Or I can just tell you what you s'posed to know."

"Heaven's sake, tell me!"

Simms paused. "I will tell you. I'm about to do that right now. But I'm gonna need something from you."

Patrice put her hands to her temples and realized tears were streaming down her face. The sun was turning a deeper orange. Soon it would blanket the entire delta in its color.

"What do you want?"

"First, tell your brother to stay out of my employee. Fact, tell him to stay out of all my employees. Ain't got the time for this."

"He's here, listening. I don't need to tell him."

"Alright, then. Next is a little bit more complicated. It's about your mama."

"What!"

"Keep your voice down. Let's try to be civilized here. All I ask is that you help me out with your connection at Bayou Bouillon. The old man with the eye patch. They say he's still alive. They say it's a true blue miracle. All over again."

Patrice listened, relieved to hear that Francois was alright. But in that same moment she realized she'd expected this. Even though they'd left him bleeding on the boardwalk, his chest gurgling where he'd been stabbed through the lung.

Leave me to the ghosts, he'd said.

Ferrar said, "What do you want with that place?"

"Just a little commerce, that's all. Want to expand my business. Cut out the middle man, or the . . . middle woman. Go straight to the im-port."

"That would be up to Francois. I can bring you there to talk to him, but what happens after that is up to him."

"That's all I'm asking. Get me the signal so's I can get in there, and you put in a good word for me. Remember I ain't done y'all no harm when I had the chance. I been straight."

Patrice looked at Ferrar, and Ferrar hesitated, then nodded.

He said, "I'll take you on the next run. No signals. You come on out there with me. We can go next week."

Simms nodded, too. "Alright then. That's all I need. Your word. I'm gonna trust you on that because I know how you do. So now all this is just between us. No need to tell your mother."

"Yes."

"So here's what it is. Ole Hutch spent the night at the doctor's, but doc ain't know what to do for him. They say he talkin to God, so they called for a priest. A sister came instead. She sat with him all night long. Prayed on him. Then she figured he had something he was trying to say, so she wrote it all down."

"Wrote what down?" Patrice asked him.

"What you think? All that stuttering and spitting he do. He talk in between that. Went on for all night, all morning. The sister wrote down what he said. Most of it didn't mean nothing."

Simms handed Patrice a bundle of papers. She glanced through them, and her gaze fell on the words:

holy holy holy holy holy holy holy mercy full mighty early
early early early and the moan moan moaning sunrise toothy
holy holy holy holy holy holy holy holy holy holy . . .

Patrice knew at once what she was reading. Trigger was using the song, "Holy, Holy, Holy" as a pigeon exercise. Just practicing on Hutch, that's all, and if the nun were Baptist instead of Catholic she might have recognized the song as she transcribed it.

Forming thoughts for other people was difficult enough. The trick was to understand their manner of thinking, so you could disguise your thoughts as theirs. But causing a man to speak words for you was extremely difficult. Patrice could do it, but she'd been the only one of the four who'd ever mastered it.

Patrice scanned the pages until she found:

tell trees not dead tell trees not dead tell pa trees not dead not
dead mama got me mama got me don't let mama lie she has
two she has two let them go now she must let them go for me
to go . . .

Patrice took a step toward Simms. "Where is she?"

"Your mother? I don't know. I'm supposed to take you with me,
that's all. You come with me, we go for a little walk, then you'll get
to see your brother and sister."

"You tell me where she is!"

His face grew hard. "I don't know that."

Ferrar pulled on Patrice's arm. "He doesn't know. Look at him.
He's telling the truth."

Patrice said, "Now she's got all of them. *All three of them!*"

Ferrar said, "Maybe she's going to try to capture you, too. So
she'll have all four."

"She made a bargain with us!"

"It might have been a trick to get you out of Bayou Bouillon,
where you were protected."

Simms said, "Look here, doll, I don't know what her game is. I
took a big risk by telling all this. She find out she gonna cut me off,
you get me?"

"I've got to talk to her myself. Face to face."

"She don't see you go off for a little walk with me, she ain't gonna
let'm go, is what she told me. You just s'posed to walk along with me
and someone out there'll be watchin. Then they let the other two go
and bring you in. She don't trust you and your voodoo, I guess."

Ferrar looked into Patrice's face. "She will trap you, you walk
with him. She wants you if only to punish you."

In the papers that were now shaking in Patrice's hands, she saw
the words the nun had transcribed at the very end:

she has my ghost but not my body she can't get to my body I
will keep my body

Patrice longed to slip into the briar, just for a moment. Glimpse Trigger. Locate Maman, and Rosie and Gil.

She knew she couldn't recede into the briar, but she could use its tricks.

Simms was pointing at Ferrar. "I done my part. No matter what happens here, we got a deal."

Patrice turned and looked at the faces lit up in the early evening glow, intensifying with every moment that brought the sun deeper onto the horizon. It filled the dark circles under the people's eyes, and the hollows at their cheeks and necks and collarbones—softened every hard line. Mother was not among them. She wouldn't be here, no, but she'd likely be nearby.

"Mother," said Patrice.

And she closed her eyes, but not to will the thorns. She had to invoke this without briar. She felt it. Cultivated from Ferrar's presence. Something that reflected back from somewhere within her own being.

She said again, "Mother."

"Mother," Simms and Hutch both echoed back.

They gave her a strange look.

"Be careful," Ferrar whispered to her.

"Mother," Patrice said again.

And she heard the people in the next camp, and Simms and Hutch once again, say, "Mother."

Patrice said the word again, letting it filter through all those people, and from the other camps she could hear the word echoing back. *Mother. Mother.*

It rippled across the lips of every person at every camp, floating from this one to that. She let it ride beyond the clearing to elsewhere. Every woman, every man, and the children all said it: *Mother.*

"Come speak to me, Mother," Patrice said.

The words washed from one end of the camp to the other, and across the thicket to the road beyond. The people on the ferry. The people across the water. Patrice felt that Gil and Rosie were saying it. Maybe even her own mother said it, too. It washed over New Orleans. They were all saying it. And after half a minute passed, they all said it again.

From somewhere off to the north beyond the trees, there came a blast of car horn. Patrice turned toward the sound.

❦

sixty-five

❦

LOUISIANA, NOW

ADELEINE SAT WITH GASTON in his tree. After she'd returned to her body, the tide had been high and they'd had to move fast in order to get back. No tar creature had been waiting at the base of the whirlpool. That thing existed in the briar only. She'd wanted to demand an explanation from Gaston but the return through the corridors of the tree had sapped their energy.

Now, they sat silently in wet clothes, Gaston wrapped in his secrets staring out into the night with tears streaming down his cheeks. She wasn't sure whether she should love him or hate him. He seemed so gentle and yet he'd killed Cheryl. And he tried to prevent her from saving . . . whoever it was below the boardwalk of the floating village. A boy who wore Gaston's likeness, if not his beard.

She put her head in her hands and vowed not to care. Her heart longed for Ethan. She loved him and she wanted him back. And she was going back, hell or high water. Now that she was healthy again she'd get back to him. Even if she had to trek through this godforsaken backwater for months. She'd find her way to civilization and she'd get back. She and Ethan would live a quiet life in a home they made together.

They'd just have to find a way to neutralize Zenon, that was all. And Chloe, too, if she was still alive.

And protect Cooper and his mother, and Bo and his. And poor Ray.

And the first step was to get out, out, out of these stupid woods.

"Dammit!" Madeleine said aloud.

Gaston looked at her. His face showed near-shock, like he'd thought himself alone and was startled to realize Madeleine was still sitting there.

She glared out the opening in the wood, beyond which the cypress trees hovered in shades of slate. First light. She would set off at first light. No matter what.

"My name is Guy Gaston LeBlanc," Gaston said.

She looked at him. The name meant nothing to her, of course, except for the surname she shared.

For the next few moments he said nothing further. Fine. She wasn't going to prod him. She'd had enough. Though dawn was not far off, the creatures who lived in the *cyprière* were singing their night sounds. Madeleine recalled the evening when she'd heard their voices coalesce into the single pulse. The horrible manipulation of their dissonance, of Severin's rhymes, of Madeleine's own breathing. Now the creatures of Gaston's *cyprière* sounded natural and easy, just like the ones of her childhood out on Bayou Black.

He spoke again. "My brother and sisters call me Trigger, though."

"Alright."

He cleared his throat. "Far as I can figure, I'm your great-uncle. One of my sisters is Marie-Rose LeBlanc."

Grandma Rosie. Madeleine nodded. Gaston seemed ten years younger than Madeleine, and here he was claiming to be about the same age as her grandmother. So this was an absurd claim. But if Madeleine had learned anything over the years, it was to accept the absurd with neither doubt nor belief and move the hell on.

"And just how old are you?" she asked.

"Depends on what year this is. I's born in 1914."

"That would make you ninety-eight years old."

He snorted, bringing a smile to his eyes though not his mouth. That expression—along with the beard that made him look like a teenager trying to pass for drinking age—for some reason it broke her heart. And then she realized she'd seen that expression on her brother, Marc, so many times over the years.

Gaston said, "Seems like an awful long time."

"So should I call you Uncle Gas?"

This time he let loose an actual laugh, that *kee-hee-hee* thing of his. "Up to you. Call me knucklehead if you want. Back when I found you in the shanty, once I got a good look at you I knew you'd come from her. My baby sister Rosie."

"I loved her."

"God, I do too. My brother and sisters been all I got even after they gone."

And then he gave her a shrewd look. "You takin all a this pretty easy. I mean, ain't this a shock to you, it isn't? Not at all?"

"I only half-believe you. Makes it easier to digest."

"That's good. Real good. Just hear it, don't have to accept it as gospel or heresy. Not for this and not for anything in your life."

"You want to tell me about what happened in the floating village? Bayou Bouillon?"

"Uh-yeah. This might be harder to understand."

"Try me."

sixty-six

HUEY P. LONG BRIDGE, 1933

THE AUTOMOBILE WAS A long scrolling line. A gleaming thing. It looked like it belonged in a parade. Nothing like the car Patrice had driven to New Orleans with her siblings.

Standing in front of the car in a gray linen skirt suit with a cloche hat and white leather pumps, arms folded tight across her chest, was Maman.

Jacob Chapman was there, too. Patrice first noticed the missing left hand and only recognized him after. He stood near Maman and looked as though he didn't know what to do with the hand he still had left.

Trigger was not here, of course. Not in body. It comforted Patrice to know that his spirit was here.

She kept walking toward the car, never slowing her pace, and Ferrar kept right alongside her as though he had no idea that he may not ever walk away from this meeting.

As she drew nearer, Patrice could see into the car. In the back sat Tatie Bernadette, flanked on either side by Gilbert and Marie-Rose. There they were, not in the briar but in true flesh and blood. Older, lengthened bodies looking worn down by cruelty. Patrice felt a wave of emotion. She wanted to run to them, throw open the door and put her arms around them. She knew she couldn't do that.

"This isn't how you said it was gonna be," Patrice could hear Chapman saying.

"Hush," Maman told him.

"Never liked the way you did with those young-uns."

"I said be quiet, you drunkard."

Patrice walked with Ferrar to where her mother stood waiting by the automobile. Jacob Chapman kept his gaze on the thicket. The sun drenched the landscape in orange and scarlet.

Patrice said to her mother: "Let Gil and Rosie go."

Maman nodded. "Very well. You come along with me, Patrice, and your brother and sister will be free to go."

"I know you have Trigger, too. I mean, Guy. You sent your bullies to Bayou Bouillon to kill him. Your own son! Only he's not dead. You've captured his mind somehow."

"He has contacted you?"

Patrice said nothing, her fury building. Ferrar grazed her arm with his fingertips.

Maman regarded Ferrar, then smiled at Patrice in the way a teacher smiles at a dull student's disappointing essay. "I take it this lumen is your companion, and not a goodwill offering to me."

"Leave him out of this."

"He has stained you."

"This isn't about him."

"This has everything to do with him, Patrice. Him and his kind, that's precisely what this is about. Because you turn your back on what you are. On me! You make his kind stronger."

"I've never done harm to you," Ferrar said, and then: "Not yet."

Chloe regarded him, his last words seeming to interest her. "So you see now it is the only way. Your kind and our kind cannot co-exist. And still you have no idea what you are."

Patrice said, "It doesn't make any sense. He's not that different from everybody else." She paused, looking from Ferrar to Maman. "Is it just the quiet inside him?"

Chloe said, "You have no idea what it means. He drains your power. What good is a gun if you have no nerve to shoot it?"

"That's ridiculous! Whatever it is that's different about him is so small. It's practically unnoticeable. That people like him are quiet inside? That's all? It's worth all this? Killing your own children!"

"You think I want that! You think I ever really wanted that! I would have made a queen of you, Patrice!"

"And yet you'd just as soon see us all dead."

"I would prefer you dead, yes, than to watch you become common, stupid pigeons."

Patrice closed her eyes. Even after all that had happened it still gave her a shock to hear it. So much ruin.

"Let Gil and Rosie go."

Chloe stared at Patrice, a long, measured look. "Your instructions were simple. You walk along the road alone with Mr. Simms. A light scratch, that is all. You would have barely felt it. And it would have been easier on you, to release yourself to me and take your place in the world of the thorns for me."

Patrice searched inside her mother's intentions, being careful not to encourage the briar to come forth, but borrowing instead from the still, blissful reflection she drew from Ferrar. She saw what her mother had truly meant to accomplish.

She said, "You would have killed him. After you trapped me, you were going to kill Simms."

"Why does it matter to you?"

Ferrar stood silently by Patrice's side. If she agreed to this, would he survive? She knew her mother and the river devils wanted Ferrar dead. Patrice had come here ready to kill her mother. But Maman held all the power, and there was no bargaining with her unless Patrice was willing to sacrifice lives.

The car door opened. Marie-Rose was pulling herself out though Patrice could hear Tatie Bernadette protesting from inside. Rosie's body was stretched long and thin. No sign of baby fat. She spilled out of the vehicle and onto the ground, pulling herself toward Patrice with her hands.

Patrice rushed to her side.

Rosie's gaze was roaming like she was blind. Her skin color had gone to ash—clearly she hadn't seen the sun in years. But something else was off. Sores and scales covered her face and arms, and her lips were the same color as her skin as though she were very cold. She smelled like vomit.

"You've poisoned her!" Patrice said.

The other back passenger door had opened and Gil was working his way out the other side. Also moving slowly and awkwardly. Tatie Bernadette was fretting after him. Both Gil and Rosie were lost deep in the briar. And only a matter of time before her mother's poison, already coursing through their veins, would finish them off.

"Listen to me. You fix the poison in Gil and Rosie's blood right now. And then you let them go."

"Remember, Patrice, that you are the only one who can save your brother and sister. You can still be a queen. You can save their lives. No tricks. Simply accept the scratch. I will remove the death from their blood and let them go with Bernadette."

"What's she sayin?" Rosie asked from where Patrice cradled her.

Patrice was shaking. She had no idea what Rosie saw there in the briar. The girl was so feeble.

From somewhere on the other side of the car, Tatie Bernadette was weeping and pleading with Gil. Ferrar put a hand to Patrice's shoulder.

Rosie spoke again. "Can she hear me now?"

Patrice squeezed her sister. "We hear you Rosie. We hear you, honey."

Her voice caught on the words. Rosie looked so grown-up and yet so helpless lying here in Patrice's arms. She knew it was fruitless to speak directly to her. Though Patrice could hear Rosie, Rosie couldn't hear anything Patrice said. Unless Patrice went into the briar. Or . . .

Or someone else did. Someone who could see past both layers.

When Rosie spoke again, her tone changed. It didn't sound like she was talking to somebody in the briar. This time it sounded like she was repeating something, like the way she used to recite the Pledge of Allegiance.

"This is what you get, Maman. This is a message from your son, Guy. I am here with Marie-Rose and Gilbert. We got them away from the tar devils. We did that."

Everyone went hushed. Patrice realized that Trigger was telling Rosie in the briar what he wanted her to say, and she let her physical body repeat his words. Easier for him than trying to speak through pigeonry. Rosie was already in his world.

Gil appeared, crawling around the other side of the automobile. He used his hands to creep on his belly like a snake, his legs trailing behind him. He too was covered in sores and ragged skin, and his coloring looked near blue.

"Gil, honey," Patrice said, and she pulled her younger sister in his direction, Rosie's feet bouncing along the grass.

Ferrar reached down and hefted Marie-Rose up from Patrice's grasp, and Patrice staggered over to put her arms around Gil. He settled at her touch the way a dog might lean against someone's knee.

From where Ferrar was now holding her, Marie-Rose spoke again in that same monotone. "What are you tryin, Maman? You tryin to keep us all or kill us all, and I ain't figured out which. But you made a deal with me and I paid my end. So now you pay yours."

Marie-Rose paused the monotone voice and asked more naturally, "What was the deal?"

Patrice looked around at the brush, the grass, the gravel road. Somewhere beneath this veneer Trigger was nearby. Maybe standing right beside her, like Ferrar was. To know that he was not dead now, Patrice couldn't bear the thought of losing him to the blackness. What would it do to his heart, his soul, his mind, to spend so much time with the river devils?

Patrice said, "Trigger, honey, you listen good. Never you mind. You hear me? I'll go along with Maman."

Marie-Rose spoke Trigger's words. "She got me already, Patrice. My body's lost. My mind barely here."

Then Rosie fell to whispering, and Patrice couldn't make out what she was saying any more. Gil whispered, too.

Patrice said, "I'm the oldest. I'm the one she wants, and I'll go." She turned to look at her mother. "But you heal these two and let them alone, and let Trigger alone. I'll give you everything I have, Maman. You can have what I am."

Ferrar whispered, "You gotta know that can't be, Patrice. Let Trigger have his way."

Gil's whispers grew loud, and it sounded like he was talking to Trigger.

Patrice said to her mother, "Quick, get it over with!"

Maman stepped toward her. Patrice looked at her mother's hand and saw some kind of raptor's talon.

"You do it you die!" Marie-Rose cried out.

And then she was weeping and pleading in her own words. "Don't go, Trig. And not Patrice. I'll go. I'm gone already."

Gil spoke. "Rosie won't say what Trigger wants her to, so I'll just say it. We all know that if Patrice goes with Maman, she'll just let herself die in there. She'll hold her faith against the river devils and waste away."

Maman said, "You all waste my time. Patrice will come with me or all of you die."

Through her tears, Rosie spoke in that monotone that meant she was speaking for Trigger again. "Here's what happens. I keep my body. I live out in the woods the way I like it. You can have my mind anytime you need it. I'm better at finding things than the three of them combined and you know it. And I'm a lot more in step with the river devils than Patrice will ever be. I'm already half devil. If you take Patrice, you will not live out the day. I promise you that, Maman. You think I ain't got skills but I got enough, I do."

Patrice shouted at her mother. "I'm the one who's going to kill you if you don't take me in right now. Right now!"

Gil said, "If she takes you, Patrice, they gonna kill Ferrar. And Maman will wind up with all of us. You can't stop her, but Trigger can cuz she can't have his body now. Let him do it."

Patrice looked at Ferrar, knowing what Gil said was true, that Ferrar wouldn't survive this. Was Gil speaking for Trigger or for himself? It seemed he was pulling toward the surface of the briar.

"Come on, Patrice, let's go," Ferrar said.

He hoisted Rosie over his shoulder like a sack of rice and was trying to lift Gil. Patrice pulled Gil upward. She looked at her mother. Mother was nodding at Jacob Chapman. Before Patrice could stop him, Chapman lunged at Ferrar.

"Stop!" Patrice cried.

But too late, something was protruding from Ferrar's neck. It looked like a cactus spine. As Patrice reached for him, she felt a sharp stab. She turned and saw her mother. And then Patrice felt a cactus spine protruding from just below her own jaw, blood weeping its way down toward her neck.

Her mother swayed, or maybe it was Patrice who swayed, and then Patrice was falling. She tangled with Gil. Ferrar went down, too, she saw. Rosie, Gil, Ferrar, Patrice, all writhing on the grass like braided snakes. Jacob Chapman was down, too, facedown. Had she herself done that to him?

She felt her blood turning to cotton.

She opened her mouth, thinking she might take a breath, a sip of water, but instead her lips formed around the name: "Trigger."

❧

WHEN PATRICE AWOKE, SHE was in a boat with Marie-Rose, Gilbert, and Ferrar, and she thought: "I am dead. We are all dead."

But that wasn't so.

Patrice could see that Ferrar's chest was rising and falling in easy breaths. And as she stirred, she saw first Marie-Rose and then Gilbert turn and look at her.

"Oh, for God!" Patrice said, and she threw her arms around her brother and sister.

They held onto one another and wept. Patrice felt rummy. This seemed like a dream, but then she remembered the cactus spine her mother had used to stick her. Her hand went to the scabbed-over welt at her neck. This was real alright. Her brother and sister were here with her.

And Tatie Bernadette, too. She was leaning against a barrel and looking at Patrice with her mouth in an O. Her body was awkward as though she wasn't sure whether to join the LeBlanc children or turn away.

Patrice said, "Tatie, I've missed you so!"

It seemed all she needed to hear. Tatie Bernadette joined them, and encircled Patrice with her arms as Patrice encircled Rosie and Gil.

Tatie said, *"Ma p'tite.* I've been waiting to tell you I was wrong."

Patrice said nothing, just leaned into her and drank in her safe, soft hug.

Rosie wept into Patrice's shoulder. "Trigger's gone. He's gone with Maman for good."

Patrice patted her, stroked her hair, stroked Gilbert's hair. They were alive, alive, alive.

"Y'all, you got the poison in you," she said.

Gilbert shook his head. "Not anymore. She gave us something to clean our blood. Already feel better."

Ferrar lay stretched next to her in the hull. He was very still, his eyes closed. She reached for him and found he was breathing easily in sleep.

"He's alright," Gilbert said.

And Rosie said, "Don't worry, we didn't kill him."

Patrice gave her sister a queer, uneasy look. It would be a while before they recuperated from the briar way. All that time spent in the company of river devils.

Gilbert said, "Maman just gave him a sleeping scratch. You, too. She figured y'all would keep her from getting Trigger otherwise."

Gil and Rosie were both still very sick but they had all their wits about them. They looked gawdawful of course. She wondered if they knew how much time had passed since that day when they left Ter-refleurs. Whether they'd seen themselves in a mirror yet. She herself had not.

Patrice looked ahead and saw the backs of two men at the helm. "Who's manning this boat?"

"Hutch and Simms."

"Oh."

And from behind they did indeed looked like Hutch and Simms. A third man stood up there with them, probably the one who owned the boat. Patrice looked around at the massive net and booms and decided it must be a shrimp boat. And it was laden with barrels of hooch or something. Heavy in the water.

The sun was hanging low but the air felt too fresh to be evening, so she guessed it must be late morning. She turned her head so as to shield the glare from the water. The boat sped past swamplands.

Where was Trigger?

She looked at Ferrar as he lay there. Still too dangerous for her to slip into the briar and see Trig with Ferrar here. Even if Maman was truly going to let them all alone, the river devils would take notice and do their hating.

It turned her stomach to think of Trigger. There had to be some way to get him out and keep them all safe once and for all. There had to be.

She watched the men up ahead at the wheel, talking and laughing and uninterested in the LeBlanc children and Ferrar. Probably Simms was anxious to get access to Bayou Bouillon for trading, and worried that Ferrar wouldn't survive long enough to hold up his end of the bargain and put in the good word with Francois. How foreign that seemed to Patrice. Never worrying whether loved ones were going to wake up in the morning occupying their own bodies, or heaven above, or hell below, or some dark corner of the shadow river that ran between the two.

She held on tight to Rosie and Gil. It felt so good to hold them, bodies and minds and ghosts all together in the same place.

sixty-seven

❧

THAN FINISHED STRAPPING THE camera around the kudzu-choked tree with green Velcro tape and said to Bo, "Turn around ten times as fast as you can."

Bo spread his hands and turned in a circle, his chin dropping to his chest, and he called out with each turn, "One, two, three . . ."

They were at Terrefleurs, Madeleine's old family property, the only place Ethan could think of to take the boys and hide. A few days ago he'd made the mistake of letting Bo's neighbor Cheryl and her son Ray meet him at his lab in Tulane to drop off Bo's schoolwork. That's when Oyster had shown up, and Cheryl had shot herself. Now she was gone, and her son Ray, wheelchair-bound and deaf, had not another living relative in this world.

Cheryl had had lots of friends—she'd been a very kind and well-loved soul—but no blood relatives. Ray had nowhere to go. And it was clear that his life was in danger, too. Ethan understood now that anyone who'd spent an extended amount of time in Bo's company had become a target. Before she'd disappeared, Madeleine had told Ethan about "the stain" and what it meant to Zenon and the others.

"Eight . . . nine . . . *ten*."

Bo didn't actually make it all the way to ten spins. He'd fallen over dizzy at nine and did the final turn on his bottom in the grass.

"Now tell me where she is," Ethan said.

Bo clicked. "That way."

He was pointing out beyond the cabins toward the bayou behind Terrefleurs. Ethan stared in that direction. South and to the west.

Ray watched Bo in silence.

The surprise was that getting temporary custody of Ray hadn't been that difficult. Ray would have gone straight to a special-care orphanage, but Ethan had gone to school with a guy who acted as a liaison with child protective services, and he made some calls. Ethan was allowed to act as Ray's legal custodian until a court hearing would determine Ray's long-term future.

Really, now that Cheryl was gone, it seemed that Bo was the only friend Ray had. There were lots of people who were kind to him. But Ray and Bo had been inseparable for years. Ray needed his friend now more than ever.

Here at Terrefleurs, Ethan thought it not only easier to hide the boys, he could protect them better, too. The place had limited access so if anyone came here Ethan had lots of warning.

"You still feel dizzy?" Ethan asked Bo.

"Little bit."

"OK, rest a minute or two."

Bo flopped onto his back.

Ethan picked up the transmitter, then waved his hand in front of the little camera now hidden in the kudzu. As soon as he waved the transmitter lit up and displayed an image of Ethan with Ray sitting just behind him in the chair.

It was a start.

Basic motion-activated surveillance equipment, nothing fancy, which was good because Ethan wasn't an electrician and didn't dare call anyone out to the property. He'd actually entertained the idea of setting booby traps but had no idea where to begin. Surveillance was a start. If anyone were to sneak onto Terrefleurs, Ethan would be aware of it.

"Can I see?" Ray said.

Ethan handed him the transmitter, and Ray examined the screen.

"OK, I'm better," Bo said.

"Do it again."

Bo hopped to his feet and started to spin in a circle again. "One . . . two . . . three . . ."

"You should do that big white house, too," Ray said.

"You think so?" Ethan said, making sure Ray could see his mouth as he spoke. Ethan wasn't great with sign language but Ray was a pretty good lip reader.

"It's a good place to hide for bad guys," Ray said.

Ray had no idea how right he was. Before Zenon had become paralyzed, the Terrefleurs main house was where he'd killed at least one of his victims. Aside from that, the old structure had pretty much been taken over by racoons and rats and vines and whatever other soldiers Mother Nature kept in her army. The main house was falling apart—the roof had caved in at places, and the whole thing smelled of rot.

Needless to say, Ethan and the boys were not staying in there. Ethan had set them up instead in two of the old workers' cabins. They, too, were old, but they were surprisingly sturdy and it hadn't taken much to clear them out for camping.

Still, it seemed one camera in the main house might be a prudent move.

Ethan turned back to Ray. "You're probably right. I'll put one in there."

Bo made it to ten and did his clicks, then pointed. "She's that way."

They'd done it four times already and no matter how dizzy and disoriented Bo was after spinning around blind, each time he clicked for Madeleine he was still pointing in the same direction.

"You sure," Ethan said.

"Yes, I'm sure."

The trouble was, the direction Bo was pointing was just that; a direction. Even if Bo was right, there'd be no telling whether Madeleine was hidden five miles, fifty miles, or five hundred miles in that direction.

If Bo was right.

Because he wasn't clicking for her the way he might click to "see" a car, or a person, or a tree. Bo was clicking in the way he used to sense when "a devil's nearby," as Bo put it. Bo said he thought he recognized the sense of Madeleine. He *thought* so. *Maybe.*

And the thing about Bo's sense, it apparently worked as the crow flies. He knew the direction only. He didn't actually know how to get there. And Bo had been pointing out into the wilds. That meant beyond Terrefleurs, into the bayou, to the shore on the other side of the bayou, continuing across various landmasses and waterways for who knew how long. A truck was no good. Hiking was fine until you hit the water, at which point Ethan would need a boat, and that would only be useful until the next landmass.

Ethan had actually gone so far as to persuade one of his old buddies to loan him a Four Winns (a called-in favor plus the promise of free consultations). So they now had the Four Winns to concentrate their search for Madeleine, but they still faced the difficulty of navigating alternating swamp and dry land. Ethan couldn't very well transport the Four Winns overland in wild swamp.

"You want me to do it again?" Bo said.

"Yeah," Ethan said, and Bo gave a tired sigh before Ethan added, "But not here." He went to his car and took out his map of the area, then drew a long straight line from Terrefleurs to the gulf in the southwesterly direction Bo had been indicating.

Ethan waved the boys at the car. "Come on, guys. We're going for a drive."

sixty-eight

LOUISIANA, NOW

ADELEINE LISTENED AS GASTON told her about when he was seventeen, when his life changed forever. He and his brother and sisters had hidden themselves in the fishing village-*cum*-rogue hideaway. When he was attacked he all but died in that water. Blacked out and found himself in the root system of the tree. It took him ages to find his way out. Time stopped making sense to him.

"Not long after I got stabbed my mother found me here," Gaston said.

"Chloe."

He nodded. "She ain't come to see me in person, no she didn't. Used her voodoo. I come to believe, the river magic only go so far here on earth. But down there, down in the briar patch, it really means something."

"You saw her then?"

"No, ain't seen my mother in real life since 1927 or thereabouts. The thing that comes to see me is part witch, part devil, and something else."

"The coldness."

He nodded. "Seems like a terrible thing, but you can use that coldness to your advantage. Sometimes you got to do things you don't have the heart to do."

"What happened when Chloe found you?"

"Well she put my sorry mess to work, that's all. My mother, as far back as I can recall, all she ever wanted was to get at them secrets. Pickin berries from the bramble, we used to call it. Trouble was, they's so many traps in there. It's a terrible place."

She thought of the sylphs and the thornflies, the creature in that oily slick. The healing fissure had been an anomaly.

Gaston went on. "So my mother, she and I struck a deal. She'd leave my brother and sisters alone. All I had to do was anything she asked."

Madeleine felt her throat going dry. She'd had her guesses but to hear Gaston say it, the full stark light of truth—it seemed unthinkable.

"So the life you knew essentially ended then, when you were stabbed?"

Gaston's voice grew very quiet. "In the old days they called them zombies. Always pictured some powder-faced ghoul. Something like what we pretended on the farm at All Hallows when we were children."

He swallowed hard, his Adam's apple bobbing in the predawn glow. "But that's what I am, a living voodoo zombie. Can't find my way to death. Just a slave. I use that cold wind whenever I need to blow any warmth from my soul, and then it's easier."

"Why haven't you aged?"

"Same way you figured out the healing. Pickin berries from the briar. I kept it hidden for a long, long time. Thought sooner or later my mother would let me go, or she'd die. And then I'd pick up my life right where I left it. Same age and ever-thing. Ain't that foolish, now isn't it? Nothing's changed in over eighty years.

"She figured it out, though. Saw what I could do. Would've been right around the time you were a little girl. She made me use it on her. My mother, she's already good and old by then. In her eighties. So I stopped it. Stopped her ageing. She continued to keep her promise. Stayed away from my brother and sisters. Stayed away from their children."

"But things have changed," Madeleine said.

Gaston nodded. "I finally told her to go to hell. I'd long since given up picking up where I left off. I just wanted to lay down for my own eternal sleep. My brother and sisters are long gone to me now. She found Zenon and started using him instead. He's already trapped. So me, I just let her have him."

"But then Zenon rebelled."

"That's right. Which is why she turned up the heat on me again. Using you like bait just like she used my sisters and my brother all those years ago. She always wants at least one of us in her pot. Something's got to give. She'll either claim me back or take you or your little nephew baby boy. Me, I just can't be this anymore. I'd just as soon die."

"Listen, you're not gonna die and she's not gonna take any of us back."

Gaston's gaze had grown distant. "If I did, if I just curled up here in this ole tree, let myself go to hard dust like these old carvings, she'd just go after your little baby nephew. Or you. And she'd get one of you, yessir. Best you can do is say which one."

"She's not getting Cooper. She caught me off guard this time, that's all. I can handle Chloe."

He was just shaking his head. "We all thought that. What happens in that case, you don't cooperate to her satisfaction and then she goes after him, too. Both a y'all's lives get ruined."

Madeleine closed her eyes, then opened them again. "We should rally together. Stop her once and for all."

He gave a laugh through his teeth. "Like stoppin a river. What you need to know, honey, is if it comes to that, if there's a tough decision, you got to let the cool wind blow on ya some. It'll numb you up good. Things won't bother you."

"Look, Chloe may not be surviving this at all. And she's got her hands full now with Zenon."

Gaston nodded. "I never thought of trying to do what young Zenon's done. He's rallying them river devils—all of them, not just his own. Pretty much doing what my mother done. Only Zenon's workin from the inside. They listen to him, as much as they listened to my mother."

Madeleine thought this over for a moment. "He spends all his time in the briar nowadays. I can imagine he's gotten to know it pretty well."

Gaston snorted. "That boy still got a lot to learn if he think he know that world."

He folded his arms and shifted position where he was leaning against the carvings. "After I got stabbed, after I wound up here, I got lost for a while. And I mean a long while. Years. Maybe even decades. Was in the briar. Armand led me into a place—very dark corner of the bramble. You can't see so well, not even with briar light. There's this . . . thing that lives in there. Sticky and weird-lookin, and he's covered in tar."

"I've seen it."

"You have? How in the Sam Hill did you get away?"

"Used another bramble berry, as you put it. I just escaped."

He stared at her. "Well I wish I'd had that bramble berry. After my brother and sisters were safe, I let that tar devil grab me and drag me down to the bottom of the tar pit. Never been so terrified in all my life. Never known so much pain, neither, not even when I'd been stabbed. He got a hold of me, and I was gone, yessir."

"Gone?"

"Lost in there. Oh, my mother still had her eye on me. Still got what she wanted out of me. That was the entire point. Don't think she realized she would have gotten a whole lot more without the damn tar devil. When I finally found my way outta the tar, I could walk along the thinnest branch like I was a lizard. Feet curled around it and whatnot. And a willow tree that I'd planted in a stump had already grown six foot tall."

She looked out the opening toward the willow. Sixteen or twenty feet high now, at least.

He said, "Time been a confusing thing, though. Out here in the bayou one day runs into the next. And in the briar time don't make a straight line, it doesn't."

"Or in the floating village? In Bayou Bouillon?"

He nodded. "Just when you goin in the back door to Bayou Bouillon, goin through this tree, that's where the whorl happens. Sometimes I go there and it's just an underwater ghost town. Big machinery ever-where for harvesting salt. Sometimes I go and the boardwalk ain't even half-built yet. It's from a time before I's born. But lots a times I go and I find my sister there. She's so dear to my heart, that Patrice."

Madeleine sat up straighter. "Patrice. That's Jane."

He nodded. "I ain't the only one who found my way back through the whorl. Far as I can tell, any of us briar folk can do it."

Of all the strange things Gaston had explained, this was the hardest to grasp. "I don't understand. The floating village exists outside of time?"

"Honey, I don't understand it myself. All I know is, whenever I go back it's a different time. Mostly, I'll find it the way it was back then. Back when I knew it. Probably because that's when it was alive, if you can refer to a place as alive. I don't know if it's haunted or I am. But others have gone back, too. We get in and out through the whirlpool though it leads to different places depending on how we go through. It's the only way I've seen my sisters over the years. Anytime I get lonely . . ."

He stopped and licked his lips, his eyes wide and glazed. But he seemed to push away whatever emotion had swept over him and he gave Madeleine a smile.

"The most confusing thing is when you see yourself in there. A copy. Lord almighty. And I'll find my sister Patrice—first one I always look for—and in all honesty I can't talk to her. We made a deal, too. And that is, it's better we don't talk. Not to each other, not to anyone on another timeline. Change something in that place and it can change everything. Believe me. I've seen it. Entire lives cease to exist. Or babies're born that hadn't ought to be born. Sometimes I have to talk to my sister, like when you were dyin. I had to find her so she could help you. But for the most part we don't talk. It's enough just to be around her. Reminds me what I'm doing it all for."

"Hence the necklaces."

"Hence the necklaces. And it's the reason why we change our names. It ain't enough to know who you lookin at, it isn't. You want to know who and *when* you lookin at."

He reached forward and pulled the click beetle carving from Madeleine's throat, snapping the leather strand. "You can't ever wear it again. You ever go back, you gotta wear something different."

"May I at least keep it?"

He shrugged. "Just so long as you don't wear it. Though why you'd want to hang on to a thing like that I can't imagine."

He made his *kee-hee-hee* laugh, and she smiled.

That's when they heard it.

Tick tick tick tock . . .

The bird call. Bo's bird call.

Madeleine scrambled to the opening of the tree and looked out. Gaston joined her. Dawn was just beginning to sweep over the *cyprière* and wisps were rising from the deepest stretch of water. There seemed to be a purple silhouette over by the shanty—so hard to trust her eyes in the darkness—but Madeleine could swear she saw a hulking shape beyond the web of fog. A boat, maybe. Maybe.

"Hello!" Madeleine called.

And all was silent. Even the birds were still.

"I don't see anything," Gaston said next to her.

Madeleine tried again. "Ethan? Bo?"

This time, something was definitely moving out there. A muffled crash.

And then she heard his voice from across the water. Ethan's voice. "Madeleine!"

She drew in a sharp breath and bucked for the opening.

"Ethan!" she cried again.

And over the distance, Bo went *tick tick tick tick tick tock.*

"Be careful!" Gaston said, grabbing her arm as she swung her leg over to the lower branch.

"Gaston! It's him! Come on, we gotta go!"

"You go on ahead, Honey."

She paused, her heart hammering in her chest. "You're coming with me, aren't you?"

His expression was obscured in the shadows, and she couldn't define the emotion behind his tone. But he stayed there a long moment, his hand clutching her arm where he'd steadied her. There was a glint in his eyes. Just the faintest shine. Tears held in.

Finally, he said, "You sure about that boy of yours?"

"Completely."

"The stain . . ."

"Gaston, please come with me. Things have changed. You don't need to go numb with that coldness, and you don't have to stay here. Not for Chloe or anyone else. You can start your life like you'd always hoped—maybe not picking up like a teenager, but you can have a new life."

"Honey, nothing's changed. Nothing has changed."

Ethan's voice calling again: "Madeleine! Where are you?"

A spotlight switched on from within the fog. It swept the shoreline and passed over near where they were.

Madeleine said, "Gaston, just try it. A few days or a week. You saved my life. I want you to come with me and meet my people."

Gaston turned his back to her.

When he spoke again, his voice was hoarse. "No, dear. You go on now."

"Gaston."

Ethan called, "Madeleine!"

"I'm here!" she called back.

She could hear him talking to Bo. The spotlight shone again; this time it landed near where she was in the tree. She'd have to climb down for him to see her.

She stepped back through the tree opening. Gaston was sitting with his arms folded over himself and his neck bent. He said nothing, but she could hear him breathing in a ragged, hitching pattern.

She knelt down next to him and wrapped her arms around his shoulders. He leaned into her. He seemed all at once that eternal boy who never grew up, and the wise great-uncle who'd witnessed nearly a century of life on this earth.

She kissed his tear-stained cheek. "Please, Gaston. I'm begging you."

He took a deep breath, shuddering. And then another. The third breath went out clean.

He gave her a nudge and spoke in a clear, certain tone. "Come find me in the briar later. We'll talk. Now get on outta here before I go down into the drowning traps. Tide's out and it'll be hell on me."

She squeezed his shoulder and turned away, heartsick, but she could no longer bridle her eagerness to get to Ethan.

She stepped through the opening again and worked her way down the tree.

"Madeleine, baby blue, I can't see anything!"

"I'm over here, Ethan!" she called. "I'm coming!"

But the light was already brighter. Colorless and soft. She was at the base of the tree and moving toward the water when she heard a splash.

She paused, eyes trained on the open water. "Jesus please us, he's hopped into the bayou."

She went in, too, splashing steps and then a surge toward the sound of him. Ethan was a loud, lusty swimmer.

"Where are you?"

"I'm right here, baby."

"I can see you!"

"I see you, too!"

They were surging toward each other with thrashing, fighting muscles, but their bodies moved in slow motion across the water. She wanted to run at him. To cry out.

She could see the boat now, too, a hulking craft that looked like the ghost of a pirate ship in the misting, gray-purple light.

And then at once she had him. He was there in her arms. He pulled her into him so tight she let go her breath and just held, not breathing, not seeing, not even thinking. Just holding. His face was in her hair. They slipped beneath the surface and for one still moment, formed a single interlocking shape. Entangled in mind and heart. Suspended in water and silence and darkness.

sixty-nine

H E'D TAKEN HER TO Terrefleurs. They lay together in a double sleeping bag inside one of the old workers' cabins. They'd made love and wrapped themselves around one another in sweet aching relief after having been separated for so long and under such ghastly conditions. But sleep eluded them. Madeleine listened to the sound of Ethan's soft, easy breathing as they lay with limbs intertwined, his finger tracing a figure eight over her arm, back and forth, back and forth.

In the next cabin, they could still hear Bo and Ray as they talked and probably signed to each other, their voices conspiratorial.

Ethan had been telling Madeleine how they finally found her. After Bo had claimed he knew the direction in which Madeleine was hidden, Ethan had used a method of triangulation to pinpoint her whereabouts. Bo located Madeleine by clicking from a point at Terrefleurs in Hahnville, and Ethan marked it with a straight line across the map. Then, Bo did the same thing from Donaldsonville, and Ethan marked that line across the same map. The point where the two lines intersected was where they found her.

"I'm just glad the boy was right," Ethan said.

"What would you have done if he was mistaken?"

Ethan shrugged. "Kept lookin. Bo's gut sense was all I had to go on, Honey. I was at my wit's end. Helped that we knew Chloe was near here."

Ethan had told Madeleine about how Oran led investigators to find Chloe, holed up in "some godforsaken house," unconscious and near death. She'd been rushed to the hospital where she was being kept alive through an artificial breathing apparatus and kidney support. Apparently she also had a very clear living will in place—that the medical staff go to any means necessary to keep her alive.

"But when you made it to Gaston's *cyprière* I wasn't even there. I'd . . . left."

She still hadn't told him about all that happened. She'd recounted her experience in broad strokes—how it had begun with Chloe and the scratch poisons, and then the floating shanty, and how she'd found Gaston, but she had yet to go into detail.

Ethan said, "Yeah, well, ole Bo was worried when his clickin didn't find you. But the triangulation method had given us a fixed point, and the GPS gave us a way to get to that point, and when we found that weird little shanty I figured you'd at least been there. By dawn, you were already back."

She listened to the sounds of the night, the sounds of Terrefleurs, so much like her own Bayou Black and Gaston's *cyprière*. The sleeping bag was open so as to cool them off a bit. Their bodies smelled like sweat and citronella, the latter of which Ethan had stocked in heroic supplies.

Madeleine said, "It's surreal, being here at Terrefleurs. Like we're on a camping trip."

Ethan gave her thigh a squeeze. "Yeah, well, I'm in good with the owner of this joint."

She smiled, snuggling deeper into him.

He said, "This is actually the perfect spot. Zenon can't send pigeons out this way as easily as he can in New Orleans. And if he does, it's a lot easier to protect the property than anywhere in the city."

True enough. As soon as Ethan had brought Madeleine and the boys back to Terrefleurs in the borrowed Four Winns, he'd spent the rest of the afternoon "reinforcing the camp," and had insisted Madeleine and the boys stay within ten feet of him the entire time he worked.

Bo's and Ray's voices kept drifting in and out on the breeze. Madeleine could still see a spark through the boarded wall where their lantern glowed. They kept it on so Ray could see Bo signing.

Madeleine said, "I'm worried about Ray, with his mother gone. What's going to happen to him?"

"I don't know, baby blue. Right now I'm just trying to make sure we all survive the next twenty-four hours."

Madeleine thought this over. "We need to see Chloe."

"She's in the hospital at St. Charles Parish."

"I know. I just need to see her."

"Why? Honey, it's not safe. There's nothing to see. She's just lying there, unresponsive."

Madeleine didn't immediately comment on that, and they fell to silence for a moment.

Then, Ethan said, "You want to see if she's in there somewhere."

She squeezed him, thinking, flipping through possibilities. Scattered leaves in her mind.

He said, "I understand why you want to go, but the thing with public places, so long as Zenon's at large, or his mind's at large, or his godawful pigeons are at large . . ."

She said, "I know. You got a look at her, right?"

"Yeah. Brain activity is reduced. She looks all sunk into herself like a crawfish chimney that got baked down from the sun."

He paused, and then: "Sounds an awful lot like Zenon's situation."

"Before he disappeared."

The notion hung in the air, transparent and drifting. Two people bedridden and physically unresponsive. Both of them, manipulators of the briar—one from within and the other from without. Each drawing loyalty among the river devils.

Madeleine said, "They're going after Cooper. Without me or Gaston, Cooper's the only one who can tip the balance."

They said nothing further, and instead listened to the night.

seventy

LOUISIANA, NOW

J ASMINE WAS BARKING.

Madeleine opened her eyes. Sunlight flooded in through seams in the wood at the doorjamb and along the roofline. They'd slept later than she'd wanted. Something disconcerting in the thought that dawn might have slipped by them unnoticed.

Ethan gave two squinty blinks and then lurched upright, grabbing his transmitter. He regarded the screen, then relaxed. "Just the wildlife. No trespassers."

Jasmine's barking had grown furious.

"Leave me alone, Jazz!" they heard Bo say beyond the cabin walls.

Ethan went to the door, stepping out onto the thin porch into the morning glare, not a stitch on him.

"What is it?" Madeleine said.

But Ethan shouted, "Bo! Don't move!"

"What?" she heard the boy say.

Jasmine continued to rage.

Madeleine was already scrambling out of the sleeping bag and pulling on some shorts and a tee from the canvas tote full of clothes Ethan had packed for her. "What's going on out there?"

But she saw it. An alligator stood at the foot of the porch steps at the cabin Bo and Ray shared. Madeleine gave a nervous smile. The creatures were really only dangerous when provoked.

Bo clicked, turning his head from side to side. "Shut up, Jazz, I can't hear'm when you're hollering like that."

"Just stay right there, son." Ethan said, and turned to put on a pair of jeans.

Bo said above Jasmine's barking, "I got to pee."

"Wait for Ethan, honey," Madeleine said.

"What's out there, a bunch of pigs?"

She laughed into her hand. "A green leather pig. With big teeth."

"Alligator!"

He clicked like mad. The general lack of concern seemed to calm Jasmine, and she now sounded more like she was talking to it and less like she was threatening it. The alligator lay grinning and motionless. Now dressed, Ethan hopped over the railing and crossed the twelve-foot divide to the boys' cabin.

But that's when it sunk in: *What's out there, a bunch of pigs?* Bo had said.

Madeleine looked across the yard and saw a second alligator, resting like a fallen oak branch next to a rain barrel.

"Look, there's another one," she said, but her mind had already zeroed in on a third beast, over by the other cabin, and then another and another. It seemed alligators were everywhere.

Ethan had taken Jasmine under one arm and was brandishing a huge golf umbrella ("baby blue, you can't imagine the hell of trying to keep a blind kid and wheelchair-bound deaf kid dry during a cloudburst") at the alligator that had started all the fuss. The thing didn't budge. Looked dead, almost.

"Ethan," Madeleine said, gesturing out toward the yard.

He finally looked up and followed her gaze. She counted thirteen of them. And even as she stared at the lumps of "green leather pigs" strewn about as if they'd fallen from the sky, she finally spotted the real pigs. Wild boar. Five of them. Black and hairy with almond-shaped eyes and tusks that looked like wood. Bo must have spread his clicks across the clearing and spotted them right away, their shapes more easily discernible than the alligators.

Madeleine watched them moving among the trees that were tangled with kudzu vine and poison ivy. Hogs are easy enough to sneak up on when the wind is in your favor because they have such poor eyesight. But between all the barking and shouting they should have scattered. Madeleine pulled her gaze from them, back to Ethan.

"Do me a favor, baby blue," Ethan said, though his gaze never left the clearing.

He was taking in each creature one by one, and then he lifted his gaze to the treetops. Madeleine looked, too.

Crows. Thousands perched in the branches as though they might have bloomed there.

Closer in, atop the cabin rooftops and roosting along the fractured staircase of the main house were grackles and starlings. No chatter; all stood silent. The only sound was Bo's incessant clicking and Jasmine's growl-whine where she stood tucked under Ethan's elbow.

Madeleine swallowed. "What kind of favor would that be, honey?"

"Would you kindly grab my boots?"

She turned to look at him and stared for half a tick, then swept her gaze over the strange gathering again and went back into the cabin. Ethan's boots lay at the foot of the sleeping bags, his gray tee-shirt draped over one of them. She grabbed the boots and tossed aside the shirt, then paused. The top of the right boot had been cut down several inches lower than the left. The handle of a pistol rose up over it, and she could smell freshly cut leather from the new holster sewn inside.

Madeleine went back out onto the porch and held them up for Ethan to see. "A few days in the holler and you've gone native."

But as she started down the steps, Ethan said, "Wait!"

"Wait what?"

"Wait for me."

"Honey."

"Baby blue, I know you can take care a yourself but just indulge me. Alright?"

She sighed. At the base of the cottage steps and off to the right a bit she saw yet another alligator. Small and vicious-looking. It's the little ones that are the most aggressive. She hadn't noticed it earlier but then again they were built to be camouflaged. Or maybe it had just now crept up.

Ethan had left the boys' cabin and was reaching for her through the stiles of the porch. She handed him the boots.

He said, "Don't use the steps, alright? Just jump on over the side."

He put the boots on the boys' porch while Madeleine climbed up onto the rail, feeling extremely foolish.

"What, you figure a bunch of crows and gators're about to lay siege upon us?"

She gave a nervous laugh but Ethan was frowning. "Wouldn't be the strangest thing that happened since this mess started."

"You gonna shoot them *all*?"

"I hope I don't have to shoot *any*."

Bo said, "I still gotta pee. Real bad."

"Just go off the side," Ethan said.

And when Bo stepped forward, Ethan said, "The *other* side. Please."

Bo turned his back to them and wasted no time. Ethan reached up to Madeleine and she put her hands to his shoulders for support and jumped off the porch ledge and down onto the ground.

The moment her feet hit the soft earth, everything started to move.

Madeleine gave a startled cry. The alligators, the birds, the hogs, and all the other things that must have been lying in wait, too, but were hidden, each of them advanced. A bobcat emerged onto the roof of a neighboring cottage. Owls. All moving. All of them. No sound other than the rustling of leather and claws and hooves and wings.

Ethan scooped Madeleine up off her feet and had her over at the boys' cabin in a solid second, hoisting her onto the porch and climbing up after her.

The creatures went still again.

Madeleine looked at Ethan. They were both out of breath, as though they'd just completed a quarter-mile sprint.

"How did you know?" she asked.

"I didn't. I was just being careful."

A single tuft of down swirled in a lazy circle and then landed on the railing. The two alligators that had been nearest were now both resting in the twelve-foot expanse between the cabins. The little one watched with a wide yellow eye, the pupil a thin sliver. The big one all but fell asleep.

Oblivious to the entire incident, probably because he hadn't been clicking while he was peeing, Bo went back into the cabin and reported the one single alligator to Ray, signing and talking simultaneously.

"Ray needs to pee, too!" Bo called.

"Be right there," Ethan said, and then quietly to Madeleine, "Any idea what's going on here?"

"I have a suspicion."

She stared at the smaller gator, focusing on that slit bisecting its golden eye.

Go back to the swamp, she told it from within her mind, from within *its* mind.

The creature did not budge. Her suggestion caught no hold.

She turned away from it and focused on a bird instead—an owl that watched from beneath the eaves of the main house. It stared at her as though furious. But the result was the same.

Severin was sitting there by the owl. She looked angry. Vengeful. Probably didn't like that Madeleine had escaped by finding her way to where Daddy and Marc were—somewhere beyond the shadow river of the briar.

Madeleine turned back to Ethan and said, "I can't pigeon them. They're already being pigeoned by someone else."

Ethan turned his gaze away for a moment, then said through clenched teeth, "Can't we catch a break for one single day?"

Unbidden, the thorns arose from the cracks in the floorboards, lengthening, curling, black and musty. She didn't try to resist them. Wasn't going to invite thornflies.

"Ethan, I've got to disappear inside for a while."

"No!" He reached out and wrapped his arms around her waist, pulling her into him.

"I don't think we have a choice."

His arms were strong around her, and she clung to him with all she had. But even as she held his physical body she felt her other self falling away.

He said, "Every time you do this I'm afraid you won't come back."

"I'm sorry," was all she could say.

Because she felt the same fear. A shudder in her throat.

Severin leaped from her perch by the owl, took up next to Madeleine. "We go now."

A sinking feeling, like Madeleine was receding toward the center of the earth. Her gaze was fixed on Severin though she still clung to Ethan.

She turned back to look at Ethan, but he was no longer there. Taking his place, his arms around her just like Ethan's had been, was Zenon.

seventy-one

LOUISIANA, NOW

ADELEINE JERKED AWAY FROM Zenon.

"You done made a miraculous recovery there, sis. Last time I saw you ya looked like you's drunk."

She saw his devil, Josh, standing there behind him. And beyond that, others. Dozens of them, silvery gray, some of them human-like, others malformed. Some quite beautiful. Armand was there. And some, like Severin, looked like children. They spoke among themselves in cackles and whispers.

Madeleine had to raise her voice in order to be heard. "What are all those creatures for, Zenon?"

"What, you mean them?" He gestured at the river devils.

"Or them?" He pointed above, as if Terrefleurs lay somewhere up above the briar world.

"Both."

He shrugged. "Had to get your attention, didn't I? You been

lyin to me. S'posta have killed that lumen kid, but the whole time, he been alive. All along. It changes everything."

"He's no threat to you. Just leave us all alone."

"Them critters up there ain't done nothin to y'all yet so why you whinin?"

"Yet."

"Well, they ain't all assembled. I turned'm loose now they'd just annoy you stupid."

Madeleine lifted her hands. "What is it you want from me?"

Zenon sat down heavily on a black log, as though all this effort was taxing him. "Well, for starters, some loyalty."

"Loyalty? What does that even mean?"

"Oh, come on. You know ole Chloe and I got a little bet going. She thinks she can find a way to lord over the briar, and I bet I can beat her to the punch."

"That's ridiculous. Chloe's as good as dead."

"No, dawlin, 'good as dead' don't mean dead."

"She's on life support. Her condition isn't the same as yours. She's sick and she's degenerating and all the machinery in the world can't keep her brain firing if it wants to quit. So go ahead and bask. You've already won."

"That's where you wrong. She ain't lived to a hunnert twenty by acceptin fate. She a perspicacious ole crow. An long as she's still breathin she's still schemin."

He waved toward the cacophony of river devils as he spoke to her. "As you can see, I got my friendlies, but she got hers, too. You gotta choose which side you on."

"I'd just as soon see you both fail."

"Don't work that way, *chère*. You can only pick one loser."

He laughed at his own irony. "An that's sort of like picking who you want to succeed. You are either for me or against me, if you are lukewarm I will spit you out."

"Playing God now."

"I *am* God, long as we're here. That's the way it's gonna be."

"Briar isn't the real world! You have your way in here, then so what?"

He smiled, slow and easy like they were discussing the ideal proportion of Bermuda grass and rye for a perfect green turf. That smile filled her with dread. The river devils continued to mill around, all hisses and whispers and snake laughter.

Zenon said, "You're right. So what? You might as well join my camp."

Madeleine tried a shrug. But her ire was rising. Thornflies couldn't be far off. She took notice, identifying the feeling of breath and life in her physical body somewhere in that cabin. She took in the sight of bramble and smell of must, the look of the river devils. With the intense observation, her fury drained. But no, not so much drained as continued its flow—coursing through her but immediately continuing out again. And she observed Zenon. Bitter, curled Zenon. He seemed sunken somehow; wild. Clearly unsteady even though he was no longer on his feet.

"Something's wrong with you, Zenon. Where's your body?"

"Wouldn't you like to know, yeah?"

"You were in a hospital for a reason. You can't just pigeon somebody to hide you and expect to stay alive forever."

"Can't I? Ain't it just a matter of shakin the right tree in the briar? Like our fine Uncle Gaston."

Madeleine caught the retort in her throat before it could escape: that Gaston couldn't live forever. He'd found a skill of longevity that stopped him from *ageing*—it didn't necessarily keep him *alive*. He could get sick and die. The healing skill, that was Madeleine's.

Zenon said, "So you show your loyalty to me, Madeleine. You tell me how you healed yourself."

"It's not something I can just show you."

He shook his head. "Liar, liar."

She looked at Severin, whose lips were wet and eyes bright. The little beast had practically purred in Chloe's lap, and now she was all too willing to side with Zenon.

Madeleine turned back to him. "If you're looking for loyalty from a bunch of river devils you're just asking for madness. They're chaos. You'll never control them for long."

"Ain't so hard. 'Idle hands are the devil's playthings,' and to them I've become the bigger devil. I give them playthings. You made me that way, *chère,* when you ruined my body and damned me to the briar. Most of these river devils are simple creatures, bored to distraction. Each gets one single human being, and each knows its human's weaknesses. But some of them are actually smart and can move beyond the one person."

He looked over his shoulder at Armand and Josh. "You work with the more evolved of the devils, and gather the rest together in a little harmonic unity."

Madeleine looked at them, and her gaze settled on Armand. The strange, sparse teeth. Dark skin and deep-voiced French patois as he argued with Josh. It took a moment before Madeleine realized the significance of Armand's presence. He was Gaston's river devil. If Armand was here with them now, that meant . . .

"Gaston . . . ?"

"Yeah, honey."

She looked. He was sitting with elbows over his knees, hidden in plain sight among all the river devils.

"I tried to get him to lay offa you, did all I could," Gaston said.

Madeleine asked, "Gaston, did you . . . ?"

Zenon cut in. "Pick sides? Yeah, he did. Picked the losing side, the stupid fuck. Chloe ain't even briar."

Madeleine shook her head. She wasn't sure what to make of it.

Zenon said, "Ain't nothin I can do about it because this here uncle of ours is already the walking dead and been that way for years. But you, *chère.* You got lots to lose. You might just listen to reason."

And his voice rose:

"For once. In your *wasted life!*"

The river devils' chatter fell to a murmur of *s*'s and *t*'s.

Madeleine felt her heart hammering even though she was disconnected from her body. This was how a person conjured that lunatic way. Other people couldn't see what was happening in the briar. Back in her body, Madeleine was probably sweating and pacing, maybe even trying to wander, with all those creatures waiting if she took a single step off the porch. Ethan was grappling with it all.

Zenon said, "Alla them here, they help me with the pigeoning. One man handling one pigeon is a piss-poor effort. But together, with all of us working in tandem, in rhythm, *in perfect fucking syncopation!* Now that, that is *something.*"

He lifted a hand and pointed at her. "But you?"

She watched him, saying nothing.

He held the gesture as though it could hold her in check. "You outta sync, girl."

She understood what he was getting at. And she knew she was already trapped.

Zenon lowered his hand. "So let's think on this a minute. Four people in a old slave cabin at Terrefleurs. A crazy woman—that's you, *chère*—and a mooncalf man, and two cripple kids. And all of God's creatures are gathered for devils' work. A balance that is downright poetic. We start with little critters. Mice. They come on in a hundred at a time. They bite some and they scratch, but more'n anything else they just give ya the willies with all their . . . *swarmin* and *scratchin,* and the *squirmin.*

"But the rats'll come next after mice, and they can actually do some damage. They a lot of rats in them woods, yeah. They bite harder. You wanna know what works to my advantage best?"

Madeleine just stared.

"Them boys. The cripples. Y'all can't get enough of that lumen stain. That deaf boy can't move his legs? He'll have a hell of a time once the rats come. You know how long it'll take for a pack of . . . no, let's call it a *plague* of rats? How long it'll take'm to dismantle a wheelchair-bound deaf boy?"

He paused for a moment, looking at her as though he actually expected an answer, then went on. "And after that, whatchoo think next, snakes or spiders? And after them come the birds. Irony is the blind boy can't get his eyes pecked out by birds. He ain't got no eyes. But the rest of y'all can. 'Specially you. Blue eyes in black skin. Oughtta be easy for the birds to find, and your mind is stuck in here with me, yeah. Won't be much use fendin *nothin* off."

"Stop it!"

He paused, a dangerous smile in his eyes. He clearly enjoyed the game, maybe even as much as his intended prize. She looked at Gaston. He looked so small, defeated; wouldn't meet her gaze.

She said, "I'll pass it to you. Just stop, please."

He raised his brows. "Comin to your senses?"

She licked her lips, breathed hard.

He stepped forward and reached for her. "That didn't take long. I didn't think it would."

But in her heart she knew she could not hand him this ability. Doing so would have a far greater impact than the four human lives trapped in that cabin at Terrefleurs. If she gave him this healing way, he would become unstoppable.

He said, "Hold my hand, *chère*. Pass it on to me. Go on now."

She grasped his hand, all of it briar illusion conjured by her brain as a way for her conscious mind to represent things that were occurring. Like watching a blip on a satellite map and knowing it represented an airplane's progression. But what if she saw what she wanted to see? If the act of holding Zenon's hand was an illusion, what if she could conjure her own illusion?

It occurred to her that the loveliest thing she could imagine right now was to see Zenon become empty of that cold void. The vacuum might be filled with warm easy strength instead. Was that even possible?

"Go on, now!" His voice was harsher.

She gripped his hands. She thought of Bo and that gentle, mesmerizing golden light that filled him. That was a different kind of healing. She closed her eyes, let the feeling of light relax from her and emanate toward Zenon.

His hands twitched in hers, and she knew he could sense what was happening. She opened her eyes and saw his expression had changed to surprised calm.

A river devil growled.

She looked and saw them staring at her. Gaston, too, was looking at her with tension in his eyes.

"What is this?" Zenon said, and his grip on her hands hardened.

The river devils were growling and arguing, and they started moving. Some came closer but Zenon raised a hand to stop them. They froze. Madeleine watched and tried to maintain calm. He managed them so easily.

Still gripping her with one hand, he looked at her. "That was plumb stupid."

He wrenched her hand. The effect was so immediate and so overwhelming that she gasped and sank to her knees. And in the same moment she felt the lumen glow vanish from her. In its place came a cold and angry hatred. Bitter and fearful; she felt defensive and at the same time aggressive. She lurched her body away from him but he held her so strongly. Thornflies swarmed. Stinging, stinging. The river devils erupted and attacked one another while at the same time they swiped and bit at her. Madeleine flailed but could not free herself from Zenon. She'd been so stupid to believe she could retrieve him with a single taste of lumen stillness.

But as she fought against him and the river devils in the briar, it occurred to her, if only distantly, that her body was acting out similarly. Somewhere in Terrefleurs.

She made herself stop. Treated the cold void the same as anger or despair or anything else, let it course through and out of her. The thornflies abated. Something was wrong, though. She felt pain and difficulty breathing. Her physical body had taken some kind of hit.

Zenon stopped it. Whatever he was doing. The river devils

calmed. Madeleine no longer felt the cold void trying to bore into her.

"Please let go of my hand," she asked him.

Gaston was on his feet. "What did you do out there in the cabin? You send the plague on them?"

Zenon released Madeleine and she fell to all fours. She was overwhelmed with a sense of grogginess and she had to double her focus just to follow what was happening.

Zenon didn't seem much better, but he yanked her by the arm and hoisted her to her feet. "There, now neither one of us got time for this bullshit!"

She swayed and pulled her gaze up to him. "The others. Ethan and the boys."

"Forget it. You're gonna take me to the place where you got that healing skill."

"I won't! Not until I know what's happened to them!"

"If you don't then you're gonna die."

"It's not that simple, Zenon! The place where the healing is, it's almost impossible to get to. You can't just walk in."

He snorted. "You managed. Now get your shit together and take me there."

The truth of it all bathed her in fire. Zenon in that beautiful place. It felt like sacrilege. Zenon, with his bloodlust, sending hordes to come after Madeleine and Ethan and the boys.

This was only the beginning. The truth struck her with an electrifying jolt. If Zenon could terrorize them into doing his bidding, he could terrorize *anybody* into doing *anything.*

Or more to the point, he could terrorize everybody.

And with the healing way he'd be able to live forever.

Zenon said, "Don't be lookin into the future, *chère.* You'll just drive yourself mad. All you got to worry about is whatcha gon do right now. Me and these devils, we can just call off all them rodents and reptiles and all the rest. If you or your folks is injured you can fix it. Ain't that right? Just do what you oughtta've done in the first place. Be loyal to your brother. I'm a lot stronger with you than without ya. Any child of the briar makes a fine right-hand man. Or woman."

He leaned in, his voice low and drawled. "Or child. Yeah, you gotta know that nephew of ours is an important part of all this."

She cut her eyes away. Little Cooper and his mother Emily never had a chance. By blood, the child was already ensnared in the briar.

"Aw, stop lookin so put out. You just show me about the healin, that's all. I call it all off and scatter my little soldiers back into the swamp. You even get to keep your stained pals. The lumen's another story but we'll take it one step at a time."

"And if I don't?"

"You and them can die. I'll be fine. Ain't in the best shape ever but alls I gotta do is go call on our nephew."

She said nothing. He shoved her forward and she stumbled, raising her gaze to Gaston. He just shrugged.

"Go on, call on your river devil," Zenon said to her.

Madeleine looked and saw that Severin was already glaring at Zenon. Clear from her expression that she, too, was loath to help him this time. But why? The little fiend was always eager to help Chloe or Zenon or anyone else who embraced the chaos.

Madeleine looked at Severin, and Severin looked at Madeleine, and Madeleine could read the look on Severin's face: fear.

"What?" Madeleine asked her.

But Severin only scowled.

And Madeleine thought, she's afraid for her life.

But as far as Madeleine knew, river devils didn't die. They were attached to a human host until—

Until that host died. And then the river devil simply roamed the briar with no real connection to the physical world. Severin didn't believe Madeleine was going to survive this. And if she didn't survive, the others wouldn't either.

Zenon said, "You got about ten seconds before we sick the hordes on ya."

Madeleine nodded at Severin.

"I don't think so much . . ." Severin began.

But Madeleine said, "Just get it over with. Like before."

"Then you must frame your mind as so!"

Madeleine tried to keep her expression placid. Severin was watching her. And then she took a step. The briar shifted. Madeleine moved alongside her with seven-league strides. And Zenon kept pace, too. Everything flashing by. Traversing islands and cliffs and mossy corners along the shadow river with the ease of a katydid walking over a globe. Some of the other river devils galloped along with them. Gaston did not.

Madeleine let her concentration ricochet all around—the levee, St. Jo's, Tulane, Terrefleurs, the state of her physical body, the floating village, Gaston's tree.

They stopped. All was quiet. The air was chilled and dank. The river was flowing somewhere nearby, but not here. Not in this grotto.

"This is it?" Zenon asked.

"It's how you get to it."

"You messin with me?"

Severin was frowning. "This is the way, so. Like before."

Madeleine nodded.

Zenon pointed at the black pool. "The fuck's that, some kind of back-ass therapeutic spring? You tryin to tell me we got to go in there?"

Madeleine turned to look. Watched the surface. It fluttered in wavering planes of light and dark.

She said, "I wouldn't recommend it."

Zenon grabbed her by the arm. "What are you up to? Where's the damn skill?"

"I told you. It's not that simple to get in! This place is a kind of a trap."

He looked like he was seconds away from losing his temper again, unleashing all those creatures in Terrefleurs onto the little one-room cabin.

She didn't know how to stop him so she just started babbling: "The way I see it, a long time ago Chloe figured out a way to send spies into the briar. Tar devils. She used them to keep an eye on her children because she herself couldn't enter the briar. I don't think she has control over the tar devils anymore. They just sort of wandered off and settled here. I think they're attracted to the healing source. Moth to flame. And they've changed since Chloe created them. Evolved."

"Evolved how?" He said it through his teeth.

She kept her eyes on his as she spoke though she sensed its advance. It wore a thick black layer of oil that also coated the grotto walls and stalactites and stalagmites and the pool itself, making it nearly impossible to discern one surface from the next. Madeleine and Zenon and the river devils were clean of it and they stood out like beacons.

She said, "They're less humanlike. And stronger. The way you get around them is the same way you get at the healing source."

"And how the fuck do you do that?"

He was looking to his left toward the pool, but the thing was coming up on his right. There might have been one coming up on Madeleine, too.

She said, "There's a bridge."

"Where is it?"

He realized what was happening. Maybe because one of the tar devils was almost upon her now. They were not fast-moving creatures but in here they were nearly invisible.

He was pointing just beyond her head. "Is that one of those goddamn things? Jesus!"

He yanked her out of the way but seemed to realize it would be pointless. There were three of them as far as Madeleine could tell.

Long, spindly limbs. One of them crept on all fours. Its face was discernable only as slick black curves and a maw.

"Where's the fucking bridge? *Where's the fucking bridge?*"

"It's not physical and it's not briar, Zenon. It leads in between them."

She closed her eyes. In her mind she saw a light beam spreading out, the beam itself invisible until it fell on things that reflected it back. That lovely light.

It didn't matter whether or not she wore a lumen's stain—now that she'd felt it she could always get it back.

Light reflected upon light. She felt her body somewhere off disconnected from the rest of her, and knew that her body shell was nothing more than tiny particles that mirrored back that illumination. Different parts of her bound together to create a single life. Electrons spinning around a nucleus to create an atom that was comprised more of space than matter.

The tar devils had probably folded Zenon into their pool by now. They would accompany him through the briar like parasites, and borrow his ghost for a while. But that was a distance away. Madeleine was already somewhere else.

seventy-two

CROSS THE WAY A fjord rose high, slate gray but freshened with green moss. She could see openings amidst the vertical rock striations—crevices like the eyes in peacock feathers; or like nuclei of smooth muscle cells. Behind her lay the cypress swamp with its floating red-and-green carpet of duckweed and black, thorny trees that stretched as high as the fjord.

She stood atop a water crossing with Gaston, and dead below them was the river. That indigo-colored river that flowed through the shadows. All sounds were rushing water, dripping water, gurgling water, and soughing wind.

No river devils at the moment, not even Severin.

Her body was healing even as her other self stood atop that bridge. She had no idea what injuries her body sustained in that cottage, but it didn't matter. She would be whole again by the time she returned.

She reached for Gaston's hand. "I'm glad you're here."

He said nothing but squeezed her fingers.

She said, "It's strange, standing here on this bridge. I think maybe I wished it here."

Gaston nodded. "You probably did."

"I didn't realize I could impose my will on the briar like a lucid dream."

"You can kind of sort of do it in either world, I think. It's a kind of pigeoning. You wished me here, too, if that's what you want to call it, and I didn't even realize it until I was already standing here with you."

"Where were you a few moments ago?"

"I don't know. Caught up with a bunch of stinkin, bellowin river devils won't shut up." He laughed.

She nodded. "I was in the grotto with Zenon and the tar devils."

They went quiet for a moment, and then Gaston said, "So if you're standing here and Zenon's not, I guess that means he's . . . dead?"

"Not dead, not yet. The tar devils got him."

"Those things is bad, but they ain't gonna kill'm."

"No, but I think his physical body's deteriorated enough to where if someone doesn't find him and get him to a hospital soon, he very well could die."

"Oh. Well, that's good, I guess. Well . . . shit."

She raised her eyebrows at him.

He said, "I thought between Zenon and my mother, Zenon was the one who had the best shot at pulling through this."

"I guess the tide's turned now."

She looked at him. "Zenon said that you had chosen sides. Did he mean you helped Chloe?"

Gaston went silent for a long moment, his demeanor heavy, and when he finally spoke his voice was rough and low. "I just want it over. All these damn years. I'd lay down and die if I could, but now . . . with you . . . It would have been easier to just disappear again if I hadn't gotten to know you."

He stopped himself, frowned.

Madeleine could see that something inside him was changing. She felt it drawing in from the corners of the briar, from the blackest reaches, the tar devil eddies at the river's edge—the cold wind. He'd drawn it into himself as easily as taking a breath.

He said, "Right. I helped my mother out a bit. Worked the ageing trick."

Madeleine listened, frowning. "But she's already in poor shape. Even if you stopped the clock on her ageing again it would only mean she wouldn't get worse. Not like you healed her."

"No. You were right to keep that one to yourself, honey. The healin."

No sarcasm in him, but his manner had lost all warmth. He sounded indifferent.

He said, "Didn't just stop the ageing. I turned it backward for her. She can be as young as she wants now."

Madeleine felt her heart drop. "You can do that?"

"Just one step deeper into the same skill."

Madeleine frowned, thinking. "It still doesn't necessarily mean she's made a complete return to health. If she's had a stroke, or if her kidneys had gone . . ."

Gaston looked at her. They both knew better. Chloe was old, and that was the only thing wrong with her. Take those aged cells and replace them with fresh pink ones, and any number of maladies could vanish within days.

Gaston said, "Between my mother and Zenon, I figured I'd pick the devil I know. Looked like she was the underdog anyhow. And I figured because she ain't really briar, she's not, she wouldn't ever get so bad as one of us goin rogue."

Madeleine closed her eyes and squeezed his hand. "I understand why you did that. It's just . . . Cooper. I probably led her straight to him. Now that she knows where he is and if she makes a recovery, she'll try to get at him."

Gaston withdrew his hand. "I don't know that kid, and I ain't gonna, I won't. I'm done gettin attached and thinkin I gotta help out."

He turned from her and walked away, his bare feet silent on the wooden bridge. Of all the places she might conjure in her mind as a way to get away from Zenon, she'd chosen a bridge. A literal translation one half of her brain created in order to accommodate an abstract one that the other half truly understood outside of words.

She didn't want him to leave yet. "Gaston, wait."

He paused and turned to her. "Take in the cold, Madeleine, that's my advice to you. Forget the people and find the cold wind."

He turned back and continued his walk over the bridge, and she thought she heard him muttering, "It's too damn long a life to be feeling every pinch and cut."

She watched him go. He stepped off the bridge and turned toward the black coils of thorns. As he disappeared into the woods she wondered why he'd chosen the black, thorny banks where devils waited, instead of the lush green cliffs on the other side of the shadowed river.

She breathed in deeply and let out the air in a slow stream.

Alone now. Damp air curled up in wisps from the river below. It felt cool and fresh. All around her, the churning water continued its rushing, dripping, constant movement.

And she thought, *It never stops. Even in a pond, water keeps moving. It's drifting amid other molecules, evaporating into the air, floating until it condenses and returns again, is drawn up through the roots of plants and then transpires back out. Always moving. Unless it freezes, pausing the energy stored in the molecular structure before releasing again upon thaw. It's always moving. It never stops.*

✦

seventy-three

✦

BAYOU BOUILLON, 1933

OR THE FIRST TIME since the long-ago Sunday when the children left Terrefleurs, though it felt like less than a week to Patrice, she opened the Bible and thought to read it. It stuck like its binding glue had gone wet, then had swelled and shrunk so many times over the years that it had sealed all the pages together. A light but firm touch, though, and the first page turned.

A dollar bill lay between that page and the next. And when she managed to turn that one, another dollar bill came free.

She pointed it out to Francois. "Look, your Bible!"

He shook his head. "Was never mine. I'd been savin it all those years for her."

Meaning his wife, Patrice thought. But she'd run off to Chicago. "Well, here."

"Ain't mine. Your'n now."

She might have argued but she knew better. Francois wasn't going to take that Bible back, nor its money. As her fingers gingerly released the pages one by one, each revealed another dollar bill—and sometimes even a fiver. It occurred to her then that the glue had not been an accident of damp and dry.

She recalled the day they left Terrefleurs. How the original plan had been to save a hundred dollars. If only they'd known they had the money all along.

But really, it probably wouldn't have made a whit of difference.

But it did now. They had this resource now. She looked down at the mildewed book in her hands. Freed another page and yet another bill.

How many pages are in a Bible? she wondered.

❧

DAYS PASSED, AND THOUGH both Gil and Rosie seemed to mostly recover from the poison, Rosie still couldn't walk and Gil could only do so with assistance.

Francois said of it, "Don't worry. They gon be fine."

Patrice believed it to be true because he himself was fine, even though he'd only recently been stabbed through the lung and left to die. They were in Bayou Bouillon now. The ghosts were around. One of them, another version of Patrice, was bound to heal Rosie and Gil.

Patrice touched the cross that Eunice had given her the day she drove out of Terrefleurs. Along with the cross, Patrice was now also wearing a new carved necklace, different from what she'd worn before. This one was made of short switches cut from willow and tangled together in a clean braid. Chaos organized into pattern. The green switches had been let to dry out—by whom, Patrice didn't know—so that the green had gone woody. Gil and Rosie and Ferrar each wore similar ones.

The four of them had had to borrow names, too, for this visit. It was part of the rules. They all went by their middle names.

They were scraping the wood down on one of the shanties and getting it ready for whitewashing. The act of doing something mundane felt good: the tension in Patrice's back, even the blisters forming on her hands and the splinters in her feet, muscles that hadn't been used in six years. She and Ferrar scraped the north wall while Gil and Rosie painted the east—the bottom half, anyway. As much as they could reach from seated positions on the boardwalk or atop crates. They spoke of what they remembered from being inside.

"It all kinda runs together," Gil said.

Rosie nodded. "Same for me. I mostly remember the sylphs."

"Yeah, a funny thing. You get to lookin at the sylphs and you forget what's goin on around you. Like the entire reason they're there is so that you don't pay attention to anything else."

Patrice listened. She herself had had the same experience, though not as much as Rosie and Gil had.

They heard a motor revving somewhere in the bayou and fell silent, listening. Another motor started up. As they continued working on the shanty, boats began moving out of the village and across to the channel.

"Tide must've healed over," Ferrar said.

And the water was indeed higher. When they'd arrived on the shrimp boat, the tide was dangerously low, and over the next several days the water hadn't restored enough to let boats in or out of the channel. Hutch and Simms were forced to stay over in Bayou Bouillon a few days. Hutch never left his shanty. He was terrified Trigger was going to possess him again. But so far as Patrice could tell, Trig had let him be.

The shrimp boat came into view among the vessels that were filing toward the channel. It rode high in the water, which meant Simms and Hutch were able to sell the barrels they'd had onboard. Even from this vantage point, Patrice could make out Simms' short tight silhouette and Hutch's tall round one beneath the overhang.

"Maman was going to kill those two," Marie-Rose said, gesturing toward the boat.

Patrice looked at her from around the side of the shanty. "Why?"

"They wanted to work *with* her, but she wanted them to work *for* her. Her man, Jacob Chapman, was supposed to give it to them when they walked you down the lane for your scratch."

"How do you know, she tell you?"

"No! Lord, no. We never spoke, never. Just the briar knowing. She wanted us to help with the pigeoning, but we never quite got it right. I think all the poisons made it too confusing to follow proper."

It gave Patrice a chill to think of it, her brother and sister suffering for so long. But now that Maman had Trigger, he wouldn't be subjected to the same poisons because she didn't have his body. His body was gone, lost in a whorl like the one that first took her to Bayou Bouillon.

Last night Patrice had slipped out and swam in the effervescent bayou by herself, letting the bubbles caress her, and she'd receded into the briar as she swam. Just enough. An underwater current wanted to pull her down, and somehow she knew that if she followed it she would never come back.

"Trig," she'd called out in the briar.

"Treese!" he'd called back.

"Where are you?" she'd called, and then, "Can you find a way out?" and, "Is there a tar devil?"

But he hadn't replied.

There had been so much to say to him. Much that they needed to figure out, because Patrice was not going to let Maman keep him forever. Patrice would put an end to it if she had to die trying or her mother would have to die, one or the other.

But oh, that briar and its way. How easy it was to forget even the most important things. Sylphs went dancing down the current in the water and it was all Patrice could do to keep from chasing them. But she didn't. She just watched. And though she didn't know where Trigger's physical body was, or even his spirit, for now she had to let it be enough that she'd heard his voice a little.

And so she sang. Sang dumb old country songs she knew from

Terrefleurs, like "Bluetail Fly." By the third song she heard Trigger singing with her. Wherever he was, tar devil be damned, he was singing. She sang every song she could think of with him, and she awoke this morning soaking wet on a pallet in the floating shanty. Ferrar was there with her, sleeping. Had her physical body climbed out of the bayou on its own or had Ferrar come and gotten her? She didn't ask. But later, she'd found his other shirt and dungarees rolled up in a damp wad in the corner.

The breeze pulled an oystery scent up from the bayou. Ferrar looked out at the boats and then gave Patrice a private nod. They'd be heading back soon now that the tide was allowing. Back to Terrefleurs, or what was left of it. Soon as Gil and Rosie were on their feet they'd take Tatie Bernadette back to the old plantation and see if anyone was still there. Patrice wondered what had happened to Eunice after all these years.

Also, Ferrar had been hinting about how they would have to figure out how to make a proper life together. That was something she hadn't thought on directly. The idea of mapping out her life with Ferrar seemed an indulgence beyond any realistic possibility. How could a child of the briar join together with a lumen? This was a thought she would set aside for another day. They'd find a way to get Trigger back and then they could figure out the rest.

For now, all they could really do was scrape down a rusting old shanty on the bayou. And now was fine. She looked at Gil and Rosie, and then back at Ferrar again. Now was fine. Now still had some blessing in it.

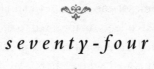

seventy-four

LOUISIANA, NOW

ADELEINE HAD BEEN THE only one who'd sustained injury. While she was in the briar Zenon had sent the animals on attack, and the bobcat had gotten into the cabin and torn open her leg. The others had minor cuts from birds and rodents. Apparently the bedlam had transpired only for about a minute before it stopped again. But in that time the cottage had gone to tatters: feathers, and shreds of fabric and paper, tufts of filling from the sleeping bags. Afterward, Ethan had watched while the gash in Madeleine's leg mended itself even as he was looking for a way to suture it up.

The cottage had felt like a hot mushroom den when Madeleine surfaced back to her physical body. Amazing how cool it had felt over the briar river when, in the physical world, she'd been sweating it out with three other bodies in an airless cabin.

When she'd come around, Ethan had been waiting.

She'd thrown her arms around him and was loath to let go despite the heat. "We're safe for now. It's OK. No more hiding."

He'd hugged her so hard it lifted her off her toes. The boys and Jasmine had simply looked on, waiting, clicking, listening, quiet and uncertain.

When they'd taken their first steps down from the porch onto solid ground, they'd found, to their relief, that none of the beasts took any notice. Some of the creatures had already wandered off. The hogs were gone. Rodents disappeared to the cracks and crevices. But some had lingered. Beasts not usually prone to daylight activity had pretty much remained where they were like spilled marbles. Most of the alligators had stayed put—more for having fallen asleep than for any other reason—though they'd wandered off one by one as they day had worn on. The birds had reduced their number by about half, too.

Ethan was not much of a hunter, but the bobcat had become his quarry when it had attacked Madeleine. He'd shot it clean and had been trying to figure out whether to take it to a taxidermist.

Now, with early evening upon them, the sound of crickets and frogs and night birds expanding with the breeze, there remained no evidence of the morning's hordes.

Madeleine sighed and rubbed the small of her back where her muscles had gone stiff. She'd been bending and lifting, loading Ethan's car. It had taken a few hours to disassemble the encampment Ethan had established for himself and the boys while they searched for Madeleine. Really, the overgrown, rotting plantation grounds had become something of a citadel the way Ethan had reinforced it. He'd finagled the toilet in the main house to become operational, though it required drawing water from a bucket and filling the tank for each flush. He'd cleared enough of the sticker bushes to allow for drive-in and boat set-in, but not so much that a person could approach the grounds unnoticed. The only real way in was from the drive or from the bayou itself, and he'd situated motion-activated cameras so that he could watch both at once while the boys were in the cabin.

Now, Ethan was standing near the tattered white main house with his cell phone in one ear and his finger pinched over the other so that he could hear. They'd loaded up pretty much all there was to load and were waiting for the transport vehicle to come collect the Four Winns from the water.

Madeleine turned slowly in a circle, taking in the sight of Terrefleurs. The buildings and trees looked like kudzu topiaries. She wondered just how far gone a place like this had to get before it was considered too far gone. Right now it seemed old Mother Nature wanted her plantation back.

The boys were exploring with Jasmine about thirty feet away by the allée of pecans. They'd devised a method wherein Bo was using a rake to gather up fallen pecans, along with sticks and other debris, and dumping the lot in a pail. Ray then held the pail in his lap and sorted the healthy nuts from the bric-a-brac. They'd already amassed heaps of good pecans.

Anxious as she was to return to civilization, Madeleine felt reluctant about taking those two boys back to New Orleans. Both Bo and Ray had very uncertain futures—Bo would return to his mother's care as soon as she was released from the hospital next week, though Esther had already received notice that they were being evicted from the trailer. Ray would most likely go to a juvenile care facility or a foster home that could accommodate his special needs. Esther wanted to take him in with her but under the circumstances, as a single mother with no job and no home of her own, her chances were slim.

Madeleine leaned against a makeshift table Ethan had put together from lumber lying around the grounds.

"I'd be careful with that," he called.

She turned and saw him walking toward her. "Can't say I'm the best carpenter in the world. That table's a good place to eat some potted meat and crackers but I wouldn't sit on it."

She smiled and rose.

He squeezed her and kissed the top of her head. "Every time I put my arms around you it gets harder to pull them apart."

She laced her arm around him as they walked toward the main house.

"Is the truck on the way?" she asked.

"Yeah. Went too far and had to double back, but the driver couldn't find a place to turn around. Should be here in fifteen minutes. It'll take a bit longer to get the boat loaded up. We'll be headed back to New Orleans before nightfall. But . . ."

"What?"

"I called to check on old Chloe."

She nodded. "And?"

"She's gone missing."

Madeleine slowed, her mouth going dry. "That fast."

She'd expected to see changes in Chloe's condition after Gaston's age reversal, but she'd assumed it would take time.

"They've reported it to the police and left messages on your voice mail. I kept after them until someone connected me to the nurse who'd been on duty when Chloe vanished. She said it looked like someone had shaved Chloe's head—there was a pile of hair on her pillow. And in the bed linen there were sheets of detritus."

"What, like dead skin?"

"Yeah. No one saw her leave, either. Security cameras showed a young black woman leaving the hospital room, but no sign of Chloe herself."

Madeleine fell silent, taking it in.

Ethan said, "And the, uh, mysterious young black woman, she was bald."

A breeze rose from the Mississippi ahead and washed back to the bayou, and with it the trees grew restless. Madeleine tried to digest what Ethan had told her. She tried to picture Chloe as a young woman. How the body might shed old cells and replace them with young ones. Even in cloning, the clone animal begins life with cells that are already at the same age as the host was at clone time.

Madeleine said, "Incredible. You really think that was Chloe on the security video?"

"I can't fathom it."

"What about Oran?"

"Far as I know, he's still in custody in association with your kidnapping. You want me to call and check?"

"No. But I need to borrow your phone. I have to reach Emily Hammond."

He handed it to her. "The reception's best if you stand over there by the ladder at the back of the house."

❧

seventy-five

❧

LOUISIANA, NOW

A GIGANTIC TRUCK WAS LUMBERING up the hardscrabble avenue that Ethan had cleared, and on the back was the Four Winns. Madeleine and Ethan and the boys followed in the Lexus as the big truck lumbered from side to side, picking its way back to the main road with the borrowed boat. Madeleine hadn't been sure how they were going to get the great vessel out of the water but the big truck had hauled it right out with its boom and placed it on the huge metal trailer, lickety-split.

The boys and Jasmine were in the back of Ethan's Lexus, chattering to each other and signing, and the trunk was packed full, the wheelchair strapped on with bungees. They followed the taillights of the big truck out toward the main road. The going was slow and bumpy, and the allée of pecan trees seemed to have gathered in tighter to see them off.

"So I was thinking," Ethan said, clearing his throat.

"Mm?" she said.

"You know how we were talking about moving in together before you disappeared?"

She tensed, thinking of trying to fit herself and Jasmine into Ethan's apartment without feeling like a marauder. "Yes . . . ?"

"Well, I know you're worried because my building doesn't allow pets. And you say your place is no good because of the noise."

"Right."

"I was thinkin we could give this ole shack a try."

She frowned. "What old shack?"

He pointed his thumb toward the back. "Here. Your family's property. Terrefleurs."

"Here?" She turned to look over her shoulder, but all she could see now were pecan trees and winks of buildings.

She turned back around in her seat. "That's an idea, but I was hoping for a place that had, you know, running water."

"I'm serious—here! Think about it. It would take a few months. Maybe a year even. We could fix up one or two of those cabins first—that wouldn't take nothin. A month, maybe. And then we can worry about the main house some other time."

"One, *or two*, cabins?"

He shrugged. "In case you want to rent it out or loan it out. You know."

She gave him a quizzical look, and he cut his gaze to the rearview mirror where the boys were signing into each other's hands. Madeleine realized what he was getting at. Bo and Esther were losing their trailer.

She said, "I'm not sure we could do that. It would cost money. I wouldn't know where to begin."

"Could harvest those pecan trees. That'd help offset the cost. I could still commute. It's only about a forty-five-minute drive to Tulane from here."

"Is that all?"

"Just seems we're in a different world, is all. But it ain't that far."

"But all that construction!"

"We could do a little of it ourselves."

She thought of all his industriousness, carrying on with the make-shift table and other things around the property, and grimaced. "You said yourself you weren't much of a carpenter."

"Yeah, I pretty much stink. But I can get some skills. How hard can it be?"

She laughed. Straight from the bottom of her belly.

Ethan said, "I know, I know. Famous last words. But, come on, now, what do you think?"

She shook her head. "I'm not sure what to think. Put it in a pot. Give a little rot."

Madeleine looked at Ethan, the waning light glinting off his strong chin. She understood what he really wanted to do here. Circle the wagons. Create a fortress. Though they had a reprieve from Zenon and Chloe for the moment, the entire matter was far from settled.

Homesteading at Terrefleurs felt like a distant, romantic idea. But not an impossible one. Not impossible at all.

The Lexus turned onto River Road after the big truck, and Madeleine leaned her head back to try to catch a glimpse of the old place. All that time spent there today—now she wished she'd taken a more careful look. Wasn't there an old piano in the parlor? She wondered what it would take to restore a thing like that.

She felt a light touch as Ethan closed his hand over hers. It felt clean and warm, and even soft—not the hands of a man who was used to swinging a hammer. But the whole notion gave her such a delight she couldn't help but grin.

Maybe.

Tomorrow they could think it through some more. Tonight they were safe. Right now they were safe. And right now was lovely.

Epilogue

LOUISIANA, NOW

EMILY SAT ON THE floor with her son. Cooper wasn't playing with his blocks. Hadn't touched them since that morning.

AUNTIE, he'd spelled out several weeks ago. It had frightened Emily. At the time, she'd broken her wrist falling down the stairs like an idiot. Later, when she'd dared come back to the attic again, she'd thrown the blocks into the square red bucket and snapped the lid closed. And then she'd packed all their clothes into suitcases. Even now most of Coop's toys were in a backpack. Only three stayed out for him to play with—the blocks, a flashing count-and-spell game, and the green dinosaur he was playing with now. And the only reason these toys were out was because they'd been in the bucket by the playpen back when Emily went on her packing frenzy.

She'd been poised to leave that very day. But she hadn't been able to, not with the broken wrist and payday still five days off. And finals had been only a week off. It had seemed silly to ruin an entire semester with just a few days to go.

She knew it wasn't Cooper doing that thing with the blocks. It was something inside him. Or connected to him.

By the time finals came around she'd talked herself out of leaving. Of all the LeBlancs, the "auntie" in question was not one Emily worried too much about. What was Madeleine going to do, march up to Wolfville and call dragons up from the sea? Zenon Lansky was the scary one, even if he was practically a vegetable. And Marc's great-grandmother—old Miss Chloe. A far cry from Emily's mom, whom Cooper was already calling Nanna. Emily's mom was sweet, if high-strung and maybe a touch overbearing. Emily wished for her now to the point of heartache.

Seven weeks had passed since Cooper'd used the blocks like that and they were still living out of the suitcases.

"Rawr," Emily said softly to her son as he wielded the dinosaur at her.

"Rawr!" he said back, eyes wide and grin wider.

The phone rang.

It wasn't her cell phone—the ringing came from the Sweet William Inn landline installed in her room. It almost never rang unless a spill needed mopping or an errand needed to be run. She looked down at her rumpled clothes, overly creased from the suitcase, and hoped whatever it was wouldn't mean interfacing with guests.

"I look like a dag-gum gypsy," she muttered as she stepped to the desk.

Cooper continued waving his dinosaur and mashing it against the toy bucket.

She put the receiver to her ear. "Hello?"

"Emily, don't hang up."

Madeleine LeBlanc's voice. Emily's fingers tightened on the handset. But as much as that LeBlanc family terrified her, homesickness arced over all of it and Emily felt a wave of comfort at the sound of Madeleine's voice.

Madeleine spoke again. "Just hear me out, OK? I'm calling because I think you and Cooper might be in danger if you stay up there."

Emily looked over at the blocks Cooper had arranged that very morning. The N was upside-down, but she could still read it just fine. It said, GRAN. She'd felt so helpless when she'd watched him do that. Didn't know what to do.

Emily still didn't say anything, but Madeleine continued. "I understand why you moved away from Louisiana. My brother Marc told you to do that just before he died, didn't he? For your own good. I think he was right to do that. But things have changed. It's no longer safe for you."

Emily said, "Why? What's changed?"

"It's no good to hide anymore. Cooper needs to be in a safe place. Up there in Wolfville, you're all alone."

"You know where I live."

"Of course I do!"

Emily was quiet a moment and then she said, "Of course you do."

And then they were both quiet.

Finally, Madeleine said, "What I'm saying, the reason I'm calling is, I'd like you to consider going back home."

"I just started up classes again."

"It's important."

Emily nodded, her heart thumping. It sounded right to her. It felt right. Time to go home.

She asked, "When do you . . . suggest . . . ?"

"Right now. You should l___ tonight. Do you understand why?"

"Not really. No, I ___ ___ ne lev_l do."

"I can try to expla___ ___ ou get home to your mother's. If you're comfortable talk___ ___ ___."

Emily nodded again, knowing Madeleine couldn't see her do it, but having lost the ability to speak for the lump in her throat. The idea of seeing her mom. Cooper's nanna. She knew that she was going to do exactly what Madeleine suggested. Pack up the car, leave tonight. Make apologies to the Inn and call the school later to formally pull out of classes.

She would be home in a matter of days. Cooper would see his nanna. Everything was about to change. Everything.